VIBEKE HIATT

The Fragmented Kingdom

Cover Designed by The Cover Collection

thecovercollection.com

First edition

ISBN: 978-1-7370140-3-4

This book was professionally typeset on Reedsy. Find out more at reedsy.com

To Brett
the man, the myth, the husband

Acknowledgement

To Mom and Dad for buying me notebooks and pens to foster my passion for writing, even when they didn't understand it.

To Deidre McCleery and Meriden Toombs, whose valuable comments and corrections helped shape this story.

To Summer Wager for her enthusiastic support.

To the online writing community for the support, insights, and good conversation.

To my followers, whose input helped me smooth out some of the trickier details of the story.

To my children for sharing me with my stories.

To my husband, Brett, who continues to encourage me every day, and who willingly volunteered to be this book's first reader.

And to God, who gave me the strength to finish when I wanted to give up.

Chapter 1

The Present

"Tell me you're ready," Meira whispered, pressing her back against the wall of the dimly-lit hallway where she and Zaric stood.

Zaric took a deep breath. "It's too late to wonder about that. Now is our best chance."

Meira peered around the corner. "It will be easy enough to create chaos. The trick will be navigating that chaos to make our escapes. It's all surprisingly simple, though."

"It doesn't need to be complicated to be effective. Just remember, by the time I reach Helen's father, I will only have enough strength to send *him* to the clearing. But I should still be able to buy us some time. I'll join you as soon as I can."

"We'll meet you at the rendezvous point. I trust Helen to do her part."

Meira gave Zaric's hand a squeeze, bowed her head in fealty, then walked out into the palace's wide foyer. A dozen people or so were passing through it—a good number for her purpose. Zaric watched from the shadows, waiting for the right moment as Meira approached one of the women and began speaking excitedly. He turned and walked down the hallway in the opposite direction.

Stephen had mapped the layout of the palace so Zaric would know exactly where to go without any unnecessary delays. He wound his way down from the ground floor to the subterranean level—the dungeon. The air was cooler there, a relief from the warm desert air above ground. Every few seconds Zaric paused, listening for a sign that so far their plan was working.

Soon, his ears picked up what he wanted to hear. The sound of many pairs of feet rushed over the stone floors not far from where he walked. He made his way to a doorway, standing back a few feet, hidden in shadow, to watch what unfolded in front of him.

"He's here!" he heard a guard shout, panic mingled with excitement. "Zaric is in the palace!"

The cry was repeated by other guards as they ran in one direction, toward the stairs at the end of the hallway. Meira had done her job to lead the guards away from Zaric's position. One face among the many looked familiar: Stephen. "Don't waste time!" he cried out to the men near him. "We can't let him get away!"

He couldn't be sure, but Zaric thought he noticed Stephen's gaze flicker in his direction for a split second as he passed. Zaric knew now that the prisoners' cells weren't far away. Concentrating with all of his energy, he stepped out into the corridor.

Staying close to the wall, Zaric walked down the hallway, moving in the direction opposite the guards. He tried not to look at them as they passed, focusing his gaze forward. The images in the periphery of his vision bent inward, distorted, as though he were walking through a tunnel of broken glass. A sharp pain pricked his forehead. The only clear image was the way ahead.

No one looked in Zaric's direction. The effort that caused him so much discomfort also made him invisible to everyone he passed. The guards' armor clanked, their feet shuffled, and their drawn swords gleamed. Still, Zaric looked straight ahead, hearing his own name repeated over and over again. Most of the guards had vacated the dungeons, leaving only a handful of men to protect the prisoners and the armory, just as Stephen had predicted they would. Zaric walked past the remaining guards and rounded a bend.

He found himself in a large enclosure of grey and brown stones, encompassed by half a dozen stone cells with thick wooden doors, set with small barred windows. The only light in the room came from a few small torches placed on the walls. There were no outside windows. Zaric relaxed and his vision returned to normal, although the pain in his head remained.

It was much quieter than he had expected. It was hard to tell how many prisoners were trapped in these cells and their condition . No one groaned, no one moved.

Zaric walked up to the first door on his left and peered inside. He saw the shapes of three men curled up on the floor. He wondered how he would know which of the prisoners was Helen's father. These men were dirty, malnourished, and dejected. All three of them looked the same.

Although Zaric had expected to feel sympathy for the men he wouldn't be able to save, the weight was greater than he anticipated, restricting his breath. His eyes burned at the corners. If only he had more energy, he would be able to transport them all. If only he hadn't used so much power to make himself invisible to the guards.

He could tell that the men in this cell were too young to be Helen's father. He dragged himself away, hoping that somehow these prisoners would survive until they could finally be liberated.

He looked through the bars of the second door, then the third. At the fourth door, the man he saw made him pause. His eyes fell on a bent and withered figure, far too thin and far too old for these conditions. The man sat hunched in the farthest corner, his arms wrapped around his knees, his eyes closed, his head resting against the stone wall. The lack of light in the cell made it difficult to make out much more than that, but something about the man's form reminded Zaric of Helen.

Zaric placed his hand near the door's handle. The metal shifted and slid within the wood and the heavy lock clicked. The door swung inward, its hinges creaking in protest. Rushing forward, Zaric fell to his knees and placed a hand on the man's shoulder.

"Cyrus," he said at the edge of a whisper. The man didn't move. Zaric repeated his name twice more before the man stirred. With great effort, his neck moving in jolts, Cyrus turned his face to Zaric and stared at him in uncomprehending blankness.

Gradually, though, his eyes focused until recognition spread across his face, growing into a weak smile on his grey and cracked lips. "Zaric!" he exclaimed in little more than a hoarse murmur. "Am I dead?"

"No, my friend. Your daughter asked me to come here to prevent that."

"Helen? She found you?"

"She made her way to the end of the kingdom to save you."

"My sweet girl."

"She's waiting for you, Cyrus, just outside the city. I'm going to send you to her."

"I am so weak," Cyrus protested in halting syllables, shaking his head. "I don't think I can leave these dungeons."

"Leave that to me," Zaric assured him.

The faint sound of commotion drifted through the dungeon and into its cells. The guards were returning and Zaric needed to act quickly. "Trust me," he continued, placing both hands on Cyrus's shoulders.

"I do," Cyrus replied, the words containing the strength of the spirit within the frail body.

Zaric closed his eyes, concentrating. In his mind's eye he saw a clearing in the mangled pine trees among the dry and scrubby hills just outside the city. He focused on this clearing—the trees, the rocks, the dirt—until everything else in his mind was pushed away. A cart and horse materialized in this mental image, with a young woman standing not far from it. His mind placed Cyrus in the clearing, near the cart. Zaric's hands dropped to the floor of the cell and he opened his eyes. Cyrus was no longer there.

Zaric placed his hand against the wall to steady himself as he rose from the floor. He turned toward the doorway just as the guards appeared.

For a few moments they stared in disbelief. They knew this man wasn't the prisoner they held in this cell. They sensed his importance. Despite the weak state of his body, his regal presence was strong.

Calmly, Zaric took three small steps forward. Remembering their position, two guards rushed into the cell and took Zaric by the arms. He didn't try to fight against them. Another man, apparently of higher rank than the others, appeared in the doorway, silhouetted against the light.

"Where is the prisoner?" he demanded tersely.

"He wasn't here when we arrived," one guard stated, his voice shaking. "We found this man instead."

"Someone will have to pay for that," the officer said. He scanned Zaric from head to toe and toe to head. "Who are you? Where is the prisoner?"

Zaric knew the advantage of his position and the intrigue he had caused. He also knew it was best to stay silent. Instead, he adopted a casual grin.

"I have a feeling," the officer stated thoughtfully, realizing this was the man all the guards were looking for, "that you are the more valuable prize. Someone who can make a prisoner disappear... Yes, Mered will be pleased when we bring you to him ."

The guards looked at Zaric, then each other, with awed and fearful eyes.

"Don't just stand there!" the officer shouted. "Let's take him to the king."

Heavy shackles were clasped on Zaric's wrists and he was pulled from the cell. They dragged him through the maze of corridors that led away from the dungeon, taking him upward through the palace. Men and women stopped and stared as the group moved past. Zaric kept his eyes forward, his face reflecting the calm he felt. No one knew him; they only sensed that he was an important man, perhaps the *Zaric* Mered had always spoken of—the one the guards were shouting about not long ago. The people the guards passed fell in line behind them, not wanting to miss what would happen when this man was taken before Mered.

The group reached a set of ornate wooden doors, set within the red stone of the palace. At the command of the official, the two men who stood guard thrust the doors open and Zaric was both pushed and pulled into the room.

Mered sat at the opposite end of the room, resting on a carved and polished wooden throne upon a dais. At the sight of Zaric, he jumped to his feet, unable to hide his shock, surprise, and excitement. This change in composure caused a stir in the room. The people who were already there turned their heads toward the door to look at the man who brought about this reaction from their leader.

"Well, well, well," Mered said, lowering himself back into his throne. "Zaric really is alive—and he thought he could walk straight into my palace unnoticed."

The mention of Zaric's name caused a murmur to ripple through the room. The guards led Zaric into the center of the chamber, parting the crowds as they went. Once their prisoner was in place, they stepped back, leaving Zaric standing alone before their leader.

"What brings you here, Zaric?" Mered asked. "Were you hoping to reminisce about old times? Or perhaps see what I've done with my kingdom? Note how I succeeded where you failed?"

A sad smile touched Zaric's lips, but he said nothing. Seeing Mered before him brought an image to his mind of the man he once knew. The face was the same, but little else.

"Or did you think that you actually have the power to fight me?" Mered went on. "As you can see, I have plenty of support, whereas you have none."

"I don't need to buy support with empty promises," Zaric replied.

"This land is mine. I have no need to make 'empty' promises. I can give away as much as I choose and still have plenty to spare."

"Yes—as much as you *choose*. But a kingdom is more than land."

Mered's face flushed. For a minute, he stared at Zaric, studying him and trying to penetrate his expression. Then he looked away with a smirk, shaking his head. Zaric noticed the scripted nature of Mered's actions, like a man playing a part on a stage. With a dramatic push on the arms of the throne, Mered stood again and stepped down from the dais. "These people don't need you, Zaric," he said with shards of glass in his voice. "They have done well for themselves without you."

"Then why do you think they need you?" Zaric returned coolly.

Mered flinched slightly. "They have lost their way," he answered with a shrug of his shoulders. "I can show them a new unity—a better way of life. With my guidance, they will no longer be sleepwalking, but will wake up to glorious possibilities. We both know that your way only brings destruction."

"As I remember it, you played a large role in that destruction. Why not give the people a choice?"

"I do!" Mered said, feigning injury. "But they rarely choose wisely. I need to show them the way—the best way."

"By force?"

"Only if necessary."

Zaric stared into Mered's eyes, trying to find a trace of the cousin beneath the guise of the pretended king. All he saw was darkness, as though he were looking into dead eyes, reignited by black fire. "I can't let that happen," he said quietly.

"Guards!" Mered shouted. "Take this man to the dungeons. We will prepare a public execution. Let's show the kingdom that the old ways—old kings—are dead. No one will oppress them. A new way of life is beginning!"

Mered stared at Zaric as the guards rushed forward, swallowing back the worry caused by Zaric's calm demeanor.

The sadness remained as Zaric looked at Mered, but his strength surged. He pictured again the same clearing as before. Just as the guards reached out to clasp Zaric's arms, he was no longer there. The shackles clanged with a heavy echo as they fell to the stone floor.

A hush fell over the room as the people froze where they stood. "Find him!" Mered called out, fury flaring in his eyes. "He can't have gone far. Find him and bring him back to me!"

The people disbursed in a chaotic muddle, leaving Mered standing alone in the center of the room. In frustrated anger, he moved back to the dais and sat in his throne, hoping that the straightness of his back would mask his fear.

Chapter 2

The Present

H elen set out before sunrise, leaving Zaric, Stephen, and Meira before the three went to the palace. She wanted to be sure she reached the rendezvous point in time. As the only one outside the palace, she had to trust that everything would play out to plan and that the others would succeed. Once outside the city, she doubted she would hear even a hint of what was happening inside.

The horse was easy to lead and the cart not too heavy for him to pull, despite the supplies it held for the journey back to Camelora. Even on foot, Helen covered the miles much quicker than she expected. Though the terrain was mostly flat, occasional inclines and declines made the city disappear from view within the first two miles, giving the land an uninhabited appearance. No doubt this was what Mered intended when he set up his headquarters in such a secluded, yet central, valley—he could exert subtle influence without attracting too much attention. At least initially.

Helen tied the horse to the trunk of a tree, then sat down beneath its branches to wait. The wash of early morning sunlight, though usually calming, did little to ease her anxieties. In this part of the kingdom, trees were scarce and she was afraid of being seen by the wrong person, despite the fact that they had chosen an old, little-used path.

There was another reason for her anxiety: if everything went well, she would soon see her father for the first time in months. Helen was eager to hear news about her mother, her home, and the people she had left there. She also worried what state her father would be in after his months' long imprisonment. She tried not to let these thoughts weigh on her mind, but sitting alone in this quiet corner of the land, it was hard to think of anything else.

The only other thought Helen could manage was how she had come to this point. The slow descent of the past few years had accelerated after she left her home in Veren. She thought on the journey to Camdor, convincing Neil to join her in search of Camelora, and the unexpected, added task of finding the keys to open the Gateway. Her heart still felt twinges of the fear she endured as they tried to outrun Ian—the man Mered sent to stop them from reaching Zaric.

She pulled herself out of her memory when an image of Siri cropped up, reminding her of the woman who had nearly fooled Neil and nearly killed Helen.

The sun climbed above the horizon, higher and higher, as birds sang and cried, rustling the trees as they left in search of food. Helen became impatient, worried that the plan wasn't working. She worried that Meira, Stephen, or Zaric—or perhaps all three—had been captured. She looked to the sky, trying to determine the time by the position of the sun. Her instructions were to wait until midday and, if the others hadn't come, assume they had been captured. In that case, she was to return to Camelora. There she would meet with the members of the council who remained in the capital and come up with a new plan.

Helen didn't like the thought of traveling all that way alone. She had traveled alone before and knew how dangerous it could be. She also didn't like the thought of leaving the others behind.

Turning in the direction of the city, Helen looked for any sign of movement. As she looked over the barren landscape, a hunched figure of a man materialized a few feet ahead of her, where nothing had been only seconds before. He sat up for half-a-second before sinking to the ground.

Helen rushed forward, falling to her knees next to him. She turned him toward her to see his face. Beneath the withered and grey skin, the disheveled and stringy hair, the tangled beard, she recognized the face of the man she knew.

"Father!" she exclaimed, tears filling her eyes as she wrapped her arms around his frail frame and pulled him to her. "You're alive!"

She eased her grip to peer again at his face. He looked at her with weary and clouded eyes. A smile slowly formed across his lips as recognition emerged. "Helen, my girl," he whispered, his voice rasping and almost inaudible. "I thought I would never see you again."

She pulled him in again and embraced him with all the strength she dared. For a minute or two she sat in this way, flooded with relief, before thinking of the danger they were in, now that he was no longer in the dungeon. The plan was in motion and she needed to be, too. A portion of her anxiety returned. She helped her father to his feet, supporting him as they walked to the back of the cart.

After helping him climb in, she sat him against the cart's wooden back. Crawling into the cart herself, she opened a water barrel and filled a cup with the clean, clear liquid, then placed the cup at Cyrus's lips and helped him drink. Once he had drained the cup, she helped him lie down, covering him with a thick blanket. Helen sat at the edge of the cart and watched as he lay with eyes closed, breathing steadily. She knew that her questions would need to wait.

Helen sat at the edge of the cart, her awareness heightened as she watched for the others, or a sign of Mered's soldiers.

As she looked out at the landscape, a man stood in her field of vision, appearing in an empty space just as her father had. Zaric. She was more prepared this time and was already next to him when he stumbled, catching him before he fell to the ground. Holding him around the waist with his arm draped across her shoulders, Helen supported her king to the cart. She helped him in, where he sat against the wooden frame, leaning his head back and closing his eyes as he caught his breath. Repeating her actions from before, Helen gave him a drink of water, then sat back herself and waited until he was ready to talk.

"Did everything go according to plan?" she asked.

"Almost exactly," Zaric replied. "My part, at least. You can never plan for everything, of course, but Mered is fairly predictable, even after all these years. I just hope Meira and Stephen arrive soon, before Mered widens his search. I'm sure he knows what I can do and that I'm not likely to be near the city anymore."

Helen hadn't realized this before, but now that she thought of it, the panic she felt swelled within her chest. She hoped she did well at hiding her feelings, though she knew that it was hard to hide anything from Zaric. "I'll let you rest," she told him, placing her hand on his.

It wasn't long before Helen heard the sound of horses' hooves on the dry ground. At first they were faint and she felt a wave of relief, but soon she also felt worried, unsure who she would see when the horses came into view. She didn't know how much more she could take of these shifting emotions, hoping for Meira and Stephen but dreading Mered's men. She doubted she could outrun a company of soldiers and knew they wouldn't move on without searching the cart, no matter what story she managed to invent. Zaric was in no state to protect her.

Her worry dissipated when the horses crested the hill and Helen recognized her friends. She lowered herself from the cart, meeting them as they stopped.

"Mered's men were still searching the palace when we left," Stephen stated, "but it won't be long before they begin searching outside the city." He walked around the cart, making sure everything was secure for its journey. He closed and secured the back of the cart. Then, he began to adjust the horse's harness, harnessing his own horse alongside the first.

"Are the others safe?" Meira asked, clasping Helen's hands. The motherly feel of her actions eased Helen's mind.

"They're resting in the cart," Helen answered, indicating the two shapes behind her.

"I'm glad the two of you are safe, too," Zaric said without opening his eyes. His voice was still weak, but there was more color in his face.

"Do you have enough strength to cover our trail?" Meira asked him.

"I think so. They may be led to this point, but I can make sure they can't follow us past it."

"We should get moving, or that won't matter," Stephen said, finishing his task. "Come sit with me, Helen."

Stephen swung himself up into the driver's box. Helen approached and pulled herself up next to him while Meira remounted her horse. Soon they were moving forward at a steady pace. Helen looked back into the cart to see Zaric sitting with his hands pressed against the planks. Behind them, the dust swirled and rose in small clouds. Any sign that they had been in the clearing disappeared.

* * *

The sergeant dreaded giving Mered the bad news, but the officers had drawn straws and he drew the short one. He delayed it as long as he could, taking his time to walk to the throne room. The situation wasn't his fault, but it wouldn't do him any good to argue that point with Mered. Defending himself would only make the king more angry.

But Mered would also be angry if he delayed telling him too long. The sergeant could only hope Mered was in a merciful mood.

The doors to the throne room opened and the sergeant entered. Stepping to the center, he bowed before Mered.

"Did you find them?" Mered asked. "I hope their absence in this room is due to the fact that you took them straight to the dungeons and *not* that you have failed me."

Gulping down the fear in his throat, the sergeant kept his gaze on the floor and replied, "We followed their tracks into the wilderness for a few miles, but we lost their trail."

"Lost their trail? How did you lose their trail?"

"The tracks... stopped."

"Stopped," Mered repeated in a flat tone.

"Stopped," the sergeant said again, his voice dropping. "The hoofprints and footprints very plainly led us to a clearing on a hill, then just disappeared. Too many old, disused paths led away from the clearing for us to know which one they took."

The room stood still—no one moved. Then Mered reached out, grabbed the nearest object at hand, and threw it across the room. The goblet rang as it hit the wall, then clattered and rolled across the floor. Next, he flung the table the goblet had rested upon, knocking it onto its side before it slid forward and banged down the steps in front of the dais.

The surprise which had made everyone in the room jump back subsided and they stood still again. Mered towered in his fury. Those who looked on expected his eyes to set something in the room ablaze.

Instead, he lowered himself back onto his throne. His face grew thoughtful, the fury evaporating. "I expected better of you," he finally stated, "but I suppose it's not entirely your fault. After all, Zaric has many powers at his disposal. Powers he will always use to deceive. Let that, as well as a week—no, month—in the dungeon, be a lesson

14

to you."

A nod from Mered was the only instruction his guards needed to step forward and detain the sergeant. They didn't want to test Mered's patience in this moment. For his part, the sergeant went without a fight. After all, he had anticipated Mered's displeasure. Protesting would only make it worse.

"Bernt, gather your troops," Mered instructed, turning to one of his nearest and most-trusted captains. "I think I know where Zaric is headed."

"Yes, my lord." The man bowed before leaving the room.

"You, there," Mered called to the nearest servant before the door closed. "I need you to send a message to all of our governors. 'My dear sirs'—"

The servant ran to a nearby desk and scrambled for paper and ink, knowing Mered wouldn't stop to allow him to prepare.

"No, 'My dear friends,'" Mered corrected,

Word has reached me that there is a threat to our alliance. A man from the north is mobilizing an army to overturn all our efforts. We must devise a plan to stop him. We will meet as soon as possible, in no later than two weeks' time. Come to my palace without delay.

"Bring the copies to me when you are finished and I will add my signature. We cannot let Zaric accomplish his task."

The servant bowed just as the captain had done, then left through the same door. Zaric turned to the dais, his mind in turmoil. He knew Zaric too well to not be afraid, but he also knew that he couldn't show this fear. Reminding himself of all he had done over the past centuries to build up his own power and strength, his mind grew a little calmer. Zaric no longer knew the man he was up against and Mered drew satisfaction from that fact.

Chapter 3

The Present

Neil pushed sleep away with slow blinks, allowing his mind to awaken at its own pace. The soft, early light of morning came through the window, reflecting off the stone floor. He lay there for a few minutes. In the distance, muted thunder rumbled.

Thunder. Neil's brow crinkled.

Swinging his legs over the side of the bed, he crossed to the window and looked out. There wasn't a cloud in the sky. *The storm must be in the opposite direction,* he thought. *Or it wasn't really thunder.*

He turned his head to get the kinks out of his neck, arched his stiff back, and stretched out his good arm. Dressing as quickly as his wrapped wrist would let him, he headed to the kitchen to grab a quick breakfast before heading out to the fields. He liked to get in an hour or so of familiar farm work, even just one-handed, before Garrick gave him his assignments for the day. Though he enjoyed working with Garrick, the work he knew well—the work he had done since childhood—helped him remember who he was and prepare him for the day ahead.

It was fortunate that the field workers didn't see his help as an intrusion. In fact, they welcomed it. Neil found that it was a good way to learn more about the people he had been asked by Zaric to serve.

As he walked to the corn fields, Neil looked up at the sky, spinning in a circle to take it all in. He didn't see a single cloud. He decided it must not have been thunder he heard after all.

Just as that thought ended, another peel of thunder rumbled. The sound was unmistakable, but no matter where he looked, Neil couldn't find a reason for it. There was no way for him to set his confusion and uneasiness aside. He went through the motions of taking a hoe from the tool shed and going about his work, while his ears were on the alert. Nodding to the other workers who had come out early, he set about his task.

Working with his left hand, Neil couldn't help feeling a wave of sadness—though not for the disadvantage it gave him. He couldn't think of his broken wrist without also remembering how it had happened. He remembered the pain as Ian pushed against Neil's sword and the feeling was dread and helplessness at being disarmed. He remembered the feeling of resignation as he decided he would rather die for Camelora than see its people harmed. And he remembered the look on Ian's face as the blow Ian struck to kill Neil mirrored back on Ian instead, sending Mered's follower to the ground, lifeless.

Just as Neil began to shake off these feelings, he perceived a man approaching him. Garrick. "I knew I would find you here," the older man said.

"You *always* find me here," Neil pointed out, stretching his back again. "How are you this morning, Garrick?"

"I'm well, I'm well. Better than you."

Garrick pointed toward Neil's wrist.

"I'm used to it," Neil shrugged. "And it's getting better, just not as fast as I would like."

"I admire your dedication," Garrick complimented.

"The fields are looking good so far," Neil went on. "We should have a good harvest."

"We usually do," Garrick said. "Camelorans are good planners and good workers. The greatest complication could be the number of mouths we have to feed. At least it's still early enough in the season to plant more crops if we need to—assuming we have the room. That's what I want to focus on today, actually. I was hoping you could help me plan where to plant the additional crops and where to set up a camp for the supporters we hope to welcome. I don't doubt Zaric will be able to round up a few."

Neil nodded his assent and the two men headed back to the city.

"I've been reading some histories lately," Neil said after returning the hoe to the shed, "and I was wondering, how big *is* Camelora?"

"That depends on what you define as Camelora. This is just the city of Camelora and it's as big as you see it. But even the size of the *land* of Camelora is debatable. Currently, it reaches from the Gateway to the very edge of the northern frontier, quite a few miles from here—about twenty, I think—and just as many miles to the east and west. Anciently, the entire kingdom was called Camelora, including your village and Helen's city."

"So, when the books refer to Camelora—"

"—what they're referring to depends on when they were written."

"How long has Camelora been hidden? The city, that is."

"Nine hundred eighty-three years."

Neil looked at his companion in surprise. "Are you that old, Garrick?"

Garrick laughed heartily. "No, it was one of my ancestors—a man called Adan—who came with Zaric back then. The people of Camelora are born, live, and die just like anyone else. Zaric excepted, of course. Mered is older than that as well."

"How is that possible?"

"With only two men able to accomplish it, I think it would be hard to find an expert on the subject. But if you really are interested in reading histories, there may be something in the library that can help you answer that question. Zaric's personal study has quite a few ancient texts, as well."

"Speaking of Zaric," Neil said, seizing the opportunity to ask about something that had been on his mind, "have you heard from him since he left?"

"Nothing yet," Garrick answered, "from either Zaric *or* Helen." He said Neil's friend's name in a knowing way, showing the young man that he knew the true purpose behind his question. "That isn't unexpected, though. We have very few allies in the larger kingdom, which means we have no couriers. We probably won't hear anything until supporters begin to arrive."

Neil was afraid of an answer like this, even if he expected it. It made him uneasy not knowing what was happening with the groups that had gone out—especially Helen and Zaric.

A faint peal of thunder halted the men. "That's the third time I've heard that," Neil stated, casting his eyes up at the sky and seeing nothing but the pale blues and yellows of early morning. He turned westward, his eyes fixed above the hills. It was then he saw a small grey cloud, streaming rain and lightning as it moved rapidly over the fields.

"That's strange," Garrick uttered.

"Yes…" Neil trailed off, remembering the time a few weeks previous when one unwanted man crossing into the borders of Camelora had caused the land to react with rain, snow, fog, and hurricane-force winds. "But we've seen much bigger storms than this."

"It's strange *because* it's so small," Garrick said. "What could possibly cause such a small storm?"

As he said this, the shadow of the cloud covered them, dragging behind it a sheet of cold rain that drenched them both, like a bucket of water overturned above them. As suddenly as it came, it passed, moving to the walls of the city and passing over the center of it.

"So much water in such a small cloud," Neil muttered.

Wiping the water from their eyes with their wet sleeves, Neil and Garrick quickened their pace. They weren't sure yet what they needed to do, only that they needed to do it right away. Around them, the air moved faster as well. It was hard to tell from which direction the wind came. Both men turned their heads back to the west to see a funnel cloud making its way toward the city—and them. They ran as fast as they could to the nearest city entrance. There was no way to cry out a warning to the people of the city.

The sound of wind filled Neil's ears, mingled with the hammering of his own heartbeat. Fear swelled inside him as the confidence drained that they could reach safety before the tornado reached them.

The men stopped beneath the arch of the gate, finding holes in the stones to hold as tightly as they could. The roar of the wind pulled them, testing their grips and threatening to rip them away in its swirl of air, dust, and debris. Using every ounce of his strength, Neil dug his hands into the crevices of the rocks, biting back the pain it caused his still-healing wrist. Crashing and breaking sounds filled his ears. He closed his eyes and rested his head against the arch.

The roar of the wind died down as the funnel moved farther and farther away. The two men stayed where they were until the sound was gone completely.

Emerging from their place of safety, they couldn't imagine what they would see, so they weren't prepared for the extent of the tornado's destruction. The cyclone's meandering path was carved into the buildings at the edge of the city. Stone and wood littered the earth. Cloth and paper drifted through the air as they made their way to the ground. Neil's and Garrick's disbelieving steps turned to a run when they saw fallen people among the rubble.

With no advanced warning, not everyone was able to get out of the tornado's path before it hit the city. Men and women lay in the street, some hit by falling debris and others ripped from the buildings as the tornado struck. A few people stood with stunned expressions while others rushed to help their injured neighbors.

"How many are hurt?" Neil asked of no one in particular, kneeling next to an unconscious woman with blood streaming from a gash in her head. Her pulse was faint. He searched for a cloth to press against the wound.

"Five or six here," Garrick answered, taking in the scene around them. "Coordinate getting the injured to the palace while I see how things look farther down. And find the council. We need to find out what's going on."

Neil nodded and Garrick ran off, pushing his way through the crowd that was forming. The shock wearing off, more and more Camelorans stepped forward to give aid. Neil worried why this had happened in the first place. Camelora's defenses were designed to protect its citizens, not hurt them. Neil's mind darted between thoughts of how to protect the city from this strange development and thoughts of how it might have started. He also wondered if Camelora would really attack itself in this way. He doubted it would. Yet, if an intruder had crossed Camelora's borders, this was not a way to repel them. Like a human being, Camelora appeared to be confused.

Neil hoped no one had been killed, and that they could solve this problem before anyone was.

Chapter 4

The Present

"Can any of you explain what's happening?" Garrick asked. He sat at the head of the table in the council room, in the chair usually reserved for Zaric. It was the first time he hadn't hesitated to sit in this seat since the king's departure. The unforeseen disaster had changed Garrick, making the man more decisive than before.

A brief pause followed as the council members exchanged glances. "No," Gowon answered, simply and resolutely.

Garrick shook his head. "I need something better than 'no.'"

"Nothing like this has ever happened before," Cynthia put in. "But I don't need to tell *you* that."

"I would have thought someone had read a book or asked Zaric to explain his defense system," Garrick went on, exasperated. "We should understand how our own defenses work."

"We have theories," Arlen stated. "It's possible that the protection of the Gateway was our real protection and now it's fading. Or, because Camelora is like a living being, perhaps she's sick. It's also possible that Camelora's defenses aren't as strong without Zaric."

"We could have an intruder like before," Zelene suggested, "but Camelora doesn't know what to do without Zaric within her boundaries. Perhaps there *is* an intruder, but the intruder isn't as much of a threat as Ian."

"Do we believe an intruder is the most likely reason?" Garrick asked.

"That's our best frame of reference," Arlen explained. "Things like this only happen when someone unwanted or dangerous enters our borders. When the Gateway was closed, this never happened. But don't forget what Zaric and the rest of the council are doing. We could start seeing all sorts of people enter Camelora with varying levels of dedication. The land is likely sensitive to that."

"How do we find out for sure if that's what's happening now?" asked Neil. "We have guard towers on the borders of the land. Has anyone noticed a large group of people approaching? Have the refugees begun to arrive?"

A commotion in the hallway outside interrupted the discussion, drawing the council members' eyes to the door and preventing them from answering. Loud voices came through the door and Neil heard Garrick's name. There was a loud, rapid knock. Neil got to his feet, but before he could reach the door, it swung open.

"Excuse me," a harried young man gasped, perspiration glistening at his temples. A palace worker stood behind him, looking on disapprovingly. "We need Garrick in the throne room. We think we've found a trespasser."

"Maybe this is our answer," Garrick said to the council before pushing past Neil and stepping into the hallway.

"You *think* you found a trespasser," Neil repeated, following as the young man led the governor down the hall. "Why aren't you sure?"

"She didn't put up a fight, for one," the young man replied. "And she isn't armed. She also seemed relieved to be found. She could be a supporter of Zaric who got lost on her way to the city, but since she's alone, we wanted to be sure."

Neil felt something ominous in the term "she," but it was only

23

a slight twinge that went away the second after it came. Half of the residents of the kingdom were female, after all. Yet he didn't brush it aside. He didn't like the sound of it. His mind filled with memories of one woman in particular—a woman who had proven to be more dangerous than he had been willing to believe, despite Helen's misgivings. Since this woman had once traveled with Ian—the man who had been defeated trying to infiltrate Camelora only a few weeks before—it was only natural that she should come to Neil's mind.

"Tell me what happened," Garrick said to the guard.

"Well," the young man breathed with a sigh as though he was preparing for an important narrative, "we—my friends and I—were hunting this morning west of the city. We thought we saw an animal through the trees, but something about it didn't seem quite right. The five of us surrounded it and closed in. As we came closer, I realized it was a woman. It's a good thing we didn't attack. The others must have realized it, too, because no one raised a bow or knife. From her clothing, we could tell she was a stranger. We asked what she wanted and she was quick to say that she didn't intend to hurt anyone. It was an odd statement. Then she said she wanted to talk to Zaric. I think we know enough not to blindly trust a stranger, either man or woman, so we searched her for weapons, took her bag, and brought her to the palace."

The council arrived at the throne room, two guards throwing open the double doors at their approach. A small group of young men stood just inside the door, but Neil barely noticed them. His attention was instantly captured by the woman standing in the middle of the room—the woman who had turned to face the door when it opened. Surprise, anger, and uncertainty froze Neil as he recognized Siri.

For a few moments, Neil stood in the doorway, his mind flooded with memories and emotions as he tried to take in what he now saw. Unaware of the recognition in the young man's mind, Garrick and

24

the council stepped past him into the room, where the governor took a position in front of the unfamiliar woman.

But Neil couldn't move. He was enraged, stunned, scared. The last time he had seen Siri, she was lying unconscious on a hilltop with a hollow reed in her hand, while Helen lay a few feet away, a poisoned dart in her neck and her life fading. Until that moment at the Gateway, Neil thought Siri was his ally—a position he defended to the point Helen nearly left him behind. He had been concerned when Siri disappeared during a storm—a storm which he later learned had been caused by Zaric himself. Now, Neil wished he had listened to Helen's fears and seen Siri as the traitor she was.

He was surprised at Siri's audacity, coming to Camelora and asking to see Zaric, as though she had a right to do so. A fire arose in his chest, making it hard to breathe. Neil thought of what the young man had said about Siri being unarmed and wondered if it was actually true. His mind tried to construct a theory as to why she was here, why she was seeking Zaric, why she had given herself up without a fight. Her clothes were specked with dirt and dust; her face was dirty and weary. Still, he couldn't think past the image of Helen on the ground.

"Siri," he finally said with more malice than he knew he possessed, breaking into the words Garrick had begun to speak. Walking to the front of the room with slow, measured steps, Neil thought he saw the woman flinch at the sound of her name and felt a jolt of satisfaction. She didn't seem very surprised to see him. Fear was in her eyes as well, but she stood straight and resolute.

"I wish to see Zaric," she stated.

Tension hung in the air as Garrick looked to Neil, unsure how to proceed. The governor knew the woman's name from the stories Neil and Helen told upon their arrival in Camelora. He knew what she had done, what role she had played for Mered, and the danger she posed. The remembrance was evident in his expression.

"You are Siri," Garrick stated, "Mered's ally."

Siri turned her eyes back to Garrick. "Are you Zaric?" she asked.

"If I was," Garrick replied, "You wouldn't need to ask. Zaric isn't here. I am Garrick, the governor of Camelora in the king's absence."

Siri said nothing for a moment, but didn't drop her eyes or show any reaction. Her gaze stayed focused on Garrick as Neil stood seething before her. "Then maybe you can help me. I came for refuge and protection from Mered."

Garrick shifted his attention to Neil, but Neil's firmness faltered. A subtle vulnerability in Siri's voice struck him. He wondered if it was possible. The young man said she was unarmed and she gave herself up without a fight. Neil slowly moved his gaze back to Siri.

But the image of Helen's cold and pale face hardened his heart again. After all, it wouldn't be hard to conceal a reed and a few darts. Siri had deceived him before with her lies. This could be another elaborate act. He didn't know the depth of her abilities to persuade someone to do what she wanted—as she had done before—and he didn't care for anyone to learn. Rage spread from the fire in his chest, filling his entire body, stiffening his muscles and burning his face.

"Protection," he spat, the anger contorting his features. "You said something similar before. No one was there to protect Helen from *you,* when you almost killed her."

"Almost?" If Siri was disappointed by this, she hid it well. Instead, she sounded relieved. "She's alive, then?"

"Garrick," Neil continued, turning to the governor, "I think we should find a cold, dark room to throw this woman in. Keep her under guard. We need to watch her every movement until Zaric returns. She shouldn't even cough without permission."

"That isn't the way we do things in Camelora," Garrick stated.

"It should be!" Neil shouted. "You've been shielded from the world for too long and don't know the best way to treat a threat."

"Gowon," Garrick said, still calm, beckoning the councilman forward.

"Neil, I can help you," Siri pleaded, clasping her hands in an imploring gesture. "I can give you information about Mered."

"We don't want your information. How do we know you won't lie to save yourself?"

"Neil, I'm sorry!"

"Sorry?!" Neil bellowed. It seemed like time stopped as complete silence engulfed the room. The deep anger that had been welling inside of Neil could now be felt by everyone there. While Neil stood with cold, piercing eyes fixed on Siri, no one spoke or moved. He considered her for a moment, growing more and more determined not to believe anything she might say.

"I think you need to calm down," Garrick said, firmly gripping Neil's arm. "Gowon, please take Neil out of here."

Gowon's hand on Neil's elbow replaced Garrick's. He placed the other on the young man's back, pushing him toward the door. Once in the hallway, Neil shook Gowon off and stormed away from the room.

For a while, Neil wandered the palace without thinking of where he was going. As he wandered, his anger subsided and a new fear grew. Finally, he found himself on the battlements. From there he gazed upon the city that had fast become his home. Looking over Camelora, he knew that he didn't want to lose it—he couldn't, even if he had to die to save it.

But if Zaric's supporters could now enter the land's borders, his enemies could, too. Siri had been discovered before she could cause any damage, but what if the next enemy had more luck? Neil realized now just how difficult the job of protecting this land would be.

He didn't know how long he had been there when he heard the heavy opening of the door and turned to see Garrick stepping through it.

"We locked the woman in a room on the third floor," he said, "and we're organizing a guard to sit outside the door. Arlen is there in the meantime. Neil, I know how strongly you feel about this woman. I remember everything you and Helen told us when you arrived. But you need to learn to temper your emotions. We need to hear what this woman has to say before we disregard her."

"Doesn't she strike you as dangerous?" Neil asked.

"No more than anyone else," Garrick answered.

Heat flared in Neil's chest, but he tamped it down. He couldn't blame Garrick for failing to see Siri the way he did. The woman had a talent for controlling how others perceived her.

"I trusted her before because I thought the same thing," Neil finally said. "She traveled with me and Helen for a few days. Do you remember the state Helen was in when we came? Siri did that."

"People *do* change."

"Does that mean she shouldn't be held responsible for what she's done?"

"No, I'm not saying that," Garrick contested. "We can discuss a punishment if one is needed, but we can also give Siri a chance to talk. If she wants to give us information about Mered, it would be unwise to ignore her."

"Do you think the people of Camelora are prepared to fight?"

"Perhaps not quite, but I really don't think one woman is a threat to an entire city."

"We aren't just talking about one woman. Think about it, Garrick. We don't know if we can trust her. We don't know if she brought anyone with her. We don't really know if protection is the only reason she came. I think it would be *unwise* not to consider that Mered could be coming."

A visible shudder went through Garrick's frame, but Neil felt no sense of triumph. Instead, he only felt the dawning of fear. Life was about to change for the people of Camelora and Neil was worried they wouldn't be prepared.

Chapter 5

The Present

A campfire lit up the clearing where the fading sunlight stopped. Days of journeying had led the travelers deep into the woods, bearing only the faintest signs of the old and forgotten path they used.

The wood was a peaceful place. The trees were a refreshing shelter from the summer heat and a welcome change from the dry, scrubby vegetation of the southern lands. As the landscape became more lush and green, the fear of being found by Mered's army lessened. The greenery also signaled that the party was drawing closer to Camelora.

Although Zaric had regained his full strength within a couple of hours, Helen's father was still frail and weak, only leaving the cart for a few short minutes at a time. The rest of the time he spent bundled in blankets, resting. Helen did her best to make him comfortable. She feared that the years added to his face by Mered's prison would never fade away, that what little strength he had now was the most he would ever have again. Helen hoped the thinness of his body would fill in once he reached Camelora and could be fed better food, but she had doubts about that, too. She wanted to wait until he was stronger to ask about his imprisonment and what had happened to their city, Veren, but now felt that time would never come.

With the camp ready, Helen stole away from Zaric and the others to spend a few minutes with her father. As gently as she could, she helped him sit up and drink a cup of water.

"I'm so glad you made it to Camelora safely," Cyrus said, clasping Helen's hand.

She only smiled, deciding not to tell him in what state she had arrived in Camelora.

"For months and months," he went on, "I worried. I wondered if I would ever know what had happened to you. Every time a new prisoner was brought to the dungeon, I asked about you, but all I received were blank stares."

"I wondered about you, too," Helen told him. "And Mother."

A shadow fell over her father's face. His eyes grew moist and his mouth quivered. Helen kept her gaze fixed on his face and he looked away, staring into the trees, his expression a mixture of pain, shame, and deep sadness. Fear enveloped Helen's mind at her father's reaction.

"What happened to Mother?" she asked, suppressing the panic constricting her lungs. The effort only heightened her dread. "Was she imprisoned, too? Perhaps in a different—"

"No," Cyrus interrupted, shaking his head. "Your mother—she never made it out of Veren. The day you escaped, the army gathered all of the prominent men and women... their husbands and wives... their children. They were angry that they couldn't find you. As punishment, the men were taken off to prison, while the women and older children... were executed."

All sensation left Helen's body, leaving behind a tingling weight-lessness. In her shock, her father's face faded away as images of the people of Veren flooded her memory, flashing before her eyes in quick succession. She thought she could hear their screams and cries—being dragged into the street, being interrogated, being separated, being executed. Those innocent people, who had always supported her father and family, killed and imprisoned because they had no idea she had escaped. The women and children dying for her, the men wasting away in dark, stone cells. Her mother—

Helen didn't know when she started to sob, but her knees were pulled up to her chin, the skirt and hands covering her face were wet.

"Please, my dear," Cyrus said as he inched toward her and enwrapped her in his thin arms. "Please, don't cry."

"They died because of me," she managed.

"No," Cyrus corrected her. "They died because of Mered. He is responsible for his orders—for his ambitions—not you."

"But if only—"

"Think of all the people who will be saved because you escaped. You opened the Gateway and reached Zaric, and now he will stop Mered's wave of oppression. The kingdom will live because of you."

Helen knew these words were true, but they did little to ease the guilt she felt. None of those lives were her mother's. She would never see her mother again, never see her people again.

Minutes passed in silent grief between father and daughter.

"I always hoped that one day I could return to Veren with you and Mother," Helen muttered as her sadness steadied and sobs lessened, "to live like we did before."

"Oh, Helen, there's no Veren to return to. As they were taking us away, the soldiers burned the city to the ground."

New tears fell as Helen imagined the city—her home—in flames. The people she knew, the places she loved—everything gone. She remembered watching as the flames reached up the walls of Neil's cottage, claiming the only home he had known. The memory fueled her imagination as she pictured fire eating away at her own home.

She knew her father was right. If the Gateway hadn't been opened, Mered would have been free to do the same thing to many more cities until he gained his desire for power and control. But if she had known she would pay for finding Zaric with the lives and homes and livelihoods of her family, friends, and neighbors, she doubted she would have done it.

"Continue to help Zaric and stop Mered," Cyrus continued. "That is how you can honor your mother and the people of our city. They were always a brave people and willing to give up their lives to ensure freedom for the rest of the kingdom."

Helen nodded. Taking a deep breath to secure her emotions, she kissed her father's cheek. "I'm glad you're safe, Father. I haven't lost everything. But I'm afraid you're tired again. All this talk of painful things has worn you out."

"Yes, but you needed to know. I'm glad I told you."

"I think you should rest now. We can talk again later."

But as Helen helped her father lie down, she knew she wouldn't have the heart to bring it up again. She knew what she needed to know and didn't need to make him relive his pains over and over.

Helen lowered herself out of the cart and rested against its side for a few minutes, closing her eyes as she calmed her body and mind. Inhaling, she opened them again and looked at the shadowed forest around her. She heard Zaric talking with Meira and Stephen not far away and allowed her feet to carry her to them.

"My plan is to go to Phara," Zaric said as Helen sat next to him. A loaf of bread was being passed around and she tore off a piece. "To the west."

"Chasing the story," Stephen stated.

Meira leaned over as the men continued to talk and whispered to Helen, "Are you all right?"

Helen felt a stone in her throat—tickling and irritating and threatening to bring her to tears again—but did her best to swallow it down. She hadn't thought of how red her eyes must be or how blotchy crying had made her face. Attempting a smile, she nodded. She knew the other woman didn't believe her when Meira sat closer and grasped her hand, not letting go. She didn't ask any more questions, though. Helen didn't want her to. But that display of support eased Helen's heart and fortified her. She rested her head on Meira's shoulder.

"Do you think you will find them?" Meira asked Zaric, inserting herself back into the conversation.

"Find who?" Helen interjected, lifting her head again. "What story?"

This wasn't the first time she had heard Zaric mention Phara. The name sounded familiar in a different way, but she couldn't recall reading about it in any books. The others seemed to understand what Zaric expected to find there and Helen was surprised that the story wasn't more widely known.

"It's a little more obscure than most," Meira said. "There's a story that tells of a person—whether it's a man or a woman, a boy or a girl isn't specified—who has an ability to make predictions that others can't make and see things that others can't see. In the final war with Mered, this person will be able to foresee what the other side is planning and help the army prepare for it."

"With this person, we would have an advantage?" Helen asked.

Meira and Stephen both looked to Zaric to answer. He hesitated. From the distressed expression he wore—one Helen had never seen on his face before—she could see the answer wasn't simple.

"Yes," he agreed, "but this ability doesn't come without its complications. It takes its toll on the person who has it. I've seen it before. You must remember that a person with abilities of this nature is still a person, not just a playing piece in a game. If Mered were to find him or her, he would likely force them to help him, by whatever means necessary, if he can't convince them to join his side. We will give them the choice and respect the decision they make. Personally, I don't care if they choose to use their abilities. I would rather they don't."

"Does Mered know this person exists?" Helen asked.

"Yes," Zaric stated simply.

Helen tried to ignore the chill that shocked her spine. "So, the story is directing you to Phara to find a person with the gift of sight," she summarized.

"Well, not Phara *specifically*," Stephen inserted.

"You see, Helen," Meira said, "this gift runs in Zaric's family and *only* Zaric's family."

Meira's words left Helen speechless. She had never thought of Zaric as a husband and father before—or at least not a father in that sense. When she thought of how long he had lived, she realized how many hundreds, or even thousands, of descendants he could have. Yet he lived alone, his only family the people who surrounded him in Camelora. She had never heard him speak about immediate family before. Were some of his descendants still living in the kingdom, or had they all died out? Did Mered know that this powerful individual was Zaric's descendant—a living member of his family? Did that only add to the person's danger?

"After the war that broke the kingdom," Meira went on, "Zaric's son, Edric, settled in Phara. It's likely that this person is one of Zaric's descendants and still lives there."

"Perhaps I can convince the people of Phara to join us as well," Zaric said. "We can't forget our primary mission. Camelora needs more support."

"That's why Meira and I plan to head southward," Stephen stated, "after we take Cyrus to Camelora."

"What is your plan, Helen?" Zaric asked.

Helen didn't know how to answer. She didn't want to admit that she hadn't thought of anything past rescuing her father. She also hadn't considered that the choice would be hers. From the beginning, she assumed she would be instructed on what to do next. Even when

35

Zaric invited her to go with him before leaving Camelora, she felt like she had very little choice. Now, if she really was allowed to choose, where she *wanted* to go and where she *needed* to go were not the same place.

"I feel I should go to Phara, too," she said. "My place is with Zaric, helping to gather support. Is that all right?"

"Of course," Zaric assured her. "You will be a valuable addition on my journey. I have no doubt you will help more than you realize."

Chapter 6

The Present

"We'll come to Camelora when our work in Phara is done," Helen said, tightly pressing her father's hand as he sat in the back of the cart. "Hopefully, the people will come with us."

"I don't doubt that Zaric will convince them," Cyrus replied. "And you will be a great help. I'm proud of you, Helen."

Helen could think of nothing to say in reply, not sure she had the same confidence in herself that her father had. Instead, she embraced him, wanting to hold onto him as long as possible. The thought fluttered at the edge of her mind that she would never see him again. She wanted to hold onto him as long as she could.

Yet they all needed to move forward: Meira, Stephen, and Cyrus to Camelora; Helen and Zaric to Phara. Helen refused to let herself cry as she and her father said good-bye. She slid to the ground and stood next to Zaric, watching the cart roll forward. It would move north as she and Zaric moved west.

Helen bit her lip as she cast her eyes back over her shoulder to watch the others disappearing into the trees. She knew there was no safer place in the world than Camelora, but she wasn't so sure about the safety of the road that led to it. She and Zaric hadn't met with any danger on the way south, but that was before they had angered Mered. It was impossible to know where Mered's men were and what they would do if they found her father again.

"Would you like to go with them?" Zaric asked, placing a hand on Helen's elbow.

"No," she replied with a shake of her head. "The thought hadn't even crossed my mind. I'm just wondering if they'll be safe."

"Watching after them won't keep them away from danger," Zaric pointed out. "You just have to trust that everything will be all right. We have our own task to worry about."

Helen nodded, but still looked back one more time. The cart was barely visible beyond the tree line. Soon, it disappeared. She inhaled slowly, telling herself that Zaric was right. She couldn't complete her own task if she was focused on how others would complete theirs.

Traveling with Zaric wasn't at all like her travels before. Helen felt an overwhelming safety and comfort with Zaric, as though she were surrounded by a bubble of protection that nothing could penetrate. She knew this wasn't entirely true, but that knowledge didn't diminish the feeling. Zaric was alert and anticipated danger in a way no one else could—a gift he used with little effort. At every fork in the path, he knew which one to take. He heard dangerous wildlife a mile away and knew how to avoid it. His sense of direction was unhindered by the thickness of the trees. This allowed Helen to worry less and rest her senses more than she had on her original journey to Camelora.

The quietness of the empty country they passed through contrasted sharply with the idea of a kingdom soon to be at war. Helen understood why it was proving difficult to win support. If she hadn't seen for herself how dangerous Mered could be, she wouldn't have believed that anything was wrong in the land. It was only when that danger took her by the throat that she was really forced to see it.

As they walked, Zaric talked. He told Helen about the corner of the kingdom they were exploring—its history and the people who had once lived there. Walking with Zaric was like being in a library. His mind held more information than Helen could ever hope to remember. He knew complete histories of every corner of this land, as well as the composition of the soil and rocks, whether or not the land was fertile, which plants were most likely to grow, the weather patterns for the different times of the year. Mostly, he liked to talk about the people and their lives. Not only their political histories, but the everyday, mundane details that gave them character. Helen knew the people were what he really cared about. Gaining power was not his idea of success, but safety and happiness were.

Despite the pleasure of listening to Zaric, Helen was glad when they finally decided to stop for the day. The terrain had become hilly and difficult to navigate, exhausting her more than she was used to. The trees were thicker in this part of the forest and Zaric chose a space to set up camp that could only be called a "clearing" in the loosest sense of the word. There was barely room for the two of them to sit around a campfire without setting the surrounding foliage ablaze. Deep shadows covered the forest as Helen gathered firewood and Zaric prepared the fire. Despite being a summer night, there was a chill in the air. Helen wrapped a blanket around her shoulders as they ate a simple supper.

Watching Zaric, a thought hanging at the back of Helen's mind came to the forefront. It nudged her until she couldn't keep it in any longer. Yet, although Zaric displayed his usual demeanor of calm and peace, Helen didn't know how to start the conversation. She didn't know where to start.

"What do you want to ask?" Zaric questioned, breaking off a piece of his bread. "I can tell something is on your mind."

Helen thought for a few more seconds, then dove in. "Why didn't you say that you had a family?"

"It was a long time ago."

"Not for you," Helen said. "Not when they're your family."

Zaric looked into the flames of the campfire, as though he were looking back through the centuries. "I think that's *why* I haven't mentioned them," he stated. "It's still and always will be too fresh on my mind. Things didn't end well for us back then."

This statement hit Helen like a stab to the heart. The image of her mother resurfaced—the worried, anxious expression on her face as she rushed to pack a simple bag and send away her only child. A too-brief embrace that Helen still felt, before she was pushed into a secret corridor of the governor's mansion, not knowing that she would never see her mother's face again. If she *had* known, she would have glanced back and taken a few extra seconds to memorize every feature, every line.

Helen realized that her eyes were wet and pushed the memories back before the tears spilled out. "Will you tell me about them?" she went on, hoping to distract herself. A pang of guilt hit her as she realized she was using Zaric's grief to ease her own, but she didn't apologize.

"Perhaps," Zaric replied. His face revealed that he was lost in memories, too. Then, he shook his head as if to shake away the images. "But we don't have time tonight. There's something else I wanted to talk about, something that I don't think can wait."

"Is it another prophecy?"

"No, nothing like that. Helen, I'm sure you've noticed that you're a very special person."

Helen looked down at her hands, feeling the color rise into her cheeks. "I don't try to be," she uttered.

"It's not a bad thing," Zaric laughed. "You handle it well because you don't think about it. I suppose I should say that you're different from others. You have certain—abilities. When you and Neil made your way to Camelora, you were able to do some impossible things."

"That wasn't me," Helen argued. "Someone else was making those things happen—someone I couldn't see. You, perhaps."

"No, Helen, it was you. Just like my wife, just like the person we hope to find in Phara, you have a special power—a special gift. But the fact that you don't realize it—even after using it—tells me that you don't know *how* to use it. I would like to show you how to control the power within you. I believe your instincts are good and you know when it's the right time to use it, but it will serve you much better if you are more aware of it."

Despite her embarrassment, Helen nodded in agreement.

Zaric shifted his legs into a kneeling position and moved closer to the fire. He reached out his hand with his palm downward, holding it over the flame high enough that the fire didn't quite touch him. Slowly, he rotated his wrist. The flame rose, curling around his hand, still without touching it. When his palm faced up, a large drop of fire floated above it, like a candle without a wick. Zaric reached out his other hand and snapped his fingers. In an instant, the fire shot up into the air and extinguished itself, leaving only a trace of smoke.

"How did you do that?" Helen asked, feeling like a child seeing a jester's trick.

"By concentrating," Zaric said. "It's as simple as that. But it's a different kind of concentration—active, intense, fully aware, intentional. You need to let go of everything at the front of your mind. Stop all intrusive thoughts and focus completely, without words or emotions. You block everything but the thing that you want to happen. Would you like to try?"

"I'm not sure," Helen said, apprehension squeezing her heart.

"You've done it before, you just didn't know it. Hold your hand out."

Helen followed his instructions, kneeling next to the fire and holding her palm down over the flames, just as Zaric had done. She sat like this until her mind stopped naming the sounds around her, forming words, or wandering and wondering. Turning her hand, the flames started to curl around it. But, at the first hint of surprise, they fell back, blending in again with the campfire below.

"That's all right," Zaric encouraged. "It takes time."

For the next few minutes, Helen repeated the same actions with the same results. She couldn't stop the thoughts from forming in her mind—the worries, the doubts. Shifting her weight, she tried from a different position, but it made no difference. In frustration, she moved away from the fire and let out a sigh.

"Take your time," said Zaric. Helen waited for more words of instruction or a speech to motivate her, but he said nothing else.

Closing her eyes, she took a few deep breaths, feeling the growing evening around her. Without looking, she saw the scene she was a part of: the fire in the middle of the clearing; Zaric sitting on the other side; the trees surrounding them; patches of sky overhead; leaves and twigs littering the clearing. One by one, Helen took these items away, disassembling the scene one piece at a time until all she saw was the fire.

Opening her eyes again, Helen saw only the orange and yellow flames now, exactly as they had been when her eyes were closed. Reaching out, she held her hand over them, then turned her hand, watching the fire curl around and lick it. With her palm faced upward, a single flame danced above it. Helen continued to push back any reaction. She raised her other hand and snapped her fingers as Zaric had done. The flame rose and blinked out.

The scene around Helen filled in again—the fire, the clearing, the trees, and Zaric. It wasn't until all of the sounds returned that she noticed they had even been gone. She let out the breath she had been holding and smiled, then giggled like a child. Zaric smiled in return. Then everything shifted and Helen reached out her hand to catch herself before she fell to the ground. Her head spun and she felt a sudden tiredness, as though all of her strength drained away. Zaric rushed to support her.

"That can happen," he said, "when you become aware of how to use your abilities. It takes some getting used to. Until then, you'll find you don't have much strength after using your power."

"It didn't happen before," she pointed out.

"You didn't know you were doing anything before. I'm sure you were only using a fraction of your power, too."

"It gets better?" Helen asked, putting a hand to her head in an effort to steady it.

"Yes, of course—with practice. For now, though, it's time to get some rest. I'll take the first watch while you get some sleep. Well done, Helen."

Helen nodded, too tired to talk anymore. She pulled her bedroll and blanket off her bag and did her best to get comfortable.

In spite of her exhaustion, though, it was a while before she was able to fall asleep. She felt that something inside of her had changed without warning and she didn't know how to feel about it.

Chapter 7

The Present

"Neil, I need you to come with me," Garrick panted, appearing only briefly before running out of the kitchen again.

Neil dropped his fork onto his plate, ignoring the few uneaten bites of his breakfast. Garrick didn't look worried, but he carried with him an air of urgency. Curious, Neil pushed his chair from the table and left the kitchen, jogging to catch up to Garrick.

Soon they stood on the rooftop of the palace, looking over the western fields from behind the battlements. A fierce wind blew, alternating between warm and cold. Though they were too far away for him to distinguish any physical characteristics, Neil could easily tell that a large group of people was approaching the city in a slow, disordered manner. It was obvious it was not an army. An army would be more organized and less weary. The guards would have sent up a call that Neil would have heard long before Garrick appeared in the kitchen. Looking through the telescope Garrick handed him, Neil saw that the group was made up of men, women, and children.

"How many do you think there are?" he asked.

"About two hundred," Garrick answered. "Maybe three. Many of them are still in the trees, so it's hard to tell."

44

"How is the campground coming along?"

"It's marked off and many of the firepits have been dug. Not the most ideal situation, but it'll do. Some of the empty buildings in the city have been cleaned, but there aren't many."

"Do you think our people sent them?"

"Possibly," Garrick conceded. "They could also be answering the call from the Gateway. Let's go and find out."

There was excitement in Garrick's voice mirroring the excitement Neil himself felt. He felt a thrill considering that his and Helen's efforts to open the Gateway had not been in vain and Zaric's plan was truly moving forward.

Their first refugees.

"Gather some guards and we'll go to meet them," Garrick instructed as they started down the staircase.

Neil obeyed. He soon met Garrick, guards in tow and umbrellas in hand, at the western gate of the city. They headed across an empty green space to meet their new guests.

The two groups met halfway between the forest and the city. As the Camelorans stood before the newcomers, Neil tried to suppress the apprehensive thoughts running through his mind as he contemplated the small percentage of potential refugees these people represented. He tried to multiply the scene in front of him, copying this group and mentally setting others like it in the surrounding space. It made him lightheaded. He knew they had room for hundreds of people, but thousands? Housing the expected refugees was the main problem they hadn't been able to solve yet.

The strangers stood in nervous anticipation. The most frightened ones in the group were mostly the children, though some of the men and women appeared to be uneasy as well, their eyes shifting from one Cameloran to another, looking to each other and murmuring.

"Do you have a leader?" Garrick asked, scanning the front line. "A governor or mayor, perhaps?"

Whispers and commotion followed as the people in the front of the group elbowed each other. An older man a few yards back said in a near-shout, "What did he say?"

Garrick, in his usual calm manner, let out a chuckle, rubbing his brow. "It's easier to talk to one person than hundreds."

One man was finally pushed forward. He stumbled but quickly caught his footing, advancing with downcast eyes. "I represent these people," he said, his voice shaking in his effort to sound official. Judging by his appearance, Neil guessed he was nothing grander than a carpenter.

"What's your name?" Garrick asked.

"Trevor," the man answered.

"Where do you come from?"

"Steren, on the west coast."

"How many are you?"

"Two hundred sixty-seven," Trevor replied. "At least, that's what we counted last night."

Neil looked to Garrick, but the man's usual optimism didn't falter. It impressed Neil how much this man believed to be possible.

"Excuse me," Trevor continued, "but may *I* ask a question now? Is this Camelora?"

Before Garrick could answer, a clap of thunder rattled the atmosphere. Neil looked up at the sky as a shadow moved towards them. He managed to raise and open his umbrella just as a large black cloud poured rain onto the field. Garrick and the Cameloran guards raised their own umbrellas or shields to protect themselves. The Stereneans weren't so lucky. Being unprepared, many of them gasped with the sudden shower of cold water, unable to avoid being drenched. Since Siri's arrival, Camelora's weather had become even more erratic and unpredictable. The people had learned in the past few days to be prepared for almost every possible weather occurrence. Within ten seconds the cloud passed on, trailing rain behind it. Those with umbrellas lowered them, shook off the water, and folded them up again.

"Yes," Garrick stated, "this is Camelora. I apologize for the weather."

Trevor's face beamed with relief as he used his hands to wipe the water from his face. He turned and shouted to his people, "We are in Camelora!"

They responded with a loud cheer that ran like a ripple to the back of the crowd. Their relief matched Trevor's.

"We heard the signal," Trevor said, again facing Garrick. "We started to move in the direction it came from, but we really had no idea where we were going or how long it would take. Are you Zaric?"

"No. My name is Garrick and I'm the acting governor while Zaric is gone. But don't worry," he stated quickly when he saw the disappointment in Trevor's face. "He will be back. He only left to gather supporters. This man here is Neil. He's assisting me and we'll do everything we can for you. For security reasons, we'll need to screen all of you. I hope you understand; it's protocol. If you will follow me, I'll take you into the city."

The guards stepped forward and walked along the edges of the group, flanking the refugees. Garrick stayed at the head and led the way back into Camelora.

"How long have you been walking?" Neil asked Trevor as they approached the city.

"Only a week," Trevor replied. "A lot of the people were reluctant to come. Steren is a prosperous place, you see. It took a few weeks to convince them, especially since we couldn't let our governor find out what we were doing."

"Your governor?"

"He's been meeting with some of the other governors, south of us.

We don't know what they're planning, but we felt it had something to do with the old stories. The call proved it. In the end, only a handful of us chose to come. Because of that, along with the time we took to pack what we needed, we got a later start than we wanted. Have many other supporters already arrived?"

"You're the first," Neil told him.

This surprised Trevor, but he said nothing.

The refugees were led to the palace, where the council was summoned to begin the interviewing process. Neil joined in the task, following the plan Zaric made before leaving Camelora. One by one, he sat with some of the new arrivals, writing down their names and skills, along with information about where they came from. He did his best to look for signs that a person was not quite what he or she seemed, or being deceptive, though past experience made him doubt his judgment in that area. Zaric wanted the council to be trusting, but not too trusting. He didn't doubt that Mered would use any deception he could think of to infiltrate Zaric's city. Despite his doubts, Neil trudged on, asking question after question, listening to story after story.

He had to admit, it was enlightening to hear about the lives of all these people. Seeing them as a group when they arrived, it was easy to forget that they lived individual lives, with individual talents and interests. They had created families and communities and friendships within their city—then left many of them behind to chase the promise of a better future, a different life.

The last of the people were interviewed and the council made their way to the main palace doors, ready to help set up the camp on the plain. As Neil made his way with the others, he was caught by Garrick, who pulled him aside.

"I think the council can handle this, Neil," he said. "It's not easy putting up tents one-handed. I have something else I would like you to do for me."

"Of course," Neil assented, relieved at the suggestion. "What is it?"

Garrick pursed his lips as he chose his words. "I would like you to interview Siri," he stated simply.

"No," Neil answered without hesitation. Remembering his position and seeing the displeasure on Garrick's face, he went on, "I would gladly do anything you ask, but I just don't trust Siri. I won't see her."

"If you're afraid she'll try to manipulate you, you don't need to worry. I won't let that happen. But I don't think she's as untrustworthy as you say."

Neil wondered if Siri hadn't already started to work on Garrick, but kept the words back. He would appear even more insubordinate if he spoke those words and he respected Garrick too much to offend him.

"Just go to her and let her tell you her story," Garrick insisted. "There are guards outside her room who will help you if you need them."

Knowing he couldn't win this argument without jeopardizing his position, Neil nodded. Garrick clapped him on the shoulder and gave him directions to Siri's room, then headed out to begin organizing the refugee camp.

The palace corridors were nearly empty, though the sound of laughter and chatter floated through the air. Most of the palace's residence would be eating dinner at this time. Evening came on outside the palace, the remaining light of the day drifting through the open windows. Neil came to a long white hallway, lit by candelabras, questioning why he was doing this. He heard the drumming of his heart and felt his apprehension rising. He wanted to turn and go back, but willed himself to move forward.

He approached a closed door flanked by two guards. Lifting his arm, he waved in greeting. The guards did nothing to prevent Neil from entering the room.

Siri didn't move as Neil came in. Sitting in a chair facing the window, the evening light fell upon her, illuminating the sadness written across her face. Her features were just as beautiful as before—her skin flawless and soft, her dark eyes mysterious despite the sadness. Her dark hair had been brushed and pulled back since the last time Neil saw her. Even in captivity Siri looked the part of the siren. A very sad, sullen siren.

In contrast to the light from the window, shadows engulfed the corners of the room. Neil chose one of these to settle himself against the wall.

"I didn't come here to be locked up," Siri stated, her cold voice penetrating Neil's heart. It frightened him to realize how little he understood about Siri's behavior. When he and Helen had found her on their way to Camelora, he had tried to befriend her, spending hours talking with her as she opened up to him. He had felt a compassion he had never felt before—but he eventually learned that she was someone he couldn't befriend. All that he had learned was like ash from an extinguished fire. He couldn't be sure now how much, if any, of it was true.

"You must have expected something like this," he returned.

"I expected to find Zaric. He would have believed me."

"He might have, but Zaric left Garrick to govern, and Garrick trusts *me*. I don't trust you. But, I thought you didn't believe in Zaric. That's what you told me before."

"Why are you here, Neil? If you intend to keep me locked in this room until Zaric returns, don't feel obligated to visit me."

"If it were up to me, I would never see you again."

A smirk touched Siri's lips. "Someone *told* you to come. For all your brave words, you still have a master of your own to answer to."

Neil lapsed into silence for a few minutes. Siri remained in the same position and it unnerved him. Sitting in this way, she looked pitiful, defeated, utterly apathetic. But he couldn't be sure that she wasn't doing this to toy with him, to make him feel sorry for her. Part of him hated to be so suspicious, but another part insisted that it was necessary in order to keep Camelora safe.

"Is Mered coming to Camelora?" Neil asked, making his voice sharp.

"I don't know," Siri answered. "Eventually, yes."

"Did he send you here? Are you his spy?"

"If I was, do you think I would say? I can play my part well when I want to. You've seen that for yourself."

Embarrassment and anger swelled in Neil's chest, but he tamped it down. He wouldn't allow Siri to bait him. "Why did you try to kill Helen?" he shot, trying to be as direct as Siri had been.

Her head snapped toward him, the sudden movement surprising Neil. Her mouth opened slightly but no sound came out. In this light, Neil saw the resignation in her fatigued expression—resignation tinged with fear.

"I had to," came her simple reply.

"You chose to."

"Are you ready to hear what I have to say, Neil?" Siri asked, a slight desperation in her words.

He wanted to say no, not wanting to believe that she wouldn't lie. But she wasn't requesting anything more than Garrick had already asked him to do. If he wanted to maintain his trustworthiness and continue to work to protect the people of the kingdom, he needed to perform the tasks given him, no matter how difficult they were. Listening didn't require believing. That would be up to Garrick when Neil relayed the story to him. Anyway, Neil could choose his own questions, probing anything he didn't fully trust.

He pulled a wooden chair across the room and set it near Siri. As he sat, he was glad to know the chair wouldn't allow him to get too comfortable. "I'll listen," he said.

Siri looked him over, her head tilted to the side. A defiance sparked in her eyes , but it soon melted and Neil found himself facing a simple, sincere woman, like any other he would meet on the streets in the city. That momentary spark was all that remained of the heat that once radiated from her amber eyes.

"You're right to think that I'm not a good person. I know I'm not. Before meeting you and Helen, I couldn't remember the last time I had met a good person. I don't know if I was always this way. My parents supported Mered. That was their choice, but I had to live with it. When I was a little girl, we left our home and moved to his palace to offer him our services."

"You told us you came from a city by the sea," Neil cut in. "Was that true?"

"Phara," Siri said in response, the name quick on her tongue. She smiled as though it left a sweet taste. "Although I was never happy with my parents, there were others I *was* happy with. I hardly remember them now. Once I realized I would never see them again, it was best to forget."

"Some things aren't easy to forget," Neil said. "I know because I've tried."

Siri let her eyes drift to the window. Neil expected her to respond to his comment, but when she spoke again, she moved on. "My parents taught me to believe Mered was a god. He has lived for hundreds of years and will live until the end of time. He has so much power—power that he has harnessed over the centuries. Growing up in his court, I soon learned how important it was to think of him first—to give my life and service to him—and then to think only of myself. That's the way it is with all of his sycophants: we think of Mered, we think of ourselves. I focused on how I could earn the rewards he so generously promised. If you make Mered happy, you live well. My parents easily gained his favor—along with a large parcel of land and everything they could ever want.

"We dined with Mered almost every night. My father led raids on nearby villages and became an effective recruiter. My mother—the most beautiful woman in his court—played hostess at all of Mered's dinners and balls. As I grew up and became more and more attractive, I became a favorite to Mered himself. My parents were pleased with this—at least in the beginning. They knew that, as they grew older and less valuable, my favor would ensure they still enjoyed the comforts that a close relationship with Mered gave them.

"But my mother became jealous when Mered began to prefer me. She was losing her own beauty faster than she realized she would—at least in Mered's eyes—so I was asked to play hostess, while my mother was all but forgotten, moving further and further down the table, further and further away from Mered when he surrounded himself with his admirers. She took it out on me. The things she said to me, criticizing every little detail of my appearance, of my behavior, believing she could tear me down to make herself important again... My father would disappear—not standing up for me, not taking her side. Instead, he did what he could to ensure his own continued importance.

"My mother—I wish I could feel sorry for her. She and my father were very proud to set me in Mered's sight. I believe every parent of a daughter hoped that someday that daughter would be Mered's favorite. I tried not to act like the others, seeing how unattractive their behavior made them. When I saw your friend Helen—free to be beautiful without trying to be beautiful, free to be covered in dirt and wear torn clothes without worrying about losing favor in anyone's eyes—I envied her. The young women in Mered's court are nothing like Helen."

Siri's words trailed off. Neil thought she was only gazing out the window, lost in thought, but he soon realized that her eyes were locked on her own reflection in the glass.

"Despite her jealousies," she went on, breaking her own gaze and casting her eyes down to her hands, "my mother was glad that Mered paid so much attention to me. I just don't think she ever realized, in all of her years of scheming and pushing, exactly where it would lead. She never considered how quickly a woman grows old in the eyes of an immortal man.

"It was my turn to have everything I wanted and what I wanted least was to sit at home to be waited upon. Mered was easily bored by women who took advantage of his hospitality. It's strange that, with all the attention we gave to him, no one else caught onto that. He never expressed his thoughts in words, but I was clever enough to watch his conduct and catch his hints. I asked Mered to allow me to train in archery and fighting. He was reluctant, but I knew how to make him give me my way and believe that it was his own idea in the first place. My mother was a great teacher in that manner. I learned the fighting skills quickly because I was determined to prove that it wasn't a mistake to let me.

"I soon joined my father on his raids and I believe Mered actually found me more interesting, for a while. His attention span isn't very long and I was lucky to be in his favor longer than most. By twenty-two, I was no longer 'young' anymore. My decision to learn to fight turned out to be a lucky one. I could still make myself useful, without being married off to some old governor and bear the next generation of Mered's followers.

"When Ian was assigned to follow Helen and stop her from getting to you, I was told to go with him, but my role was merely to observe. Mered only wanted me to assist Ian when it was absolutely necessary. It irritated me, as though he never truly believed I could do the job as well as any man. That may have been when my trust in Mered began to waver. But life with him was all I had known. I wanted to prove that I was still valuable to him. After Ian failed twice, it became my task to get your book and convince you to join me. I think I was even close to succeeding, wasn't I?"

She looked at Neil with a half-mocking smile, but it quickly faded, replaced with the warmth of shame. Neil felt uncomfortable at the memory of how close he had been to falling for Siri, how he had almost fallen into Mered's trap. A shudder cascaded through him.

"But 'close' wasn't enough," Siri continued. "You never would have joined me. Whatever it is you feel for Helen, it was too strong for me to break completely. Everything I wanted changed when the snowstorm came. Do you remember that? In that tiny moment with the snow and fog thickening, when you had to decide whether to reach out for me or Helen, you chose her. I realized then that there was never a possibility you would have chosen me.

"I couldn't find you in the snow. Then it grew harder to breathe. All I could think was that I was going to die and I would die alone. I was so scared—more scared than I have ever been in my life. When everything started to go black, I gave up. I woke up in Ian's camp. I thought he might have captured you and Helen as well, but he told me you weren't there when he found me."

"We were told that *you* weren't there when *we* were found," Neil interrupted. Siri stayed silent, visibly confused.

"I guess it doesn't matter, really," she went on with a light shrug, but Neil thought she was still turning the phenomenon over in her mind. "Ian told me that since we had failed in everything else, we now needed to stop you and Helen from reaching the Gateway. The only way to do that was to kill you, or so Mered said. While I was with you and Helen, Ian had managed to find it. His plan was that I go to the top of the hill while he waited in the valley below. If he didn't kill you, I was supposed to. I realized, at the last moment, that I didn't want to."

"Yet you tried, anyway."

"No, actually, I tried not to. I learned about poisons when I lived at Mered's palace. Like I said, I wanted to know *everything*. I knew which poisons would work quickly and which would work slowly. If it wasn't for the fact that Mered always checked my bags before I left his palace, I would have taken something that wouldn't work at all. But I knew that if I used a slow poison, you might be able to get Helen to Zaric in time to save her."

"What if I *didn't* get her to Zaric in time?" Neil returned, frustrated with Siri's reasoning. "What if she died before we reached Camelora, or Ian killed me and I didn't make it to Helen at all? What sort of plan is that?"

"The best I could come up with. I'm not like Helen. I was never taught to think like her. None of those things happened, anyway. You reached Camelora and Zaric, and Helen is fine."

"You didn't have to do it," Neil insisted. "Why not poison Ian instead?"

"If you knew Mered," Siri retorted, raising her voice, "you wouldn't wonder. I didn't want to kill anyone, but I didn't want to lose my own life. I don't know how to be good, Neil. I'm trying, but I still don't know how. I'm not Helen."

These last words were measured, deliberate. Neil was sure the pang he felt was just what Siri had hoped to inflict.

He shook his head, seeing that there was no way to convince Siri she could have made a different choice. "Why are you here now?" he asked. "You don't belong in Camelora. This place was never meant for someone like you."

Siri winced, but held back the sharp words on the edge of her tongue. Though her eyes were wet, she didn't allow the tears to escape. "When I returned to Mered," she said, "I couldn't forget what I had seen with you and Helen. I've never met people like you. Helen was so determined and nothing could stop her from finding what she was looking for. She was looking for protection, not domination. And not for herself, but for her family and her people. I started to imagine what it would be like to be that kind of person. The thought of Zaric intrigued me, too. I began to believe that he wasn't the man Mered had always described him to be. If Zaric is the man you say he is, then I am *exactly* the sort of person he would invite to Camelora.

"It was harder for me to hide my disdain for Mered. I knew that if I didn't escape and try to make my way to Camelora, Mered would discover my doubts, imprison me, and execute me. I told Mered that I wanted to head north to gather support. He had a new, young, beautiful distraction by then, so he allowed me to go with three of his men. We were instructed to enter the places a larger army could not.

"I played the part of an obedient follower until I knew I was far enough away from Nubiim—Mered's city—to break free and reach Camelora, before the men could tell Mered that I had gone. I took first watch one night, gave the men something to help them sleep, then slipped away. I tried to keep myself moving for as long as possible until I reached this land. You know the rest of the story."

Neil sat silently, watching the fading daylight streaming through the window. Pity tapped at his soul when he looked at Siri, seeing a woman who only felt beautiful if others saw her as beautiful, a woman who had been raised to think only of herself, to destroy others before they could destroy her. In her eyes, Neil saw defeat.

So he refused to look in her eyes. "Excuses," he muttered. He got to his feet and crossed the room toward the door.

"What?" Siri exclaimed, jumping up. Her voice was full of fury, hurt, and indignation.

Halfway across the room, Neil stopped, turning to face Siri. "Why should I believe you?" he asked. "You risked our lives to save your own."

Siri's eyes flashed and her face turned red in anger. "You don't seem to realize, Neil, that I have known all along that Zaric is real, but you can't say the same. You've shown your power over me by having me locked up, but I will not allow you to speak to me. From this point forward, I will only speak to the governor or Zaric."

She turned again to the window, the haughty expression returning and holding firm as she held her head high. Neil stood in the middle of the floor, trying to think of something biting to say, giving him the last word, but he could think of nothing.

Neil left the room. He heard the guards lock the door behind him, but didn't turn around. He kept his eyes and his focus forward.

Chapter 8

The Past

I
n times of peace, everything was more vibrant and beautiful, from the colors to the people to the nature that surrounded them. The smile of the Eternal One upon the land was almost visible. At least, that's what the people said. Peace had been established before any of the kingdom's current citizens were born. The stories came down from their parents and grandparents. The people had mostly stopped noticing, but not Zaric. He never failed to see the beauty of the kingdom and the beauty of peacetime.

He breathed in the fresh air with contentment. He was glad he had chosen to spend the day working in the fields with the farmers. Of all the inhabitants of Camelora, these were the ones he felt closest to. His respect for the farmers ran deep. They knew just when to plant their crops, just how to take care of them, tending to them with a gentleness that helped Zaric see how to care for the Cameloran people. The only thing they couldn't control was the weather, but even to some degree they could control the impact the weather had on their crops. They respected the land and the conditions of each day, making adjustments to ensure that the harvest would be provident. So much of what they did wasn't even for their own benefit, but for the survival of their fellow citizens. Zaric had been working with these farmers for years, gaining every insight he could from the work they did.

"No one really expects you to do that, do they?" a familiar voice said behind him.

Zaric straightened his back and turned to see Mered. His cousin's expression of mock-distaste was overshadowed by the jovial light in his eyes. With his dark traveling clothes, dark hair and eyes, tall frame and tanned skin, Mered could have been mistaken for a highway robber if it wasn't for that obvious light of friendship. The trail of horses and servants dressed in his father's livery also worked to give nobility to Mered's character.

"Mered!" Zaric exclaimed, dropping his shovel and striding forward, warmly embracing him. "What brings you here?"

"Have you been working in the sun too long, Zaric? I'm here for the celebrations, of course—for the peace anniversary."

"But the anniversary is a month away. The celebrations don't even start for two weeks."

"The official celebrations don't, but that doesn't mean we can't start the *unofficial* celebrations. We can't pass up an excuse to have a good party."

"I have too much work to do," Zaric stated, looking at the fields. "Everything needs to be done at just the right time to ensure a good harvest. The people in the capital still need to be fed, in spite of our celebrations."

"So, you really *are* expected to do this?"

"*I* expect me to do this. Why should I expect the people to support me when I can easily support myself?"

Mered shook his head and sighed. He turned and gave instructions to the servants to go ahead to the palace before resuming the conversation with Zaric.

"It's hard to see how your father could have a son like you. The two of you aren't very much alike at all. At least I know that your princely duties matter to you, too. You have a guest, Prince Zaric, and that guest needs an escort to the palace. If you will take me to my uncle, I would be much obliged."

With a soft smile, Zaric looked to the overseer, who excused him with a nod of his head.

Zaric knew Mered was right. He would always have to find this balance between royal duties and human responsibilities, especially if he planned to one day be the sort of king he envisioned—not quite as regal as his father, but deserving of respect both as a king and as a man.

They found King Edric in his study with his advisors, going over details of the upcoming celebrations. Before the peace, these advisors would have served a more necessary function, but Edric had never needed them for anything more than minor disagreements between noblemen and arranging royal parties. Neither had his father before him, nor his father. It was Edric's great-grandfather who had established the peace a century before. The kingdom had forgotten what it was like to be afraid of their neighbors.

Edric gave a broad smile when he saw Zaric and Mered coming through the door, but didn't even falter in his words. He finished his meeting, made sure his instructions were understood, then waved his advisors away. It was only when they were gone that he stepped forward and warmly clapped his nephew on the shoulder.

"Mered, how good it is to see you," the king said. "I wish I could say I'm surprised to see you so early, but I'm not surprised at all. How is your father?"

"Very well, I thank you."

"Good, good. And things are going well in your duchy, I trust?"

"They couldn't be better."

"Excellent. I'm glad to have two men I can trust so well to take care of that corner of my kingdom. I look forward to seeing your father as the celebrations begin, but for now I'm pleased to be able to host his son within our walls. Has Zaric been showing you the improvements we've made?"

"Zaric is too busy working, Uncle. I've only seen the fields."

"To be perfectly frank," Zaric put in, "he only just arrived."

"Nonsense," Edric said, ignoring his son's statement. "Zaric has plenty of time to show you around. The farmers can take care of the fields and Zaric will be your personal guide while you are here. Now go on, I have work to do."

Once his father's back was turned, Zaric shook his head, knowing that, not being the designated day to hear disputes, his father had nothing more important to do than plan meals, parties, and renovations.

King Edric had redecorated a number of rooms since Mered's last visit to the palace and Zaric was sure this was what the king wanted his nephew to see. The king and his brother enjoyed competing over who could create the most lavish palace in the kingdom.

Mostly, though, the tour was a chance for the two cousins to catch up. Despite his carefree attitude, Zaric knew that Mered played an active role in governing his duchy. As long as he sprinkled the conversation with statements about furnishings and how much they cost, the prince knew his cousin wouldn't mind talking about government things. Once every newly-furnished room had been shown, the cousins made their way to the ramparts at the top of the palace.

"Just think," Mered said, leaning lazily on the stones as he looked out over the wakening Cameloran land, "one day all of this will be yours."

"You know that doesn't matter to me," Zaric replied, embarrassed by his cousin's statement.

"That doesn't make it less true."

"If I could only know that I'll be worthy of the responsibility. I sometimes think of what it means to be a king and I feel so inadequate. I think I'll be dead before I feel like I even deserve it."

"You think too much," Mered laughed. "It's just like you to be philosophical about the whole thing instead of just enjoying it. I imagine you'll be the best king these people have ever known."

Zaric doubted that. He gazed out over the land, thinking about the people living in the kingdom and all of the things they needed. There was so much they didn't *know* they needed, and that thought often worried Zaric. One hundred years of peace made the people complacent and unprepared for any difficulty that might come their way. They couldn't sense what Zaric did. Sometimes for a split second—a moment so brief he wondered if it wasn't just a fraction of a blink—the colors of the land faded slightly and Zaric felt that the peace was slipping away. More than once he had asked his father if they should begin to prepare an army for any unforeseen threats, but the king laughed at such ideas. They had good relations with their neighboring kingdoms, over land and sea. The thought of any of them attacking Camelora without warning was unfathomable. Since Zaric wasn't able to provide any more reason than his feelings of uneasiness, Edric was certain the guards and soldiers they already had were more than enough to combat any minor dispute.

What unsettled Zaric now, though, was what his eyes caught as he stood with Mered—something so definite he had no reason to wonder if what he saw was real. As he looked out over the land, hearing Mered's statements about the future, the brightness of the colors in his vision faded and, this time, it didn't return.

* * *

The banquet hall was full of allies of Camelora—men and women

Zaric had rarely ever seen. They sometimes met for trade talks, either in Camelora or their home kingdoms, but those were infrequent. The Cameloran royal family visited neighboring kingdoms for various celebrations, but Zaric had only begun accompanying his father after his mother's death two years before. The celebration of one hundred years of peace, though, was the most anticipated and most important event in all the kingdoms. No one wanted to miss it. Zaric even noticed two or three families from across the sea. A visit from those kingdoms was even more rare than a visit from their land allies.

Zaric sat at the head table, not far from his father. To Zaric's left was Queen Ersilia of a southern allied kingdom. He had visited her on state business two or three times before. At his right was King Yarkko of an eastern land, a man who had a reputation for being eccentric. Not many allies visited Yarkko's kingdom unless it was absolutely necessary, but he didn't seem to mind that. In spite of all the stories Zaric had heard—most of them from Mered—he enjoyed his conversations with the king. His honesty was refreshing and his stories interesting. Queen Ersilia hardly said a word to Zaric at all.

As the meal ended, Edric rose and the conversations in the room died down. "My dear friends," he said jovially. "It is a great honor to be blessed by your company. The air of this occasion is much different from the one we are here to celebrate. The feeling of friendship had not yet grown between the kingdoms which assembled to sign my grandfather's treaty of peace. But years of fighting and the death of thousands of citizens showed the leaders of the kingdoms that there had to be another way to work together. My grandfather's ideas were still unproven, yet your own ancestors were willing to try a new way, to spare the lives of their people by working together. Since that time, we have all conducted our dealings with each other in a fair and reasonable manner. I hope that we can now see the value of the treaty my grandfather created—a copy of which hangs in every council room in every allied kingdom. As we conduct our business, we are reminded of the reasons why we no longer go to war.

"So, I ask you all to raise your cups as I propose a toast to our ancestors. May they smile down upon us as we carry on their legacy, fulfilling today the promises they made to each other one hundred years ago. To our ancestors!"

"To our ancestors!" The statement rang throughout the room, every voice in unison. Edric sat again in his chair and the conversations and laughter once more filled the hall. Zaric turned to speak to Queen Ersilia just as she turned to the neighbor on her left. The eccentric King Yarkko stared blankly at the far side of the room, his open demeanor now closed. Careful not to show his relief in enjoying a moment free of conversation, Zaric took the opportunity to cast his own eyes over the assembled monarchs, nobles, and dignitaries. It was easier for him to manage state visits when he could take a few minutes to quietly gather his thoughts. Formulating trivial topics of conversation was a great chore. Mered sat not far away, chatting comfortably with a foreign princess, while Mered's father laughed with a king. Both uncle and cousin resembled each other in a way Zaric envied, knowing too well how different he was from his own father.

Although Zaric felt most comfortable working with the people, he was not uncomfortable with the leaders of the kingdoms. He found that his intimate knowledge of the workings of Camelora gave him the experience that he needed to speak freely with the men and women with whom he made agreements. He knew what his own people needed and could present that when brokering pacts. Still, when it came to offering inspiring speeches—as his father had just done—Zaric felt inadequate and knew that he had much to learn.

When the banquet ended and the men and women began to make their way to the ballroom, Zaric felt a hand on his arm. Turning, he found his father, standing with a duke from one of the overseas kingdoms.

"Son," Edric said with his most royal smile, "I was wondering if you would show Duke Saerin to the library. His king has asked him to find an old treaty that has become lost in their own land. You know the library better than anyone else and I'm sure you will know where to find it."

"Of course," Zaric replied, thankful to avoid the ballroom a few minutes longer. He greeted the duke with a customary bow of his head, then led him through the palace to the library.

Despite the vagueness of the duke's description, it only took a few minutes for Zaric to find what they were looking for. Edric had been right when he said that Zaric knew the library better than anyone else. Writing a short note, Zaric set the treaty on the desk of the clerk who oversaw the library so it could be copied in the morning. The two men turned to the door when a movement in the corner of the room caught Zaric's eye.

"Do you think you could find your way back to the ballroom?" he asked Saerin. "I just want to check something else before heading back."

The duke bowed, leaving Zaric with a simple expression of thanks.

When he was sure the duke was far enough down the corridor, Zaric walked between two rows of shelves as he cast his eyes around. "Hello?" he called out. "I know someone's there."

A shadow passed at the end of the row just before a man stepped out. Zaric jumped at his sudden appearance, his heart pounding in his ears. The man wore dark clothing and had dark hair and a dark beard. This, combined with the dim light in the room, caused his entire form to blend together, making his face difficult to distinguish. Yet his presence didn't give Zaric any uneasiness and his heart soon calmed down.

"May I help you?" Zaric asked. "If you're looking for the king, I'm afraid you won't find him here."

"Actually, Zaric," the man said with a smile, "I'm looking for you."

Zaric flinched when he heard his own name. No one was ever looking for *him*. Squinting, he tried to get a better look at the man, thinking that he *must* have met him before. "For me? Do I know you? Do you need my help with something?"

"No, I'm just hoping for a little chat."

Zaric stared at him, trying to remember where he might have seen him before. He didn't look like any of the servants in the palace or any of the workers in the fields. Zaric was familiar with most of the families in the village and this man didn't belong to any of them. His clothing was not that of a nobleman and Zaric hadn't seen him in the banquet hall. Stepping closer, Zaric was able to make out the man's features and saw that his face was middle-aged, yet ageless. His appearance and manner were non-threatening and casual. Though he was certain he had never met him before, Zaric felt like he knew the man very well already—as though they were old friends.

"Who are you?" Zaric finally asked.

"I'm a traveler," the man replied simply.

"Travelers don't usually enter the palace unannounced. The king likes protocol to be observed. Did a servant show you in?"

"No, I found my own way. You see, Zaric, I have questions that only you can answer. Tell me, what do you think about the state of Camelora?"

This was an odd question, considering the celebration that was taking place at that exact moment. "We've been at peace for a hundred years now. The people are prospering and life is good."

"But?"

Zaric hesitated. He didn't think he had indicated any doubt. The thought of the dimming landscape flashed in his mind—the thought that something was changing, even though he couldn't tell what. "But everyone is too comfortable. We're no longer prepared for something to go wrong."

"Do you think something will go wrong?" the man asked.

"Yes," Zaric answered without hesitation, feeling like he couldn't hold anything back in this man's presence. "But it's just a feeling. I don't know what it will be."

"I can tell you, your highness, that something is stirring, but it isn't coming from where you think. The threat isn't outside, but inside."

Zaric was stunned. He found it difficult to find the words to respond. "How do you know this?" he finally asked. "Are there traitors meeting without the king's knowledge?"

"No, no one has resorted to treason. I know the signs; I've seen them before."

"Before? Are you traveling from another land? You seem to know a lot for a man who is simply a traveler."

"I've been to other lands, other times. I'm a man who has seen much and experienced much. One man with enough anger is all you need to bring the kingdom down."

"What are we supposed to do, then? We can't govern men's thoughts."

"You don't need to do anything yet. I only want you to be aware. Pay attention to the kingdom and be a better king than your father—though I'm not saying he isn't good. I am confident that you will become the greatest king this kingdom has ever known. Keep your eyes open, Zaric, and I will tell you more when I return."

The man smiled at Zaric then turned and walked away, going around the end of the shelf. Dumbfounded, Zaric couldn't move. The man's words were enigmatic and confusing. He didn't know what to make of them. It wasn't until the man's cloak could no longer be seen that Zaric found his feet.

"Wait!" he called, jumping forward. He rushed to the edge of the bookcase, but stopped. The corner of the room was empty. No sound—footsteps, breathing, rustling clothing—could be heard. The man had disappeared.

Chapter 9

The Present

E arly in the afternoon, Helen felt a subtle change in the air. The atmosphere felt sticky and strange, creating a mugginess that caused her clothes to cling to her body. She looked up at the overcast sky just to be sure it wasn't drizzling. A salty smell touched her nostrils. "Is it over the next hill?" she asked, feeling and sounding like an eager child as her skin tingled.

"No," Zaric replied. "We still have a long way to go before we reach the sea."

Helen's anticipation deflated. She looked ahead, imagining what the sea must look like and how it would feel when she finally saw the wide expanse of water stretching out ahead of her. She wondered if she would be excited or afraid, or somewhere in between.

As she glanced over the rising and falling terrain, grass and dirt, rocks and trees, something caught Helen's eye. Climbing up the hill to her right, clusters of large, grey stones dotted the grassy ground. They were too ordered to be natural, as though they had once been part of a man-made wall. Next to her, Zaric slackened his pace. Helen glanced over to see that he had noticed the stones, too.

"What is it?" Helen asked. He didn't answer.

In Zaric's mind, the voices of soldiers and the sounds of clashing

70

swords and clanking armor rang out. Instead of clusters of stones, he saw a tall stone fortress, stretching out on the crest of the hill. Its thick and rounded walls, slits of windows, and jagged parapets rose toward the sky. From its depths, he heard the voices of confrontation—his and his son's screams, his wife's cries, Mered's laughter....

"What is it?" Helen asked again, bringing him back to the present moment.

Zaric shook his head as if he were shaking out the memory. "Sometimes, hundreds of years ago can feel like yesterday. I've lived so long and seen so much."

Helen slowed her pace in order to focus her eyes on the king, noticing for the first time that, despite his young appearance, she could see the years of his life on his face, though she couldn't describe—even to herself—how. She thought that she was seeing the Zaric of nine hundred years ago and the Zaric of today at the same time.

Helen's thoughts were broken by a sudden silence in the clearing around them. The wind ceased and the birds stopped chirping. Nothing moved in the grass. The feeling that came with this silence was one Helen knew too well. Memories of Ian came back to her, though he had been dead for weeks now.

It was apparent that Zaric felt the silence when he stopped walking, too. They both strained their ears, trying to pick up any sound they could. "There," Helen said, not daring to speak above a whisper as her ears picked up a distant commotion.

"A rumble," Zaric replied. "Movement. We're still too far away to hear the sea and it's not thunder."

"I can't tell where it's coming from. It seems to be everywhere. Could it be a caravan? Perhaps on its way to Camelora?"

Zaric shook his head and closed his eyes to focus. "I don't hear cartwheels, but I do hear horses. Not many. There's the sound of metal, like armor. Marching, not walking." He snapped out of his trance, shifting his focus to Helen. "I don't like it. We need a place to hide until we know we're safe."

Now that they needed shelter, the clearing around them seemed to expand. There was nothing but grass and small stones, barely large enough to hide a fox, within safe distance. The crumbled, ruined walls were too far away. Still, Zaric pointed to them, wordlessly communicating to Helen that they needed to make their way to them. She sighed. The ruins were at least two hundred yards away, but at least closer than anything else. She nodded and they ran.

Halfway to the walls, Helen glanced over her shoulder and saw a small militia marching down the hill behind them. She was glad to know that they weren't running toward them, but her heart fell when she realized that, even if they reached the walls, they couldn't do it without being seen. Then, it was only a matter of time before the army caught up with them. The momentary relief disappeared completely when another group of men came over the hill in front of them, and a third appeared over the hill to their left. Helen and Zaric slowed, took a few steps backward, and turned in circles.

The battalion surrounded them. Fear compressed Helen's chest as they waited for the battalion to descend into the clearing. Ideas raced through her mind as she tried to think how they could evade them, trying to fight the dreadful swelling of resignation that moved forward from the back of her mind, but nothing she could imagine seemed possible. She wondered if Zaric had the strength to escape all these men. She knew that she didn't.

Zaric gripped Helen's hand while the men were still too far to hear, bent down to her ear, and whispered, "Don't say anything."

As the men closed in, one mounted soldier pulled ahead of the rest. His expression disarmed Helen in a way that reminded her of Ian, but somehow this man seemed harsher. The coldness in his dark eyes lacked Ian's impulsiveness. She imagined this man must be calculating and cruel—not likely to make mistakes. He guided his horse expertly, taking his time as he approached his prey. His appearance was tidy, his brown hair sleek and groomed.

Helen inhaled slowly, but it didn't diminish her fear. The mounted man halted and the battalion followed suit, stopping a few yards behind him. He dismounted and a soldier ran forward to take the reins of the horse as the man approached Zaric and Helen. Standing a little bit taller than the king, he towered over them.

"It's unusual to see wanderers so far from any village," the leader said, his voice hard and icy. "Where are you going?"

Zaric kept his mouth shut, a defiant smile raising the corners of his lips. Helen gripped his hand tighter.

"Where do you come from?" the man tried again, but his question was met with the same response. "I see. You believe you don't need to answer me. Maybe you are too stupid to notice the battalion surrounding you. It is within my power to arrest you and hold you until you tell me what I want to hear. No one is permitted to travel without authorization. Do you have papers from your governor?"

Helen's face reacted before she could stop herself, unable to suppress her surprise and confusion. Although the different regions were governed by their own governors, the freedom to travel between them had never been restricted before. Without a central government, there was no one to impose such a rule.

Zaric still remained silent.

"You will either show me your authorization," the man stated, his voice rising as his patience faltered, "or I will take you back to His Majesty King Mered to do with you what he will."

"Mered," Zaric scoffed, "is no king."

The leader's eyes flashed like sparks and his face grew red. Understanding erupted in a smile. "So, it *is* you," he spat. "The 'great' King Zaric. I will enjoy taking you before Mered myself. You won't escape this time." He raised his voice and shouted, "Seize them! They're under arrest."

Half-a-dozen men rushed forward and took Zaric by the arms. He twisted and tried to pull away, but those who caught him held on too tightly.

Helen stepped back, but it only placed her closer to the reach of an armor-clad soldier who threw his arms around her, trapping her own arms against her body. Helen resisted, too, kicking and turning, but her captor had the advantage. The leader turned his back, walking to his horse. The man who held Helen easily lifted her off the ground, but as the soldiers dragged Zaric forward, he dug his feet into the earth. He tried to reach out to Helen, but the soldiers pulled his arms behind his back.

"You're a puppet!" he shouted. The leader turned, his expression firm. "Mered won't share power with anyone. He will discard you like an unwanted fool."

The leader rushed at Zaric and grabbed him by the collar, his face red with anger. "I don't care who Mered thinks you are. I don't believe in his superstitious stories. Your life isn't worth my trouble."

He stepped back and pulled out his sword, then lunged forward. The blade struck one of his own soldiers in the chest, sliding against his armor. He cried out, surprised by the blow.

Zaric was no longer there.

"Zaric!" Helen called out.

Silence fell over the battalion as the leader's eyes grew wide with terror. "Search the area! Find the man and bring him to me. Dead or alive, we can't let him escape!"

Chaos reigned as the men dispersed, running toward the rocks and trees, armor clanking. Some soldiers examined each other, believing Zaric had somehow disappeared into their ranks.

"Keep her alive," the leader instructed Helen's captor. "If this man really is Zaric, he'll come back for her. Don't let her out of your sight."

The leader moved to the center of the clearing, turning a circle as he scanned the landscape. Helen struggled against the soldier who bound her, but he was too strong. She kicked her legs with all the strength she had. She knew there wasn't much of a chance she could get away, but she wanted to make this as difficult for the soldier as possible. Simultaneously, she tried to piece together the last few minutes, wondering where Zaric had gone.

Her experience taught her not to be surprised by the unexpected or even the impossible, but knowing that Zaric could make himself disappear did nothing to tell her where he was. Of the things he had taught Helen so far, transporting herself to another place was not one of them. She wondered if she even had the ability. Zaric might have gone to Phara, but having never been there before, she had no idea what it looked like.

A thought came to Helen and she hoped it would work. There was no time to question it. She pulled her arms to test her guard and his grip tightened once again. Holding her breath, Helen relaxed and focused her mind, spreading her fingers wide. A current of sparks skipped up her arms.

With a shout, the man let go of her and shook his hands as though he had been burned by fire. Anger flashed in his eyes. Four more soldiers rushed to his aid. In the second before they reached her, Helen raised her arms out at her sides. She pulled at the moisture in the air. An icy whirlwind formed around her like shards of glass, cutting the hands of the soldiers as they tried to reach through it.

"What are you doing?" the leader asked. "Stop her!"

Again, Helen held her breath. Blue flashed in front of her eyes for a fraction of a second, then her vision went black.

Helen gasped as her body was plunged into and engulfed by frigid water. She tried to push herself up to the surface to breathe, desperate not to gulp down any of the liquid that held her down. The waves pushed against her. Her vision clouded and she couldn't focus. Kicking her feet, she felt the sea floor beneath her, just at the tips of her toes, but the wet sand slipped and shifted. The grey sky above and dark sea around her dimmed as her consciousness drifted. In a last attempt, hoping against fear, she raised her arm before awareness slipped away.

Chapter 10

The Present

N eil walked to the ramparts, looking out over the city. It grew busier every day, with all of the refugees arriving from outlying cities, towns, and villages. The men and women in the government were growing busier in response. Neil hardly had time for a moment's peace.

At home in Camdor, he never would have realized how many people lived in the land. Life at home revolved around his village and his village alone. Even the governor of the province never bothered to visit Camdor. From the stories he had heard from his grandfather, most of the province lived in pretty much the same way. Almost every governor lived a life of ease, cutting himself off from his people, governing in name only.

But now the people were coming from everywhere, tired of the treatment they received from their governors, seeking unity without any idea how life would change, chasing the stories they had consigned to the backs of their memories. For the first time, Neil realized that, throughout the kingdom, there were other grandfathers like his own, telling the old stories to their grandchildren, preparing them to follow a signal, not knowing where it would lead.

This migration was only the beginning. The refugees who had

arrived were only a fraction of the inhabitants of the land.

Soon, the governors would notice their people leaving. Word would pass to Mered. They would try to stop it in order to retain their authority. Neil read about this in the records in the library and felt a twinge of nervousness as he thought of it now. Eventually the kingdom would be united again and subject to one king, but Neil didn't know yet whether that king would be the good Zaric or the evil Mered.

Neil heard footsteps coming up the stairs and turned to greet the arrival. A pageboy emerged through the doorway. Neil recognized his face, but couldn't remember his name.

"Eric?" he guessed.

"Jared," the boy corrected with no sign of offense. He took a few steps forward. "I was wondering if I can speak with you. Garrick is busy and suggested that I find you."

"Well, I'm *not* busy," Neil reassured the boy. "What's on your mind?"

"I noticed something strange in the woods this morning," the boy said, pointing uncertainly towards the setting sun, "while I was taking a morning walk. I wasn't sure if it was important, but it's been on my mind all day."

Neil looked westward to where a dark cloud hovered over the forest, pouring down rain and flickering with pent up lightning. "The storm?" he asked. "I'll admit it's strange that it's been in the same place all day, but we've had so many of those lately that they aren't exactly unusual anymore."

"I think I found what's causing the storm," the boy went on, unruffled. "There are some strange metal sticks in a clearing in the woods. I've never seen anything like them before. They gave me a weird feeling and I didn't like being around them."

Neil looked at the forest again, looking at the storm with more attention. If he remembered correctly, the storm marked a spot not far from where Siri had been found by the hunters.

"Thank you for telling me about this, Jared," he said. "Is there anything else?"

The boy shook his head.

"I'll see what I can find out," Neil said. "Please, don't mention it to anyone else for now."

The boy nodded, hesitated self-consciously in the doorway, then went back down into the palace.

The sun rested just above the treetops. Neil knew it would be too dark to find anything useful in the forest by the time he reached it. He would investigate as early as possible in the morning. But, with this mystery hanging over his head, he wondered if he would even be able to sleep.

* * *

The grey pre-dawn light washed the forest. Within the trees it was still night. Anticipating this, Neil had brought a torch from the palace. He walked with nimble, careful steps. He told no one about the pageboy's story. Garrick trusted Neil enough to send the boy to him and he was determined to figure out what he could before taking his suspicions to the governor. He was afraid he might be wrong.

Yet he believed there must be something here—something interfering with Camelora's defenses. And he believed he knew who had brought it.

Thunder rumbled overhead and a light mist of rain fell. It frightened him to think of what he might find, but it frightened him more to think that he would miss it altogether. As he went further, he began to hear a faint hum, a sound distinct from the wind and rain—a sound foreign to the woods. It grew louder as he came toward a space almost too small to be called a clearing. Emerging from the trees, he found himself facing the source of the sound.

Three black staffs topped with rounded knobs, coming as high as Neil's waist, were set into the ground, forming a triangle in the forest floor. They could have gone unnoticed by anyone not looking for them, resting close to the trees. He was surprised the young hunter had even seen them. Could the young man have heard them if he wasn't searching for something odd?

Neil stood next to one of the staffs and reached for it, but drew his hand back. It radiated coldness and sent a strange, tingling sensation through his fingertips. He had never seen anything like this. It made him nervous.

An instinct inside of him told him to turn and leave, but it was an instinct he knew not to obey. Fear couldn't help him protect the people. He needed to know what this was and if it served the purpose he suspected. With a little more confidence, he reached out again and placed his palm on top of the bulb that capped the staff, wrapping his fingers around it. The metal was like ice beneath his hand—a burning cold that bit into his palm. The hum grew louder. Sparks pricked his hand and he pulled it away again. Neil looked at the other two staffs and saw sparks dancing over their heads. Dread washed over him. A violent beat pounding his heart, he tried to think of a way to stop the humming and sparking.

In that instant, jagged, luminous streaks flickered in the middle of the triangle. Hanging in the air, a ball of sparks grew.

Then, too fast for him to see how, the ball transformed into an apparition—a transparent man standing with his back to Neil. Neil's reflexes told him to hide, but the man cast his eyes over his shoulder, looking directly into Neil's eyes, as though he sensed his presence. A heavy weight settled in Neil's stomach. As the man turned to face him, an aura of shade emanated from his form. He wore dark clothes and his brown hair fell in waves to his shoulders. There was a shadowy glint in his dark eyes. What disturbed Neil the most, though, was the leer that parted his lips. His expression showed a frigid triumph and arrogant confidence.

Not thinking twice, Neil swung the torch at the staff nearest him. It toppled to the ground, but the apparition remained. Frantic, Neil dropped the torch, fell to his knees, and took the head of the post between his hands, gritting his teeth against the pain from the sparks. He twisted. The knob snapped off. The image in front of him quivered and dimmed, but didn't disappear. Neil dropped the knob and ran to the second staff, breaking off its head, too. The man in the center of the triangle spun as his form diminished, following Neil's movements, showing no hint of concern. Neil trembled. He felt exposed, like he was trying to hide in a dream, but couldn't move fast enough to avoid being caught. When he snapped the head from the third staff, the image sputtered and dissipated, fading to nothing. Neil pulled air into his lungs and sighed it out.

He knew without wondering that he had just seen Mered—and that Mered had seen him. Somehow, the man had managed to infiltrate Camelora's borders. The fears of the council were correct. Garrick and Neil hadn't been able to prevent it. Neil's thoughts went to Siri, locked in a room back at the palace.

Clutching one of the knobs, Neil strode back in the direction of the capital, his anger focused as he formulated a plan.

He entered the front doors and headed straight for the main staircase, noticing but ignoring Garrick, who waited for his assistant at the bottom of the stairs. Not slackening his pace, Neil climbed the steps two at a time.

"What are you doing, Neil?" Garrick called, running up behind him.

"Not now," Neil replied shortly.

"What did you find?" Garrick persisted.

"I said not now."

"Neil!" the governor shouted with authority. Neil disregarded him.

"I know where you're going," Garrick continued. "I've been talking to Siri—"

"I can tell you something about Siri," Neil retorted, spinning at the landing to face Garrick, who stood two steps lower. The rage in Neil's eyes made Garrick flinch. "She will tell you exactly what you want to hear and make you believe what she wants you to believe. That's how she works. And you want to hear that she has the best intentions. She wants you to believe that. You could never imagine someone would be manipulating you. If you had any experience in the world, you wouldn't trust her so easily."

"So why is it that you were able to trust her before?"

Neil couldn't tell if Garrick's tone was cold and critical, or simply inquisitive, but the words Garrick spoke pierced him.

"You yourself saw what came of that 'trust,'" Neil said.

"You might want to remember your place before you speak to me this way."

"Punish me if you want—take away the position Zaric gave me—but I won't be stopped from asking Siri about this." Neil held up his hand, showing Garrick the knob he carried.

His face falling with shock and confusion, Garrick said nothing. When Neil turned his back and continued to Siri's room, the older man followed in silence.

Neil opened the door to see Siri lying on the bed, staring at the wall. She wore a coarse, simple nightgown, but was on top of her blankets. Her hair, unbraided for the first time, fanned out over the bed, giving her an even more pitiable appearance. She didn't move her head as he entered, or even flinch.

"Will you get up?" Neil asked, his voice biting. Yet, his anger faltered. Siri's position disarmed him.

"Neil," Garrick whispered, a quiet warning in his voice.

In a slow but steady movement, Siri raised herself and swung her legs over the side of the bed. She stood on her bare feet and turned to face Neil.

He went to the table and dropped the metal knob on its surface. It bounced slightly, then rolled back and forth on its side. Siri showed no reaction. "Do you recognize this?"

"Yes," she answered without hesitation.

"Do you know what it is?"

"Yes."

Neil waited, but Siri didn't seem inclined to elaborate. "Is it a communication device?" he asked, his frustration intensifying his anger.

"Yes."

Closing his eyes and trying to swallow back his irritation at her short replies, Neil chose a different approach. "Please explain it to me."

"We need your help, Siri," Garrick gently added.

Her face softened as she looked at the governor. She crossed the room to the table. As she drew next to Neil, he took a step back. "It's a Triad Communication Device," she told them, "created especially for Mered. Whenever a battalion leaves Nubiim, he gives the commander one of these. He can call them with instructions or they can contact him with information or in case of danger. It's set up whenever the battalion makes camp."

"Could it ever work as a transportation device?"

"No," Siri scoffed with a snicker, "of course not. The other person will appear as an image—which could make someone believe they are actually there—but this is only an illusion. Where did you find this?"

"I think you know where I found it."

"What is it going to take to make you trust me, Neil?" Siri asked, exasperated. It surprised him. Tears welled in her eyes as she said the words, but she blinked and shook her head to push them back.

"The truth," was his reply, though his determination not to believe her waned.

Siri reached out and picked up the knob, weighing it in her hand, then dropped it again with a look of disgust. "Believe what you will, but I wouldn't have brought anything that might allow Mered to find me. It's unusual to find one unattended. A lone traveler would only place it in the ground when needed. If you were able to find it without being caught, someone was confident it wouldn't be found. Or they're careless. Either way, I would guess they're still nearby."

Neil's heart beat faster. "Or you were using it when you were caught by our men," he stated, but he wasn't sure how much he believed it anymore. The person who had left it in the woods, under a perpetually active rain cloud, *was* careless, and his experience with Siri told him that she was not. Someone within Camelora's borders was in communication with Mered, and that person posed a risk to them all.

Siri crossed back over to the bed and sat down. "You can think I'm lying if you want to. Maybe an invasion of Camelora is what it will take to make you see that I'm telling the truth."

"Did you lead someone here?" Neil persisted. "An army, or even just one man? Were you followed?"

Garrick placed a hand on Neil's arm, then crossed the room to kneel in front of Siri. "I believe you," he told her.

Siri's face relaxed. Her posture became more open and her manner almost enthusiastic. "I can help you," she said. "I can lead you to them. If I know Mered well enough—and I'm sure I do—he would rather protect his pride than admit that one of his favorites has escaped. I can be a useful spy for you."

"And if you lead us into danger?" Neil asked, unable to contain the words. "I won't allow you to lead our people into a trap."

"If there's any hint of that happening, you can kill me on the spot."

Siri's voice was calm, her face unmoving. In that moment, Neil didn't just believe her, but felt there was no reason *not* to. "I would rather die than go back to Mered."

Neil studied Siri. For the first time since she had been brought to the palace, he looked at her with curiosity instead of fear and hatred. There was more helplessness in her expression and bearing and words than he had allowed himself to see, or even imagine possible.

"That's a good idea," Garrick agreed. "I mean, not killing you, but letting you be a spy. If Mered's followers know you as well as you think, they might be glad to see you and share their secrets."

Garrick patted her hand and she gave him a smile in return.

"Won't they suspect you're working for us?" Neil questioned, wanting to consider anything that could go wrong with this plan.

"They might," Siri conceded, "but I can play my part very well."

"Yes, you can," Neil said, but his words lacked the bite they had before.

He picked up the knob from the table and put it in his pocket. Without turning his gaze back, he left the room. He no longer knew what to think.

Chapter 11

The Present

Her perception was grey and clouded. Panic seized her breath as Helen wondered why she couldn't see clearly. The world around her shifted beyond her control. The sound of movement over the hill terrified her. She knew without seeing that a battalion moved toward her and she needed to hide before she was found. As she turned her head to look for a hiding place, large slabs of stone appeared, forming a semi-circle around her. Lifting her feet, she tried to move behind one of them, but it was like trying to step out of deep, wet mud. She looked down and only saw dewy grass, but it soaked the hem of her skirt, making it heavy. The gloss of the water looked like solid metal.

The sound of the battalion grew closer. The pounding of Helen's heart accelerated. She looked back to the hill, then back to the boulders. Not knowing why she did it, she continued to shift her gaze from the hill to the boulders. Every time she looked at the boulders, they moved farther away. Every time she looked at the hill, it came closer. Fear mingled with frustration as she realized she couldn't control her own actions. The next time Helen turned to look at the hill, the battalion stood only feet away.

Her heart jolting in her chest, Helen spun around and tried to scream, but the sound drifted away from her like smoke. She stepped back and tripped over an unnoticed rock, falling to the ground. Trapped, she looked at the battalion. The leader stood in front of her with a smirk on his face. His brown hair waved in the wind as he walked toward her. Helen wanted to speak, but her mouth wouldn't open. His eyes were disconcertingly calm. His face was Ian's, and yet, at the same time, it wasn't.

Still silent, the man now stood over her, holding his sword as though it were part of his arm. He pulled it back, then thrust it into Helen's stomach.

With a gasp, Helen opened her eyes and raised herself up onto her hands, gulping in air. For a brief moment she thought she felt a pain in her abdomen, but when she looked down there was no sign of a wound. She sat in a bed, all alone in a bedroom that she didn't recognize. Light came in through the window, telling Helen it was morning. Confused, she studied the plain and unadorned wooden walls, the white sheets on the bed, the faded curtains at the window, and the lack of any furniture aside from the bed, a wooden chair, and a small table. With slow movements, Helen drew back the corner of the blanket that covered her legs and set her feet on the floor. The floorboards groaned as she started to stand. She froze. She wanted to walk to the door to see if it was locked, but she was sure every step could be heard with a resonance that spread throughout this place.

With an abruptness that made Helen's nerves jump, the door flew open. By instinct she reached for her crossbow, but her bag wasn't over her shoulder. She noticed it on the floor in a corner of the room too far away to reach. That in itself gave her pause. Her bag was there. Whoever had brought her here didn't try to take it.

A woman stood in the doorway.

Taking in her appearance, Helen wavered. The woman didn't look like any Cameloran—from either the new or old kingdom—she had ever seen before. Her face was more round with a flatter and wider nose than Helen had ever seen. Her skin was smooth and the color of a stone reflecting sunlight. Dark hair was pulled back from her face and her large, dark eyes were unlike any Helen had seen in any of her travels. Helen wondered how far from Camelora she had strayed. Perhaps she had transported herself across the sea.

She could only look at the woman with pleading, resigned fear. She was vulnerable and defenseless, unsure if this woman was a friend or an enemy. But the woman surprised her: she smiled. In her arms she bore a tray with a plate of food and a clear glass of water.

"I brought you breakfast," the woman said. "I wasn't sure if you were awake today, but I hoped you would be. I'm glad to see I was right."

"Today?" Helen asked, catching the oddity of that one word.

"You've been asleep for three days," the woman responded. "Why don't you sit down and eat? You must be starving."

With trepidation, Helen sat on the edge of the bed, her eyes following the woman's movements as she set the tray down on the table. Looking at the plate of eggs, bread, and cheese, Helen realized what the pain in her stomach was.

"You don't need to be afraid," the woman continued as she sat in the chair. "I won't hurt you."

Glancing over the woman one more time, Helen relaxed. She had a kind look that Helen knew couldn't be feigned, like the look of a mother determined to care for her children and anyone else who crossed her path. Helen also didn't sense she was in any immediate danger. Being fed was a good sign.

"Oh, how rude of me," the woman exclaimed, as though she had just remembered something important. "I haven't introduced myself. My name is Lena. I'm the innkeeper here."

"Here?"

"Here," the woman repeated, waving her hand in an exaggerated motion.

"I don't know where I am," Helen admitted.

"Oh," Lena exclaimed, her brow furrowing in confusion, then she relaxed and laughed. "My husband and I joked that you must have fallen from the sky."

"That's not far from the truth."

"Well, then, you fell into the bay in Phara. We found you in the water. I don't believe in mermaids, though, and I don't believe people can fly."

"This is Phara?" Helen blurted, half question, half statement. "We were trying to find this place. But how did I get here?"

Puzzled, Lena twisted her face , staring at Helen for a minute before speaking again. "You don't know how you got here?"

Helen shook her head. "Not really."

"My husband and I found you at the beach. At first, we thought you had washed ashore after a shipwreck, but there was no debris or evidence of that. We can't understand how you got there, since there's no way to get to that part of the beach without passing through the village. We didn't see you pass. I was hoping you could tell me where you came from." Silence passed for a moment, then Lena continued, "What's your name? Who are 'we'?"

Helen hesitated. She wondered how much she should tell Lena. If Mered's influence had reached Phara, giving this woman too much information could impair Helen's errand.

Yet she felt that she could trust Lena. The woman had a trustworthy quality about her. The comfort Helen felt in Lena's presence was stronger than her own reluctance. "Helen," she answered. "My name is Helen."

"And what brought you to Phara, Helen?" Lena asked with no sign of recognition.

Before Helen could answer, a distant bell rang. "I'm neglecting my customers," Lena stated in a muted tone, hurriedly standing. "You eat and rest. I'll come back later for the dishes. And tonight, we'll continue this conversation. Is that all right?"

Helen nodded and Lena left the room.

Moving closer to the table, Helen began to eat. In the quiet, her mind went to Zaric. He knew the land much better than she did and had better control over where he would end up. Not knowing how far Phara was from the place where she had last seen him, Helen wondered if he had also come here, how she would ever find him again, or how she would find her way back to Camelora. Mentioning that city could be a dangerous move—or it could be met with blank stares. A new feeling overwhelmed her as Helen realized just how lost she was.

By late afternoon, Helen had moved the chair to the window, looking out at the sparkling sea. She was amazed and a little bit frightened when she saw it from this view. Her eyes were mesmerized by the mass of blue water that had no end, with rolling white foam and streaks of silvery yellow light cast by the sun. Faded wooden docks reached into the water with boats of assorted sizes tethered by sagging ropes. A few boats sat out on the water, crewed by men and women actively working with nets to bring in a decent catch. Helen heard a strange shrill sound overhead and looked up to see large white birds flying in lazy circles.

The rhythmic sound of a hammer reverberated through the air, mingled with voices in conversation and children's shrieks and laughter—the sounds of people living their everyday lives, of people who felt no sense of danger. They were sounds she missed. People passed every few minutes on the street below: some alone, some in couples or groups.

Helen was too frightened of this strange place to want to leave her room. What she saw from this window was a small glimpse of the village as a whole and until she knew more about its people, she had no desire to venture out on her own. She also felt physically and mentally weak, despite her long sleep. Her worry for Zaric only grew.

Lena brought Helen another tray of food at lunch time, but was too busy to hold a conversation. Helen stayed in her room until the light outside faded almost completely and the sound of voices downstairs died down. When she believed it was clear enough, she cautiously opened the door and peeked out.

The hallway was empty. She stepped out and walked with light steps, hoping the wooden floor wouldn't creak. Clenching her teeth to ward off her apprehension, she paused at the top of the old wooden staircase before descending. She tiptoed down halfway and looked into the large dining area below, where Lena stood among the tables and chairs, chatting with a diner. The room appeared empty besides them. Helen waited. She thought she saw Lena glance out of the corner of her eye toward the stairs, but there was no break in the flow of her words.

"But we can't stay here talking all evening," Lena stated, bringing the conversation to a close. "Your wife must be wondering when you'll finish talking to your friends and come home."

"True, true," the man sighed. *"She* was the one who invited our daughter and her children back into our home..."

In spite of his reluctance, the man rose and left the inn with a cheerful goodbye. After a few seconds, Helen finished her descent.

"Have you had the rest you needed?" Lena asked, standing in the middle of the floor, her hands resting on her hips.

"I think so," Helen answered.

"Have a seat and I'll bring you something to eat," Lena said, heading through a swinging door into the kitchen.

Helen obeyed the command. The muffled sound of cupboard doors, plates, and silverware floated from the other side of the door . Helen looked around the room. The rest of the inn was just as bare as her bedroom. Plain wooden tables and chairs were scattered throughout the dining area, thin white curtains drawn across the windows, and the wooden walls bare.

Soon the kitchen noises stopped and Lena appeared again, carrying a plate and a cup. She set them down and Helen smiled at the sight of roast beef, roasted potatoes, and an assortment of vegetables. She hadn't eaten anything like this since leaving Camelora.

"I like having a few minutes in the evening to enjoy the silence," Lena stated with a smile, lowering herself into the chair across from Helen. "I hear so many voices all day, my brain needs time to air out."

She spoke of it as though it were laundry, something that could be washed and cleaned. It was an idea that appealed to Helen. She wished she could air out the thoughts in her own mind.

"Is your inn busy?" Helen inquired as she took in the number of tables and chairs filling the room.

Lena nodded. "The dining room is, anyway. It's convenient. Close to the water, in the center of the busiest street. Many of the fishermen come here for their meals. I'm a better cook than most of the women in this village," Lena confided, dropping her voice to a whisper as her eyes twinkled with mirth. Then, her voice returned to its usual tone. "There are less people here than there used to be, though. We don't often see outside merchants or tradespeople anymore—maybe once a year." Lena's smile took on a wistful, dreamy quality, revealing on the outside the memories she held on the inside. "The rooms upstairs go mostly unoccupied. Traders don't stay long when they *do* come and the residents have no need for the rooms."

The front door flew open, startling Helen and setting her heart drumming. She snapped her head around, afraid that she would see a large group of people spilling into the room, knowing there was no time to hide. After what Lena had told her, she knew that the sight of a stranger would draw attention she didn't want.

Her alarm lessened when Helen only saw two people enter—a man and a young girl. Lena rose and rushed forward to greet them, catching the man in a brief embrace and touching the girl's cheek. Helen was struck by the appearance of these newcomers. The man's features were more familiar to her—a tall man with the appearance of a Cameloran. His eyes were much lighter than Lena's, as was his wheat-colored hair. The girl, though, looked like a miniature version of the woman who greeted her. Lena's husband and daughter, Helen guessed. Curiosity filled the girl's face as she gazed at Helen. Then, she looked at her mother, her eyes asking an unspoken question. Lena nodded and the girl ran up the stairs.

The man looked over at Helen. "I'm glad to see you awake," he stated.

Helen bowed her head in acknowledgement, not sure what to say. Lena took the man's hand and led him to the table. "This is my husband, Connor," she said as they sat down.

"I'm Helen," Helen told him. She looked down at her plate, still hungry, yet suddenly feeling awkward eating as the two innkeepers watched.

"Oh, don't mind us," Connor hurried to say, understanding the expression in her eye. "We're used to talking with people as they eat. We've all had our dinner, anyway."

Relieved, Helen continued her meal. "Where did the people go?" Helen asked between bites.

"I beg your pardon?" Connor asked, confused.

"I was telling Helen about the village," Lena explained, "and how there are less people now than there were before." She turned her attention back to Helen. "I don't want to bore you with a long story. Basically, they left to see the world, to find a better future than they could in Phara. I traveled a lot as a girl so I can understand the desire.

You see, my father was an ambassador from across the sea. Have you ever heard of Ancloru?"

Helen shook her head.

Lena went on. "Our emperor was curious about the stories of a kingdom that had disappeared from our histories. He sent my father to find it. My father didn't want to leave my mother and me behind, so we came with him. And we found Phara. His plan was to stay here for a time and document what he found. We had only been here a few months when he fell ill and died, leaving my mother and me with no way to get back to our homeland. So, we built a life here. Phara may have its failings, but the kindness of its people is not one of them."

Connor reached out and placed his hand over his wife's, but fixed his gaze on Helen. "You have traveled far," he stated. "I can see it in your face and clothes. Where do you come from?"

Helen looked down at her clothes, travelworn and now caked with sand and salt from the sea. She hesitated, wondering where to start.

In that moment of hesitation, the door opened again and she felt the same reaction as before, her nerves still on edge. This time, a solitary man walked into the dining room, a hooded cloak concealing his face—a cloak she knew well. He sat at a table just inside the door and raised his head just enough for Helen to see his features. Their eyes met and she relaxed.

Lena crossed to the man and greeted him, her manner more guarded with this stranger than with Helen. After a few brief words, he handed her a couple of coins and she disappeared once again into the kitchen. A minute later, she returned with a plate of food and a cup identical to Helen's. Setting them down before the man, she said a few more words before returning to Helen's table.

"I'm originally from Veren, in the south," Helen said, continuing her story in a lower tone.

"Veren," Lena repeated, the name visibly striking a chord.

"It's gone now," Helen stated, looking down at her plate. She pushed it away, her appetite gone.

"We've heard the rumors," Connor said. "We never know how much to believe, being as far away from everything as we are."

The tears sprang to Helen's eyes and she covered her mouth in an effort to suppress the sobs that swelled her chest. But there was no way to control the emotion that overwhelmed her. Lena moved quickly into the chair next to Helen's and wrapped her arms around her. Silently she sat, not trying to say anything to stop the flow of tears. Helen felt that this woman understood her feelings. Her embrace was the embrace of a mother, something Helen hadn't felt in a long time, something she missed more than she could tell.

The tears gradually lessened. Helen was soon able to accept the handkerchief Lena held out to her. She dried her eyes and cheeks, and blew her nose. Still, she kept her head down. "My mother is gone," Helen uttered weakly. "Everyone and everything I knew... My father was captured, but he was the only one who survived."

"Do you know where he is?" Lena asked, her words steeped with concern.

"Yes. We managed to free him not long ago. He's on his way to safety now."

"We?" Lena questioned. "You said that before. Who are 'we'?"

"My—my traveling companions," Helen stuttered, not sure how much she should say. "We were separated."

Lena knew Helen held back something important , but didn't press her. "You managed to escape," she stated. "From Veren, I mean."

"My mother sent me away. That's a long story, though."

"You're her, aren't you?"

The voice and words startled Helen. She turned to see Lena's daughter sitting on the stairs, watching through the rails of the banister. Helen wondered how long she had been there, listening.

The girl hadn't spoken yet and her soft, sweet voice was unexpected. Her eyes shone brightly, mingling hope and excitement.

"Aurelie," Lena scolded gently. "You know how I feel about eavesdropping."

"You're the girl in the stories," Aurelie went on.

Helen's wonderings were confirmed. People outside of Camelora knew the old stories. In much of the land, they had been lost so long ago. Those who knew them, she had started to believe, didn't care about them anymore. But if this young girl knew the stories, perhaps this journey wouldn't be as difficult as Helen had imagined. She smiled at Aurelie and nodded.

"Then it's true!" Aurelie exclaimed. "The forgotten king is coming for us."

"How do you know about Zaric?" Helen asked, the girl's enthusiasm brightening her spirits.

"From the stories she reads," Lena explained. "Aurelie loves to read stories. She found some rare parchments and books forgotten and unwanted in the village hall library and archives. Sometimes she tells them to me. I've always thought they were simply fairy tales, but she believes that every word is true."

"I *know* they're true," Aurelie argued. "But none of them tell me the king's name. Zaric. I like that."

The girl got to her feet and skipped down the stairs, running into the dining room to sit beside her father, who draped an arm across her shoulders and kissed the top of her head.

"What happened here, in Phara?" Helen asked. " In my travels, I saw an entire city that was completely empty, except for a man and woman who were on their way out. But in their case, it was a matter of safety. They weren't looking for a better life, just a way to preserve the life they already had. They supported Zaric and Zaric's greatest enemy didn't like it."

"Strange things are happening, I suppose," Lena stated with a shrug.

"It's strange that so many villagers would decide to leave all at once," Helen continued. " If Phara is anything like Veren was, you don't want to take a chance in a region where everything might change so suddenly."

"I'm afraid the idea to leave wasn't born in Phara." Lena looked to Connor to catch his nod of agreement before she went on. "Some men came—traders, we thought—from the sea. They asked to stay a few days. They paid us well and we wouldn't have refused them, anyway. Business is business. We were a little confused when they didn't bring goods from their ship, though. It became obvious they weren't traders at all. We couldn't understand why they had come. They spent their time sitting here in the dining room, talking to the people. Nothing out of the ordinary, just talking about the mundane things of life. It didn't take long for them to get to know nearly everyone in Phara. Knowing what I know now, I would love to say that I had a bad feeling about them, but I'm afraid I didn't. They seemed like average, ordinary men.

"One day, one of the men climbed onto a table. Everyone stopped talking. He told us that, after getting to know us so well, he felt sorry for us. Never before had he seen a city living on so little when they had the potential to accomplish so much. He told us about a man who had plans to reunify the old kingdom. He was looking for men and women who were willing to work for him in a diplomatic capacity, to go among the governors of the land and convince them to create alignments and treaties."

"They were recruiters," Connor inserted.

"The families that chose to help," Lena went on, "were promised lands and cattle and crops, gold, jewels, wealth, and anything else they could desire. It was then that things didn't feel right to Connor and me. How could he promise such things? What would others lose for us to gain them?"

"Do you remember who they were?" Helen asked.

"I don't remember those men's names specifically, but they had been sent by someone else. It's a name I couldn't easily forget. His name was Mered."

Helen held her breath, even though it was the name she had expected to hear. Her mind filled with questions like water bubbling up through a hole in the bottom of a boat.

The man near the door coughed. The sound startled everyone at Helen's table and Lena jumped up from her chair. "I'm so sorry!" she exclaimed in a way that told everyone she had forgotten he was there. "I've been neglecting you."

She took a few quick steps toward him, but he was already on his feet, crossing the room to their table. Lena sat down again haltingly, watching him with curiosity and confusion. "How long ago was this?" the man asked.

"Twelve years," Connor replied cautiously. Whatever secrets this family held, Helen could now see they didn't like to share them with just anyone.

"And did you know of Mered before this?"

No," Connor shook his head. "We had never heard of him before. But his name has been coming up more and more again lately. Do you know him?"

"You could say that," was all the man offered. Then he asked, "How many went with these recruiters?"

"More than three-quarters of the city left with them," Lena said. " In the end, Mered took so much of what he promised to give. If you walked through the streets, you couldn't have helped but notice all of the empty homes, falling apart because no one is there to take care of them."

"And what did *you* lose?"

The silence that followed this question stretched out, but the stranger was in no hurry to speak again. "My sister," Connor answered eventually. "And her husband and daughter."

The man nodded, but still said nothing. Connor continued. "There was nothing wrong with our lives. We were all happy without Mered and his ideas of wealth and ambition. I don't mind those things when they come honestly, but I had the impression that Mered was willing to get them in less-than-honest ways. My sister didn't agree with me. She always wanted more than Phara could offer. We argued about it for days."

Lena took up the story. "More and more people were deciding to join Mered's supporters. Connor's sister saw her friends and neighbors agree to go. She begged her husband to take her and their daughter to Mered."

"I don't think it took much to convince him," Connor scoffed. "My brother-in-law was much like my sister and couldn't get out of Phara fast enough. But our niece..."

"She was almost like a daughter to us," Lena said, memories rising in her eyes. "She spent most of her time here at the inn with me, helping in the kitchen. When her parents wanted to go to parties—which was often—Connor and I watched her. Her mother didn't seem to mind letting someone else take care of her. Since I had wanted a child for so long, I was glad to have her around. But in the end, she wasn't ours. When we saw that Connor's sister was determined to go, we asked if our niece could stay with us, but she accused us of trying to steal her daughter. It was only then that the girl seemed to matter to her.

"Two more ships came—empty ships. We saw then that the men had planned all along to take our people with them. They gave us one more day to decide whether or not we would join. Those who did not would be left behind."

"My sister chose to go, and we did not," Connor stated. "I wish

I could say that I miss her, but I'm afraid I don't. Not her, not her husband. Just their daughter, Siri."

"Siri!" Helen exclaimed, almost jumping out of her chair. In her mind, thoughts clicked together like magnets. Phara and Siri—that was how she had heard of this place before. The name was familiar because Siri had mentioned it as her home. The lie she had told upon meeting Helen and Neil was tinted with truth. Memories overwhelmed Helen, both images and emotions—dread, fear, and darkness.

Lena stared at Helen, hopefulness and the fear to hope both written clearly across her face. "You know Siri?" she asked.

"I met her a few months ago."

Lena's eyes regained the brightness they had gradually lost as she and Connor told their story.

"You've seen Siri!" she exclaimed in a hushed tone, as if the statement were sacred. "Is she doing well? Did she manage to escape from Mered?"

For a moment, Helen was tempted to lie. Lena was so hopeful, it felt harsh to shatter those hopes and tell her just how much evil Mered's followers were capable of, no matter how good they had been before. But a lie wouldn't help Lena or Connor. They would eventually learn the truth and their trust in Helen would falter. Out of the corner of her eye, she saw the man nod slightly. "She was working for Mered," Helen said, keeping her words plain. "She tried to mislead my friend, and when that didn't work, she... she tried to kill me."

"So that's what Mered does to his followers," Connor stated, his voice flat. "That's what my sister chose for her child. They turned her into a liar and murderer."

Heaviness engulfed the room. Lena looked toward the window, her mind thrown back to a different time. With a sigh and a smile, Lena looked back at Helen and said, "Aurelie came to us only a couple of years after that—a gift from the Eternal One—a reward for our decision to stay behind."

Helen looked at Aurelie, taking in the girl's sweet air and innocence as she sat cradled beneath her father's arm. Her eyes were unmarred by the family's tragedy and loss.

"I'm afraid we'll be seeing the same situation again," Connor said, returning to the subject of the city. "There are rumors that our governor—in the comfort of his grand home, locked away from the world—has been meeting with an ambassador from Mered. They say that he will be sending men again to gather supporters."

For only the second time since he had entered the room, the stranger's and Helen's eyes met and locked, as though they were speaking without words.

"You can be sure," the man said, "that Mered's men will come back. I saw a small battalion headed toward Phara only a few days ago. It won't be long before they arrive. And it's not like Mered to take some people from a city and let the rest stay without trouble. That's one thing we have all learned from Veren. He wants power and anyone who doesn't recognize his complete authority will be destroyed. We can make sure that doesn't happen, but we don't need to follow Mered to do it."

"How will we do it, then?" Lena asked.

"We'll teach the people about Zaric," Helen stated.

"Do you think they will believe without any other proof than your word?" Connor wondered.

"They won't have to," the man said, "because I am King Zaric himself."

Chapter 12

The Present

O nly a handful of people sat scattered among the library's tables and chairs. It was often like this. Neil didn't mind. He had awoken that morning with an idea in his head, but the demands of the morning didn't allow him to act on it. It wasn't until after lunch he was able to snatch an hour to search the records, looking for some way they could defeat Mered. So much of what they were doing had been written about before, predicted by the writers and storytellers of the past. If there was any indication of how to finish the threat of Mered for good, Neil realized it was likely to be in the records kept in the palace's library.

So far, he had found nothing. He didn't know where to start or what sort of records to search. At the moment, he hovered over what appeared to be a centuries-old text, but it was written in an almost indecipherable hand, making it impossible to tell. With a sigh, he flopped back in his chair, rubbing his eyes.

Running footsteps sounded across the floor—faint , but growing louder. The library door burst open and a guard spilled in, out of breath. "We need you outside, Neil," he stated between gulps of air.

"Is something wrong?" Neil asked pushing back his chair and jumping to his feet in the same motion. With a smile, the messenger shook his head. Neil followed the young man as he rushed back out.

They passed through the open front doors of the palace into the late afternoon sun. As they ran down the palace steps, Neil saw a cart approaching. A red-haired man sat in the driver's box while a black-haired woman sat in the back—a man and woman Neil instantly recognized, though he had only seen them once before. A calm fell over him that he didn't know he needed.

When the cart stopped, the horse shifted its weight uncomfortably, panting, tired from a long journey. Stephen jumped down from the box and went to the horse, rubbing its head. A woman came running from the direction of the stables, carrying a bucket of water and some hay.

"I wondered when I would see you," Neil said, approaching the cart as Meira let herself down from the back.

"Hello, Neil." Meira's manner was as warm as he expected. She embraced the young man as a mother would.

Stephen left the horse to the care of the stablewoman and walked to the back of the cart, extending his hand to shake Neil's.

"I'm glad you're here," Neil said, feeling a relief he hadn't anticipated. "Have you seen Helen and Zaric?"

"Yes," Meira answered, "but we can talk about that later. Right now, we have someone for you to see."

She indicated the back of the cart with a gesture of her hand. At first, Neil only saw a pile of blankets. But, as Meira climbed back in and approached it, he realized it was actually a person wrapped in quilts. Gently, she touched a shoulder, startling the person awake. A grey-haired head appeared, eyes blinking rapidly at the sudden awareness of daylight. Meira helped him into a sitting position. His hands trembled as he leaned against the back of the cart, unable to support himself in his still-waking state. Neil took in the man's aged and wrinkled face, the skin that seemed to hang straight from his bones, his plain and ill-fitting clothes, and his feeble frame. Embarrassed that he didn't recognize the man when it was obvious that he should, Neil looked into his eyes.

The man blinked away the cloudiness of sleep and age, then beamed at Neil. "You look so much like your father," he stated, his voice soft from the dryness of his throat, "but I see your mother in your eyes."

"Cyrus," Neil responded, just above a whisper. He wanted to jump into the cart and hug him like his own father, but he was afraid that he would break him.

"It's been too long, Neil," Cyrus said. "I'm so sorry that I wasn't there when your parents…"

"I'm glad you're here now, Cyrus," Neil told him, showing the old man that he understood. "I'm glad you're safe."

Cyrus nodded to Meira and Stephen, who helped slide him to the edge of the cart. Neil motioned to a nearby guard and the two of them helped lower Cyrus to the ground. With Neil's arms bearing his weight, Cyrus steadied himself and stood as straight as he could.

"If only I didn't feel so weak," Cyrus apologized. "There is so much for us to talk about, my boy, but after all of those days in the cart, I am so tired."

Neil smiled and nodded his awareness. He turned to the guard. "Is there an empty room close to mine? I want Cyrus to be near me, if possible. And make sure he gets everything he asks for. He's Helen's father," he added, feeling that the fact warranted greater care and attention. The guard nodded and rushed up the palace steps, disappearing through the open door.

"Stephen, Meira," Neil went on, "if you can trust Melda to take care of your horse and cart, I'm sure Garrick would like to see you. Let's go to the reception room."

Stephen chuckled as they started to walk, taking Cyrus's other arm so that Neil wasn't left to support him on his own. "You sound very official, Neil. Camelora has changed you."

Once inside the palace, Neil beckoned to two more guards. Leaving Cyrus in their care, Neil went with Meira and Stephen to the reception room. They found it empty—no citizens waiting to settle a dispute, no guards taking a quick break away from the unusually hot day, no children hiding to play or read a book instead of doing chores. They crossed the colonnaded room, across the luminous squares cast by the sunlight coming through the skylights above. Chairs sat in alcoves throughout the room and Neil chose one by a window.

"How are Helen and Zaric?" he asked before any of them sat down.

"They were both well when we left them," Stephen reassured him. "Zaric wanted to go straight into his next mission and Helen chose to go with him. They would have lost too much time returning to Camelora first."

Neil nodded, trying not to show the disappointment he felt. He didn't want to admit that he hadn't thought a return to Camelora was impractical. But he realized now just how much he had wanted to see Helen again. Although he was glad to see Cyrus, the father was no replacement for the daughter.

The squeak of hinges announced Garrick's arrival in the room. The governor scanned its periphery until his eyes fell on the alcove where the three sat. A broad grin covered his face and he wasted no time in crossing the room.

"I don't think I need to ask who you are," he stated as the three stood to greet him. "Meira, Stephen, I've heard so many stories about you."

"Hmmm," Meira let out, skepticism infusing her manner.

"Really, I have," Garrick restated. "You're some of Zaric's most loyal supporters."

"Meira and Stephen have brought Helen's father to us," Neil informed the governor.

"Cyrus," Garrick said with reverence. "He's alive and well, then?"

"Alive, at least," Stephen corrected. "The months have not been kind to the governor of Veren."

"Our Cameloran nurses will take good care of him. They know the best herbs and cures in the kingdom. As for us, I want to know everything you have to tell me. Leave no detail out."

"How are things throughout the kingdom?" Neil interjected.

"Mered has increased his military presence," Meira answered. "His own palace is busy and he is gaining more and more support from the governors. They meet with him regularly. We saw many of them arrive as we were living in Nubiim. Troops are stationed in many of the regions throughout the kingdom. If Zaric's supporters aren't on the move already, it will soon be difficult for them to make their way to Camelora—especially now that Mered knows Zaric is moving freely to gather support."

"I'm afraid part of our plan involved alerting Mered to Zaric's presence in the kingdom," Stephen explained. "His *active* presence, that is. It was Zaric's idea. Not that it should be much of a surprise to the false king. How he's managed to build so much support is beyond me. The governors I can understand, but as for recruiting the regular citizens of the regions, how can they not see through him?"

"I can understand it, unfortunately," Meira said. "He makes such grand promises. Their greed blinds them to the fact that something about it isn't quite right."

"We have already received some of Zaric's supporters," Garrick said. "You say it will be difficult for them to make their way to Camelora. Difficult, but not impossible?"

"Nothing is impossible," Stephen assured him. "That's what Zaric would say."

"Stephen and I plan to leave again, after a couple of days' rest. We want to recruit supporters until there are no more supporters to be found."

Neil rested his elbows on his knees and pressing his fingertips together, disappointment sending another pang through him. He had hoped that Meira and Stephen would stay and lend their support in Camelora—ease some of the burden on Garrick, the council, and himself—but he knew that Zaric's greatest allies had a better chance than anyone else at rallying support elsewhere. "I think that would be best," he agreed. "We haven't received nearly enough support yet to take on a battalion."

"I agree," Garrick said. "Of course, you are governors in your own right and don't need my permission to do what you like."

"We appreciate the backing all the same," Stephen said.

"Have our own citizens arrived yet?" Meira inquired next.

"They were some of the first," Neil replied. "They've been trickling in over the past two weeks, with different groups from all over the northern lands."

"We would like to see them as soon as possible," Meira said, smiling with relief.

"And have you seen Alan yet?" Stephen asked.

Neil shook his head. "I assume he's trying to find Zaric's supporters, too. He was already preparing when Helen and I saw him, just before opening the Gateway."

"That's something Zaric has," Meira put in, "that Mered does not: *true* loyalty. Eventually Mered's promises will turn to dust and he will lose the confidence and support of everyone he has deceived."

"I hope you're right," Neil sighed, not feeling as certain as Meira apparently did. Though he didn't mention it to the new arrivals, the knowledge that they likely had a traitor in their midst caused many of his old doubts to resurface. It was a situation they hadn't spoken of and Neil was afraid it would prove to be their undoing.

Chapter 13

The Present

After supper, Neil made his way to Cyrus's room. He had wanted to speak with him all day, but knew how much the old man needed rest. Instead, he busied himself with gathering what details he could from Meira and Stephen as he followed them around the refugee camp, marking on a map of the kingdom the areas of concern they brought up—places where Mered's influence was too strong for them to expect much support. Garrick felt that supporters from these regions who independently made their way to Camelora would require additional scrutiny.

"Neil, my boy," Cyrus exclaimed hoarsely when he saw the young man. He placed his thin fingers on the armrest of the soft chair where he sat and pushed himself to his feet, his legs shaking from the effort.

"Don't stand up for me," Neil said, rushing forward and helping Cyrus sit down again. Then, he sat in an identical chair across from his parents' old friend.

Cyrus's tattered clothing had been replaced and his body was clean, which took a few years off his face. Neil saw now just how much the dirt and fatigue had added to his age before. His thin white hair was washed and combed, hanging long against his shoulders. It was a comfort to see that his blue eyes were still as bright as Neil remembered. Still, with a shawl wrapped around his shoulders despite the summer warmth, he looked much older than he should—a fact that pained Neil's heart.

"I'm glad you're finally here," Neil said. "I'm sorry for everything you've been through."

"And I for you," Cyrus stated. "I'm sorry we weren't there for you when your parents died. We wanted to be, but—"

Neil cut him off by placing a hand on his arm. "I understand," he said. He looked into Cyrus's eyes so the man could see that this statement was true. He raised the corner of his lips and squeezed Cyrus's hand. Inside, he dreaded what he needed to ask next, but he knew that it was important and tried not to let his dread show in his face. "What happened to Veren?" he asked.

His eyes clouding, but his posture resolute, Cyrus related his story about Mered's occupation of his city. When he spoke about Helen's mother, Neil's heart dropped, then beat ferociously. He thought of what Helen must be feeling at her loss. She had clung to hope throughout the months she was separated from them that she would see her parents in the end. Knowing that Helen would never again see her mother, knowing how they had parted without a proper goodbye—it was worse than the way he had lost his own parents. He had at least been able to stay with them, talk to them, listen to them, watch them take their final breaths, and ensure that they were not alone.

"How is Helen?" Neil asked, the twinge of missing her touching him unexpectedly.

"She's so much stronger than she ever was before," Cyrus said with an expression of wonder, shaking his head from side to side as he thought of his daughter. "She has grown so much. When my wife and I talked about sending her away, I worried that she wouldn't make it—that she wasn't really the young woman mentioned in the stories—but I realize now that I was being unfair. I was worrying like all fathers do, without seeing the strength of my own daughter. Helen is capable of taking care of herself. Now, she has gone off to help Zaric and to prove that to her old father again."

"Everything she has done and everything she continues to do is because of you. It doesn't surprise me at all. Helen has a deep belief in this cause."

"You have changed, too," Cyrus continued with enthusiasm, his eyes twinkling. "It's been years since I last saw you, but I'm amazed at the man you've become. The little boy I knew gave no signs of ever being able to govern a city."

"I'm only helping. As far as growing is concerned, I didn't have much of a choice. You didn't see what I was before Helen came to me. Once she did, there was no way for me to stay the same."

Cyrus opened his mouth to reply, but instead a cough rose up through his dry throat, turning into a fit that he couldn't stop. Feeling a surge of panic, Neil crossed the room to a small table where a pitcher of water sat next to an empty glass. He filled the glass and took it to Cyrus, who drank gratefully. A few more coughs came after he drained it, but they were less violent and soon subsided. He set the glass on the windowsill.

"Zaric must trust you a great deal," Cyrus finally went on. "Giving you such a charge. But the stories always indicated that it would be so."

"I still don't know how much confidence I have in the stories."

"Well, I suppose it's different when they're about *you*."

"And I'm not sure how well I'm helping with Camelora."

"You look out for the best interests of the people, surely."

"But how can I be sure we're really keeping them safe?" Neil asked. "There are already people in Camelora who don't belong here—who mean to cause us harm. We just don't know who they are. How do we stop them?"

"Conspirators in Camelora?" Cyrus questioned, fearful yet unconvinced.

Neil told Cyrus about the device found in the woods. He told him his frustrations about not knowing where to start or how to figure out what they were up against. The flow of his words led him to Siri, their history, and the stories she had told him about herself and Mered, as well as her offer to help find whomever was trying to communicate with their enemy. He reiterated what she had done to Helen, trying to convey just how close they had come to losing her.

"You're a governor," Neil stated, "and a father. I'm sure you must have an idea of what to do in a situation like this."

Cyrus was thoughtful as he looked down at the floor, tapping the arm of the chair with his fingertips. Neil had seen the tears gather in the old man's eyes when he told him about Helen, but they didn't spill. When he lifted his gaze to look at Neil, they were the calm, clear eyes of a leader. "What does Garrick think?" he asked.

Neil was stunned. He had expected a different reaction, one that was more emotional and less diplomatic—the reaction of a father who had nearly lost his daughter, despite Neil's appeal to him as a governor.

"He thinks we should trust her," Neil admitted, hating the words.

"Zaric trusts Garrick enough to leave Camelora in his care. *You* need to trust *Garrick*. If you want to do what is best for these people, listen to their governor."

"But there's no knowing what Siri will do. She hasn't proven herself trustworthy."

"Then *let* her prove herself. Do you believe Garrick will allow anyone to destroy this city in Zaric's absence?"

"No," Neil admitted.

"I'm sure he has a plan in case she betrays the trust placed in her. In the meantime, do as Garrick asks. If you have a concern and know that it stems from more than just your own prejudice, I'm sure he will listen to you."

"Would *you* trust her?"

"I don't know; I've never met the woman. And, remember, in the end, I didn't do enough to prepare my own people. My judgment is questionable."

"Don't say that," Neil argued. "From what I've heard, you did more for your people than any other governor has done for theirs—Meira and Stephen excepted. Most of them are only thinking of themselves, not their people. But you—Mered saw you as a threat. There was no way to know the extent to which he would go to stop you."

"Well…" Cyrus cut himself off, lost in thought. When he spoke again, he retraced the steps of the conversation. "What do your instincts tell you about Siri?"

The question frustrated Neil. He wanted Cyrus to tell him what to do, not ask him what he felt. But Cyrus sat with a calmness that eased Neil's frustration and helped him to think. He took a minute to let go of his anger towards Siri and examine his deeper feelings—the instincts and intuitions that helped him to prepare the people, and that Zaric had seen in him to put him in this position.

"I don't know why," Neil said, measuring his words, "but I feel like I can believe her. I *should* believe her. Her fear of Mered seems to be genuine. Everything that I know about Mered leads me to believe that Siri's story is true. If she's sincere, any information she can give us would be invaluable."

"Even Mered's strongest supporters are capable of change," Cyrus stated, his simple words striking Neil like a blow to the chest.

"I don't know if we can say that she has ever really supported Mered," Neil admitted. "Siri has been used and manipulated and has done all that she could to please him, but that was to stay alive. At least, that's what she told me and Garrick."

"This is the reason Zaric chose you to help govern Camelora in his absence," Cyrus exclaimed with more emotion than Neil had seen yet, reaching out to squeeze the young man's hand. "Your instincts will keep Camelora safe, just as they helped you come here with Helen."

"You think I can trust Siri, then?"

"I think you can answer that question yourself."

"And if my instincts are as good as you think they are, I will be able to determine if she tries to work against us."

"I would never advise you not to be cautious." Another fit of coughs attacked Cyrus, coming from deep within his body. Neil winced at how painful it sounded, growing more and more concerned. The conversation had visibly wearied the older man. Neil refilled his glass with water from the pitcher, then placed a hand on Cyrus's back as he drank.

"I should let you rest again," Neil said, holding out his arm. Cyrus nodded and allowed the young man to help him to his feet, then into his bed. He settled into the pillows and covered himself with the blankets.

"Thank you for your advice," Neil continued. "I'm glad you're here."

"I'm glad to be here," Cyrus replied as he closed his eyes. Neil was surprised at how soon he was asleep. He adjusted the blankets around his friend's frail frame, then left the room with careful steps, softly closing the door behind him.

The conversation with Cyrus repeated in Neil's mind as he walked through the palace, greeting everyone he passed with only a smile and a nod. He didn't want anything to dissuade him from his purpose. Looking from this new perspective, he could see how unfair he had been to Siri. Zaric would have treated her differently—with fairness and understanding. He understood now just how embarrassed he still was to have fallen into Siri's trap all those weeks ago. Regret wasn't much help to Camelora. Neil was determined to change his present course.

He no longer believed that Siri was trying to deceive him. He had wanted so much to be right about her because he had been wrong about her before, to see now the deceit he hadn't seen then. Now that he was faced with it, he saw what a foolish choice that was. Zaric would never have made that mistake. He would never allow his personal feelings or past errors to cloud his judgment. Neither would Helen. At least, he didn't believe she would.

Neil thought of everything Siri had said to him since arriving in Camelora. He thought of her desire to speak to Zaric, of her offer to help the people in their fight against Mered, and especially of the story of her life she had told him. He thought of how she had lived up to this point, of her parents and how she had been raised. The pity he felt was one he had never felt before. Although he had lost his own parents, he knew that they loved him and that they would never have used him as Siri's parents had used her. From his parents and grandfather—and even from Helen and her parents—Neil had never felt anything but love and acceptance. He found himself admiring Siri for fighting against everything she had been taught, every habit she had formed, to become something better. She knew that it was wrong and was willing to leave her parents and everything they believed in—the life she had always known—for something greater.

Taking a deep breath in, then slowly letting it out, Neil attempted to release his anger and stubbornness with the air from his lungs.

He found Garrick in Zaric's study. The governor looked up in surprise as his assistant burst in, but Neil didn't want to give Garrick time to greet him before he spoke, afraid that he would lose the courage he had built in his walk down the hall.

"I want to work with Siri," Neil blurted. "I haven't been fair to her; I didn't see how valuable her information and skills can be to us. And

I'm willing to admit now that you might just have some knowledge of the world outside of Camelora after all."

Garrick stifled a grin, but his eyes still laughed at the young man. Neil knew he couldn't be angry; he had been arrogant and that arrogance was bound to be humbled.

"I'm glad you can see that," the governor stated, sitting up taller in his chair. "Zaric has been preparing this people our entire lives to face the eventual threats which would one day come. It may be harder than we realized it would be, but we aren't ignorant to them. Are you saying you finally believe Siri?"

"I'm getting there," Neil admitted.

"Good," Garrick replied, patting his young assistant on the back, "because I've decided to allow her to help us. Tomorrow, I would like the three of us to meet and decide where we go from here. In the meantime, I will be removing Siri from the palace and bringing her into my own home."

Neil knew his fear of Siri hadn't dissipated completely. Nothing he had said could have given Garrick the impression that it had. This statement caused that fear to bubble again. Every nerve in his body tingled. "Are you sure that's a good idea?" he asked, being careful with his words.

"You know my wife, Neil. Do you think anyone could easily fool her? Anyway, I think she would be good for Siri."

"But your children—"

"But Zahra. She can handle it."

Neil was reluctant to concede to Garrick's plan, reluctant to allow him to remove Siri from a place where she was so well guarded. But he was not the governor and did not have the final say. Knowing he couldn't win this argument, he nodded in assent.

"I appreciate that your heart's in the right place," Garrick went on, "but you can trust me. Come back here after breakfast tomorrow morning. We have important work to do."

"All right," Neil agreed. He couldn't help wondering what he was getting himself into. This could either be a good idea—or a mistake of immense proportions. His imagination could create many terrible scenarios. He hoped none of them were true.

Chapter 14

The Past

After a period of mourning, the court scheduled Zaric's coronation. A sudden illness took Edric sooner than anyone expected—decades, Zaric thought, before he was ready. The new, young king couldn't imagine holding celebrations for as long as his father would have, but he *did* agree to a week of dinners and parties leading up to the main event, then a week of parties following it. His heart beat harder in his chest as he watched men and women arrive from all over the kingdom. More and more people filled the palace, permeating its usual quiet with too much noise. All of those years in this grand space, all of those years watching his father, all of those years training to one day be the king—and Zaric still felt inadequate when he was surrounded by the nobility of Camelora.

"Does this make you uncomfortable?" a soft and gentle voice whispered behind Zaric on the first evening of parties.

The voice startled him. He thought he was well-hidden in the shadows just outside of the ballroom, watching the people dance through a crack in a side door as they awaited the new king's entrance. He turned to find a young woman standing next to him, the top of her head only reaching his shoulder. Though most of her dark hair was pulled back in elaborate twists and braids, a couple of strands

117

framed her tanned oval face. Wide, dark blue eyes twinkled up at Zaric, complementing the kind smile that set the king at ease. A deep blue gown covered her slight frame, elegant in its simplicity. She was the most beautiful woman Zaric had ever seen. With the training of a true noblewoman, she bowed her head and curtsied when Zaric turned to fully face her.

"A little bit," was all Zaric could manage in reply. "My name is Zaric," he added, then closed his eyes in embarrassment. She already knew who he was. Everyone in the palace did.

"I am Althea, your majesty," she said, taking no notice of his awkward statement as she bowed her head again.

"I don't like parties," Zaric told her. "My father always did, but I never could get used to them."

"I can understand that," Althea said. "I only like the *right* kind of parties—when I can be surrounded by people I like and when I know that the conversation will be refreshing, not dull. But I also understand the importance of diplomatic parties. I can always encourage myself to do my duty, especially when I know that it will be over in a few hours."

Zaric had never thought of that. The task of governing the kingdom didn't bother him, just the socializing at parties with small talk and pretending to be interested in finery and other superficial things. He had never thought to remind himself that it would soon be over and he could move onto more important tasks.

"Is that what brings you out here?" Zaric asked. "Is this the wrong kind of party?"

"Not at all, your majesty. I'm simply trying to avoid—someone—who is paying too much attention to me. No, if you find the right people," Althea went on, "even a party like this can be pleasant."

"Do you know the 'right' people?" Zaric looked into the room again at the menagerie of men and women, of all ages and every noble status.

Many he already knew, many he did not.

"I like to think so," she answered, looking into the room as well. Zaric glanced down at her profile and was struck again by her beauty, seeing now not only her face but something of the woman inside. She wasn't like most of the women he met now that he was the king. She didn't wear an artificial air, hoping to catch his attention. Her face was honest, and that honesty was refreshingly different.

"Can you show me the ones I should know?" he asked.

"If you like," Althea answered. "But I think you should let them announce you. Then, we can meet properly and talk in the light."

She gave him a smile that made his stomach flutter, then passed through the door into the ballroom, where she made her way to a group of men and women, standing to the side and watching the dancers. An older man—perhaps her father—greeted her with a warm smile and a kiss on the top of her head. She curtsied to the others in the group. Zaric watched her for another minute or two, marveling at the grace with which she moved, talked, and cast her eyes around the room.

He took a deep breath, knowing he had delayed his own entrance long enough. Besides, if he wanted to find Althea again, speak with her, and get to know her better, he would need to enter the room. He stepped away from the door, walked the few feet to the main hallway, and approached the ballroom.

The men and women clapped as the servant announced his name. As he moved forward, Zaric didn't know what to do first. It would be ill-mannered to walk directly to Althea and her group. In the past, his father orchestrated every introduction, utilizing his son as he saw fit. His sudden death prevented him from teaching Zaric how to do that for himself.

But Zaric didn't have to wonder for long. Two men approached him before he had walked very far—heads of state from minor neighboring kingdoms, both wanting to be the first to catch his ear. Zaric searched the crowd as they talked, looking for Althea's face or the group she had joined. It was harder to find her from this new vantage point. The party-goers in the room wouldn't stop moving. The circle of men and women hoping to speak with him grew larger and larger as well. Minutes passed with no hope of relief in sight.

A hand on his arm filled him with dread. He turned slowly, expecting to find someone else who wanted to talk about trade, but relief filled his body when he saw Althea standing next to him again.

"Excuse me, ladies and gentlemen," she said with that same polite bow of her head that Zaric now realized was second-nature to her, "his majesty promised to dance with me. Since this is a ball and not a meeting, I'm sure you will all understand."

Zaric nodded to the men and women standing around him, who hid their disappointment beneath polite smiles. He led Althea to the middle of the floor.

"Thank you," he said to her as the music began.

"I promised that I would introduce you to the most interesting people," Althea replied. "They were not them."

Althea stayed by Zaric's side for the next two hours. Citing decorum, she had tried to step away at one point, but the thought of navigating this room without her filled Zaric with dread. He quietly begged her to remain with him. It took little convincing for her to oblige.

They moved from group to group, meeting men and women who felt the honor of being graced by the king's presence without fawning. They were interested in what Zaric had to say—and disagreed with him in the most polite terms when they felt to disagree. When they spoke of matters of state, it was in a natural style, not trying to convince Zaric to think in one way or another. Zaric learned about their kingdoms and duchies from the stories they related, not from ideas or policies they tried to force upon him.

"Which Cameloran customs do you intend to keep, Zaric?" one eastern nobleman asked.

"All of them," Zaric answered without much thought. Then he amended, "Well, most of them."

"The ones you like?" a small, middle-aged woman asked.

"The ones that mean the most to the people."

A murmur of approval arose throughout the group.

"Is there one that will remain for certain?" the original questioner asked.

"I believe there are similar customs in other lands, but every autumn, we gather to thank the Eternal One for the blessings of the harvest."

"May His name be praised," many of those gathered uttered together.

"And what would you do away with?" the small woman questioned.

The inquiry was unexpected. Zaric could never imagine anyone asking his father the same thing. Changes would happen as a matter of course, but no one in Edric's circle would have been bold enough to ask what he intended to change. Tradition was sacred in Camelora, even the most simple and basic ones. That didn't mean Zaric didn't have ideas of his own on how to govern the kingdom.

"There is a thought I've been turning over in my mind," he confessed, the manner of the conversation emboldening him. "At the moment, the King's Council is made up of noblemen. I worry that the common people are not being properly represented. I want them to have a say in how they are governed."

"A council made up of commoners?" one Cameloran duke asked.

"A council made up of both commoners and noblemen," Zaric corrected. "We want to be sure we're hearing a variety of voices, not just the poor, not just the rich."

"You don't trust us to relay the wishes of our people?" the duke pressed, although there was no hint of offense in his voice.

"I do, but we can't be sure the people are fully informing their dukes on matters in their duchies. Allowing the common people to be directly involved with the council will, hopefully, empower them and give them a better system to speak their minds."

"Fascinating," a third man stated, speaking up for the first time. "And you will listen to both noblemen and commoners?"

"I will do my best."

Positive remarks accompanied by smiles ran through the group.

"We'll be paying close attention to how things work out for Camelora," the small woman said. "How do you expect to fill the seats on your council? There are many common people, after all."

"An election," Zaric replied without hesitation.

An excited murmur flowed through the group now. It had been some time since any of the kingdoms had held an election. It was a thrilling prospect.

Despite all the attention he received, Zaric didn't forget the woman standing next to him throughout every conversation. What pleased Zaric most about the evening was what he was able to learn about Althea. He was right when he guessed that the man she had gone to before was her father, Evander. He was a minor duke from a southern duchy—Veren—a widower who had raised his only child to think and choose for herself. It was rare for women to inherit power and titles, but Veren cared little for how things were done in the rest of the kingdom. Althea would one day become the duchess of her region and her father had every confidence in her judgment already. Where other fathers had tried for years to place their daughters before Zaric, Althea's father didn't appear to be concerned about what the new king thought of his daughter. As the duke of a well-coordinated region, Evander had little reason to ever come to the capital himself.

Throughout his various conversations, Zaric learned that Althea spoke little and listened a great deal. Initially, he couldn't tell if she agreed or disagreed with the things she heard, but after a while he noticed that she would sometimes nod ever so slightly when she heard something she liked, and shake her head at the things she did not. Yet she never interrupted or inserted her own opinion.

"Why don't you say anything?" Zaric managed to ask as the two of them walked from one group to another. As the evening wore on, Zaric felt more at ease and found that he was actually enjoying himself. "When the subject of government comes up, I mean," he added, thinking of all that Althea said when the subject was *not* matters of state. He liked hearing her voice and found himself staring when she told a story, watching the expression of her eyes and the movement of her mouth.

"I've found that people often put too much confidence in my opinion," she admitted. "Whether I think an idea is good or not, I tend to be right."

"Right? How?"

"I don't really know. Instinct, I guess. People have noticed and sometimes they expect me to offer an opinion. I've found it's best if I don't. It gives me a headache. Plus, it makes me feel too serious."

"I don't care if all you talk about is the weather," Zaric assured her. "I just want to hear you talk."

"Thank you, your majesty," Althea said, releasing a weight on a sigh, lightly placing her hand on his arm. "But I want to say, I like your idea of a king's council. Creating a council of both nobles and commoners—it's a revolutionary idea. If I may be so bold, I can't imagine your father would ever have come up with anything like that, but it is exactly what the kingdom needs. The nobles have too much power and the people are being ignored. Something is happening, I just can't quite see what."

"Don't worry," Zaric told her. "I see it, too. Perhaps, if you and I can spend more time together, we can help each other discover what it is."

His own forwardness surprised him and he hoped that Althea didn't notice him holding his breath. Instead, she smiled—a wider, brighter smile than any other she had given him that night. "I would like that," she said.

Two or three times throughout the evening, Mered found Zaric and declared that the party was better than any Edric had ever thrown. He was pleased with the music, the company, and the beauty of the young ladies. He looked at Althea with a great deal of interest as Zaric introduced them, but Althea's politeness was shorter with Mered than it was with everyone else. She was more quiet with him—a quietness that seemed to be accompanied by uneasiness. Zaric made a mental note to ask her about this, but the opportunity didn't come up that night.

The day of the coronation came and went. By the end of the celebrations, Zaric found it easier to manage the feasts and parties. Mered and his father were on hand throughout it all, but Zaric found himself spending more and more time with Althea and *her* father. By the end of the coronation week, he announced his intention of forming a king's council of his own. The announcement shocked the current council—those men who had been selected by Edric and who believed they would continue in their roles with his son. The idea's reception among the nobles was mixed, but there was more favor for it than against. Zaric hoped it would remain that way.

* * *

Elections for the council were soon underway in the kingdom's duchies. The intent was to find twenty-four nobles and twenty-four commoners to represent the people and help Zaric as he governed the kingdom going forward. In this way he hoped to placate the nobles who showed discontent over the roles they currently played while also giving the common-born people a chance to express their ideas and wishes. Althea and Evander returned to Veren to oversee the elections in that region of the kingdom, sharing in Zaric's optimism that this change would make a great difference in the land. Yet the feeling of heaviness still hung over Camelora. Zaric still felt that he could see imminent change hanging on the horizon, but he still didn't know what it was.

The day-to-day demands on his attention prevented Zaric from working in the fields as he had before, but he managed to find some time after one particularly busy day of listening to disputes and problems and pronouncing judgments to wander outside the castle grounds. The workers had gone to their homes for supper and the fields were empty. The smell of earth and grass and natural life comforted Zaric. He crouched in the field and took up a handful of dirt, letting it slip through his fingers, calmed by the soft, cool, familiar feel of it. He rubbed a few grains between his thumb and forefinger.

A shadow fell over him and he looked up, surprised to discover he wasn't alone.

He jumped to his feet when his eyes focused on a memorable face—a face without a name. It was the man who had approached him in the library long ago, the mysterious man who asked questions with complicated answers and knew of things that hadn't yet happened.

"Hello, your majesty," the man stated, bowing.

Zaric could only stand still, dumbfounded. A simple greeting seemed out of place. Questions ran through his head, but he didn't know where to start. He wanted to know who the man was, where he came from, how he knew so much, and what he expected was going to happen next.

"You haven't been king for long," the man continued, "and already you have started some great improvements."

"I'm not sure they're enough," Zaric said, still trying to clear his head.

"It doesn't feel like anything has changed."

"Your perspective has changed. That's something."

"But can that make a difference?"

The man only smiled and Zaric could see that he had no intention of answering. "Who are you?" Zaric went on.

The man didn't look like he intended to answer this question, either, but he finally stated, "My name is Alan."

"Alan? Alan who? From where?"

"Just Alan. I've never needed another name or title."

"Men need titles, to distinguish themselves."

"I don't need to distinguish myself. As difficult as it is to believe, men can be very happy without distinctions. Tell me, your majesty, how are the elections coming?"

"Very well," Zaric replied.

Ideas formed in his mind. Alan knew about the elections. *He must live in Camelora,* Zaric thought to himself, *or at least nearby.* Zaric wondered how much to tell the man, but, at the same time, felt that he could trust him, despite knowing so little about him.

"The people like the idea of having a hand in how they're governed," Zaric went on. "I like it, too. There is much that I haven't experienced and I want to know that the people are being treated and represented fairly."

"What do the nobles think of your plan?"

"They accepted it more readily than I anticipated. Perhaps because those who support it the most enthusiastically have a great deal of influence. The nobles still have a measure of control in their own duchies and I'm doing my best to give them equal representation on the council."

"And yet you don't feel that this has changed the future of the kingdom."

Zaric hesitated. "In a way, it has," he said cautiously, "but in another way it hasn't. I still feel that something troubling is coming, I just don't know what. But who exactly are you, Alan? How do you know so much about what is coming?"

"I wouldn't say that I know what is coming," Alan answered. "Like you, I can feel that something *is* coming, but unlike you, I know how to read the signs. That's what brought me here today. Your majesty, I want to offer you a gift."

"A gift?" Dismay washed over Zaric. Since becoming king, he had received many gifts, but mainly they were veiled efforts to buy favors.

"I promise you, it's not like the other gifts you receive," Alan went on as though he read Zaric's mind. "This gift won't just benefit you. In fact, it may not feel like a benefit to you at all. Its purpose is to benefit the kingdom of Camelora."

Zaric's curiosity was piqued. He remembered the impressions Alan had made at their first meeting. There was nothing dangerous in his manner, nothing self-serving. His knowledge of Camelora extended far beyond Zaric's own understanding, yet he did nothing to make a display of it. So far, he had asked for nothing for himself and Zaric sensed that he would continue on in this way. "Go on," the king said.

"I would like to extend your life," Alan stated.

The simplicity of this statement left Zaric dumbfounded . "Is it in danger?" he finally asked once he found his voice.

"No more than you would expect, but darkness is coming to Camelora. She will need a king capable of leading her through it, no matter how long it takes. A king who will die in seventy years cannot offer Camelora the help she needs. You are the king Camelora needs, if you will allow me to extend your life."

"I've only been king for a few weeks. How can you be so sure?"

"Trust me, Zaric, I am sure."

Nervousness gripped Zaric, causing his arms, legs, and neck to tingle. A life longer than other men's was incomprehensible to him, filling him with fear as though he stared into a dark void. "How much longer would I live?"

"As I said, as long as it takes. You don't need to accept the gift right now. In fact, I don't think you should. I want you to think about it—consider it as long as you need to. As you do, you will see why this is more likely to benefit the kingdom than it does yourself. Long life requires more sacrifice than most people are willing to give. When you see me again, you can give me your answer."

Again, Alan bowed, then turned and casually walked away. A part of Zaric wanted to call him back, but the rest could only stand speechless and motionless. He felt that a heavy burden had been placed on his shoulders and he could do nothing to remove it. He knew he had questions to ask, but the words wouldn't form in his mind. After standing for a few minutes, unable to focus his eyes on anything around him, he slowly started the walk back to the castle.

Chapter 15

The Present

Since arriving in Phara—which he managed much less dramatically than Helen—Zaric had been staying in a cave by the sea. Although it was hidden from view from any vantage point on the beach, it was still where it had been centuries before. Back then, it had been a fun discovery for Zaric's son, Edric. Now, the water and waves had carved it deeper, lending atmosphere to the loneliness and darkness of the space.

Zaric had seen Helen arrive, splashing and thrashing in the water, but couldn't reach her before she was found by Lena and Connor. Every day he walked past the inn, looking through the windows when he was least likely to be noticed. It wasn't until he saw Helen sitting in the dining room that he ventured inside.

Now, he sat with her at the entrance of the cave, watching the fishing boats bob on the morning sea. Although Lena and Connor had given Zaric a room the night before, he felt that Helen needed fresh air—and the two of them needed to create a plan without being interrupted.

"I believe Lena and Connor will make good allies," Zaric said, "despite their reservations."

"They don't seem too sure about the stories," Helen pointed out.

"But they have it in them to believe. Most people in this kingdom

129

didn't grow up with believing parents like you did. We'll befriend them and give them time to make their choice. Then, I hope they will be willing to help us find more supporters. They know the people of this village better than anyone."

"Do you think we'll be able to find much support?"

"A fair amount. The people are divided, though. I didn't realize we would have to fight against Mered's influence. Not so strongly, anyway. And if this is where those soldiers we met are headed..."

Helen didn't need Zaric to finish the statement to understand the weight of it. She was surprised they hadn't seen the soldiers yet. They were certainly headed in this direction.

"What would you like me to do?" Helen asked. "I don't want to waste any time."

Zaric laced his fingers together and rested his chin on his hands, looking out at the water as he thought. What he came up with surprised Helen. "What do you think you should do?" he asked.

Although she had expected him to give her instructions in the way any king would to a subject, Helen was glad Zaric was leaving the decision to her. She had already thought of how she wanted to help.

"Lena mentioned a library," she said. "I thought I would ask Aurelie to take me there. Perhaps I can find something that will show us what happened to your son and his descendants."

"That's a good idea," Zaric agreed. "Get a start on that, while I work with Lena and Connor. If they agree to help us, we'll start meeting with the other Pharans. Hopefully, we'll be able to find the support we need and the person we seek at the same time."

Helen caught a note of eagerness in his voice. She felt she understood what Zaric was feeling—the anticipation of finding family he hadn't seen in so long. Her separation from her father had only been a few months, but to wait centuries, the feeling of hope returning where it had been lost... She only hoped he wouldn't be disappointed.

Helen wanted to be sure she did everything she could so that wouldn't happen.

"But, right now," Zaric said, changing his tone, "I want you to practice some more. Who knows how much time we'll have or if you'll even have a chance again later? We don't want to draw attention to ourselves if those soldiers *do* come here."

Helen looked out at the boats on the water—too far away to make out more than the forms of people, but still near enough to make her nervous. "Aren't you afraid of being seen?" she asked.

"Yes," Zaric replied, "but this is the best opportunity we have."

Helen didn't want to admit how little confidence she felt. Her arrival in Phara had been less than graceful. But Zaric was right. They didn't know what their future in Phara looked like or if there would be another opportunity for learning. The day might come when Helen would be grateful for what little preparation she could get.

She nodded her acceptance.

"Just like with the fire…"

Zaric held out his hand over the water, his relaxed fingers pointing down. The sea's surface jumped and danced, then spun, creating a small whirlpool. Instead of spiraling downward, though, it wound up, forming a mound of water that grew higher and higher. When the rounded top of the mound was only a few inches away from Zaric's hand, he slowly turned it, catching a thick drop that floated above his cupped palm. Straightening his fingers, the spell broke and the water splashed across his skin.

"Now you try," he instructed, wiping his hand against his thigh.

Helen took a deep breath. She held out her hand as Zaric had done, though hers was less steady. She was tempted to extend her fingers as she had always done when focusing power, even before she knew what she was doing. But Zaric's hand had been relaxed. It must be possible to focus while staying relaxed.

131

A few small ripples spread out beneath Helen's hand, but the water became still again. She exhaled in frustration.

"It's all right," Zaric assured her.

"It seemed easier before," Helen argued.

"You weren't overthinking before. Relax your mind."

"How can I relax and focus at the same time?"

"You've done it before."

Helen looked out again at the boats on the water. She imagined the fishers looking in the direction of the cave, sensing that something was happening there, even if she herself knew no one was near enough to see the instruction going on.

"What if it goes wrong?" she questioned.

"I'll help you stop it if it does."

With another inhale, Helen closed her eyes. She imagined her doubts like pebbles, rolling before her eyes. Forcefully, she flicked them away. She held out her hand, relaxed, above the water. The coolness of the sea air floated upward and ran through her fingers, to the palm of her hand, to her wrist and up her arm. Ripples pushed their way from a central point. They began to swirl. The swirl built up, turning into a rounded mound that grew toward her hand.

"Helen?"

The shout came from behind, startling her. She dropped her arms and jumped to her feet just as Zaric did the same. Lena stood on the beach with Aurelie, waving to her.

"You're doing well," Zaric said, placing a hand on Helen's back. "You can practice on your own if you like, but we need to be careful how much we reveal to the people of Phara, even our good hosts. We don't know how any of them will react."

It was a relief to Helen that she had been able to affect the water without it growing out of control, but the doubts remained. The fear of facing Mered's lieutenant nagged the back of her mind, as well as the rush of water that had engulfed her when she first arrived at the beach. It was the first time this power had gone wrong and Helen worried it wasn't the last. Without Zaric next to her to help her, she feared the next mistake would be fatal. It would have been better, she thought, if they had left the power alone.

* * *

The governors sat in plain wooden chairs around a plain, long oval table. A stiff formality engulfed the room. No one sat at the bottom of the table. No one wanted to face Mered directly. His own chair sat at the head, larger than the rest and decorated with ornate scrolling designs. It sat higher than the other chairs, too, preserving the perspective that Mered was higher than the governors, that he was the one who could do for the land what none of them were able to do themselves.

Not many conversations took place as the men waited. They sat with a mixture of disdain and discomfort. It was true that the governors were cordial with each other, but they were also wary of each other. They all knew the story of Cyrus and Veren. They dreaded the thought of Mered finding some flaw in the people of their own regions and some excuse to strip them of their office and possessions. If one governor wanted more power than the rest... They didn't trust each other for protection against Mered's temper. Each man was more likely to fan its flames than try to tamp it down.

The double doors leading into the room opened and Mered swept in, his head held high. Two servants trailed behind as he made his way to his seat. He sat with a flourish, a tight smile that bordered on a sneer crossing his lips.

"Gentlemen," he greeted, "I am glad you could join me again in Nubiim so soon. Our plan is progressing beautifully and it is time for us to begin to deploy the next phase."

This statement was met with silence like an unsteady wall. Though they tried, the governors couldn't hide their uncertainty about the progress of their plans, but no one dared to contradict Mered.

"Come now," Mered said with a laugh. "You aren't going to tell me that the soldiers you have provided to offer protection to the land aren't making great advances."

"We've heard rumors—stories," one man finally spoke up. "We believe it's the same man you warned us about in your letter. Word of him has reached our citizens. They're saying some old king is sending out representatives, telling the people that he wants to unite and protect the land."

"And what do *you* say?" Mered questioned, his words sharp like the tip of a sword.

The governors were caught off-guard. "We tell them of *you,* of course," one brave governor finally stated, hoping his words sounded as true as he wanted them to. "No one can protect the land as well as Mered. For some reason, though—" The man cut himself off, second-guessing the statement he was about to make.

"Go on," Mered prodded. He gave the man a look that compelled him to speak, without any falsehood, even if it was against his will.

"For some reason, this old king inspires optimism where the name of Mered cannot."

Apprehension engulfed the governors. Every pair of eyes fixed themselves upon the man at the head of the table. They knew this governor would never have spoken these words under his own power. Each man wished he could close his mouth and his thoughts, to never be forced to tell Mered anything that would displease him. As he had done with this man, he could do to them all, and force truths they didn't wish to tell.

"I told you," Mered scoffed, shaking his head. "I warned you that this man—this 'king'—would come down from the north and try to steal your people and your regions away. So far, all of my warnings have come true. He thinks of himself as some sort of immortal, invincible and above everything your regions stand for. He wants you to believe that he will help you, but he will take the government of your lands away without a second thought. His only thought is for his own glory."

"But who is this man?" another governor asked. "I remember some old folk tales from when I was a child about a king living in exile in the north, but I didn't think they were real. Now, we have someone coming out of the north, calling himself a king, and making promises to our people. Are the old tales true?"

Mered shook his head again. "This is why we need to move forward with our plan. This man, Zaric, is taking advantage of some old stories in an effort to gain support. If you have allowed your people to become too superstitious, I'm afraid they will easily fall for it. Phara."

Startled at the mention of his region, the governor of Phara sat up a little bit straighter in his chair. "Yes?" he responded nervously.

"I am sending one of my best men—a man named Bernt—to your region with a small company of soldiers. He will help you recruit more supporters for our cause. If you travel quickly, you should make it home before he gets there."

"Why Phara?" one governor inquired, a derisive laugh in his voice.

Mered shifted his gaze to the man, his face twisting as though the name left a bitter taste on his tongue. "Camdor," Mered replied. His expression was both hot and cold at the same time, with nothing in between. "I have my reasons. And anyway, I don't expect very much help to come out of your region. The opposite, in fact. Did you know that you lost a young man out of one of your villages?"

Confusion crossed the Camdoran governor's face. "I know a farm in one of the border towns burned down suspiciously, but I was assured no human remains were found at the site. I assumed it was an abandoned cottage that some of the local youngsters were using for their own amusement. Other than that, I haven't heard of any unusual activities. You can't expect me to track the movements of all of the people in my region. None of us could. Though I do try."

The governor of Camdor looked around the table, expecting the others to agree with him. No one said a word.

"I wouldn't be concerned if he was an insignificant young man, leaving Camdor to find a better life in another region. No doubt, if someone wanted to, they easily could. But this particular young man is directly responsible for the threat we are now seeing from the pretended king. He made his way north and is now plotting to overthrow every one of your regions. You have been lax with your people, Camdor."

"One young man," the governor of Camdor reiterated. "How is anyone supposed to keep track of every single citizen, every young man in their region? If he wasn't living in such a way as to bring attention to himself, there is no reason for me to know of his existence."

"Well, you see, Camdor, this young man and his ability to so easily leave his home has caused me to take a deeper look at the work you have done for me since our first meeting. You and I have been in communication for a decade or so, and yet I have received very little support from you. The men and women you have sent to Nubiim to add to my numbers are only a fraction of what your compatriots have sent. Within Camdor itself, very few people recognize my name when it's mentioned. You seem content with enjoying the gifts I provide without showing any gratitude for them."

"If there are failings in our relationship," the governor said, his tone more nervous and his words less smooth, "I'm sure I can do more to strengthen it. I am terribly grateful for the support you have shown to Camdor and I vow to more fully do my part. When I return home,

I will send out recruiters of my own to gather soldiers for your army. Your name will be taught in every village. The people will know of your generosity and goodness to us. Whoever this young man was, I'm sure he will be long forgotten, while your name is praised for generations to come."

Mered stared at the governor, the glare in his eyes not letting up. He uttered no response. Tension hung in the air, making everyone shift uncomfortably. Even the stoic guards at the door and posted around the room found it hard to stand still. They knew what Mered was capable of. If they found that the governor of Camdor had been turned to stone in his chair, none of them would have been surprised.

But the governor still moved, still breathed.

The meeting moved on. Mered spoke a few brief words to other governors, commending them for the men they had sent and promising to repay their support. After that, he dismissed the meeting and the governors stood to go. The governor of Camdor hesitated and hung back, certain Mered would say something more to him, but Mered made no move to detain him and the governor eventually left the room.

Mered motioned for a guard to come toward him, his gaze following the governor's steps until he was out of sight.

"Once Camdor reaches his room," he instructed, "I want you to arrest him. I would rather install someone of my own choosing to govern his region than to allow him one more day of freedom. Allow a rumor to flow among the rest of the governors. They need to know what will happen if they don't do all they can to serve me."

The guard nodded and left the room to follow the governor.

Mered dismissed the rest of the guards, wanting to be alone for a few minutes. He hated to admit it, but he was frustrated with the state of his plans. Ian was certainly dead, he knew, and now Siri had gone missing. Bernt was the best man in his employ, yet he couldn't swear that he would be successful. Though he sent spies throughout the land to track Zaric's movements, he could never predict where his old nemesis would go or what he would do. Zaric had a talent for being invisible when he didn't want to be seen. With reluctance, Mered trusted that Bernt would be able to find where the old king was hiding. If Mered's reasoning was correct, he was confident Zaric would make his way to Phara.

And that man he had sent to Camelora—Mered couldn't even recall his name—was certainly not the best he had. He was the best of the most expendable, though, which was all Mered could expect. And, in it all, perhaps someone could find Siri and bring her back to answer for her betrayal, for turning her back on the man who had given her so much.

At the thought of Siri, the anger surged in Mered's chest. He grabbed a candlestick from the windowsill and flung it across the room as he roared like a deceived and wounded animal. He would not lose all he had gained because of a woman. No woman would prove to be his downfall. Siri had been trusted too much—and it was all the fault of those parents of hers. Their daughter's disappearance did nothing to stop her hag of a mother from trying to worm her way back into Mered's favor.

Mered determined to make an example of them, too, just as he planned to do with the governor of Camdor. After all, they had raised an entitled young woman who thought she could use Mered and then abandon him. He would destroy the parents, then find and destroy the daughter, showing the people how severely he punished betrayal.

Chapter 16

The Present

"Y ou still don't trust me."

The words cut through Neil's thoughts like oars through water. He looked at Siri, his eyebrows raised. In the ten minutes they had been sitting together in Zaric's study, she had shown no sign of even *wanting* to speak to him.

"No," was Neil's simple reply. He didn't care how it sounded or how Siri would react.

She surprised him by saying, "Good. You shouldn't."

Neil searched her face for a hint of sarcasm, but saw none. The haughtiness and arrogance he expected were not there. Though Siri didn't quite look humble or contrite, her expression was something close to it. Resigned and determined, perhaps, but no longer proud.

"How could anyone change in such a short amount of time?" she mused wistfully, staring off as she spoke the thought.

Neil wasn't sure she was even speaking the words to him, but he still felt a twinge of guilt. He had once believed it was impossible for people to change, especially in such a short amount of time, but Helen had seen things differently. She saw that Neil could change. She believed he would. As they traveled to Camelora, her faith in him was stronger than his doubts.

But Neil had never tried to kill someone in cold blood.

"Cyrus believes I should give you a chance," Neil told Siri. Her confused expression prompted him to add, "Cyrus is Helen's father."

"Garrick told me about him," Siri said, recognition dawning. "He was a governor in the south. Mered once spoke of him, too."

A spark of fire roared in a corner of Neil's heart, but he held it down. "If Cyrus is willing to trust you, I need to try to trust you, too."

The door flew open and Garrick rushed in, wearing his usual smile. "Sorry I'm late," he stated. "With the camp growing, there's so much more to organize now than there was before. Now, let's not waste any time. We need to come up with a plan to flush out whomever is trying to communicate with Mered."

"I must point out," Siri said, measuring her words to get them just right, "since Neil destroyed the communication device, if the traitor has gone back to it, he or she knows that we are aware of their presence in the land."

"You're going to blame me?" Neil argued.

"She has a point, Neil," Garrick said. "It's not blame, just a statement of fact. I would have done the same thing. Who knows what danger we were in with that device functioning? But Siri's right. We have to consider that we are now trying to find someone who is more alert, more cautious."

Neil had to concede that this was true. He didn't admit it out loud, though.

"This brings us to another thought I had," Garrick went on. "As the governor, I feel like I need to go on as usual, receiving refugees and preparing Camelora for battle. Anything else would reveal that I know we have a traitor in our midst. If I act as though I know nothing, our enemy may lower his or her guard."

"Give them a false sense of security," Siri put in. "I know the tactic well."

"Good, you understand," Garrick said. "I would like to place you, Neil, in charge of this operation. Work with Siri and try to find who may be behind this betrayal. Your arm is still healing, anyway, so any other work you can do is limited."

Neil wasn't sure how he felt about this idea, but he knew how he was expected to answer. "Of course," he said. "I'll do whatever you need me to do."

"May I offer a suggestion?" Siri asked.

"Of course," Garrick replied, a little more readily than Neil would have.

"Don't tell the council what we're doing," Siri instructed.

"Excuse me?" Garrick questioned, his brow furrowing in confusion.

"The traitor could be anyone—even someone on the council. If you tell them about this operation, it might tip them off."

"I won't distrust my council," Garrick said with a firmness Neil didn't often hear in his voice. It was the first sign Neil had seen that the governor wasn't willing to agree with Siri completely.

"I'm not asking you to," Siri defended. "I'm simply asking that we keep this quiet until we have more information. Once we know who's involved in this, we can bring the council in. There isn't much they can do at the moment, anyway."

Garrick kept his eyes on Siri as he considered her opinions. "All right," he finally agreed. "I want the two of you to work together. Meet me back here every morning to give me updates. I should probably get back to my own duties now. This room is yours for the rest of the day. Please, for the good of Camelora, do your best to work together."

He made his exit, leaving the other two in silence.

"Well," Neil sighed, "you sure have Garrick wrapped around your finger."

"Do you have a map of the city?" Siri asked, ignoring the remark.

"Of Camelora?"

"That's the city, isn't it?"

Neil went to the table where Zaric kept his maps. The parchments were stacked neatly, but there was no order or method to the stacks. It was also hard to tell what each map was documenting. Many were labeled "Camelora," but they looked nothing like the city. Remembering what Garrick had said about the kingdom, the region, and the land, Neil wondered how old the maps were and how long Zaric had been drawing them.

When Siri came to look over his shoulder, Neil grew even more agitated. He didn't realize how difficult it would be to find what he was looking for; he didn't like feeling incompetent with an audience.

"That's it!" Siri exclaimed, snatching a map out of Neil's hand just as he picked it up.

"How do you know?" he asked.

"I know."

Siri took the parchment to the desk and sat in Zaric's chair. A wave of nervousness went through Neil seeing this woman sitting at the king's desk. He watched, unsure how to react, as she took up a pen and piece of blank parchment and began to copy the map out.

"What are you doing?" Neil asked.

"Coming up with a plan," Siri answered, not taking her eyes from her work.

He watched as she roughly sketched the streets and buildings, writing in their names with a practiced hand. Whenever Neil tried to speak, Siri shushed him. As the minutes passed, he was forced to sit on the other side of the desk and watch her work.

When her map was complete, Siri drew light squares over the top of it, creating a grid that divided the city into small blocks. Nothing was left out. Streets and buildings, gardens and homes—all were broken up in the squares she made. She finished with a flourish and set the pen down.

"What is it?" Neil asked, limiting his words to avoid being silenced again.

"A system," Siri answered.

"What *kind* of system?"

"The kind we're going to use to search this city. We'll move square by square until we find what we're looking for."

"You don't really think we'll be able to search every home, do you? I don't think that sort of thing is allowed."

"Hopefully we'll find what we're looking for before it comes to that. But, if it's necessary, that's what we'll have to do."

"The people's homes are off-limits," Neil stressed, bristling at the thought of someone entering his own room without his knowledge or permission, whether he was hiding something or not. "That's not the way we do things here."

"Oh," Siri said, realization dawning. A genuine emotion followed that Neil didn't expect: Siri blushed.

Her embarrassment was obvious. She didn't try to explain away what she had suggested, or ask Neil what he meant, or even try to press her point. What came next was just as unexpected as the redness in her cheeks. "I'm sorry," Siri said.

She turned back to the map, working for the next few minutes without speaking.

Neil was the first to break the hush. "So you expect me to walk up and down the streets of the city with you."

"I don't expect you to do anything, Neil. What you do is up to you. But Garrick has asked us to work together and I don't see any other way to catch the traitor in Camelora without going out into the city."

"To do what?"

"To watch."

Neil had been watching the people of Camelora for weeks now—long before Siri appeared. He hadn't seen anything suspicious.

143

If he had, he wouldn't need her help.

But he did need her help. As much as Neil wanted to be the one who came up with an idea to find Mered's spy, he couldn't think of anything better than what Siri suggested. Siri only humbled him more by asking, "How were you expecting to find the traitor?"

Neil didn't answer.

"I suppose you don't have a map of the refugee camp," Siri went on.

"It's a camp," Neil laughed. "We've tried to keep it as organized as possible, but that isn't easy to do with tents and masses of unpredictable sizes."

"That's what I assumed," Siri said, taken aback. "We'll just have to do the best we can."

"Why not search the camp first?" Neil asked, wondering why he hadn't wondered before. "If the traitor arrived with the refugees, isn't that the most likely place we'll find him?"

"Because the traitor could very well be one of your own."

"You suggested that before, but how could that have happened? These people have never left this land."

"Well, obviously, the original traitor came with the refugees," Siri admitted. "But, I imagine, he or she has been working to turn others in Camelora against Zaric. It's not impossible. Anyone turned would act more suspicious than someone who came from Mered's base. That's why we search the city."

The thought chilled Neil, but once it was in his mind, he couldn't shake it. The more he thought about it, the more it took root, sprouting and growing until it was all he could think about. He saw the possibility in what Siri suggested. Many of the refugees spent their days within the city, anyway. It would be a good place to look.

"After we wander the city, *watching,* what do we do then? Is there more to your plan?"

Siri needed no time to think before laying out her thoughts. "We look for anyone acting strange. Signs of deception. When we find someone who seems suspicious, we surveil them for a few days, watching their every step until we know we're right. After that, it should be fairly simple. I'll work my way into their trust, saying that Mered sent me here to spy for him, that I've managed to gain your trust by saying that I ran away from Mered. From there, I just need to play it by ear until we find out what they're planning."

"You think it will be that simple?"

"Of course. I'm good at what I do." She leaned toward him and mock-whispered, "I've done it before."

"Are you doing it right now?"

"Neil!" Siri exclaimed in exasperation. "What's it going to take for you to believe me?"

"Not betraying me, for one. Only time will show me that. Taking this seriously for another. Not teasing me."

Siri looked ready to respond, but cut herself off, gulping back the words. She looked off in the opposite direction and remained silent.

"We interview everyone who comes here," Neil continued. "Zaric set up the process before he left. We take notes during those interviews. Would it be possible to find the traitor through those notes?"

"Because everyone is honest? Have you had anyone tell you straight out that they're a spy for Mered?"

"Not every lie is hard to see through."

With her eyes on Neil, Siri considered this idea. "Yes, it could be possible," she conceded. "If someone's story is too perfect, too average, everything you would expect it to be—it could be a sign of deceit."

This statement threw Neil's mind back to the day he and Helen met Siri and to the story she told. It mirrored Helen's own story too much. Helen saw it. Neil did not.

"Are you ready to start?" Siri said, snatching the map from the desk and getting to her feet.

"Remember, Siri: you're the one trying to prove yourself, not me. I will give the orders and you will follow them. Is that clear?"

"Yes," she conceded. Neil waited for another retort, but none came.

A lull in the arrival of refugees gave Camelora a feeling of something almost like normalcy—at least within the city. Neil tried to be as alert as possible, not allowing Camelora's peaceful atmosphere to cause him to drop his guard. He wished he could say he had noticed something out-of-place before, but he hoped he could say it now.

"Locked in that room in the palace," Siri said as they walked, "I could hear the sounds of the city. So full of life, full of peace. I wanted to see it, but I only caught glimpses."

"Your choices have consequences," Neil stated. He hated how heartless and unfeeling it sounded. It felt like he had taken a step backward.

"Yes, Great Philosopher, I'm aware of that. This place... It's everything Mered wants to create, but everything he's incapable of creating. He wants order, but not happiness. Fear, not laughter. He believes that submission equals respect and adoration, and that the only way to achieve submission is by forcing it."

"Even with the promises he makes?"

"Everyone who follows Mered knows how easily those promises can be broken. We learn it quickly. It's a reality we live with every day."

Siri's openness and sincerity surprised Neil. They caused his heart to react with a pity his head wanted to deny.

"Do you mind if we walk through the market?" Siri asked, her tone changing again. "It's been years since I saw one."

Neil wanted to say no. He worried what Siri might do in such a crowded setting. But the thought struck him that the market would be the best place to see as many people congregated as possible. Since the arrival of the refugees, the newcomers had joined the Camelorans in setting up stalls and selling goods. So, Neil agreed.

He relaxed at the sight of Siri in the Cameloran marketplace, admiring the scene and sounds and tastes, like a child seeing the world for the first time. She listened attentively to the men and women at each stall as they told her about their goods. She admired the feel of the fabrics and the tastes of the foods and the craftsmanship of the furniture and furnishings. What surprised Neil the most was her laugh. It rang sincere, unlike her laughter in their previous travels. Siri was comfortable in a way Neil hadn't expected.

Then Neil remembered. Siri was good at playing a part. *More* than good. His own past gullibility stung him, shooting a cold river through his veins. Anger flared as he thought of Siri deceiving these innocent people as she had done him. The Camelorans had no experience in the world, no experience with deception or how to detect it. Annoyance flooded his mind, burning his neck and cheeks. He grabbed Siri's arm and pulled.

"What are you doing?" she demanded, wrenching her arm away from his grasp.

"We're going back to the palace," Neil answered through gritted teeth. "I brought you out here to see if you can spot anyone out of place, not for you to take advantage of the good people of this city. You aren't even paying attention."

Siri narrowed her eyes and opened her mouth to make a hasty reply, but then closed her mouth and eyes, taking in a deep breath. After a slow exhale, she opened her eyes again and asked, "What do you see when you look at this street?"

Neil gazed at the people walking around them, the children running, the men and women talking and laughing as they bartered and traded. Citizens walked in ones and twos, chatted in threes; they spoke in light tones and serious tones, telling stories about their families or their occupations or their opinions of the things that were likely to occur now that refugees were arriving in large numbers. It was a normal Cameloran market on an average Cameloran day.

"I see the people of Camelora going about their business," Neil answered, his annoyance and anger subsiding into embarrassment. He saw nothing out of the ordinary and the realization made him see just how much he had overreacted. How could he expect Siri to see something that wasn't there?

"Do you see that man over there?" Siri asked, pointing out a young man standing behind a market stall. "He's nervous, but not in a criminal way. He's holding a small bunch of flowers at his side. Unremarkable flowers. My guess is that he plans to ask someone to marry him, but he isn't sure she will say yes.

"And that girl walking up the street? She's too preoccupied to notice all the people saying hello to her. Walking in the direction of the palace—she's probably going to be interviewed for a job and she's afraid that she won't make a good impression on the housekeeper. I've seen the housekeeper, by the way, and she has reason to be worried. Not even the cleanest floor makes a good impression on that woman.

"People enjoying their day, catching up with friends, making plans. No one on this street is acting suspiciously, Neil. I've studied every single one of them. Living in Mered's court, you learn to study people without showing it. It only takes a few seconds. We were always studying each other, waiting for someone to slip so that we could take advantage of their fall."

The discomfort burned in Neil's face now where the anger had before. Taking a deep breath—and with a great deal of reluctance—he said, "I'm sorry, Siri. I jumped to a conclusion that wasn't fair. I've been asked to give you a chance and I haven't made a very good start."

"No, you haven't," Siri agreed. "I'm trying to help you. You need to allow me to, and to let me do it in the way I know how. Please, try not to make a commotion yourself."

Neil looked again at the young man behind the market stall, who took a deep breath and walked down the street in resolute strides. Looking in the opposite direction, he could just make out the retreating figure of the girl as she moved toward the palace. He thought of the housekeeper that Siri suggested she was going to meet. Neil knew the woman, too, and Siri was right—nothing pleased or impressed her. He brought his eyes back to Siri, then scanned the people on the street, seeing no signs of danger or deception.

"Let's move on," he said. "There doesn't seem to be anything to find here."

Neil led the way down the alley and Siri followed. After a few seconds, though, he noticed she had fallen behind. He turned to see her gaze, for a brief moment, focused on something he couldn't make out.

"Is there something wrong?" he asked.

Siri shook her head and smiled. "It's probably nothing. Let's go."

"But it could be something," Neil prodded.

"There isn't enough…" Siri's words trailed off, like she didn't have the words to finish the statement. "We can come back to the market later. I'm guessing it's the area of the city that sees the most movement, so the people we see will likely change. Let's find a street where that isn't as likely to happen."

They left the crowded business district behind and headed for a residential area of Camelora. There were fewer people to watch here. Neil couldn't help noticing the difference that came over Siri as they encountered more families and less merchants. Her manner among the people of this area was different from her manner in the marketplace. She showed a shy aloofness—especially as she watched the children—that contradicted the easy confidence she had shown before. The look in her eyes was filled with curiosity and envy. Unlike in the market, Siri didn't chat with anyone as they walked, as though she didn't want to bring attention to herself.

Neil didn't realize how much he had been staring until Siri's face changed. Grasping his arm, she said his name and pointed over his shoulder. Around them, the people erupted into commotion and ran toward the center of the city. Neil turned to see what Siri pointed at and what had caused so much concern.

Smoke rose near the center of the city. It was hard to tell exactly where it came from, but it couldn't have been a campfire. There was too much for it to be a chimney.

The palace. Once the thought struck, it consumed Neil's mind. Running down the street, Neil no longer worried about being noticed. He didn't need to look over his shoulder to know that Siri had followed.

Chapter 17

"I've heard that a battalion isn't far away," Lena said in a hushed tone as she and Helen washed dishes after supper. Most of the fishermen had returned to their homes, but a few stragglers remained in the dining room. The drone of Connor's voice drifted through the closed door as he chatted with the men while he cleaned the tables.

"We knew it was only a matter of time," Helen responded. "When Zaric and I ran into them, we weren't too far from Phara. That was days ago."

"Will it hinder your plans?" Lena asked. "The promises we rejected years ago are probably much more welcome to the people of Phara now."

"Zaric promises something greater. I hope they can see that."

Lena looked thoughtful, hesitating to make another statement. "I don't want to offend you," she finally managed, measuring her words carefully. "I know what Zaric means to you. But, can we be sure his own promises are real? In the end, it could be that neither man is working in the best interests of the people."

Though these words gave Helen a pang, they didn't offend her. Instead, they helped her to see why it was difficult to gain support.

151

Without realizing the threat Mered posed, they couldn't contrast it with the hope Zaric brought. Her mind drifted to the stories she had heard growing up, told to her and Neil by his grandfather. Neil's parents believed them. Her own parents did, too. As a child, she had never considered *not* believing in Zaric. This world where his name was unknown was a foreign world to her.

But even Neil had convinced himself that they were only fairy tales. To say that it hadn't been easy to convince Neil to believe in the story again would be to understate the truth. The thought now crossed Helen's mind how difficult it might be to convince people to believe a story they had never heard to begin with.

"In my travels," Helen stated, "I have seen so much. Too much to dismiss the power Zaric has. I've been to Camelora. I've seen the people there and the preparations Zaric has made. It may be hard to believe that he's the man from the stories—that he's lived as long as he has—but I promise you, it's all true. I know you haven't known me long enough to know whether or not you can trust my words, so I hope that Zaric and I can prove them to you."

Lena contemplated Helen, locking her eyes with the young woman's. Helen let her, determined not to look away. Finally, Lena nodded.

"Your governor won't give up Phara so easily, though," Helen said, wanting, more than hoping, to be right.

"The governor doesn't care about Phara," Lena scoffed. "No one has seen him in years. His mansion is a safe place outside of the village and he doesn't need to trouble himself about what goes on in here. I think he regrets not leaving on the boats when he had the chance. We've been left to ourselves for a long time."

Helen dried and put away the last dish. "Where is Aurelie today?" she asked, realizing that she hadn't seen the young girl since lunch.

"She wanted to go to her library," Lena answered. "With your help this afternoon, I decided it would be all right for her to go earlier than usual. I think she had an idea when she woke up and wanted to research it."

"You mentioned the library the other night. I'd like to see it, if Aurelie doesn't mind showing it to me."

"I'm sure she would love to. Aurelie loves sharing the books as much as she loves the books themselves."

When Lena told her daughter about Helen's interest in the library, the girl's face beamed. They set off the next morning as soon as breakfast was done—Aurelie, in her eagerness, leaving her plate half-full.

The young girl still seemed unsure how to act around Helen. She was sometimes reserved, sometimes open and talkative. She asked questions about Helen's travels, what the land was like outside of Phara, and what it was like growing up inside a governor's mansion. The enthusiasm she showed made it easier for Helen to talk about her land and her family without too much sadness.

The abandoned library was in a different part of the village, which gave Helen a chance to see more of the place than she had before. She wore her cloak, despite the summer heat, pulling the hood up and around her face. Not many people knew that a stranger had been found on the beach and she wanted to keep it that way. She hoped that she and Aurelie wouldn't run into too many villagers, though.

Phara wasn't the colorful, vibrant city Helen imagined when Siri first spoke of it. It was actually quite the opposite. The streets and buildings were dark and dingy, even with a blue sky overhead. More than half of the houses appeared to be empty and falling down. The smell of fish hung in the air, overpowering the smell of the sea. The two of them met very few people. Some appeared friendly, while others ignored them. The village lacked a sense of community.

But Helen knew now that it had been some time since Siri was last in Phara. The place she spoke of no longer existed—if it ever had at all.

When they reached the old city hall, Helen was surprised. It was a large and imposing structure—probably the largest in Phara, aside from the Government House not far away. It was made mostly of stone, cut into precise bricks. Most of the windows were broken, gaping wounds in a once-magnificent edifice.

As they approached the wooden front door, Helen noticed it stood ajar. She paused, but Aurelie simply pushed past her, unphased by the fact. The hinges creaked as she pushed the door inward.

"What if someone's inside?" Helen whispered.

"No one's ever inside," Aurelie replied. "Only me."

Once they were through the door, Helen waited to allow her eyes to adjust to the lack of light. The dark walls reached to the high ceiling, webbed with cracks and shadowed with missing pieces. A few pictures hung askew around the entrance hall while others had fallen to the floor. Tables and chairs sat against the walls, broken and leaning. A layer of dust muted the colors of the space. Dead leaves had been blown in through the broken windows. Straight ahead, a wide, magnificent, and ornate staircase led upstairs. The banister was smooth and polished, but many rails had broken away, leaving gaps along the sweeping flight.

Half a dozen doors led off the hall. Only one stood open. Aurelie walked through it, ignoring the scene that captured Helen's attention. Sweeping her eyes over the entrance one more time, Helen followed.

She found herself standing in a room lined with shelves, filled with books of various sizes and bindings. One shelf even contained a pile of scrolls. Though not as high as in the hall, the ceiling reached at least twelve feet. Rolling ladders rested against the shelves on each wall, free from the dust that plagued the rest of the house. Two or three tables were clean as well.

"So, this is your library," Helen remarked.

"It's not *my* library," Aurelie stated, though her face lit up with pride in a way that betrayed her words.

"Can you tell me about it?" Helen asked.

Aurelie composed herself as she went from shelf to shelf, taking on a mature manner, telling Helen about the books she would find in each section. This library had a little bit of everything: truth and fiction, history, philosophy, theology, and science.

Helen was surprised to see different cities and regions represented as well. Many of the books had been brought to Phara from other parts of the kingdom. Most of the people within the boundaries of old Camelora had stopped interacting centuries before, but whoever had maintained this library through the generations had gone to the trouble of bringing in books and records from all over the land. Perhaps some had come with the traders who still dared to make their way to Phara.

As Aurelie pointed out the books from the southern region, Helen was pleased to see a few familiar titles from Veren.

It was obvious Aurelie was not particular about the books she read. Most of them were free of the disuse evident throughout the rest of the building.

"Which subject is your favorite?" Helen inquired, fingering the spine of one especially old tome.

"History," Aurelie responded without a pause.

"What do you like about history?"

The girl shrugged. "I don't know. I guess I just like to learn about the people who came before—how they lived and what they were good at. Some stories make me sad, though. Like the story about the forgotten king."

"That's right, you said you found that book in here. Do you remember which one it is?"

Aurelie went to a section of shelving and scanned its contents. She smiled when her eyes fell on one book and she pointed it out to Helen. It was too high for either of them to reach. She pulled over a ladder, climbed up, and retrieved the book.

"It's really old," she said as she handed it over. "Some of the writing isn't very clear. The person who wrote it had bad handwriting, too. But it's a good story."

"Even if it's sad," Helen inserted with a wink. She opened the book to a page near the middle and read a few lines. Realization dawned as she recognized the writing. "I knew the man who wrote this. He was my friend's grandfather."

"I didn't mean what I said about his handwriting," Aurelie stated quickly, looking embarrassed.

"He would probably agree with you," Helen chuckled. "He passed away years ago. But he *did* know how to tell good stories. Do you mind if I take this? It might have some differences from my own book of stories."

Aurelie shook her head. "No one cares about these books. I'm the only one who ever comes here and I've read that one three times already. There are so many more I still want to read."

Helen tucked the book under her arm and went back to searching the titles.

"What are you looking for?" Aurelie asked.

"I'm hoping this library has some records of Zaric's descendants," Helen told her.

"Descendants!" Aurelie exclaimed. "He looks too young for that."

"I had the same reaction, too. But it's true. You've read the story of the forgotten king, so you should know that Zaric is hundreds of years old. He had a son and that son settled in Phara. We believe someone here could be one of Zaric's great-great-great—"

"Lots of greats," Aurelie interrupted with a giggle.

"Lots-of-greats-grandchild," Helen agreed playfully.

Aurelie stood with her hands on her hips, surveying the room. "Those are the oldest records here," she said, pointing to the shelves with the scrolls. "I don't look at those because when I tried to unroll one, it fell apart. If you know how to do it, you might be able to find something there. There are some books of records, too, though."

"I'll have to ask Zaric about the scrolls," Helen sighed. "So, in the meantime, I'll see what I can find from the books. Thank you, Aurelie." She placed a hand on the girl's shoulder and Aurelie lifted her chin, pleased to be useful.

Aurelie showed Helen where to find the genealogical records, then left Helen to find a book for herself. A book of her own in hand, the young girl went to a corner of the room, where she sat upon an old, worn cushion to read.

Helen turned to the bookcase and examined its rickety ladder, wondering if she dared to climb it to the uppermost shelf. She decided against it for now, choosing instead to look through the books nearer the floor. The older books would only show her the start of Zaric's line. There was a greater chance that she would find what she was looking for in a newer book. At least, that was what she hoped.

Many of the books had no titles. Those that did were mostly faded. It would be hard to tell what they contained without looking through each one.

Helen chose a selection of books at random. Turning to a nearby table, she set them down and took a seat. As she opened the first book, its spine crackled, revealing its years of being ignored on the shelf. Helen soon discovered why. The keeper of this house and library had apparently valued all knowledge and the knowledge contained in this book—weather records, fishing yields, farming reports—was just the sort of knowledge that would bore any casual reader. Glancing over the bookcase again, Helen could see the two dust-free books which had been read before Aurelie decided to abandon this section for more interesting stories elsewhere.

Helen flipped through the pages of the book, careful not to disturb the spine too much, but the only names it contained were those of the men and women who had submitted the reports. Closing it softly, she set it aside and took up another volume. It was a continuation of the records she had just examined. Helen put this down, too.

Every book she had selected contained these types of reports.

For a couple of hours, Helen searched, one shelf at a time. It wasn't long before she fell into a routine of selecting a book, flipping through its pages, scanning its contents, and replacing it on the shelf. Some of the records looked more interesting than others and she wished she had the time to read as Aurelie did, but with the reports of the battalion coming toward Phara, she wanted to find what she was looking for as quickly as possible.

Helen changed her method. When she found a book that looked promising, she set it aside to take back to the inn. She wouldn't use her time reading them right now. With a growing pile and feeling too tired to search anymore, she scooped them up, carrying them beneath her arm. "Are you hungry?" she said to the corner of the room where Aurelie had disappeared. The girl's head popped up and nodded. "Let's go back for lunch."

Commotion met them as they emerged from the building. Helen's heartrate increased at the sight of so many people, all rushing toward the center of the village. Despite the Pharan clothes Lena had given her, she was afraid of standing out as a stranger. The temptation to run and hide was strong—or at least to ignore what had captured everyone's attention and continue to the inn—but Aurelie ran down the steps of the building, excitement written across her face. The girl fell in with the crowd and Helen had no choice but to follow.

No one paid any attention to her. They were too consumed with what was happening at the village square. Helen realized she would have been more conspicuous if she had gone in the opposite direction.

She and Aurelie pushed into the throng to stand among the other villagers—not too close to the front, not too far in the back. Helen placed her hands on Aurelie's shoulders to ensure she stayed with her.

Phara's small squadron waited in the square, wearing everyday clothes instead of sharp uniforms. Their straight lines looked pitiful in spite of their efforts to look impressive. Only a few men carried weapons.

But no one was paying attention to the squadron. The object of their fascination was the battalion coming down the village's main street, dozens of soldiers marching in rhythm with armor clanking, swords at their hips swaying, heads pointed forward. Bernt rode at its head, his horse groomed with great care and his own armor polished so the sunlight gleamed off of its surface. A few people near Helen gasped and smiled as they looked on. The statement of the battalion's appearance seemed to say, "We're here to protect you."

Helen saw it differently. The armor they wore would only protect themselves.

Her grip on Aurelie tightened ever so slightly.

Bernt dismounted and approached the commander of the squadron with an arrogant manner and outstretched hand. The commander, visibly nervous and just as visibly trying to hide it, put out his own hand and shook Bernt's.

"Mered is grateful for your service," Bernt stated in a volume the whole crowd could hear, "but he has decided Phara needs the security that a small village squadron cannot provide. Our battalion will take over now. You will assist us and report to me."

If the commander was offended, he was wise enough not to show it. "We will gladly follow your command," he said in a voice much quieter than Bernt's.

Bernt then turned, with an air of amiability, to the crowd surrounding the square. "Friends of Mered," he said, his voice ringing up and down the street, "there are new threats rising up in the kingdom. We are here to give you protection and secure our borders. Our regions have been divided far too long and there are those who would take advantage of that situation. I am confident we can work together in harmony and complete unity to root out every threat."

Applause broke out, spreading through the crowd. Helen joined in so as not to stand out, but she was glad to see that Aurelie did not.

Bernt returned to his horse and remounted, turning toward the governor's mansion, which loomed on a hill just outside the village. He moved forward and the battalion followed, turning down a side street, with Phara's small squadron attaching themselves behind. The crowd parted to let them pass, then stood still until the last soldier disappeared beyond the buildings. Helen tempered her steps as she pointed Aurelie in the direction of the inn, walking at a natural pace instead of the quick one dictated by the rate of her heart.

"We saw soldiers!" Aurelie blurted as she rushed through the door. Every head in the dining room turned and every voice abruptly stopped. Connor stood next to a table, looking first at Aurelie, then at Helen, who nodded in confirmation.

Lena appeared in the doorway of the kitchen. "Go and wash up for lunch," she instructed Aurelie, her calm tone belying the anxiety in her face. Aurelie's obedient footsteps clattered up the stairs and the buzz of conversation little by little returned to the room. It wasn't hard for Helen to pick out what everyone was talking about. Some of the patrons spoke with fear while others spoke with excitement.

Lena approached Helen and Helen wanted nothing more than to spill out everything they had seen, everything she felt. They still didn't know who in the village would give them support, though. "Go to the back room," Lena whispered, then walked back to the kitchen.

Helen obeyed.

She found the room empty. Sitting in a chair facing the door, she waited. Zaric soon came in, but he left the door open, forcing Helen to remain silent a little longer. His face was emotionless, betraying no hint of what he did or did not already know.

Connor appeared a few minutes later, closing the door behind him.

"Bernt is here," Helen exclaimed as soon as she heard the click of the latch. "Mered's battalion has arrived."

Zaric didn't react. He crossed the room to the window, staring out at the inn's backyard through the thin curtain. Connor acted with more agitation, pulling a chair close to Helen's and sitting on it backward, resting his arms across the back. "Did they come for recruits?" he queried. "Like they did before?"

"They came to 'protect' you," Helen replied. "That's what he said. But it's obvious this is an occupation—just like Veren. It doesn't seem the Pharan governor is going to do anything to stop it. He didn't show his face and the Pharan squadron was more welcoming than intimidating. It wasn't much of a surprise, since Lena says you haven't seen the governor in years. What do we do, Zaric?"

Zaric took some time to gather his thoughts before responding. "We continue to do what we have been doing, only with a little more caution. We can't abandon our mission, especially our *primary* mission. Bernt's arrival makes that even more clear. Let's see how the battalion acts. I still feel there are people in this village who will support us."

"How will we be able to gather supporters when we're surrounded by a battalion?" Helen asked, her voice and unease rising.

"Lena and I still know the people of this village," Connor stated, gaining some composure. "We know who to trust. Are you ready to start meeting with villagers?

Zaric turned to face Helen and Connor, the thoughts still rolling through his mind. "Yes," he finally asserted, with a nod. "We'll start tonight if we can."

"Then we will provide people to listen," Connor stated.

Helen knew she should have more confidence in Zaric and his plan, and she felt guilty that she didn't. She was glad to be moving forward. But her mind wandered back to the scene in the square while her ears still rang with the sound of applause.

Chapter 18

The Present

T he crowd of people thickened the closer Neil got to the palace. They were too distracted by the chaos caused by the fire—some running toward it, some running from it, and some standing still in shock—to notice the governor's assistant and make way for him. He was forced to push his way through, not caring how rough he had to be to move the people aside. Frustration built up in Neil's chest along with his feelings of helplessness.

Trying to remember where to find the well nearest the palace, Neil ran toward the stables instead of the front entrance of the edifice. Siri was at his heels. Even from this distance he could see that his fears and suspicions were correct. A chain of men and women wound around the palace, disappearing around a corner. Further away he could see the dark, heavy smoke as it rose above the palace roof. Neil inserted himself into the line from the well, helping to pass buckets back and forth. Siri materialized a little further down.

"What happened?" Neil asked the man to his left as they worked.

"I have no idea," the man shrugged. "I looked up and saw the smoke, so I came to help."

Neil turned to the woman on his right, but she shrugged as well and shook her head before he got any words out. Pushing the questions to the back of his mind, he decided to focus on fighting the fire before looking for answers.

From this vantage point, it was impossible to see what difference the water made. The people continued for some time to work with an urgency that told Neil that the fire was very much alive. He wished he had taken a place further along the line, where he could see what they were fighting. He hated to move now, disrupting the flow of the water. The people didn't let up. They continued to work. Eventually, the smoke decreased, the dark wisps lightening and thinning.

The urgency of the task subsided and Neil jogged off, heading toward the front of the palace to get a better look. He found a few people pouring water onto the smoldering remains of that fire. Water continued to be added until the ash turned to mud. Neil got as close as he dared without getting in the way.

The furthest window of the ground floor of the palace was shattered. Charred wood and black soot surrounded the hole where the glass used to be. The soot climbed the white stone wall of the building, reaching for the window above, which was stained and smeared black. Inching closer, Neil could see into the room that had taken the brunt of the fire. It dripped with water and smoldered with the steaming remnants of the items that used to occupy the room. What remained of the wood of the ceiling was also charred, black, and scarred with the effects of the fire. Through the gaping window Neil could see the solid oak door. It had done its best to contain the fire within the room, but it now hung crooked on its hinges, threatening to collapse.

"It could have been worse." Garrick's unexpected voice hit Neil with a jolt. He hadn't noticed the governor in the crowd outside the burnt-out room. Neil turned to see Garrick at his elbow and Siri not far behind.

"Did everyone get out?" Neil asked, wondering how many people would have been in that corner of the palace at that time of the day.

"As many as we could get," Garrick answered. "Everyone in immediate danger was evacuated, at least."

"And the damage?"

"Too early to tell. This room is a loss, obviously. The room above must at least be unstable. When it's safe to inspect the damage, we will do it."

Neil's mind flooded with more questions, but he knew it was too soon for anyone to have the answers. Who had done this? How? Why?

Something on the ground glinted in the sun and caught Neil's eye. He stooped to pick it up, but Siri was right there to place a hand over his, preventing him from touching it.

"It's another communication device," she stated. She took it up, placing her fingers at the edges, careful not to touch the silver metal on its sheer, rounded faces. "A primitive one. Not anyone's *first* choice, but good enough if your first choice is destroyed by your enemy. Someone was careless to have dropped it. Very careless."

"How does it work?" Neil couldn't help asking.

"You rub it between your thumb and forefinger," Siri replied. "That's why I stopped you. You don't want to open a line of communication again, do you?"

"No," Neil admitted. "Do you think this has something to do with what you saw, Siri?"

"What did you see?" Garrick asked. But before she could answer, he held up his hand. "Wait. Why don't we continue this conversation in Zaric's study?"

He glanced around at the citizens standing near the corner of the palace. Most of them were too focused on the damage caused by the fire to notice the governor, but Neil understood his desire to be cautious. Siri slipped the coin-like device in her pocket and the three of them headed to the palace's front entrance.

"Tell me what you saw, Siri," Garrick instructed once they were

165

settled .

Siri hesitated, looking from Garrick to Neil and back again.

"You saw something," Neil urged, "while we were walking through the city. What was it?"

"I couldn't have stopped this," Siri argued, defending herself haughtily before revealing anything. "I couldn't be sure of what I saw or felt."

"No one is accusing you," Garrick reassured her in the gentle tone he adopted when speaking to Siri. "We understand how difficult it must be to pick out one suspicious person in a city full of strangers, no matter how much experience you have. If you have any insights, though, we would like to hear them."

Siri braced herself before speaking. "I saw a young man. That was all. A young man walking down the street, trying not to be noticed."

"Is it possible he was heading to the palace?" Garrick asked.

"It's possible," Siri stated. "It's also possible he had nothing to do with this."

"Would you recognize him if you saw him again?"

"I have a good memory for faces."

"Do you think it's time to bring the council in on this?" Neil asked Garrick.

"No," Siri inserted firmly, gripping the arms of her chair. "I can do this."

"We're not saying you can't," Neil assured her. "But the council can help."

"We still don't know if any of them are involved," Siri countered. "The fire started at the palace, after all. They all have access to it."

"*Everyone* in Camelora has access to the palace," Neil argued.

"You both make good points," Garrick interposed. "With the limited information we have at the moment—not knowing where the fire originated, not knowing how many traitors are involved with

Mered—let's continue as planned for now. I'd like the two of you to go back into the city. See if you can spot the young man you saw before, and anyone else who seems suspicious. I'll work with some of the city's builders to investigate the fire. Bring me what you have tonight and we'll speak again. Hopefully, we will all have something to share."

Neil wished he could work with Garrick and investigate the fire. Perhaps he could find more evidence, like the communication device that had been dropped outside. Which reminded him...

"Siri," Neil said, tapping the desk in front of him.

"Oh, right," she replied. She pulled the coin-like device from her pocket and dropped it on the desk, the metal ringing.

"Do the best you can," Garrick said encouragingly as the two walked to the door. "I'll see you this evening."

Chapter 19

The Past

F or days Zaric was absorbed with the idea Alan had planted in his mind. He had very little appetite, had trouble sleeping, and found it difficult to focus on his daily tasks. At times he wondered if it had been a strange dream, at other times he was bewildered that the idea Alan presented was even possible. It frightened him.

But as the days went by, the shock of the idea waned. He still thought of it frequently, but it became easier to manage. It consumed less of his energy and stopped interfering with his work.

Althea arrived in the capital to deliver a report on the progress of the elections in Veren—though her presence also served as a much-needed personal distraction for Zaric. He received letters from candidates on a daily basis, hoping the king would speak for and endorse them—in essence guiding the people for whom to cast their votes. Determined to remain impartial, Zaric replied to each of these letters in the same way, politely pointing out how unfair this would be and excusing himself from any such interference. What embarrassed him the most were the unwanted gifts the candidates sent, which he was obliged to return. Having Althea by his side to advise him gave Zaric more confidence. She assured him that his stance was right. The task became easier to bear.

To everyone else in the palace, Althea became a familiar figure. The more she stayed, the more Zaric thought it would be a good idea to make her presence permanent. He wrote to her father, inviting him to come back to the capital when the elections were over, hinting at his intentions. Only a week or so after sending the letter, word reached the capital that Evander had withdrawn from the election in Veren. For the duke's sake, and the sake of the government, Zaric hoped Althea's feelings truly did complement his own.

Zaric was glad when Mered came for a visit. They had seen little of each other since the coronation. The arrival of his cousin, in addition to the presence of Althea, made Zaric feel less like a king and more like a normal person. Mered also did his best to charm Althea and the two of them seemed to get along well, even if she was still more reserved when he was around.

"I don't envy you," Mered said to Zaric one evening after a private dinner. Althea had excused herself to write some official letters, leaving the two men to catch up. "In most respects, anyway. So many people making demands or asking you to solve their problems—it would wear down my patience within hours. The only thing I *really* envy is the beautiful woman by your side."

"She isn't exactly 'by my side,'" Zaric argued. Yet he blushed at the mention of Althea, noticing the twinkle in Mered's eye as he spoke of her. "I'm accountable to the people of this kingdom," Zaric went on. "They need someone they can rely on. I just happened to be the one born into this position."

"It's a position that could do so much for you, yet I don't think you ever think of that. Not many men would be so good-hearted."

"I think about myself often enough," Zaric countered with a light laugh.

Mered nodded, but said nothing. Zaric looked at his cousin for a minute, thinking of the long history they had together. Since childhood they had always confided in each other. Despite the differences in their temperaments, they had managed to keep that friendship intact. If there was anyone Zaric knew he could talk to, it was Mered.

"I've had something on my mind lately, actually," Zaric stated.

"I heard that you haven't been quite yourself," Mered replied. "You seem very pensive, even for you."

"I've received a somewhat unusual offer," Zaric went on. "You've heard the legends of people with extraordinary powers."

"Ah, yes. People who have been blessed by the Eternal One to do great things beyond the abilities of normal men. But there are also those whose powers are used for evil. Stories our parents told us to make us believe that anything is possible, but also to scare us into being good. Personally, I'm not sure if I believe—"

"I believe I've met one of those men," Zaric interrupted. "One of the good ones."

Mered scoffed, raising his goblet to his lips and taking a swig of its contents.

"No, it's true," Zaric went on. "He hasn't done anything extraordinary yet, but I feel that he's not like other people. He's a stranger and I've met him twice now. At our last meeting, he told me that there is evil on the horizon and that Camelora needs a good king who is willing to live for as long as it takes to save the kingdom from ruin. He says that I'm that king and he offered to extend my life."

"Are you sure he's not one of the candidates from a distant duchy who you've dismissed without a second thought?"

"Mered—" Zaric began with warning in his tone.

"Extend your life how?" his cousin went on. "What does that mean exactly? A few more years? Decades? Are we talking about immortality?"

"I don't really know. 'As long as necessary,' he says. I don't know what threat we're facing, but I've felt it coming, too."

Mered smirked, looking away and falling silent. Then the smirk disappeared. Zaric could see his cousin's mind turning this idea over, studying it from different angles. After a minute, he said bluntly, "I think you should accept it."

Zaric chuckled. "It didn't take you long to come to that conclusion."

"It didn't need to. I know you, Zaric. Perhaps better than anyone in this kingdom. If this man is right, if this land really is in danger, you are just the man to protect it. I also know that you will do everything you can to make that happen. You see kingship as a responsibility and not an opportunity, as most men would. So, you should accept this man's offer. Then we'll know for sure whether or not he's bluffing. He's probably just a crazy old man. He'll wave his arms around, imagining he's doing some great magic, and you'll be embarrassed that you even believed him. Don't worry, though. When that happens, I won't tell anyone. The sad truth will remain between you and me."

Zaric tried to laugh with Mered, but the thought that Alan could be making all of this up didn't settle into his mind. Mered hadn't met the man, listened to him, heard the tone of his voice or felt the power of his presence.

Zaric wasn't convinced that Mered took it as lightly as he said he did, either. Something in his expression told the king that his friend thought there was truth to Alan's offer.

"I do agree with his assessment that you are a great king, though," Mered continued. "As a great king, I was hoping you would be willing to do me a favor."

"Oh? And what would that be?"

"With these elections going on, it would be a great advantage if I had the king's endorsement."

"Not you, too," Zaric huffed. Knowing his cousin, he had feared

Mered would make such a request. "I thought you just said you know me well. You should know I can't be partial in this election."

"But we're family!"

"The people need to know that I will accept their will, whatever it may be. Anyway, I'm sure you won't need my endorsement in the end. The people in your duchy like you, as well as those in the neighboring duchies. From what I've seen, you don't have much competition. Trust your people."

"One word from you..." Mered let the words trail out, rich with meaning.

"Just let it play out, Mered."

"Well, it was worth a try, even if I did know what you would say before I asked. Sometimes, Zaric, I really hope you'll surprise me."

Zaric caught a fire in Mered's eyes he had never seen previously, despite the acceptance in his cousin's words. Never before had Mered stirred fear inside Zaric , but the king felt a flicker of it now. Although Zaric knew it wasn't a mistake to refuse this request, he couldn't help feeling that his refusal had changed something he wouldn't be able to change back.

Chapter 20

The Present

Helen and Zaric no longer dared to venture outside the inn. Mered's soldiers roamed the streets, familiarizing themselves with the layout of the village and entering homes at random, under the guise of sociable protectors. As the restaurant filled with customers for dinner, the pair confined themselves to Lena and Connor's private sitting room upstairs—Zaric making plans while Helen studied one of the books she found in the library.

Helen and Zaric didn't speak again of honing her powers. It was too dangerous. If she failed to control herself or something went wrong—or they were interrupted by the wrong person—it could destroy all of their progress and prevent them from saving the people of Phara, as well as Zaric's undiscovered descendant.

With no chance to continue her training, Helen had even more time to devote to studying the records of Phara. They taught her interesting details about the residents of the village over the past few centuries and how their city functioned as a trading hub in this corner of the land. Nothing she read so far mentioned a family connected to Zaric, though—or Zaric's name at all.

When activity in the inn slowed for the first evening of the

173

battalion's occupation, Zaric went to the back room to meet with the potential supporters Lena and Connor had invited throughout the day. He had been gone for less than a minute when his face appeared in the doorway again, wearing a half-smile and an expression of amusement and disbelief. "You need to see this," he said before disappearing again.

Helen jumped from her chair and rushed to the door, knowing from Zaric's smile that the news wasn't bad, but curious to see what could surprise even him. She composed herself, though, before going down the stairs, remembering that she didn't want to draw attention.

Opening the door to the back room, shock kept Helen from stepping inside. The room was filled to capacity with at least three times as many people as she expected—a much greater number than Lena and Connor had promised. They occupied the chairs, sat on and leaned against the tables, with some sitting on the window sills. Heavy dark-colored curtains had been added to the windows to keep the light of the lamps and candles from escaping.

Connor appeared out of the crowd, approaching them. "This is too many," Zaric whispered. "They're going to attract too much attention."

"You can thank the battalion," Connor defended. "There were more who wanted to join us, but we convinced them to wait a few days. You will have enough to fill this room for at least three more meetings—and those are only the ones we managed to talk with today."

Connor retreated to the edge of the room. Helen followed him, while Zaric went to the opposite wall. Most of the people watched him as he walked, curious about this stranger their hosts had told them about —a man who materialized at just the right time. Others couldn't help turning their eyes to Helen, noticing that Zaric wasn't the only stranger in the room. Even when Zaric began to speak, they frequently looked back at her. She tried not to stare back, but the attention warmed her cheeks.

"I'm sure Connor and Lena have explained the need for discretion here," Zaric began. "You were invited because they trust you to protect our cause. I must stress the importance of secrecy and tell you that I am grateful so many of you are willing to help us in our fight against Mered."

"We don't want to *join* Mered," one man said from the middle of the room, "but we don't necessarily want to *fight* him, either. We feel uneasy about him, but we also don't know you or if we can trust you."

"We're here to find protection for our families," a woman put in. A murmur of agreement arose.

"We can provide protection for your families," Zaric responded, "but that protection can only last so long if we don't defend ourselves against Mered and his army. And I assure you, the time will come when we can't avoid the need to defend ourselves."

"Mered is powerful," a second man argued. "Even before the battalion arrived the rumors reached Phara. We know that our governor has met with him. If we go against Mered, how can we win without losing our lives?"

"Mered *is* strong, but we can be stronger. It isn't numbers that make strength, it's confidence in your cause. At this moment, many other people around the kingdom are gathering, preparing to fight Mered when the time comes. I can't guarantee that lives won't be lost, but if we don't try, what kind of life are you living?"

"Will we even be able to defend Phara?" another woman asked. "Can we get them out of our land?"

Zaric shook his head. "I'm afraid that opportunity has passed. As your neighbor said, your governor is in league with Mered and too many citizens agree with him. I'm not sure our numbers can take the city."

"Then what are you planning to do?" another man exclaimed. "You say that we don't need numbers to fight Mered, but then you say that we can't protect our homes, our city."

"I understand your desire to protect Phara," Zaric stated. "I once did everything I could to protect my own land—and lost more than you could imagine in return. But this isn't about one city. If you save Phara, what then? Mered will still have the rest of the kingdom. You may defeat Bernt and his battalion, but Mered will only send a larger unit until he finally defeats you. He will show less and less mercy until none of you are left. He's done it before."

"In Veren," someone stated. Zaric nodded.

"These people you mentioned, those who support your cause, where are they gathering?" the first man asked. "Where do you propose we go?"

"Once we've found everyone willing to, we will take you to Camelora."

A confused quiet fell over the room as the people looked at each other, shaking their heads, shrugging their shoulders, casting quick glances at Connor. "What is Camelora?" one woman finally ventured to ask. "How far from here is it?"

"It's a land to the north, where the people have been protected from Mered for hundreds of years, and where they are preparing to fight him when their forces are strong enough."

A disharmony of voices grew.

"Hundreds of years! Are you trying to say that Mered has been around that long?"

"That's ridiculous! No one can live that long."

"Lena and Connor must have gone crazy."

"Who are you, anyway?" the first man asked, his skepticism apparent in his tone. "Like I said, why should we believe you?"

"My name is Zaric."

Helen held her breath for a response, some sort of wave of encouraged recognition. None came.

"Connor told us that, but it doesn't tell us who you are."

A wave of sadness slammed into Zaric, pressing against his chest. He wished his name would inspire a glimmer of hope, but in Phara, he now understood, he truly had been completely forgotten. It was evident that his descendants hadn't chosen to pass on his name and purpose. His own son had decided to forget him.

"I am a man who wants to help you," Zaric replied. "My whole life is devoted to that purpose."

"So, you want us all to go with you to this 'Camelora.' How do you propose doing that? Our governor has just welcomed in a battalion."

"They're surrounding the city. There's no way for us to get out undetected."

"How are you going to protect us from *that?*"

"I have a plan, but I need something from you first. I'm not asking you to pledge your support right now. No one should ever be expected to make such a hasty decision. I would like you all to go to your homes and think this over. Consider your options. Choose what's best for you, for your family. I only ask that you promise to avoid discussing what has been said in this room in public. We don't want this information to fall on the wrong ears. Connor and Lena invited you here because they trust you, and I hope that you will not betray that trust."

He bowed to the room, then stepped back. The buzz of hushed conversation commenced from the group. Helen circled the room to stand with Zaric while Connor let the people out two or three at a time to avoid suspicion. The crowd thinned until only Connor, Helen, and Zaric were left.

"Perhaps I should have spoken, too," Connor said.

"I'm not sure it would have made any difference," Zaric told him, "but, next time, I will give you a few minutes, if you like. You know the villagers better than I do. I only wish they knew the history of this place and the kingdom. But I can't fault anyone here for that."

"You're forgetting that Lena and I learned about you from the old book Aurelie found in the library. The history is there, if anyone cares to look for it."

"I will look for some more records tomorrow," Helen inserted. "I have confidence that some of these people will recognize you for who you are. It's the truth, after all."

"We're making progress," Zaric smiled. "And we can't force anyone to join us, anyway. I'm sure some people will be willing to support us. I'll be glad to take them away from here to a place of safety. In the meantime, we won't stop trying."

Despite his optimistic words, Helen detected something in Zaric he had never shown before. She suspected it had been centuries since he felt it, but Zaric's usual certainty was wavering.

Chapter 21

The Present

They didn't speak much as they walked the streets of the city. Siri occasionally pulled out the map, comparing it to the buildings and side streets around them. Though her actions were deft and discreet, Neil had the impression that she was not only memorizing the map but the city it represented. He tried to suppress his feelings of admiration.

Every once in a while, Neil asked if she had seen the young man from the street again. Each time, she shook her head in response. He had seen too much throughout the day to question her. At one time, Siri made the comment, "I wish I had said something when I saw him the first time."

Neil didn't press her. He understood the feeling. If she had said something, she might have prevented the fire that damaged the palace. They would have had a target to follow to find the traitors they were looking for. But they also might have hampered their own mission, revealing too soon what they knew about Mered's infiltration of Camelora.

"There," Siri said quietly, snatching Neil out of his thoughts. He was disappointed in himself, realizing he had once again allowed his attention to drift.

179

"Where?" he questioned.

Siri pointed with her head. He followed the invisible line in the direction she indicated.

A young woman walked down the street, alone. She kept her head forward and her neck straight. By focusing on her, though, Neil was able to see her eyes shift from side to side, taking in the street around her.

"Look away," Siri said, taking Neil's hand and pulling him near a shop window. "She'll notice you."

Neil worried they would lose sight of the girl, until he realized Siri was watching the reflection of the street in the glass. Following her example, he watched as the girl stopped for a few seconds, glancing around for the first time. He saw something fall from her hand before she moved again.

"What's that?" Neil whispered to Siri.

"A signal," she replied. She watched as the girl continued down the street, then hurried to the spot where the item had dropped.

"What are you doing?" Neil argued as he watched Siri pick up a delicate-looking scarf. "Don't you want to see who comes for it?"

"I'll learn that later," she returned. "For now, I'm going to be a good citizen."

She looked down the street, picking the girl out again in the crowd. When Siri moved after her, Neil had no choice but to follow.

The evening was coming on, throwing much of the city into the shadow of its buildings. Siri and Neil hurried their steps to close the gap between them and the girl as much as they dared. With the fading light and all the citizens anxious to return to their homes, they could easily lose sight of her.

Soon they found themselves on another residential street. There were fewer people here than on the streets they left. The girl approached a tall, narrow house, lit with a lantern above the front door. She opened it without knocking.

Her home.

Siri stopped a few yards away from the house and pulled the map out of her pocket, consulting it for a few short seconds.

"Should we come back in the morning?" Neil asked. "Hopefully catch her on her way out to—whatever it is she does?"

"No," Siri chuckled, flashing a familiar, bright smile. She folded the scarf up neatly and approached the door.

"What are you doing?" Neil asked as he followed. He wished he could read Siri's mind, especially when it became so focused.

"I don't have time to explain," was her only response.

She reached the door and knocked without hesitation.

A stout, middle-aged woman opened it, her face betraying the surprise she felt at receiving visitors.

"Good evening, ma'am," Siri said. "I'm sorry to trouble you, as I'm sure you're about to sit down to supper, but I was on a merchant street a few minutes ago and saw a young woman drop this scarf. I picked it up and tried to call after her, but she didn't hear me, so I followed her. I believe she came through this door just a moment ago. Is there a young woman here?"

"I have a daughter," the woman answered, "but I've never seen that scarf before. Riva!" she called out, turning her head toward a staircase against the wall.

A few seconds later, they heard a creak at the top of the stairs. The girl they had seen on the street soon appeared. She was younger than Neil, with dark hair, dark eyes, and a serious face. Much like Siri, Neil couldn't help noticing, but with plainer features and less animation in her manner .

"Riva," her mother said as the girl neared the door, "these two people think they saw you drop a scarf on the street. Is it yours?"

Riva kept her face straight, but she couldn't hide the flicker of anxiety that ignited her eyes. Neil knew that if he could see it, Siri could as well. Siri held out her hand, showing the scarf to the girl.

"I'm sorry," Riva said, attempting a smile. "It isn't mine."

"Are you sure?" Siri asked. "I was certain it was you I saw drop it."

"It must have been someone else," Riva persisted. "We Camelorans all look the same."

"Oh, dear," Siri said. "I thought I was so careful, but I must have lost the girl I was following. Are there any other young women living on this street? I would hate to have to knock on every door."

Between Riva and her mother, Siri and Neil left the house with the recommendation to check at least five other homes. They wished the family a good night before the door closed.

"That was her, wasn't it?" Neil asked as they stood in the shadow of a lean-to at the corner of the house.

"Of course," Siri maintained. "Her denial just makes it even more obvious that she dropped the scarf as a signal. Someone else was meant to pick it up. You saw how worried she was when she saw it. We interrupted some sort of plan."

"At least we know where she lives now."

"Exactly right. You're learning, Neil."

"Should we go back to the palace? We can tell Garrick what we've learned and come up with a plan for tomorrow."

"Oh, no," Siri contradicted. "We still have five more houses to visit."

"But we already know where she lives."

"Yes, but if we head straight for the palace and she's watching, she'll know that we know. We have to go on with this ruse, even if it means pretending to look for a young woman who dropped a scarf."

Neil wanted to argue that they were wasting time, but he had to admit to himself that Siri was right. He didn't have to tell her, though. He sighed audibly before following her down the street.

*　*　*

They found Garrick in Zaric's study when they returned, eager to receive their report. Excitement and a measure of pride tinged Siri's voice as she related what they had discovered. Neil didn't mind letting her tell the story. She knew what to say and what to discern from it. Once the details were related, they were able to frame a plan for the following day.

"Neil, do you have a few minutes?" Garrick asked as Neil and Siri made to leave the room. "You can wait for us," Garrick added to Siri, seeing the apprehensive look on her face. "I'll walk home with you after I speak with Neil."

Siri assented and left the room while Neil lowered himself back into his chair.

"What's going on?" Neil asked, confused by the governor's behavior.

"I think there's more to this rebel plot than Siri realizes," Garrick stated.

"Do you think she held something back?"

"No, I don't think it has anything to do *with* Siri. I can't be sure, but I don't think so."

"What's going on?" Neil repeated more emphatically.

Garrick carefully considered his next words before speaking them. "Weapons are going missing from the armory," he answered.

"Weapons ? Are you sure?"

"We keep track of these things. Everything that goes in, everything that goes out. Some items aren't where they're supposed to be."

"And you think it's the rebels."

"It seems like the most likely answer, but I can't be sure. That's why I don't want to tell anyone else yet. Not even Siri. No need to alarm anyone until we're certain. With your wrist still healing and unable to do the work everyone else is doing, I thought this investigation might be a good job for you."

"On top of this job with Siri?"

"Well, that doesn't have to take up your *entire* day. Devote some time to this, too."

"I'll do what I can," Neil said, hoping his words sounded more sure than he felt, "but I don't really know where to start."

"I can't help noticing an unusual coincidence," Garrick went on. "You've been looking for a way to defeat Mered, weapons are going missing… It's possible you've already started."

"You think Mered already knows what will defeat him."

"I think he has an idea. It can't hurt to proceed under that assumption."

"No, it can't hurt at all," Neil agreed. "I'll look into it."

"Thank you, Neil. And, like I said, let's keep this between the two of us for now. For once, I agree that we don't know who we can trust."

Chapter 22

The Past

Zaric sat at his desk, looking over the last of the election results. They had arrived by special messenger that afternoon. He read the letter detailing the tallies from his uncle's duchy three times. It was very clear. The winner won by a large majority with no room for doubt. Zaric dropped the letter and rested his forehead on his hand.

A rapping knock sounded on the door. "Come in," the king instructed.

"Your cousin is here to see you, sir," the servant said as he opened the door. He hadn't finished the statement before Mered pushed past him, knocking the servant off balance.

"You've received the letter?" Mered asked, though it was more a statement than a question.

Zaric waved the servant from the room and the man closed the door as quickly as he could. "I was just reading it," the king responded, indicating the letter on the desk.

"I'm sure it was rigged," Mered spat, sweeping up the sheet, glancing over it, then throwing it down again. "I demand a full investigation."

"That is your right. I will point out, though, that your own father oversaw the election."

"My father is a stupid, senile old man. You should never have trusted him to oversee anything. And you could have prevented this, you know."

"Me?"

"If you had spoken for me. I *am* your cousin. I would have won if you had spoken for me. A kind word from my cousin and best friend would have shown the people they could trust me."

"Your own actions should show the people they can trust you. I told you before: as the king, I couldn't interfere."

"Yes, yes," Mered said with an impatient gesture. He took a deep breath, then stood in thought. With a calmer tone, he continued, "You can still fix this."

"Fix what? Nothing is broken."

"Keep the results to yourself. Announce that I was the winner."

"I will not lie to my people," Zaric said, pronouncing every word carefully to disguise the anger that built in his chest as he slowly raised himself from his chair.

"Make a special appointment," Mered persisted. "Create a place for me on the council. I *am* family."

"That would undermine everything, Mered. The people have chosen their representative. If I make a special appointment, they will feel I'm ignoring them. They will think I don't trust them and they will stop trusting *me*."

"It's all about *you,* is it?"

"It's about the people." Zaric gripped the desk, finding it hard to tamp down his annoyance. His heart beat rapidly, the sound flooding his ears. "I'm doing what is best for the kingdom."

"You are my cousin!" Mered emphasized through clenched teeth, jabbing his finger on the desk.

"I am your king!" Zaric shouted in response, bringing his fist down. Items on the desk rattled as the echo of the slam filled the room with a wave of anger, frustration, and truth.

Fire shone in Mered's eyes. He took a step back and smirked, his eyes locked on Zaric. Then, he raised his hands, making a gesture of surrender. "You're right," he said with forced calm. "The people have spoken. I need to resign myself to their will." He allowed a tension-filled pause to settle over the room before he resumed. "I wonder, though: how brave would you be if you allowed the people to choose their king?"

Zaric stood stunned as Mered swung around and stalked out of the room, slamming the door behind him. The silence that followed was thick and heavy. Dropping into his chair, Zaric watched as all the color drained from his vision. A dread settled over him. Something had shifted between him and Mered in the last few minutes and he knew it would never shift back . Searching his mind and memory, he examined what he had done and wondered what he could do to fix it, but realized that he could do nothing. Mered had changed and he couldn't change him back. Zaric himself had changed and he didn't *want* to change back. The parallel paths the two men had walked their entire lives had diverged, and they would never intersect again.

There was also a haunting inkling in Mered's words: if the people were allowed to choose their king, would they even choose Zaric?

* * *

Over the next few days, Zaric expected Mered to return to the palace. He dreaded meeting him again. Yet, he also dreaded not seeing him.

The dread gradually lessened as Mered failed to materialize. A different anticipation grew. With the end of the elections came the return of Althea and her father. A gathering would soon be held for the members of Zaric's new council, but he made sure that the Vereneans would arrive a few days before that.

Once he saw Althea and spent a few minutes with her, Zaric knew he was making the right choice. As he dined with her and her father, he had to make a great effort to keep from staring and divide his attention between the two of them. The anxiety Zaric suffered at the prospect of speaking to Evander, and then to Althea, only proved to deepen what he felt *for* her.

"You seem distracted, your majesty," Althea stated as Zaric finished his meal, setting his spoon at the edge of his plate. She and her father followed suit.

"I think I am, yes," he responded, his cheeks burning. He couldn't stop the smile spreading over his face.

"Is there anything I can do for you?" Althea asked.

Zaric had no response. Althea's father studied the king, then turned to his daughter. "Althea, my dear, do you remember those items I asked you to bring from Veren to show his majesty? I believe tonight would be a good time for it, if you don't mind fetching them for us."

"Not at all," Althea responded, pushing her chair back. She looked from one man to the other, sensing that they both knew something she did not. She was too polite and too skilled to do anything other than smile it away.

The two men stood as she left the room, then sat down again.

"You gave me some very strong hints in one of your recent letters," Evander stated, surprising Zaric with his direct manner. "Strong enough to convince me that I should drop out of the election in Veren."

"Yes," Zaric replied, feeling himself blush again. He watched Althea's father, waiting for him to continue speaking, but the older man only looked back with a glint of challenge in his eye and a slight raising of the corners of his lips. Zaric wasn't sure how to read this expression—if the duke meant to toy with him or simply encourage him.

"When I met your daughter…" Zaric went on, but the words trailed off. He wasn't sure where to go with that statement and thought he had started in the wrong way.

"I never expected…"

Still, the beginning wasn't right .

"Althea is unlike anyone I ever knew before. I'm surprised I *didn't* know her before…. She has made a great impact on me and I was wondering… hoping… I think very much that I would like her to be my queen. Or I should say my wife. Or both. I would really like for her to be both. I'm sorry, this is all very new to me."

"I should hope so!" Evander exclaimed. "My daughter should never be any man's second choice."

Zaric gaped, caught off-guard. He was confused, too, unsure how to react to the father's statement. "I've never looked at any woman the way I look at your daughter." Once these words were said, he was afraid of how they were heard. "What I mean is, what I feel for Althea is something I have never felt before. When I'm not with her, I want nothing more than to be with her again. When I *am* with her, I feel like I can be everything I need to be."

"That is as it should be."

"And, in a practical sense, she is everything a woman should be if she is going to be a queen. I know that, in that respect, I could not make a better choice."

With expectation, Zaric stared at Evander. The man said nothing, only stared back. Zaric shook his head at himself, sure he had misspoken. Maybe, he thought, he needed to say it again in a different way.

But as he opened his mouth, Evander held up a hand. "There's no need to explain yourself further," he said. "I don't know how anyone could fail to see how you feel about Althea. You are not the first man to show an interest in my daughter, but you are certainly the best. And, I should add, you are the first that she has shown an interest in return. There is a genuineness about you that most men don't have—especially among kings. I would be honored to have such a man as my son-in-law.

"Also, you could not have chosen a better woman for your queen. My late wife had high hopes for our daughter. When I knew Althea would be my only child, I put all my effort into shaping her into the greatest duchess the land of Veren would ever know. Now, she can use that training to be the greatest queen *Camelora* has ever known. The only inconvenience you're giving me is, now I have to find a new heir."

"So, I have your permission to marry your daughter?" Zaric asked, his heart lightened by Evander's words.

"You have my permission to ask my daughter to marry you," Evander clarified. "It's her choice whether she accepts or not. Let's hope I'm not wrong about my daughter's feelings."

There was a sound at the door and Althea reappeared. "Just maybe not tonight," Evander whispered as his daughter approached the table, carrying the books and trinkets she had retrieved.

Despite the duties that demanded Zaric's attention, he found time the next morning to stand at the wall of the palace with his hands resting on the cool stone as the day dawned, taking in its peace. Even if he had wanted to propose to Althea the night before, all of his courage had been used up speaking to her father. Zaric needed this morning to build up that courage again. Grey clouds spread across the sky, but there was enough of a gap on the horizon to allow the light of the approaching sun to shine through. Zaric took a deep breath.

He failed to hear the nearing footsteps and was startled when a hand covered his own. He looked down at the slender white fingers and felt a wave of emotion at the tender touch. He looked down into Althea's smiling face and was captivated by the way the morning light brought out the variations in the color of her eyes. In that moment,

Zaric realized that this was exactly what he wanted, to be standing in the waking light with Althea at his side.

"I thought I would find you here," she said, pressing her hand a little harder over his.

Zaric's heart swelled and he lost his thoughts in the feel of Althea's hand and the depth of her eyes.

"Will you marry me?" he asked before he knew what he was saying. He thought it would be harder to ask, but knew now just how easy Althea made it to say what he wanted to say.

Althea stood with her mouth open, speechless. Her brow contracted in a visible sign of thought. She looked away, then back at Zaric as a smile flickered over her lips. "Yes," she said, lifting Zaric's hand and holding it between both of hers. "Yes. You surprised me. I wasn't expecting you to ask so abruptly. But I want nothing more than to be your wife."

With laughter on his lips, Zaric freed himself from Althea's grasp and held her face in his hands, kissing her before he thought twice about it. He felt her lips smile against his.

When he pulled back, Zaric looked into Althea's face, studying it. The sincerity and genuine love he saw there told him he had chosen the right woman. For the first time in his life, he was not a prince or a king, but a common person with real emotions. As king, though, he was glad the choice was his own. He had always thought his marriage would be an alliance between two kingdoms, that he would have to learn to love and respect his wife after she had gained that title. He never imagined he would be allowed to love first.

"Will you mind being my queen, too?" he asked.

"As long as I can spend my life with you, I don't mind what else I need to be," Althea responded. Zaric liked the way her lips said the words and he couldn't help kissing them again.

"I think most kings would have to get the approval of their advisers before they could ask such a thing," she went on. "Did you?"

"I asked your father last night, and my advisers haven't been assembled yet. They will have to settle for hearing the news without giving their opinions. And, as my future queen, I would like you to sit in on every council meeting as often as possible, as *soon* as possible. Your ideas and opinions are the ones that matter most."

An alarm crossed Althea's face, but it evaporated as quickly as it came. "I hope I don't disappoint you. What if the opinions I've offered up to this point are all I really have to offer?"

"Then you will be my wife and queen, and what more could I ask for? I still remember what you said the night we met. I value the ideas you have to offer."

Althea bowed her head in thanks.

"Which reminds me," Zaric went on. "I noticed something that night that I meant to ask you about. My cousin Mered."

Althea pulled back and broke eye contact. "I know the two of you are very close," she stated.

"We always have been. Growing up, we were like brothers. But I don't know if that's the case anymore."

Zaric told her about his last meeting with Mered —the things his cousin said, his demands and manner, and the anger with which he left. He related the uneasiness he felt and the rift he sensed, which he didn't believe could be mended.

"Mered has changed," he said. "When you first met him, I could sense you felt something."

"I'm not surprised you did. Beware of Mered."

"Why? I need to know."

Althea placed a hand on the wall, looking out over the fields to the horizon, where the sun crested the hill, fighting off the grey clouds. "Mered is dangerous," she finally said. "He envies you, though I'm sure that's something you have already noticed. If he had been born to a different brother, all of this would be his, not yours. He knows that. He feels he has just as much right to the kingdom as you—perhaps more. You are not what most people think of when they think of a king. The day will come when Mered isn't afraid to try and take the kingdom. All he needs is support."

"How do you know all this?"

"Because I see it. The night we met, you asked why I was so quiet. I told you. When I give my opinion, it isn't wrong. Somehow—and I'm not sure why—I have an ability to see how things are going to play out. Perhaps not all the time, but enough of the time to make a difference. I don't want people to take advantage of that. Perhaps it's selfish, but I want to have as normal a life as possible. And it gives me a headache."

"Althea," Zaric said gently, taking her hand in his as she had done before. "I promise you that I will always respect *whatever* this gift is, and your decisions on when—or if—to use it. You will never be pressed to give information. If you do, it will be your choice. As my wife and my queen, you are free to act as you feel best."

Althea smiled up at Zaric, then rested her forehead against his chest. He wrapped his arms around her and kissed the top of her head. For now, he didn't want to think about kingdoms and envies and possibilities. He only wanted to hold Althea close, and he would do that as long as he could.

Chapter 23

Meira and Stephen left Camelora. After spending some time with their own citizens, they were confident their people would help prepare the kingdom—and they felt the pull of the task to bring in more support. Having Meira and Stephen in Camelora was, to Neil, almost like having Zaric there, but he also knew that Garrick trusted them more than anyone else to convince the refugees that what Zaric offered was worth the risk.

After seeing them off, Neil and Siri took up a position outside Riva's house. It was their fourth morning there in a row. Impatience coursed through Neil's body as the morning wore on, but Siri was unruffled. It wasn't unusual, she explained, for an enemy to become more careful for a time if they thought they were under suspicion. This was why Siri chose the shadows of an alley down the street instead of one across from the front door of the home to wait, watching as the occupants came and went. At times they thought they might have missed Riva, only to see her appear in the doorway, shouting after her brothers or emptying a dustpan into the street. She hadn't left her house—that they knew of—in the time since they approached the door with the scarf.

"I wish we had someone to watch the door at night," Siri voiced as they waited.

"We could always bring someone else in," Neil suggested.

"Still too soon," Siri answered.

The door of the house opened and Riva came out, carrying a basket over her arm. Closing the door behind her, she glanced up and down the street before heading off purposefully. Siri waited until there was enough distance between them before following. Neil took the cue and walked with Siri.

For a few blocks they trailed Riva, stopping when she stopped and moving when she moved. The basket she carried was covered and she never once reached inside of it. Neil wondered what it contained and what she intended to do with it. Was it an innocent basket, or something more dangerous? There were questions he wanted to ask Siri, but he knew they would have to wait. In the time they had spent watching, she had made it clear that any conversation in public needed to be superficial and unrelated to the task at hand.

Riva left the residential streets and entered the more industrial area of the city. Her tidy appearance contrasting with the more rugged, hardened appearance of the workers who walked the streets, yet no one questioned it. Everyone in Camelora was free to roam the city as they wished. Anyone who saw Riva was free to make their own assumptions about her presence, and none of those assumptions were likely to be menacing.

They reached a street lined with warehouses on one side and smithing workshops on the other. Riva stopped between two buildings on the warehouse side, checking her basket for the first time. She lifted her head again to scan the street. Siri pulled Neil in front of her, forcing him to face her while using him to shield her from Riva's view. He didn't argue, not wanting to give them away, though he was worried about not being able to see what Riva did next. Although her eyes were on Riva, Siri kept her face turned toward Neil, a broad smile covering it. Again, she masterfully played a role.

Neil only knew something had changed when the grin dropped and Siri walked again, taking his arm. He skimmed the street for Riva, but couldn't see her.

"Where did she go?" he asked, trying his best to cover his annoyance.

"Into that warehouse," Siri answered, nodding at a building on the opposite side of the street—a solid wall with one door, and windows near the roof.

"What do we do now?"

"I'm thinking."

Neil still wasn't used to seeing Siri this way, concentrating on a task instead of standing at ease, charming everyone around her.

As she thought, Neil felt eyes watching them. Looking over, he noticed the blacksmith in a nearby workshop staring at the two of them. Neil worried they had lingered too long, attracting too much attention.

When the blacksmith approached them, Neil knew they couldn't just slip away.

"I'm sorry," Neil said. "We're probably disturbing you. Come on, Siri."

"Oh, no," the man said, "you're not disturbing me." The man's eyes glanced up and down the street around them.

"I have such a fascination with the work you do," Siri complimented, touching Neil's arm to tell him that the blacksmith's manner hadn't escaped her. "Would you mind showing us how it's done?"

The man waved toward the forge, then led the way. He picked up his abandoned tools and continued his work where he had left off.

"You're Neil," the man stated, "the governor's assistant."

"Yes," Neil assured him. "Do you need something?"

The man glanced around again, making sure no one else stood nearby. "I've been noticing strange activity on this street. At the warehouse, over there. The one you were watching." He nodded in the direction of the building across from his forge. "We keep winter goods in that place and there's no reason for anyone to go in there so often at this time of year. Especially not the type of people I've been seeing."

"How often do they come?" Siri asked.

"Two or three times this past week."

As Siri and Neil turned to look at the warehouse, a young man in foreign apparel approached it. His steps slowed as he neared the door Riva had gone through and he glanced around to see if anyone was watching. Siri elbowed Neil, turning her own eyes back to the blacksmith. Reluctant, Neil pulled his eyes away, too. After a few seconds he looked back, just in time to see the young man slip through the door.

"And it started about a week ago?" Neil asked.

"It could have started before then," the blacksmith admitted. "I'm not always paying much attention to the street."

"How many people?"

"Five or six?" the blacksmith responded. "I haven't counted."

"That's all right," Neil said. "Knowing it's more than one or two helps. Do they come at the same time every day?"

The man nodded.

"Should we check it out?" Neil asked Siri in a low tone.

"Are these the only two so far today?" she asked the blacksmith, seemingly ignoring Neil's question.

"That I've seen," the blacksmith answered.

"Not yet," Siri said in response to Neil. "Let's see if more come."

For the next few minutes, she stood watching the blacksmith work in rapt attention, playing the part of the eager student. The sincerity of her praises made the smith beam and he added a bit of a flourish to his actions. If he gifted his finished product to her without a second thought, Neil wouldn't have been surprised.

Meanwhile, four more people entered the warehouse . Each person slowed his or her steps, sweeping their eyes over the street before opening the door. Each person failed to notice the blacksmith's forge across the road.

Siri gave a slight nod, signaling it was time to investigate the warehouse.

"Is it all right," Siri started, placing a gentle hand on the blacksmith's arm, "if we meet back here after our investigation? I'm anxious to see your progress, but we don't want to lose our chance to see what's happening in that building."

The man nodded his understanding.

"Stay here," Siri instructed, turning her attention to Neil. "I'll see what's going on and tell you what I find out."

Not waiting for a reply or acknowledgement, Siri crossed the street. She was much more discreet as she approached the door, displaying more skill than any of the young people they had seen enter the building up to this point. If Neil hadn't been watching, he was sure he wouldn't have noticed. Distrust swelled again and he ignored Siri's instructions.

"Is there another way into that warehouse?" Neil asked the blacksmith.

"There's a door around the back," the man answered. "Most people don't know about it, unless they live in this neighborhood."

Waiting until Siri slipped beyond the door, Neil used a sudden flow of people to his advantage as he made his way across the street.

Once he was in the alleyway across from the forge, Neil looked for the back door. He found it about halfway down the wall. The smith had been right. Being flush with the wall, it was barely visible. When Neil tried the knob, he found it was unlocked. The hinges were silent as he swung the door open and slipped through.

Once inside, Neil found himself facing a large stack of boxes. The boxes were piled to his right and left, too. In fact, this back entrance was completely blocked from view within the warehouse. There was a good chance the rebels hadn't discovered it.

The boxes were set a few inches away from the wall, but still too close to allow Neil to pass easily behind them. He was forced to slide against the wall, holding his breath as he looked for an opening, all the while trying not to knock over any of the crates in the process.

The hum of voices told him where to find the assembled group. Siri's voice was among them. Careful not to make a noise, Neil made his way to the voices, finding a gap between the supply stacks where he could see and hear without revealing his presence.

Siri leaned against a wall of the warehouse, her manner bored and her presence towering, despite her slight stature. The people they had seen entering the building now sat in a semi-circle of crates, their shifting weight and avoidance of Siri's eyes betraying their discomfort in her presence. Their discomfort only added to Siri's distinction.

The highness of the windows in the warehouse walls and the stacks of boxes and crates dimmed the natural light that entered the space. A few lanterns and candles had been lit to negate this effect, but cast shadows that made the features of the people difficult to distinguish. Still, Neil recognized Riva, looking not only uncomfortable but irritated. The expression of her eyes when she glanced at Siri showed her contempt for the older young woman.

The other rebels were a mixture of young men and women, both Cameloran and foreign. All appeared to be Neil's age or younger. None of them carried themselves as Siri did, with the air of confidence and authority of one who knew the seriousness of the task they were involved in.

"You followed me, didn't you?" Riva spat, her arms folded across her chest.

"It wasn't hard," Siri said in reply. "You were careless."

"I did what I was trained to do," the younger woman defended.

"Yes, but you failed to notice *me*. Whoever your leader is, he's not exactly working with the best."

There was an outburst around the circle as each member tried to argue with this assessment. All it required for Siri to silence them, though, was a raise of her hand.

"You should know better than to make so much noise," she stated, her manner still cool and undisturbed.

"Why did you let this woman in?" Riva questioned, glaring at the young man who sat next to her.

"She knew the password," he answered.

"Mered sent me," Siri stated.

"Did he?" a man's voice asked, drifting through the stacks of crates, startling Neil and increasing his heartrate. He steadied himself, checking again to make sure he wasn't visible from anywhere near the warehouse's main door.

The rebel group jumped, too, with audible intakes of breath. Only Siri stayed still, unphased by the voice. "Step out, then," she instructed. "Let's see who you are."

The man stepped into the light of the lanterns and candles, taking slow steps and allowing the shadows to pass over his body and face. Siri rolled her eyes at the drama of his entrance.

"You remind me of Ian," she said. "Let's hope you don't end up like him."

"Ian disappeared," the man stated. "Mered knows exactly where I am."

"Ian was killed by the governor's fool. Though, one could argue he was *actually* killed by his own arrogance."

The leader flinched at the word "killed," but covered his discomfort by raising his chin a little higher. "You disappeared, too, Siri." The man stressed her name as though he were making a great revelation. "Don't look so surprised"—though Siri did not—"of course I know you, even if my friends here do not. Everyone in Mered's court knows about the versatile and beautiful Siri."

"Then you are expecting me," she stated. Her voice was calm—the voice of a woman who knew she had command of her audience.

"No," the man answered. "Mered said nothing about you."

"Ah, yes, that's right. How can you communicate with him when you've allowed two of your devices to be discovered by your enemy?"

"I still know my duty. Mered gave me clear instructions before I set out."

Siri chuckled. "He must not trust you, then."

"Of course he trusts me," the man retorted. "He trusts me enough to burn Camelora to the ground."

"Is that what you were trying to do?" Siri mocked, her calm unaffected. "If he trusts you so much, why did he feel the need to send me? You aren't a part of his inner circle, or even his outer circle. You do realize you know who I am, but I have no idea who you are."

Seeing the offense on the man's face, Neil was baffled by Siri's tactics. This man looked ready to kill her and abandon her body in a dark corner of this warehouse, rather than share his secrets with her. How would Neil and Garrick learn anything then?

The man's mouth twitched, then softened. "I'm Spenser," he said.

"But is it?" Siri questioned. The man said nothing. "All right, *Spenser*," Siri went on, finding a crate to sit on, "why don't you tell me what Mered needs to know."

"You're in contact with Mered?" Spenser questioned, interest in his voice.

"I'm part of his circle—as you know. He needs someone in Camelora who knows how to use her head."

"How could I know—"

"You should *always* know someone could find your device. That's why you keep it with you."

"It was a risk I had to take."

"We'll see."

"We?"

"One mistake could mean nothing, or it could mean everything. *Two* mistakes..."

"What's the second mistake?" one of the young men of the group asked, his voice shaky.

Siri appraised him before answering his question. "The fire," she said, her tone bored and irritated.

"The fire was not a mistake," Riva defended.

"I see it differently," Siri said with indifference.

"What would you know?" Riva went on, her temper flaring. "You, who stay with Garrick and pretend to be in league with him. You walk through the city with that assistant of his as though you're one of them. How do we know that's just an act? At least we aren't pretending to turn our backs on Mered's cause."

"Don't confuse calculation with weakness," Siri responded. "I've lived in Mered's world; you never have. In this world you've chosen, you have to navigate the calculations if you want to remain relevant."

The girl sank back at these words, flushing with embarrassment.

"I see that none of you are afraid to turn on your own people," Siri added.

"They were misguided," Spenser explained. "All their lives, Zaric has been feeding them his story. That isn't their fault."

Siri stared at Spenser, tapping her fingers on her knee as she allowed the seconds to pass in silence. "Well," she finally said, "you've certainly gotten the governor's attention."

"Hopefully, his isn't the only attention we have," Spenser said.

"I'm in a position to help you," Siri pointed out when Spenser failed to elaborate. "I can direct the governor's thoughts wherever I choose. You only have to let me in on your plan."

"Mered didn't tell you the plan?"

"You know I won't fall for that. Mered didn't come up with your plan. If he had, he would have sent his own men to carry it out, instead of instructing you to recruit these children—"

The four recruits shouted in indignation. "We aren't children!" the young Cameloran man stated sharply.

"—to help you," Siri finished, ignoring the outburst. "Soldiers with experience."

"You can't come in here and talk to us like that!" the young refugee woman cried.

"Yes, I can!" Siri shouted back. "You have done nothing yet to prove to me that you even belong in this cause. Setting fire to the palace, dropping signal scarves in the marketplace... That isn't going to get you very far with Mered."

"It's all part of a larger plan," Spenser explained, waving down the protests of his small band. "We need to shake the refugees' trust in Zaric and the people of Camelora. They need to see that, in the end, only Mered can protect them. I mean, Zaric isn't even here to welcome his new supporters. He's off doing who knows what, expecting those he left behind to defend his 'kingdom' while he does nothing to help. We, at least, can see that Zaric has abandoned his post, only planning to return to claim the victory if it's won."

Again, Siri stared at Spenser. The man's back was to Neil, preventing him from seeing his expression and how well it held up under Siri's scrutiny. His posture, though, revealed part of what Neil needed to know. His shoulders slumped slightly, unable to bear the full weight of Siri's gaze.

"And that's all," Siri questioned in a statement.

"That's all for now," Spenser answered.

"We're on the same side, Spenser."

"Are we, Siri? Don't forget: Mered put me in charge of this mission. All I have is your word that he asked you to come as well. What sort of soldier would I be if I took you at your word without confirmation?"

"Confirmation you won't receive," Siri pointed out, "since you allowed your communication device to be destroyed."

"Spenser is only giving us bits of the plan at a time," the young Cameloran man explained.

"We plan to create chaos," Spenser hastened to assert. Neil didn't miss the bladed look he cast at the young man. "That's all you need to know for now."

"With so few of you?" Siri questioned.

"There are more. Or there will be. I'm not done recruiting. Plus, you don't need large numbers when you have a solid plan."

"I hope you formulate one soon," Siri shot. "Otherwise, the governor may take action before you're ready. Frightening the refugees—is that all you're after?"

"We're also—" the Cameloran man started, but Spenser cut him off.

"You've all been away too long. I won't give you any new assignments today. We'll meet again tomorrow. Same time, same place."

"Not tomorrow," Siri said.

"Why not tomorrow?" Spenser asked.

"You'll attract attention—more than you already have. Meeting at the same time and place will only get you caught. As much as I hate to admit it, if I figured out your pattern, someone else will, too. A different time, a different place."

"I live here," Spenser pointed out.

"Live somewhere else. No one will notice you in the camp."

Spenser started to argue, restating the words of indignation he had used before. Neil knew he shouldn't stay to hear it. The others were shifting and standing, preparing to leave the warehouse. He wanted to reach the blacksmith's forge before Siri exited and discovered he had followed her inside.

Finding the gap leading to the back door wasn't easy, and leaving silently was even more difficult. As the hum of the group's voices dulled, Neil hoped Siri would be the last to leave.

From the alley, he saw the members of Spenser's traitorous band hurrying down the street, spaced out to avoid detection. He pressed himself against the wall, trying to be as invisible as possible. When he felt it was safe to step out, he hurried back to the shadowy corner of the smith's forge.

A few minutes went by with no sign of Siri. When she arrived, she came from down the street instead of across it. Neil did his best not to look surprised, remembering that he wasn't supposed to know the meeting had ended.

"How did it go?" he asked eagerly. "Were you able to learn anything?"

"Thank you for your help," Siri addressed the blacksmith, ignoring Neil's questions. "We appreciate you telling us what you noticed. We will be sure to tell the governor of your assistance."

"I don't mind doing my duty," the smith replied.

"Let's report back to the palace," Siri said to Neil, keeping her voice low. "This street isn't the place for sharing sensitive information."

Neil remained quiet for a minute or two, but didn't want to appear too complacent. "What did you learn?" he whispered as they walked, keeping an eye on the people around them, watching for the traitors he had seen in the warehouse.

"Do you even need to ask?" Siri asked in reply. Neil tried to think of something to say, but words wouldn't come. "Next time, I would appreciate a little more trust."

"What do you mean?" Neil didn't need to see his own face to know how much he failed at feigning confusion.

"I saw you, Neil. You're lucky none of the rebels did, too."

205

"I just thought it would help for both of us to hear the plan."

"I know what I'm doing."

"And you think I don't?"

"I *know* you don't. Don't jeopardize my work by inserting yourself where you don't belong. If you get caught, they'll suspect us both."

"Are you sure Spenser trusts you?"

"He would be a fool if he does," Siri said, surprising Neil . "Mered teaches us not to trust each other too much. But I was there when Spenser told his rebels the time and place of their next meeting, so I'm safe for now. Stay out of this and I might stay that way."

Chapter 24

The Past

T he council arrived in the capital. Zaric was familiar with the noblemen, but the commoners elected by their countrymen were new to him. Yet he knew many people like them from his interactions with the people of his city. It wasn't difficult to treat the newcomers with the respect their new positions demanded.

Their first meeting went better than Zaric anticipated. None of Edric's former advisors had been chosen in the elections, so advising a king was new to them all. Zaric purposely created an agenda that would avoid any major changes or controversial topics. There was plenty of time for those later. Still, it wasn't easy for the nobility and commoners to find common ground, but seeds were planted. Plans were made to improve the affairs of the kingdom. Needs were addressed, concerns were raised, ideas for the next meeting were drafted. Although the new council didn't agree on everything, the excitement of this new venture made them all a little more willing to try.

Zaric and Althea announced their engagement. Zaric didn't want to put the wedding off any longer than they had to. Fortunately for him, Althea felt the same way. Within a month the ceremony was performed and Althea settled into life at the palace.

All the while, Zaric watched for Mered. The king's uncle attended the wedding celebration, but his son was nowhere to be found. In the brief moment when Zaric was able to ask about his cousin, he was told that Mered disappeared not long after the elections—following an argument with his father similar to the argument he had with Zaric—and no one in his region had seen him since. The only information they had was that he was seen traveling east.

Zaric thought about Alan as well. Both times he had seen him previously were at major celebrations. Zaric expected this celebration to be just the sort to draw the man out. Zaric had spoken to Althea about Alan's proposal. They discussed it for days, looking at the positive aspects as well as the negative ones. In the end, though, the decision they made was based more on the inklings they had than logic. The king was ready to give his answer.

But Alan did not come.

Months passed. Days came and went—days filled with common, everyday moments and official, administrative ones.

The feeling to journey out of the palace came on an ordinary day. Zaric awoke from a dream where he saw a familiar grassy hill in the middle of a forest, a day's journey from the capital. Unlike images in other dreams, this one didn't fade. He believed he needed to travel there. Althea agreed.

The hill was exactly as Zaric had seen it in his dream. The trees stood where he remembered them, every stone was laid out in the same place—even the color of the blue sky and shape of the white clouds were identical. Zaric dismounted his horse, secured it to a nearby tree, and climbed the hill as though he were entering a holy place. Once he reached the top, he waited.

The air was just the right mixture of cool and warm. Birds sang joyfully, glad to be past the winter's cold. Light green buds of leaves dotted the branches of the forest, which swayed in the slight breeze.

At the top of the hill, Zaric watched and listened, finding that his worries and anxieties slipped away on a draft.

As he watched, Alan stood before him, appearing in a spot that had been empty only a second before.

"I thought I would find you here," Zaric said, unsurprised.

"That's what I wanted you to think," Alan responded. "You received my message."

"The dream? Yes. My wife advised me to listen to it. I thought we would see you at the wedding."

"That day was not a day for business. But I did enjoy it."

Zaric's brow furrowed in confusion. "You were there?"

"A man doesn't have to be noticed in order to be somewhere. I didn't think you would mind. I love weddings."

"I don't mind, I only wish I had seen you."

"If you had, you would have wanted to talk about the proposal I made at our last meeting, while all I wanted to do was enjoy a wedding celebration. I wanted you and Althea to enjoy it, too. This is a much better setting for such a serious matter. Have you thought about my proposal?"

"Yes," Zaric responded quietly.

"Have you looked at it from every possible angle?"

"I believe so. I discussed it with Althea. We've been over it again and again. But there only seems to be one possible answer. You made the proposal for a good reason, even if we can't see exactly why yet. The only real option is to accept it."

Alan showed no reaction as he stared at Zaric. The king thought the man couldn't just hear the words he spoke, but every feeling behind those words, and every thought, every conversation that had gone into making this decision. After a minute or two, Alan nodded once.

"I have a question, though," Zaric inserted. "Can Althea be granted this gift as well?"

Alan stood like a statue, his face betraying no expression. Zaric wondered if he needed to repeat the question, but just as he opened his mouth, Alan replied, "It is not her path."

Zaric felt like his heart stopped. Then, it beat again harder than before. He had rehearsed that question in his mind for hours until he was sure he knew what the answer would be. He knew what he *wanted* it to be. With the passing time, he had convinced himself that Alan couldn't fail to see how important it would be for Zaric to have Althea by his side for the untold years, decades, or even centuries until his task was complete. Although Zaric hadn't gotten up the courage yet to ask Althea what she thought of the idea, he couldn't imagine that she would want anything else.

Now, the thought of living without Althea caused a heavy fear deep within Zaric. "I don't know if I could live so long alone," he said. Embarrassment tickled his mind once he had said it. The words—and the thoughts behind them—made him feel like less of a king, a man unworthy of the title he held.

"It isn't too late to change your mind," Alan told him, not moving an inch. "You are free to reject the proposal, if you so choose."

Zaric inhaled deeply and released the breath slowly, then shook his head. "No," he answered. "I have already made my decision. I will accept your proposal and everything that comes with it."

Again, Alan nodded. "Well, then, let's get started."

Chapter 25

The Present

Zaric entered the inn, his face half-concealed by the hood of his cloak. It was between mealtimes and hardly anyone sat in the dining room. Those who were there were men and women whom Zaric knew and trusted. He lowered his hood.

Lena looked up at him and smiled as she cleared plates from a table. The kitchen door swung open and Helen came through, carrying two cups of water. Sitting at the nearest table, Zaric waited for her to join him.

"Is everything ready?" Helen asked in a low voice as she took her seat, setting one of the cups in front of her king.

Zaric nodded. "I've hidden carts with provisions a few miles from the village," he said. "Hopefully we can reach them before anyone notices that so many people are gone. Do you have confidence in the plan, Helen?"

"I do," she replied. "It's more of a plan than I had when I left Veren. I have confidence in you. That's what matters the most."

With a shake of his head, Zaric cast his eyes over the others in the room. "We've only reached a fraction of the people in this village," he said after a brief pause. "I wish we had more time."

"Apart from standing in the village square and making a public

211

announcement, I'm not sure what else you could have done. That wouldn't have done us any good, anyway. Being captured by Bernt wouldn't save anyone."

Zaric inclined his head in agreement and acceptance. He took a long drink of water, draining the cup.

"I haven't accomplished what I wanted to, either," Helen said, sipping from her own cup. "I feel like I'm very close to finding the record I need, but not close enough. What if the person we're looking for stays behind in Phara, not choosing to come to Camelora? If we learn that after we get home, we won't be able to come back."

"I worry about that, too," Zaric admitted. "I wish I could have done more to help."

Another pause followed.

"I'm looking forward to seeing my father and Neil again," Helen admitted, staring forward as though she were looking across the distance separating her from the people she loved the most. "I've missed them."

"I believe you will see them within a couple of weeks," Zaric said, "if everything goes to plan. Tomorrow night will be here before you know it."

They spent the rest of the day in quiet preparation. Secret notes were taken from the inn to various supporters throughout the village. Short replies came back in return. Lena took care of the dining room in her usual way, as though nothing were different, while Connor stayed in their living quarters, making sure they had what they needed for the journey. He also spent time destroying papers he didn't want to be found after they were gone. He hid valuable items in a secret panel in the wall, hoping they would be able to return for them when everything was over—whenever that might be.

With so little time left, Helen was determined to devote every moment she could to finding the person they had come to Phara to protect. If she could find a record that went back further than five hundred years, she was certain she could find the clue she needed.

Venturing to the library was no longer safe. In the first few days after Bernt's arrival, Helen and Aurelie secretly made the trip to retrieve the books that looked the most promising, but those trips ended when patrols of soldiers were stationed on the block where the library was located. They didn't want to be caught with the books and questioned about what they were doing. Helen packed away some of the records while keeping others out to search until the time came to leave.

She had been over these records many times. They didn't tell her anything new. She contemplated risking another trip to the library to fetch more books, but she knew that Aurelie would insist on going with her. Attracting attention at this time would only put them both in danger and she didn't want to take that risk.

And, anyway, she didn't have time. The final day had come.

Late afternoon sunlight filtered through the curtains as Helen gathered up the papers scattered across the desk in Lena and Connor's study. These loose sheets had been stuffed between the pages of one of the books she and Aurelie had taken, hidden well enough that Helen believed they must be important. Although they were family records, they didn't go back far enough to tell Helen where the family started.

She leafed through the papers, thinking more than reading. She didn't *need* to read the names to know them. Some of these families had chosen to join Zaric on his journey back to Camelora. None of them showed any connection to the king or his son. She feared the prophecy was wrong and that Zaric's family had died out. Still, Helen also felt these papers held an answer of some kind.

As she turned the papers over, one toward the middle of the stack caught against the tip of her finger. It felt thicker than the rest. Puzzled, Helen held it up and shook it. It moved stiffly. Holding it with both hands, she examined the edge. The thickness was that of two sheets, not one. She placed the paper on the desk and flicked the corner a few times with her thumb. A second corner of paper came loose.

With a bit of gentle effort, Helen took each corner between a thumb and forefinger, peeling the sheets apart and freeing the bottom sheet from the top. Her heart jumped and she couldn't stop the smile that crossed her lips as she realized she hadn't gone over this record before.

A knock on the door pulled her out of the thrill of discovery. Not knowing who was outside, she put the sheet of paper on top of the stack, then covered it with a book.

There was another knock as Helen crossed the room and threw open the door. Relief washed over her when she saw Zaric standing on the other side.

"We need to get ready," he said just above a whisper. "We leave in a few hours."

"I was just doing some last-minute research," Helen explained.

"Have you found anything new?" Zaric asked, his eyes brightening.

"I found a piece of paper I missed before. It's probably nothing, but if I can have a few minutes, I would like to be sure."

"If you don't mind watching Aurelie while Lena helps me, you can have all the time you need until we leave. Put her to work and I'm sure she won't be any trouble."

"Yes, of course," Helen agreed.

A few minutes later, Aurelie was sitting on the floor of the room, looking through a book for the tenth time. The sun had set. Helen lit the lamp on the desk and crossed the room to the window, pulling the heavy curtain closed, blocking the light from pouring into the street. Too much light attracted too much attention. She sat at the desk with the paper in front of her.

The handwriting at the top of the page was old—much older than on the other records she had seen. The lettering was old-fashioned, too. It was hard to make out exactly what was written, especially since the ink had faded over the years. Not even Neil's grandfather's writing was this hard to decipher. As her eyes moved down the page, though, Helen noticed that the handwriting changed. It looked as though a handful of people had written this record over the years. Yet the ink was no more readable at the bottom than the top—likely the result of being stuck to the page that had been pressed over it. Helen wished she had more light to read by. Each word took too long to make out.

She sighed, feeling like she was making no progress, tempted to fold up the paper and wait until they were away from Phara and in the daylight.

But a word caught her eye. She peered more closely and made out the name "Edric." The name of Zaric's father and son.

Her heart thumped in her chest. Smoothing the paper out on the desk beneath the light of the lamp, Helen read the title across the top of the sheet: "The Family of Edric." Below this line were written Edric's name and the name of his wife. Their children were listed next, with the names of their children. Helen didn't see Zaric's name. This must have been his son and grandchildren. Reaching the bottom of the paper, Helen realized the genealogy didn't end with this sheet. As though the pieces clicked into place, she now understood the importance of the other papers she had studied.

She pulled the stack of loose pages toward her and studied them one by one, looking for the continuation of this list. Page after page, generation after generation. Looking at it now, she wished she had read it before instead of only skimming it.

Still, Helen laughed, unable to contain her excitement. "What is it?" Aurelie asked, setting her book on the floor and rushing over to the desk, where Helen laid out the sheets of paper.

"I think I found what we've been looking for," Helen replied.

Aurelie jumped up and down, her hands clasped together as she squealed in delight.

Each family line was listed with the births, marriages, and deaths of its individual members. The recordkeepers had tried to keep some order throughout the years, but it was difficult with so many different people recording the events of Edric's—and Zaric's—many descendants, the lines of the family growing and growing with each successive generation. Helen struggled to follow the lines that had been written down.

Some members had moved away from Phara and what happened to them became lost. Of those who stayed, many of the lines died out, leaving no living descendants. The growing family started to shrink. From what Helen could tell, maybe only half-a-dozen of those who remained in Phara were still alive.

There were still a couple of pages left to examine when a knock came to the door. As she had done before, Helen gathered up the papers, but this time she rolled them into a tight scroll and tied a bit of string around it before putting it in her pocket.

"It's time," Zaric said.

Helen nodded and went to the corner, where her bag sat, ready to go. She slung the bag across her body and blew out the lamp on the desk. Aurelie looked up at her, the color sapped from her face, her smile disappearing, and her lips pressed tightly together. Helen did her best to smile in reassurance. She knew what it felt like to leave her home, not knowing when or if she would return. Putting her hands on Aurelie's shoulders, she pushed the girl forward and out of the room.

Those who chose to follow Zaric had been quietly slipping out of the town throughout the day in groups small enough not to attract attention, at various exit points along the border of Phara. Connor was one of the first to leave, making his way to the meeting place a few miles away to organize the people once they arrived there. Zaric accompanied some elderly supporters, while Lena agreed to take three children of a widowed mother of six . Not wanting to make any of these groups any larger, Helen agreed to take Aurelie.

As they made their way through the village, Aurelie was unusually subdued. Helen knew that her mother had instructed her to stay quiet while she was with Helen, but her normally excited manner was depressed. In every action, she held back. She said nothing as they hid in the shadows and hesitated to emerge when their way cleared. Helen knew that Aurelie was like any other child—talkative and playful at times, quiet and studious at others—but she had never shown any signs of this fear before. She had been excited at the thought of leaving Phara and seeing the world beyond. Something in her manner made Helen uneasy herself, as though a different little girl stood beside her.

"You don't need to worry," Helen risked whispering as they stood with their backs pressed against the wall of a narrow alley, waiting for two guards to pass at a corner a block away. "I'll do everything I can to keep you safe."

Aurelie nodded, but her mouth stayed shut and her expression didn't change.

"Is something the matter?" Helen asked, eager to ease the girl's mind.

The girl was reluctant to answer, but Helen waited through the silence. Taking a deep breath, Aurelie asked, "Why did Zaric come to Phara? He could have gone anywhere."

"Why do you ask that?"

"I'm just wondering," Aurelie shrugged.

"Do you think that Bernt and his battalion would have stayed away if Zaric had gone somewhere else?"

After another moment of hesitation, Aurelie nodded. "We're not going to make it," she whispered, almost as though she were talking to herself.

Helen took a deep breath and knelt on the cobbled ground, making sure she stayed as close to the wall as possible. She didn't want to tower over Aurelie while she spoke to her. "I don't believe I've ever told you what started me on this journey. I thought it would be too scary for you, because it was scary for me and I'm so much older. You've heard us talk about Mered. Well, one day, his soldiers came into my city—where I lived with my mother and father. Zaric hadn't been seen in hundreds of years, so it wasn't because he was there. He was actually hundreds of miles away. My father refused to help Mered and that made Mered angry. The men occupied Veren just like they're occupying Phara. Every day my mother became more and more worried until, finally, she sent me away to find Zaric. She knew that Zaric's presence would help us, not hurt us.

"You see, Aurelie, Zaric's goal—his purpose—is to protect the people from Mered. That's all he wants. So far—as far as we know, at least—Bernt doesn't know for sure that Zaric is in Phara. He came, anyway. When Mered wants something, he doesn't care who he hurts to get it. That's why Zaric came to Phara. He knows Mered and he knew Mered would come here. There are important people here who need to be protected before Mered can find them and hurt them."

"But I'm so afraid that Zaric's plan won't work," Aurelie said, echoing her previous statement, tears filling her lower eyelids like puddles.

"What makes you say that?"

"I had a dream last night. Two armies facing each other outside of Phara."

"You've heard the stories about the war that was fought here hundreds of years ago," Helen replied, hoping the reminder would explain the dream.

Aurelie shook her head. "My father was standing next to Zaric. The battle hasn't happened yet."

Helen stared at Aurelie, an idea sparking in her mind. In that moment, the last piece fell into place and the truth hummed.

Zaric's heir.

The sound of a rock skidding along the cobbles brought Helen's mind back to the present and made her stand up straight again. They both pressed themselves against the wall and waited.

A guard on the main road passed the alleyway. When he had walked a few feet beyond it, he stopped, turning to face the street. Helen held her breath, hoping he would turn again and continue on his way, but moment after moment passed with the guard casting his eyes around the area, taking in every detail. She couldn't help feeling like he was guarding their position.

Her heart beat faster and faster, her anxiety growing. Instinctively, she held out her arm to cover Aurelie. Plans started to form in Helen's mind for overpowering the guard before more guards came. She shook the thoughts out of her head. They didn't want to bring attention to themselves. Doing so might endanger others who weren't far enough away from Phara. The shadow of the alley was deep enough to cover both Helen and Aurelie. She tried to convince herself that the guard's actions were only routine, but she couldn't shake her nervousness.

Looking down the alley in the opposite direction, she saw that the shadows thickened farther down. With a slight wave of her hand, she indicated to Aurelie that they were going to move that way. Pushing the girl forward, they slid along the wall, stepping carefully to avoid making any sound.

When they reached the end, Helen craned her neck to investigate the small street separating the town's buildings from its wooden exterior wall. The road was empty. Because Zaric valued good contingency plans, Helen knew that there was a spy gap not far away, leading out of the village. She grabbed Aurelie's hand and took a deep breath.

Leading the way, Helen ran for the gap.

They slid easily through the space between the boards. Standing close to the outside of the wall, they studied the path ahead of them. The land around was empty. Beyond the wall were a few yards of sloped grassland leading to the forest, where Helen was confident the trees would hide them as they made their way to the rendezvous point. Not letting go of Aurelie's hand, she ran again.

The appearance of half-a-dozen men, stepping out of the trees, brought them to an abrupt halt. Helen turned and saw another handful coming toward them from the gap in the wall. She saw the same scene to their left and right, forming a box around them that they couldn't escape.

Helen thought back to the day she and Zaric managed to evade from Bernt. She also remembered the pull of the water when she landed where she didn't intend to. Zaric hadn't had the time to teach her anything else, and she lacked the confidence to try to disappear with Aurelie in tow.

Like a mother bird, she wrapped her arms around Aurelie, protecting the girl as much as she could as the men closed in.

Chapter 26

The guards pushed Helen to the hard stone floor. The rope binding her hands behind her back bit into her skin. But she worried more about the pain Aurelie felt. A few feet away, the girl knelt in the same position, tears streaming from her eyes as she tried to suppress her sobs.

"Please," Helen pleaded, "she's just a child."

Something hard hit the side of her head and the sting of the pain engulfed her. For a few moments, her vision spun. As the shock of the pain subsided into a dull throb, Helen tried to think of a way out of this place. Guards surrounded them, most of them holding swords, staffs, and other weapons. One guard stood not far away, holding the straps of Helen's and Aurelie's bags in his large fist.

"Well, well, well," a casual voice said. The guards parted, moving aside to let the man through. Helen looked up and tried to focus her eyes as the man crouched down. Bernt. "It's Helen," he went on, "Zaric's pet. I had a feeling Zaric was here."

"Zaric isn't with me," Helen said through her teeth.

"Not *here*, no. But I have a feeling he's nearby. Probably wondering where you are. Now that I have you, I think it will be a lot easier to bring him out, too."

"You overestimate my importance."

"Helen," he chuckled, "you seem to think we haven't heard the stories. What sort of man would Mered be if he didn't study his opponents? We know just how valuable you are. And if I doubted that Zaric would come out of hiding for *you*, we have the little girl. Zaric isn't going to sacrifice a little girl."

Aurelie turned her pale face to Helen, her frightened red eyes spilling tears. Helen tried to reassure the girl with a smile. Another blow hit the side of her head.

"Don't break her!" Bernt exclaimed with annoyance. "Zaric won't come back for her if she's dead."

He crouched down, holding Helen's swaying head between his hands to direct her eyes toward him. "You can make this easier," Bernt went on, "by telling me what Zaric is planning. Where is he, Helen?"

Returning Bernt's glare, Helen pressed her lips shut.

He stood again, towering over her. When he spoke again, his words were cold. "Surely whatever it is isn't worth your life. Where is he? What is he planning?"

He paused.

Silence.

"Is he going to attack the city? Is he fleeing?"

When Helen still didn't respond, Bernt only thinly tried to contain his frustration. "It's all right, though. There are other ways to bring Zaric out. You are an enemy of Mered's kingdom. That alone is enough to warrant a death sentence. We will spread the word that you and the girl are to be executed— No," he cut himself off, thinking. "No, not that."

Bernt waved a guard over, then lowered his voice conspiratorially. "Start a rumor," he instructed. "Have the guards throughout the city drop a hint that Zaric and his followers plan to burn the city to the ground. If we haven't captured Zaric in three days' time, that is *exactly* what we will do. The prisoners will die and the remaining people in Phara will lose all trust in Zaric—if they ever had any. No one will doubt Mered after that."

"Zaric has more important things to worry about than us," Helen stated, trying to sound calmer than she felt. Her heart threatened to beat out of her chest.

"That may be so, but Mered told me all about Zaric. His weakness is that he can't bear to leave his friends behind. And I know about you, too, Helen. I've read the stories.

"Guards," he shouted, "take our prisoners to the dungeon. Then, send out a decree that we have captured two enemies of the state trying to flee Phara—no doubt in an effort to undermine Mered. That should bring Zaric out."

As the men stepped forward, Bernt held up a hand to stop them, a visible thought running across his cold face. He approached one of the guards and took the man's staff. Walking back to Helen, he raised the weapon and heavily struck it against the side of her head. As she fell to the ground, the room went black.

* * *

When she regained consciousness, Helen found herself in a cool, dark room. Aurelie's anxious face filled her vision. Helen felt the girl's small hands cradling her head.

"Are you all right?" Aurelie asked.

"I think so," Helen responded, her voice weak. "My head is throbbing. Did they hurt you?"

Aurelie shook her head.

Helen tried to raise herself up, but her head felt heavy, like her skull was full of rocks. From what she could tell, they were in the dungeon. Stones made up the floor and walls, while a wall of bars cut

223

the room into two. Five other people sat or laid on the floor of the large cell—four men and one woman.

With Aurelie's help, Helen managed to crawl to the wall and lean against it. In a far corner of the room, she saw where the guards had tossed her and Aurelie's bags . At least they hadn't taken their cloaks. This would give them something to use as a pillow or cushion.

As Helen took in their surroundings, she caught the eye of one of the men who shared the cell. He smiled. She returned the gesture and the man looked away. The other people seemed too worn down and weak to care about the newcomers.

After a few minutes had gone by, Aurelie laid her head on Helen's lap. Helen set her hand on the girl's arm and felt her shiver. Pulling the cloak off herself, Helen draped it over Aurelie like a blanket. The young girl relaxed. Helen stroked her hair, trying to comfort her in some small way.

"Don't worry," she whispered, hoping she sounded tranquil. "Zaric will find a way to help us. He always does."

* * *

Zaric and the refugees waited at the rendezvous point, deep in the forest surrounding Phara. Minutes passed, then an hour, without any sign of Helen and Aurelie. Zaric knew what the news would be before it was relayed to him: they had been captured. It took no time for his plans to change. He wouldn't leave them behind.

Light spread on the horizon as the refugees reached a nearby hidden dale. Like an ocean wave, they descended its slopes, Zaric leading the way. A grassy mound rose up near the dale's center.

"Will we make camp here?" Connor asked when they reached the valley floor. His voice shook almost as much as his hands, which were doing their best to support his pale and shocked wife. Their fear for their daughter was palpable.

"No, not quite," Zaric answered. He motioned for the rest of the group to stop, then went on alone, skirting the mound and walking toward its eastern side. Excitement and sadness mingled in his chest as he tried to anticipate what he would see. It had been so long since he was last here.

As he approached, more and more stones appeared, scattered around the base of the mound, rising up among the long grass. A broken and collapsing stone doorway gradually came into view. Zaric paused to light a candle. Bending down, he passed through the doorway into the darkness.

The light of the candle tried to fill the large chamber beyond the doorway, feebly catching the outlines of large stones lining the chamber to form walls, dotted with small cavities filled with smaller rocks. Occasional patches of grass grew through the cracks. In the center of the chamber stood a single stone tomb, the effigy of a crowned woman adorning its lid. Tears filled his eyes as Zaric walked forward with reverence.

"Althea," he said, barely above a whisper, placing his hand on the figure's chiseled stone cheek. In his mind, Althea's face appeared before Zaric's eyes, the colors and details exactly as he had once known them, replacing the face of stone. A smile spread across her face as she looked up at her husband.

"Zaric," Connor's voice echoed around the chamber, breaking into the memory.

"We can camp in here," Zaric said in reply, blinking away his tears as he pulled his hand away from the chiseled face. "It will be tight, but I believe we'll be safe. We'll post guards in the woods to watch for any patrols Bernt might send out."

Connor nodded and went back out again. Zaric cast another glance over Althea's stone face, then straightened his back as he swallowed back his emotion.

Chapter 27

N eil wasn't surprised when Garrick agreed with Siri's idea of infiltrating Spenser's group of rebels. The governor didn't really have a choice. Siri had inserted herself into the situation without consulting anyone and it would look suspicious now if she backed out. And Neil had to admit, it was a good idea.

She still insisted on keeping the council out of the mission. She felt, and Neil agreed, that the group in the warehouse didn't represent all the members of Spenser's band. Others could have met separately and Spenser spoke of continuing his recruitment. The next challenge, Siri felt, was to figure out how this recruitment was being carried out.

As much as Neil still wanted to keep an eye on her, he knew there wasn't time to follow Siri all day while trying to figure out why someone was stealing weapons from the armory. The armory was open to everyone in Camelora, so there was no reason why anyone should feel the need to hoard weapons. The city's blacksmiths added to the collection regularly, growing Camelora's supply in preparation for the anticipated war.

None of the weapons were special, either. They were all standard swords and standard bows and standard shields, with no distinctive embellishments to cause envy amongst those called up to fight. There was no reason for anyone to believe any of the weapons had more power than others, aside from their level of craftsmanship.

The events of the past couple of weeks had distracted Neil from his previous assignment of searching for a way to overcome Mered's dark powers and defeat the pretender once and for all. Garrick still wanted to keep this research secret. He recognized, too, that Neil couldn't watch Siri and research the thefts at the same time. They had to let someone else in.

Considering the members of the council, they settled upon Genevieve. She and Garrick had been children together and he knew her better than anyone else in Camelora, his wife excepted. Stressing the importance of secrecy, she was assigned to work with and watch over Siri.

As Siri and Genevieve went out into the city to learn all they could about Spenser's plan, Neil went back to the palace library. Perhaps the answers to his two questions could be found there, in its books and scrolls.

Setting himself up at a table near the door, Neil pulled some books of history from the shelves, thumbing through their familiar stories and less-familiar legends. He read about the settlement of the city of Camelora, not long after the fall of the kingdom. It was possible whatever Zaric had done to rid the kingdom of Mered back then was recorded in these books.

Neil scanned the neat handwriting on the pages . He read more thoroughly when he found any mention of Mered's name. Sparse details of Mered's younger years jumped out—his relationship with Zaric, his bid for a position in the king's government, the assembling of his army and recruitment of allies as he tried to take over the throne. None of them spoke in any great detail. The chroniclers who, by their brief autobiographical sketches, had been born in the new city wrote little about the past, focusing instead on the threat Mered posed in the future. It wasn't an attempt to hide the history of the old kingdom, but simply a general lack of knowledge about it.

One thing was clear: Zaric had been the one to defeat Mered. Whatever information existed on the subject would likely be found in the king's study.

While Neil was putting the books back on their shelves, a young man walked into the room. Neil immediately recognized the young Cameloran from Spenser's small gang, having only seen him the day before. Neil remembered how the young man had started to speak about something in the warehouse—some part of Spenser's plan—but was cut off. Something about an additional assignment.

Standing still, Neil watched around the edge of the bookcase as the young man filled a table with books, then settled down to look through them.

Neil was better able to study the young man in this setting. He realized he had been right when he guessed the boy wasn't much younger than himself. His gaunt and lanky figure hadn't filled out, accentuating the height he only recently gained. Bright reddish-orange hair covered his head in an unruly crop. Freckles covered his face. Neil was sure he had seen the young man before with his family, but he couldn't recall the family name or the names of the boy's parents. They were of the population of Camelorans who commonly escaped notice.

Once he was sure the young man was at ease, Neil approached him. "The governor has you doing research, too," Neil stated, startling the young man.

"Y-yeah," he stammered, snapping his book shut in his nervousness.

"What's your name?" was Neil's next question.

"Rufus," the young man said, looking like he regretted his ready answer as soon as the name escaped his mouth.

"Glad to meet you, Rufus," Neil went on, holding his hand out .

Rufus's grip was reluctant, but he shook the offered hand. "What does Garrick have you looking for?"

"Garrick the governor?" Rufus asked uncertainly.

"Yes, that one," Neil nodded.

When Rufus hesitated to answer the question, Neil snatched up one of the books in front of him, ignoring the stifled protest as he flipped through its pages. "Weapons?" he asked.

"Um, yes," Rufus answered. "I work with a blacksmith and the governor wants us to make stronger weapons."

The thoughts webbing through Neil's mind wove into place. The stolen weapons and the solution to defeating Mered: he now believed he and Rufus were looking for the same object.

"How long have you been an apprentice?" Neil went on.

"A year or two," Rufus hesitated, unable to hide the uncertainty in his answer.

"Yes, you do look about that age. Have you done any training with the armorer yet?"

"I've never been near the armory." Rufus offered the statement too readily. The pieces clicked into place in Neil's mind, but he hoped Rufus was too flustered to notice.

"These old men," Neil sighed, dropping the book back on the table. "Nothing's ever good enough for them. He has me researching old plans of the city because he believes the rumors about a secret exit in the outer walls. I'm sure I'm not going to find anything. I doubt you'll find any method for making weapons that's any better than what you're already doing."

"You're probably right," Rufus replied with a nervous chuckle.

"Good luck with your weapons," Neil called over his shoulder , walking out of the library.

Neil didn't stick around to see what Rufus did next. Zaric's study held a number of books about weapons and Neil didn't want to waste any more time before starting his more focused search.

Chapter 28

The Past

The growing plants looked beautiful in their regularity, reaching out in straight lines and standing a foot out of the ground. Zaric crouched down and pulled up a weed, knocking the dirt from its roots. He looked a few feet behind himself and smiled at the sight of his ten-year-old son, Edric, doing the same.

"Do all princes do this work?" Edric asked, tossing the weed into the sack that hung at his hip.

"The princes of Camelora do," Zaric answered.

"Did your father make you?"

"I *chose* to," the king corrected gently. "Do you feel forced to work in the fields?"

Edric shrugged, pulling up another weed. "Sometimes."

Zaric studied the young boy's face, noticing his slight frown and the crease of his forehead. Edric had never complained about the field work before and Zaric sensed his irritation at this moment had very little to do with their task.

"Is something troubling you, Edric?" the father asked.

"I haven't seen Mother all day," the boy moped.

"She has a headache."

"She *always* has a headache."

The worry Edric felt for Althea drifted through the space between father and son, entering Zaric's heart. It had been like this ever since Alan had given Zaric his gift—he often felt what others were feeling.

That wasn't the only reason Zaric understood his son's emotions, though. It was at about Edric's age that Zaric lost his own mother. He had never thought such a thing was possible until it was too late. A sudden illness took her from her husband and son, giving them very little time to say goodbye.

But Zaric knew what caused Althea's headaches. He knew it wasn't likely to be fatal. Camelora was changing. Whispered threats drew closer and closer to the kingdom, despite all the good the King's Council had been able to do in the past thirteen years. Rumors circulated that Mered had been seen at the southern edge of the kingdom. Zaric wanted to believe that his cousin had set their differences behind him, but Mered failed to appear at the palace. Without a conversation to prove to Zaric that their relationship could return to what it once had been, he was forced to imagine the worst.

The rumors coupled with Althea's visions of war and bloodshed told Zaric the truth he didn't want to acknowledge.

Zaric did his best to enjoy every moment with his son, especially on those days when Althea was unable to leave their bed. He didn't only make Edric work. They made up games to play, Zaric allowed Edric to join him in meetings, and he found moments to teach him the history of Camelora and their family. Evander visited the capital as often as he could, too, occupying his grandson while the king saw to government business.

But nothing could compare with the relationship Edric had with Althea. As they left the field, bags full of weeds to be disposed of, Edric ran ahead. Zaric didn't even try to call him back. He knew where he would find the boy.

Once Zaric completed his tasks, he made his way to the residential wing of the palace. Edric was right where he thought he would be, sitting next to the bed where his mother lay, listening to the story her son enthusiastically told her. For a minute, Zaric watched the two of them, not wanting to interrupt the moment while taking in the scene of love between mother and son. Edric was the only one of their five children to live more than a day and both parents cherished the time they had with him.

The scene in the room also tightened Zaric's resolve to protect his kingdom from the threats the queen sensed. Although Alan's warnings shot through his mind, telling him the threat might not be eradicated for decades or centuries to come, Zaric was determined to stop any war as quickly as he could. He trained soldiers, despite the complaints from the Council that so many soldiers were not needed in times of peace. He instructed the blacksmiths to forge shields and weapons. And he had fortresses constructed at strategic places throughout the kingdom, places of refuge no matter where a battle might find them.

As he readjusted his focus on his wife and son, he relegated these thoughts to the back of his mind. For now, he had done all he could and he wanted to enjoy time with his family. He didn't know how much more time like this they had left.

Chapter 29

The Present

The Pharan people filled the cavern, huddled together in families. Some people slept, some talked in hushed tones, and some simply sat staring, the fear of what might happen next written across their faces. Despite the warm summer weather outside, the stones and earth made the air in the cavern cool. Zaric placed two guards at the entrance while armed men patrolled the forest surrounding the dale.

A commotion drew Zaric's eyes to the entrance of the mound. Confusion etched on his face, Zaric stepped closer to the opening, trying to hear what was going on. Soon, two guards burst into the chamber. Zaric moved faster, eager to hear their news.

"The information we had was right," the first guard stated, panting from his run through the forest. "Helen and Aurelie are being held in the dungeon below the Government House. That's not all, though. The people in Phara are saying that you and your followers plan to burn the village to the ground."

"Bernt is trying to discredit me," Zaric stated.

"Is Aurelie all right?"

The question came from over Zaric's shoulder and he turned to see Lena. He hadn't noticed her and Connor walk up behind him. The mother's strength amidst her fear was evident despite her husband's comforting arm encircling her. But the courage she had shown since entering the mound was beginning to crack and worry showed through. Connor looked like he needed support just as much as Lena did.

"Have they hurt our daughter?" Lena went on.

"There is no reason to believe they have," Zaric assured her, placing a hand on her arm. "They're trying to bring me out. They don't really want Helen and Aurelie and we will do everything we can to get them back."

"You can't give yourself up!" Connor exclaimed.

"Not without a plan, no."

Zaric glanced over his shoulder. His eyes rested on the stone casket in the middle of the room, his mind filled with Althea. He missed her and her wisdom—a wisdom he needed in this moment.

He thanked the guards, then stepped out of the mound. He needed the space to be alone and think.

* * *

The floor of the cell was hard and cold—impossible to sleep on. Their cloaks could act as either pillows or blankets, but not both. Helen let Aurelie rest her head on her lap when the girl needed to sleep. The others in the cell placed their heads on each other's shoulders, getting what rest they could. Sitting against the wall, Helen stroked Aurelie's hair as a mother would, leaning her own head against the stone and closing her eyes.

Though she didn't remember opening her eyes again, Helen found herself surrounded by trees. She couldn't understand where she was. A shadowed form stood in front of her, more the suggestion of a figure than an actual person. Helen tried to focus on the form, but she couldn't make out who it was.

"Aurelie?" she asked, though she knew that it wasn't the girl. Hazy panic pressed on her mind as she wondered where Aurelie had gone. Frantically, she spun around, searching, but the girl was nowhere to be seen.

The shadow appeared in front of her again, flickering as though the person were trying to materialize. "This is sleep, Helen," she heard in Zaric's voice. "Aurelie is still with you."

The face of the king flashed on the form, but it didn't stay. Helen closed her eyes and shook her head in frustration, hoping the action would fix her focus on the shadow. When she looked again, Zaric stood before her, translucent as a ghost and not fully formed. Only his head and torso were solid. The rest of his body faded away into nothing.

"What's happening?" Helen asked. "Are you real?"

"In a manner. I have no other way to get a message to you. Not without it being intercepted or putting someone else in danger, anyway. I know you've been captured and what Bernt plans to do, but don't worry. We're coming up with a plan."

"You can't come for us. It's just a trick to get you to come back."

"I know that. Mered would do the same thing if he were here. But that doesn't change who I am or what I need to do. I won't leave the two of you behind."

"Maybe I can figure something out. You're too important to lose, Zaric."

"Helen," Zaric replied, his form drifting forward as though he took a few steps toward her, "I need you to realize that you're important, too. And I intend for you to help us. Remember what I taught you. Remember what you've done before. You have a gift. Use—"

A banging on the cell's bars jolted Helen out of sleep. She wanted to scream, a different panic gripping her now as she wondered what

Zaric was about to say. Her heart beat hard against her ribs.

"Food," the guard said as he tossed some hard rolls through the bars. The prisoners scrambled to the stale bread, eager to have what little sustenance they could. Helen shook Aurelie, who had already raised her head, her eyes still glazed with sleep. One of the other prisoners handed them a roll to share.

As she chewed slowly, trying to make the meager meal last longer, Helen turned Zaric's words over and over in her mind. How was he planning to come for them and how was it going to work? How did he intend for her to help? What could she do?

Her memory brought up the evening by the campfire, when Zaric tried to teach her to harness the power surrounding her. She tried to remember his words, reconstructing his teachings until her head ached. She was too weak to focus on the memories for long. Silently she prayed that another opportunity would come for her to speak with Zaric, that he would tell her exactly what to do.

* * *

Zaric sat at the entrance of the mound as the rising sun tried to break through the grey clouds lingering on the horizon. He felt Connor and Lena approaching before he saw them.

"Helen and Aurelie are still alive," he stated, a reassuring smile on his lips.

"You know that how?" Lena asked, more out of disbelief than doubt.

"It's hard to explain and I'm not sure you would understand. But I fully intend to go back for them."

"How will we do that?" Connor asked.

"We speak to the people and make a plan. I want input from anyone willing to give it. We also need everyone's support."

Lena's face showed just how doubtful she was, but Connor put a reassuring hand on her arm.

"It seems unfair to ask the people to risk themselves to save our daughter," he stated. "But if you believe they will, and if you will lead us, I trust you to do it."

Zaric, Connor, and Lena returned to the cavern, finding the people preparing for the new day. A restless buzz hung in the air. From the doorway, the sight of these supporters peeled back hundreds of years of Zaric's own waiting for some event to change his routine days. His mind flooded with images of life before his exile, when the kingdom looked to him for guidance and the weight of their expectations made Zaric feel inadequate. How he saw himself had rarely aligned with what was required. Now, he was invigorated in a way he didn't often feel. Though he felt inadequate still, he was grateful that the time had come to reunite the kingdom, to solve what he couldn't solve before—to move forward with his long life.

"If I can have your attention, please," he said, his voice echoing around the room. His voice was the voice of a king, carried through the burial chamber to every person in the room. The chorus of voices stopped. The people turned toward him, curiosity, eagerness, and relief etched on their faces. Parents held their children or stood behind them, placing hands on their shoulders as the children fidgeted in their natural way. The men and women stood unmoving in their anticipation.

"Not everyone made it out of the city safely," Zaric began. "I'm sure most of you have heard that by now. I know we had planned to move on by this point, but my companion, Helen—a woman who has helped all of us—was captured as she tried to leave with Aurelie, Lena and Connor's daughter. I'm sure you all know her, too. I have no intention of leaving them behind. That isn't in my nature. But I also have no intention of losing anyone in rescuing them. So, I would like your help in making a plan. It is only a matter of time before Bernt threatens their lives. If we leave without them, or make any move to, I'm certain he will kill them. I know that their capture is a ploy to convince me to trade myself for them, but I think knowing that gives us an advantage. We don't have to do what he's expecting. I want to put it to you—you who know Phara so well—to suggest how we accomplish this impossible task."

An array of expressions looked back at Zaric at this statement: confusion, disbelief, hope, doubt. Children continued to squirm, neighbors whispered to each other.

"When you came to Phara," Connor said, "you told us how you used yourself as a distraction to free Helen's father. Could you do that again?"

"It *is* possible, but Mered wasn't expecting me to be there and was ill-prepared to deal with my presence. Bernt could be prepared to stop me from doing the same thing here. After all, I'm sure he knows what I did to save Cyrus."

"What if we draw Bernt and his men out of the city?" one of the guards said from the entrance, turning to face the cavern.

"Our group is small," a woman shouted from the back of the chamber. "How could we be threatening enough to get them to leave the safety of the city walls?"

"You can help us, Zaric, can't you?" another man questioned. "The legends say that you have great powers."

"Yes, I can, but you must know that I can't use any power without using physical strength. The greater the task, the more energy it uses. I will do what I can—if that's what you all wish—but we must face the fact that it may not be enough."

Silence draped the space as the people thought.

"You know, Zaric," an old man said, stepping forward through the crowd, "you came to Phara when we didn't know we needed you. Mered sent men to our village years ago and enticed away many of our family and friends, despite the fact that some of us knew the stories about our forgotten king. It was *their* choice, I'll admit that. But we didn't do much to stop them. We didn't connect our reality with the legend.

"Now, Mered has sent men to occupy our village, giving us very little choice in the matter. We didn't stand up to them. Our governor abandoned us. He's safe in his walled compound with his own flatterers and doesn't think anything about the people he left behind. You came and gave us the option to escape. You and Helen. But escape isn't enough now. We didn't fight when Bernt took over our village. It's time to fix that."

The room was silent as the men and women took in what the man said. Even the shifting of pebbles on the walls could be heard. A baby fussed and its mother shushed. Sharp and brief whispers rose and fell.

"Our friend Fidelis is right," Connor said, breaking the silence. "This is our village, not Zaric's. We can't expect him to fix everything for us. So far, most of our proposed plans have been about what *Zaric* can do, but *we* are the ones who let the occupation happen without a fight. Before we move on to Camelora, we need to show Bernt that we aren't going to give in easily. Let's give him a taste of what is to come—something he can tell Mered. Phara is ours to come back to when this war has been won."

"Helen and Aurelie aren't the only ones left behind," Fidelis continued. "Not everyone had the chance to choose to follow Zaric. Do we all agree that we go back for our own, no matter what happens to us?"

A few voices broke out in assent, then more, then many, until the whole room reverberated with shouts of approval.

"If this is really what you want," Zaric said, "I will help you in any way I can. If you Pharans don't mind accepting outside help, I will send a small group of guards to go out and see if they can find anyone—another village, a traveling group—who is willing to increase our numbers."

"If no one can be found," Connor said, "our numbers aren't great enough for us to fight Bernt head-on. What can we do then?"

"If you don't mind humoring an old man," Fidelis said with a sly smile, "I think I have an idea."

Chapter 30

The Present

Most of the palace's occupants were asleep when Neil emerged from Zaric's study. It had been a long day and he felt no closer to finding what he was looking for. As he carried his candle past the reception room, he noticed the door was ajar and light was coming from inside. It was uncommon to see light in there at night, especially when the people rarely went in during the day. He approached the door with caution, not even trying to guess what he would find .

The light came from one of the tables near the windows. A woman sat with her back to the door, slouched in her chair. Her hair was coming out of the clip that held it in place, but she didn't seem to care. She stared out the window, her eyes fixed on the darkness. It took a moment for Neil to recognize the posture as Siri's, but less time to realize how exhausted she appeared.

Hanging on the doorstep, Neil had a choice to make. He could go in and approach Siri, finding out why she was in the castle so late at night—when she should be at Garrick's home, under the governor's watch. Or he could ignore her and go to his own room, leaving her alone with her thoughts.

He asked himself what Helen would do. Not the Helen who had

been poisoned by Siri, but the Helen who had heard her stories and seen her determination to help Neil and Garrick find the traitors in their midst.

Neil stepped into the room. He didn't try to lighten his steps or disguise his presence, yet he still managed to startle Siri when he came up beside her. She jumped in her chair, looked up to see who was there, then nervously giggled as she covered her face.

"What are you doing here so late?" Neil asked, sitting across from her.

"Thinking," she responded. "A little too deeply, too, it seems. What time is it?"

"Late. I would have thought you had gone home with Garrick."

"He left a long time ago. I wanted to stay here, ponder over some things."

Siri allowed her gaze to shift back to the window. It was dark outside and almost impossible to see anything through the glass, especially with the glare from the candle reflecting on it. Neil knew there was nothing out there for her to watch and didn't try to do the same. Instead, he watched Siri, trying to read her closed face.

"Is there something wrong?" he finally questioned, reading nothing in her expression aside from a frown. "Something with the rebels?"

"Apart from the fact they exist? No, nothing like that. I'm worried about me."

"You chose to do this—"

"No, no," Siri cut him off. "I'm not worried about my safety. Not my *physical* safety, anyway. I'm worried about what I chose to do when I decided to infiltrate the rebel group. I wanted to prove to you that I could help you—you and Garrick—but it's a dangerous position to place myself in. I was part of Mered's world for so long, what if I slip back into it?"

Neil didn't know how to answer this question, or even if Siri expected him to. His thoughts went to the young man he had been only a few months before. The stories he had grown up hearing had become meaningless to him. True, he had never imagined the stories were about him. It didn't really matter to him who fulfilled the stories, or even if *anyone* did. Once he had chosen to believe, though, he knew he could never turn back. The fear Siri faced had never crossed his own mind.

"Do you feel you want to go back?" he questioned, uneasy about the possible answer to the question.

"No," Siri scoffed, brushing the idea aside. "I want to take Mered down."

"They can't really sway you if you don't want to be swayed," Neil stated. It seemed only logical to him.

He expected Siri to look relieved, to praise him for his wisdom, to thank him. But her concerned expression persisted. The tension and worry remained. Looking Neil in the eye, she simply stated, "I hope you're right."

* * *

After the flood of refugees Camelora saw in the beginning, the flow slowed to a trickle. Fewer and fewer guards were needed to meet them. Groups of hundreds became groups of dozens. Looking out over the camp outside the city walls, at the gathered thousands, Neil thought that he should be happy with the support they had, but he couldn't help feeling that it could be more—that it *should* be more.

"Garrick, I think we have a problem," he said one morning as his meeting with the governor wound to a close. Lately, Siri hadn't been attending the meetings, speaking with Garrick alone instead before going straight from his house to her daily assignment.

"What kind of problem?" Garrick asked.

"Did you see the group of refugees who arrived yesterday?"

"Yes."

"Did you notice how small it was?"

"I couldn't help noticing that. Or the group before it, or the group before that. I want to assume we're only seeing the results of small communities and settlements that couldn't gain any more support, but I'm sure you're going to try to convince me otherwise."

"Spenser said that one of their goals was to make the refugees doubt us," Neil pointed out. "You remember that?"

"I remember."

"Rumors are spreading. They're moving through the city, through the refugee camp, and I wouldn't be surprised if they're going out even farther than that. What if word is getting to those who are heading to Camelora that this place isn't safe? If the people believe Mered's threat is larger and closer than it actually is—"

"—they might just turn back," Garrick finished with reluctance. "From Siri's reports, this group of rebels isn't that large."

"And Mered isn't that close. But they don't have to be. All they need is a suggestion. Stories grow, especially as they get farther away from the source. A minor problem becomes a large one and the threat of a battle becomes an all-out war."

"Siri's reports show that the group is growing," Garrick stated, visibly thinking. "It's still small, but growing. With both Camelorans and refugees, many of them young people. But we still don't know everything they're planning. She has confirmed that Spenser is looking for a powerful weapon, as you suspected. How is that search coming?"

"I still think I'll find the answer in Zaric's study, but he has a lot of records to go through," Neil said.

"Keep up with the search throughout the day, but I want to give you a special assignment for this evening. Siri tells me the group will be meeting after dark this time. Once I get the location, I'll give it to you. I want you to go there and see what you can discover. Find out if Spenser is giving instructions when Siri isn't there. I know she has confidence in her own abilities, but it doesn't hurt to be cautious with an enemy like Mered or any of his followers. If Spenser doesn't trust her and is hiding something from her, I want to know what it is."

Neil agreed. Once he had, though, it was difficult to accomplish his own task, going through Zaric's books. His mind was in the city, wishing he could see the players and details of the plot against the government, to know what was happening. Instead, he could only speculate and hope they would stop the plan before it started. Frustration built as he waited for the daylight to shift and night to come.

* * *

The streets of Camelora lay in almost complete darkness. Very few windows released any light and the overcast sky blocked out the moon and stars. Although Neil was nervous to carry a torch, it would be too difficult to find his way without one. He decided to use one when he left the palace, then extinguish it a couple of blocks away from his destination. If he knew the streets as well as he thought he did, it wouldn't make too much difference.

Still, the torch's light was like a beacon on the dark street. Anyone hiding in the shadows would be able to spot Neil, but he would not be able to spot someone in the shadows.

Siri had given the location of the meeting to Garrick, who then passed it to Neil. She also told him that some sort of attack was planned for that night, though she didn't know yet where the attack would be, or who the intended target was. This prompted Garrick and Neil to adjust their plan. Guards would be stationed and hidden in a nearby street. Neil would arrive early and try to find the meeting spot, listen for any necessary information, and inform the guards when he knew the target of the attack.

Neil dropped his torch on the ground, rolling it and stepping on it to snuff the flame. Placing his hand against a wall, he felt his way forward, relying on the solid stone to keep him on track.

Arriving at the spot where the group was meant to meet, Neil found a cluster of shops with residential dwellings above . In the darkness, with every curtain drawn, it was difficult to see which shop was the shoemakers Siri had mentioned. It was an odd place for the rebel meeting, surrounded by Camelorans sleeping with windows open to allow for the flow of air on this warm summer night. The lightest sleeper would awaken at the slightest sound of voices.

As he waited, the stillness surrounding Neil grew heavy. Not for the first time, Neil found himself thinking of Helen, wishing she were here to help him make sense of his situation. His mind told him he was missing a piece of the problem, but he couldn't figure out what. His mind also told him that Helen would know. She would be able to see what he couldn't. Her intuition would reveal gaps that went unnoticed. Helen would help him form a plan or tell him a story that would answer all his questions.

Every sight, every sound, every feeling created a story that played out in the corner of Neil's mind. The players and plot were shadowed, but the scene was there. When he tried to turn his head and see it, it shifted to a different time and place, always out of reach.

There was no sign of the rebel group or Siri. The time for the meeting was approaching and Neil would lose the opportunity to learn what he could before Siri arrived. Uncertain, he stepped under the shadow of a shop's awning. Perhaps the location had changed, perhaps the time.

A shuffling sound in a nearby alley caught Neil's ear. At first, he thought it could simply be an animal, but he soon picked out human footsteps. The fear that crawled along his spine made him question whether or not the steps were real. He pressed against the wall, focusing on the sound, trying to place its echoing, shifting source.

He sensed the blow before it hit, but there was no time to move out of its way. With a cry, Neil fell to the ground. Reaching for the knife hidden at his waist, he swung the blade and fended off the next blow.

It was impossible to make out more than just the dark mass of his attacker. Man or woman—he couldn't tell which. Whomever it was, they made no vocal sound. Neil relied on his instincts to block the blows he couldn't see coming.

The sudden, burning sting of pain in his side brought out an involuntary shout. Kicking as hard as he could and brandishing his own blade, he managed to push his attacker away. The attacker stumbled to the ground. Neil pressed his left hand to his side while holding out the knife with his right, bending in pain. The sticky warmth of blood gushed around his fingers.

"Guards!" Neil called out. He could already hear their running footsteps, responding to his first cry. "Guards!"

Candlelight appeared from windows above the street, accompanied by hushed voices, awoken by Neil's shouts. The thudding sound of the guards' feet on the street's packed dirt preceded their appearance. Shadowed faces looked down at the scene below.

Another form emerged from the alley, hovering over Neil's attacker. "We need to go," the newcomer said in Siri's voice. "Now."

"But my mission—" a young man's voice began.

"You should have slit his throat when you had the chance," Siri interrupted. "It's too late now. Come on."

She pulled the young man to his feet and down the alley, disappearing before the circle of light from the guards' torches touched them. The governor's guards entered Neil's sight, their forms merging in the intensity of his pain.

"That way!" Neil managed through gritted teeth, pointing to the alleyway. Two guards peeled off from the group.

"What happened?" another guard asked as he lifted Neil to his feet.

"He rushed out," Neil said. "Attacked me."

Gingerly, he raised the side of his shirt to reveal the wound, though it was hard to make out more than the blood in the flickering light.

"We need to get him back to the palace," the leading guard ordered. Then, he said to Neil, "Do you think you can make it?"

Trying to walk with the support of the guards, Neil took a few painful steps. It was too much for him and his legs went slack. The guards took hold of him—careful not to aggravate the wound—and carried him instead.

When they reached the palace, one guard was sent to find a physician while another was sent to fetch Garrick. The rest took Neil to the infirmary. There was no way to anticipate when the waves of pain would strike and no way to prevent the cries they caused.

As a resident of the palace, the physician arrived at the infirmary not long after the others. Neil had already been placed on a cot where he waited for the man to examine him. It was the same young physician, a man named Reddel, who had been treating Neil's arm. Neil was embarrassed to be injured again. The man took a look at the slice in Neil's side but said nothing.

"Someone get me a bucket of water," Reddel instructed as he went to the supply cabinet. Another guard disappeared, nearly colliding with Garrick as the governor rushed into the room.

"What happened?" Garrick questioned, his eyes darting between the guards and Neil, then casting a quick glance at the physician.

"I'd like to know that, too," Reddel stated, taking his seat next to the cot.

Neil related his story as well as he could, the intakes of his breath

CHAPTER 30

hissing as the doctor did his work. He didn't worry about details. Only the general idea mattered, enough to give an idea of the situation in as few words as possible.

"It isn't too deep," the physician assured him.

"Just painful," Neil responded, squeezing his eyes shut against the pain.

"The knife didn't reach the inside, so I don't think anything there has been damaged."

"Did you find Siri's group?" Garrick asked. "Is that why this happened?"

"Siri," Neil said with a laugh. Regret followed as a spasm of pain shot through his body. Neil couldn't decide if he was angry or hurt by her new betrayal. "I'll tell you about Siri."

"What about Siri?" Siri's voice drifted into the room before she appeared in the doorway, leaning against the frame. When she saw Neil on the cot, though, she pulled away and stepped in, her cool demeanor evaporating in her concern.

"I believe Siri betrayed me," Neil went on, his words directed to Garrick although his gaze was fixed on the woman who approached him.

"I did *not*," Siri refuted, lifting her chin.

"When I arrived at the meeting place—which *she* told us about—I saw no sign of anyone. Siri helped my attacker escape, too, when I called for the guards."

"I needed to protect my cover."

Anger flashed through Neil's vision, triggering another wave of pain. "You said he should have slit my throat! Is your cover more important than my life?"

"You're only making my job more difficult," Reddel said with a meaningful frown. "I can't stitch you up when you allow yourself to be so agitated."

"How did he know I would be there, Siri? Did you tell him?"

"Why would I have done that?" Siri spat back. "It might have jeopardized my own position. Anyway, we don't know that he meant to attack you. What would you have done if you found an enemy outside your meeting place?"

"I would capture him, not kill him."

"That's not how Mered trains his followers. He teaches them to kill without a second thought."

"Something you know very well."

The unveiled fire in Siri's stare could have ignited torches in the room, but she fell silent, saying nothing in return.

"Garrick," Neil continued, his tone infused with a cold fire of his own, "I think we should pull Siri off this assignment. I believe she might have been compromised."

"I haven't, Garrick," Siri returned, falling to her knees next to the governor as she looked pleadingly into his eyes. "I don't know exactly what happened tonight, but you can't stop this operation now. We haven't learned all we need to and you won't be able to infiltrate the group with anyone else. Not at this point."

"Did you learn anything tonight?" Garrick asked her.

"No," Siri admitted after a pause. "Everyone scattered because of the attack. The meeting didn't take place."

Garrick drummed his fingers on his knee as he sat in thought. When Neil tried to speak, the governor stopped him with a wave of his hand. The stern look from Garrick and the glare from the physician were enough to show Neil that his arguments were done.

"Siri," Garrick said, turning his attention to the young woman, "I know you say you had nothing to do with this attack, but could there be any reason to believe Spenser has discovered your true motives?"

"No," Siri stated, resting her hands on Garrick's knee. "I know what I'm doing."

"I'm not questioning that. This might have nothing to do with your words or actions, but is there anything in Spenser's behavior to indicate that he knows what we're doing? Do you believe, even just in the smallest way, that you've been compromised?"

"No," Siri repeated firmly. "He would have attacked *me* if that was the case, not Neil."

Garrick took a moment to silently consider this truth.

"We can't risk it," Neil blurted, unable to stay quiet any longer. "Pull Siri off the mission."

"Please, Garrick," Siri pleaded.

"Siri will stay in this for now," Garrick relented. "We need to know what these traitors are planning. But at the first hint of trouble, we will stop this and bring them in. Is that understood?"

"Yes," Siri said with a relieved sigh.

Garrick turned his eyes to Neil, expectant. Swallowing back his frustration, Neil conceded. "Yes, Garrick," he said, focusing his eyes on the ceiling.

"Good," Garrick smiled, getting to his feet. "Let Reddel finish his work, then get some rest, Neil. Guards will be right outside the door. Will he be all right, Reddel?"

"I'm confident he will be," the physician answered, not looking up from his working hands. "I should be finished soon. Then, it will just need time to heal."

"You really need to stop getting hurt, Neil," Garrick said. "Just when your wrist was almost fine, too."

He crossed to the door, motioning for Siri to go with him. "We'll plan our next steps," he told her. "We need to take another look from every angle. Nothing like this can ever happen again."

Neil watched them leave, angry at being left out and angry with himself for being in this situation. He had let his guard down, letting himself trust too much. Even if she hadn't betrayed Camelora, it was clear that she hadn't completely gained Spenser's trust. Neil should have considered that instead of blindly following her instructions. Without some sort of upper hand in the rebel group, they were no less in danger than they had been before.

Chapter 31

The Past

The capital fell. Mered's siege lasted three months, his men bombarding the walls by catapulting boulders at their stones, until Mered himself had mastered the power he needed to bring them down with only his will. Aside from the long life he had been given, Zaric knew no magic and couldn't counter what Mered threw at them. He knew it would be important to gain some sort of power, but he had no idea how. At his last meeting with Alan, there had been more pressing matters to discuss. If he survived this war, Zaric knew he would have to ask his old ally if there was anything he could teach him.

The first time Zaric had seen Mered use just a glimmer of power, he realized what his cousin had been doing in the east. Beyond Yarkko's kingdom there was a land rumored to be shrouded in darkness. Men devoted their lives in this kingdom to imitating the power they saw in the wielders of good. For a fee, they would share what they had learned. Mered showed now that he had gained some of this volatile knowledge.

Mered's new power was too strong and unbridled, though, bringing down the village and palace along with the wall. The earth rumbled. Bricks, beams, and stones fell as the people fled, leaving everything behind. Many didn't make it out, the rubble coming down on them too fast, burying their screams under dust and stone. Abandoning their defensive plans, Zaric tried to corral and remove the people as fast as he could when the first tremors began. They left the city through a secret pass that had been added before this battle, leading directly into the forest.

But it was impossible to save everyone.

He was glad Edric had been sent with his grandfather to the safety of Phara a few weeks before, but for hours Zaric had no idea where Althea was. Trying to ignore the growing dread and fear tearing at his chest like a bleeding wound, Zaric kept himself busy with looking after the safety of his people. He surrounded the civilians with soldiers as they moved through the trees. The ground shook as more and more of the city fell behind them—each vibration cutting into Zaric's heart as he thought about the people left behind. Directing some of his commanders to lead the people to the nearest stronghold seven miles away, he stayed at the back of the group, gathering as many confused citizens as he could and pushing them forward.

Then she appeared. Zaric wondered if she was alive or a ghost—a vision of his hopes. A haunted expression consumed her face. Tears and dust ran in streaks down her cheeks as she stumbled towards her husband. "I wish I could have saved them," she whispered, her body shaking as she melted into sobs and buried her face in Zaric's chest. Forgetting everything else around him, he held her in his arms, tears silently pooling and spilling from his own eyes.

"I didn't see what was going to happen until it was too late," Althea said, her words bringing more sobs. "I don't know why. Maybe I didn't want to. I was too selfish—"

"Shhh," Zaric responded, pulling her close again. "It's all right. None of us saw this coming."

They found the next stronghold—a round tower with slits for

windows running up its exterior. A few smaller buildings sat at its base, encircled by a thick stone wall. More structures ran around the wall, with another thick wall protecting them. It was barely large enough to hold the refugees. Zaric knew they wouldn't be able to center the command of their armies from this place. They would need to move on, find a place with the provisions and numbers they needed to have a fighting chance to win this war.

Zaric gathered all the commanders he could find. They couldn't move forward without planning their next strategy. He found sixteen men—all that remained of the Council the people had chosen in the last election.

They met around the dusty, unused table in the stronghold's council room. Althea sat next to Zaric, her face pale and her eyes disturbed by memories of Camelora. Though she didn't say anything, Zaric worried that she was haunted by new visions, too.

"Mered's powers are new," the first commander stated. "He doesn't know how to control them yet."

"That's both an advantage and a disadvantage," another commander inserted. "He can't control the destruction he causes, but he doesn't care whether or not he causes destruction. All we can hope is that he hasn't learned to use it whenever he wants to."

"Does the queen have any advice for us?" one new general asked. He had been staring at Althea for several minutes.

Zaric cast his eyes at his wife, placing a gentle hand over hers. Her eyes darted from person to person, aware of what they expected from her, then shook her head, her cheeks flushing pink.

"We know what Mered is capable of," Zaric stated. "We need to decide how we will combat it. This place isn't big enough to maintain and defend the entire kingdom, though it is strong. It is safe enough for the civilians and some soldiers, but the army will need to move on—soon. Do we know anything about Mered's movements?"

"Our spies tell us that he's moving south, towards Phara."

The image of his son's face flashed across Zaric's mind. The tension in Althea's hand told him she had thought of their son as well. Young Edric was still at the point between boy and man. Too young for this war, too old to be spared from his duty.

"How are our defenses in Phara?" the king asked.

"It is well-fortified. A double-wall surrounds the city, like the one here, with regular watchtowers along the way. It wouldn't be as easy for Mered to bring the whole thing down as it was at the capital."

"The capital was fortified in a time of peace," Zaric said, trying not to let his words sound bitter. He was embarrassed at the lack of forethought shown by his predecessors. He himself hadn't taken the time to add to its defenses. The thought that Mered would attack the capital first hadn't occurred to him. By the time Althea had her first dream of the siege, it was too late for such a project.

"Phara is much older and better prepared for an event such as this," Zaric added.

"It has an independent armory and soldiers are already stationed there," the first commander said. "If the civilians are to stay here, we can set out soon and reach Phara before Mered does."

"The addition to our forces would give us a better chance," another commander added.

Zaric only needed a moment to consider these suggestions. He nodded. "We will leave a third of our forces to protect the people we leave here. As for everyone else, we will move on, to Phara."

* * *

Zaric climbed the stairs of the Pharan keep. He stopped at one of the slits in the wall, surveying the courtyard below. From this height, he could see everything. The blacksmiths were hard at work crafting swords, lances, and arrowheads for the soldiers. The rhythmic sound of their hammers rang through the air as the knights tested their skills with trained swordplay, the sound of steel on steel creating a complementary rhythm of its own. Soldiers carried bags of grain to the storeroom, weaving their way through the commotion. Beyond the castle walls, smoke rose from the cook-fires of the camp. The voices and shouts and laughter reminded Zaric why their victory was so important. Taking a deep breath, he continued up the stairs.

He soon reached a heavy wooden door. He rapped his knuckles against it, then opened it, not waiting for a reply. The room beyond was mostly bare, its only furnishings consisting of a desk, three chairs, a fireplace with poker and shovel, and tapestries hanging on the walls. Althea sat at the desk, poring over a stack of papers and maps. Zaric was struck by the beauty of her profile as she stared intently at the map in front of her, just as much in love with her now as he had been when he married her seventeen years before.

She was too intent on her work to notice her husband come into the room. He walked to her, placed his hands on her shoulders, and kissed the top of her head. She looked up and cast a quick smile over her shoulder before returning to her work.

"I don't want you to wear yourself out, Thea," Zaric said, taking a seat next to her.

"I want to help," Althea countered.

"It drains you so much. I'm just not sure it's worth the cost."

"We need to defend ourselves, Zaric. We need to protect our people. We can't lose any more of them. I've made progress, anyway. Do you see this valley, here? Mered intends to come at us from every side. He believes that he can surprise us by fanning out his army from this valley. If we can bring a part of our army around the back of this hill, we can box him in as he moves forward."

Zaric looked at the map, studying the marks Althea had made. He didn't ask if she really believed this plan would work—as he would with any of his other advisors—because he knew it would. That was part of Althea's gift. So often she could see Mered's movements before he made them. For all the years Zaric had tried to protect her from the strain of this gift on her mind, he was uneasy with her determination to use it now. Zaric wished it wasn't necessary. If she were simply protecting her family from everyday dangers, he wouldn't worry so much. He hated that she felt compelled to use it to direct a war and strategize battles.

"How much time do we have?" he asked, suppressing a sigh and resigning himself to the fact that this was what she wanted, and needed, to do.

"Five days," she replied. "If we wait any longer than that, it will be too late."

"We'll meet with the commanders this afternoon and show them your plans. Until then, I want you to rest."

Althea stood, shaking her head as she looked down at her husband. "I feel like I'm missing something," she stated in frustration. "There's an image—a commotion—in the corner of my mind that I can't focus on. It feels important."

"You know that it doesn't help to obsess over it," Zaric told her, getting to his feet and looking into her eyes, his hands on her arms. "The more obsessive you are, the harder it is for you to see, and the greater the toll it takes on your mind. Get some rest and maybe it will be clearer. You've done great work and I believe your plan will help to give us an advantage."

Althea nodded, leaning into his chest as he wrapped his arms around her. "I want this all to be over," she said softly.

"So do I, Thea. Perhaps this battle will decide the outcome of the war."

"I can't help feeling that this is only the beginning of something worse. But maybe that feeling has nothing to do with my gift."

Zaric let a minute pass, allowing himself to enjoy the peace of holding his wife in his arms. "Have you given any more thought to Alan's agreement?" he asked. "I'm afraid that if we don't give him an answer soon, he'll change his mind. I don't know what I would do if I couldn't have you with me."

"That's why I've decided to accept it."

Warmth filled Zaric from head to toe and he held Althea tighter, kissing the top of her head. He took her face in his hands and kissed her lips. When he pulled back, a smile covered Althea's face and he kissed her again.

"We can talk to Alan after the battle," she continued.

"Not before?"

"When he extended your life, you slept for two days afterward. I can't afford to lose two days of planning."

A fear crept up Zaric's spine, but he suppressed it by squaring his shoulders. He told himself that the delay wouldn't make a difference. Alan was certain that Zaric would be needed in the future and Zaric knew that he would enjoy his lengthened life a thousand times more with his family by his side. He chose to focus on that thought.

Chapter 32

"I know what they're planning," Siri exclaimed, bursting into Zaric's study.

Garrick and Neil sat on opposite sides of the desk, going over their daily plans. Startled, they turned to the intruder on their meeting. Wincing at the pain, Neil put a hand on his side. Days after the attack, he was still learning new ways not to move.

Urgency radiated around Siri, mingled with excitement and fear. "An assassination," Siri continued.

Tension coursed through the men's frozen postures, replacing the stillness of curiosity with the stillness of fear.

"When Zaric returns?" Neil finally asked, reaching for the first idea that came to mind.

"Before," Siri stated with a shake of her head.

"Before he reaches Camelora?" Garrick queried.

"Zaric isn't the intended target," Siri clarified. "Not yet, at least. They intend to assassinate you, Garrick."

"Me," Garrick said, shocked. His mouth hung open, though no more words came out. "You could at least look more concerned about it," he went on as he found his voice.

"But we have the upper hand," Siri stated. "We *know*."

"When?" Neil asked.

"I don't know that yet. I don't know how, either. All I know is that they intend to kill the governor, throw the government into turmoil, and complicate Zaric's plans before the king returns."

Garrick and Neil looked at each other, each willing the other to speak first. "Do we arrest them?" Neil finally asked.

"You won't be able to catch them all," Siri argued. "After the attack on Neil, Spenser is being more cautious. His group is growing, but he still doesn't invite everyone to every meeting. I don't think I've met them all yet. If you try to arrest them, someone will slip through the cracks. The plan could still move forward."

"And we still don't know what Mered is planning next," Garrick pointed out. "Killing me won't stop Zaric."

"Should we post extra guards?" Neil suggested.

"Any change in security will tell Spenser that you've been warned," Siri said. "By tightening his circle, he's creating a benefit for himself and a risk for you. If you act on the information I give you, he's more likely to discover it was me who tipped you off."

"So we do nothing," Neil stated, not afraid to show his frustration.

"We make a plan of our own," Garrick corrected. "Siri is still learning all she can. Spenser can't plan an assassination without sharing some details. When we know more, we come up with a counterplan."

"In the meantime—" Neil began.

"In the meantime, we do what we're already doing," Garrick stated. "Keep looking for the item Mered doesn't want us to find , continue to learn Spenser's plans. How likely are we to arrest the entire group at some point, Siri?"

"If I can learn what part each member of the group is meant to play in this assassination, we will know where to find each of them when it's time."

"But if he's only meeting with part of the group at any given time,"

Neil said, "how will you know what everyone else is meant to do? Will they all have a part in this plan? If you truly think you can learn everything, has Spenser stopped suspecting you?"

"Of course he still suspects me," Siri countered. " He just doesn't suspect me of passing information to you. I may not be able to find everything out from Spenser, but I will be able to learn it from the others in his band. Most of them haven't learned to be distrustful yet."

"All we need to do is act with more caution without being cautious," Neil stated.

"You finally understand," Siri said with her prettiest smile.

"And are you sure you're telling us everything you know?" Neil questioned, his words following the flow of the conversation. A part of him hoped to catch Siri off-guard.

"Everything," she stressed, looking straight into his eyes.

"Come, Neil," Garrick sighed. "We all trust each other here, don't we?"

Neil stared at Garrick, unwilling to agree with his statement. Siri's voice rang through his memory, chastising his attacker for not slitting his throat. She could have said anything. Was it really necessary to advocate for his death? But he needed to trust Garrick's judgment. By now Neil had learned that he wasn't the only one with wisdom. Neil had the advantage of worldliness while Garrick had the advantage of time.

Neil nodded.

"Saying that," Garrick continued, "I think it's time we bring Siri in on our other little project. Who knows? Perhaps she can help."

"What project might that be?" Siri asked, swallowing hard. It was impossible for Neil to hide the satisfaction he felt at the deflation in her tone.

"Neil is looking into thefts from the armory," Garrick replied. "We believe someone from Spenser's group is responsible, and we believe we know what he's looking for. How close are you to finding what Rufus wants, Neil?"

Neil challenged Garrick with another stare, though he knew there was no escaping an explanation now. "It's in this room somewhere," he replied, his eyes moving to the shelves surrounding them as he waved his hand. "I just need more time. Do you know anything about it, Siri? Since Garrick hopes you might."

"No one has mentioned it in my hearing," Siri said, "But I do know Rufus. He's a fool, not very bright. A little too much zeal with too little sense. I doubt he'll find anything before you do."

"Thank you for the vote of confidence."

"Take the day," Garrick said to Neil, pushing back his chair and gathering the maps in front of him as he stood. "Forget anything else I've asked you to do. There isn't much you can do while your new wound heals, anyway. Let's leave him to it, Siri."

They left the room, with Siri casting a last look over her shoulder before exiting.

Neil rubbed his forehead. Over the past few days, he had searched these books until his eyes ached. So many pages, so many words—and so few hints. But Zaric believed there was a way to defeat Mered and, if Zaric believed it, it must be true. The only reason Neil had for doubt was the fact that these were Zaric's own books. They were more personal and important than those in the library. Neil couldn't help wondering how something so important, so pivotal to their defense, could have escaped Zaric's notice.

Walking up to the shelf where he left off the evening before, Neil took up the next book.

"This must be tedious work."

He looked up to see Siri standing in the doorway, one hand resting on the frame as she smiled at Neil.

"Important, though," Neil answered. "I don't mind being bored if it makes a difference."

"Another difference between the two of us."

Neil didn't feel like responding. Instead, he opened the book in his hand and started to scan its words.

"Listen, Neil," Siri went on, stepping into the room again. "I didn't properly apologize for what happened to you. Or even explain it. Spenser changed the meeting place at the last minute and there was no way for me to tell you. I don't know why. My guess is that he was watching the original place to see if someone would come, and you did. If your injury had been more serious… I would have felt like I had attacked you myself."

Her words surprised Neil. He was glad to know what happened to the meeting that night, but he was even more annoyed with Siri's tone of indifference.

"You didn't know how serious it was," he said sharply. "You're also responsible for your words and actions at the time."

"I was playing a part!" Siri defended, her own irritation reddening her cheeks. Closing her eyes, she took a moment to calm herself before going on. "I'm sorry , it's just— Actually, there's no excuse. I'm sorry. Truly, I am. I wish I had reacted differently—better."

Seeing her face, Neil's own emotions softened. He saw the sincerity of her words. He felt it. If only Helen was here to tell him whether or not he could trust his instincts…

"I hate to admit it," Neil said, "but I do understand how difficult it must be for you to decide when to protect us and when to focus on the plan."

Siri exhaled as though she were letting out a great worry. "Who knows? When we stop these traitors, perhaps you'll finally trust me when I say I want to be on your side."

"Perhaps."

A silence followed. Unable to think of something else to say, Neil took his book to his chair in front of the desk.

"Would you like some help?" Siri offered eagerly. "There are so many books and documents to go through."

"Even if it's tedious?" Neil asked in return.

"Well, maybe just for a little while," Siri said.

"Fine," Neil said after a moment's consideration. He explained what they were looking for and Siri took a book from the shelf, then sat in Zaric's chair. For the remainder of the morning, she hardly said anything to Neil, giving all of her attention to the book.

After a couple of hours, Garrick returned to the study, looking for Siri. He wanted her to see what more she could learn from Spenser. Neil would have to continue his search alone.

Part of him hoped that his luck would turn, that he would find what he was looking for in the first book he picked up, but the rest of him knew how improbable that outcome was.

For the next day or two, Neil closed himself off in the study. Finishing one record only gave him a deeper desire to search one more. He poured over every book, every scroll, skimming the words for any sign of significant weapons, stopping to read when a word or phrase jumped from the page. Weapons lost or weapons taken. Histories, fairy tales, folk tales—every story whether plausible or not. It had been four days since Neil had seen Cyrus. It had been days since he slept more than four hours. Neil was mentally and physically exhausted, but he was determined.

Five bookcases had been searched and there were two more to go. Every book ever written seemed to be in this palace, and every book of significance seemed to be in Zaric's study. Centuries of stories and ideas were contained in these works and Neil didn't know how much time he had left to search them. He dropped into Zaric's chair, took a bite of fruit, and rested his weighted head in his hands.

Neil thought of Rufus, searching the library for the same record he was looking for. He thought of Garrick, welcoming the dwindling groups of refugees, preparing the people for a battle while knowing someone in the city was plotting his death. He thought of Siri, gathering information Neil still wasn't sure they could trust. And he thought of Mered, out in the wider kingdom and how little they knew about his plans.

Walking to the next bookcase, Neil pulled a stepladder against it and climbed to the top. As he reached for the first book in the row, he noticed something further down the line. A small, thin, worn book rested between two larger ones, making it invisible from the floor. Extending one arm, he steadied himself by holding onto the shelf with the other. A dull pain radiated from his side, reminding him to be careful of the wound still healing there. He used his fingertips to pull out the book, then pinched it between his index and middle finger. Pulling himself straight, he took a good look at it.

This record looked promising. There were no words on the front or spine and not many pages between the brittle leather covers. Neil took it back to the desk.

The first page told him this book was a copy of a copy of an ancient text. This replica had been commissioned by King Edric to commemorate the seventy-fifth anniversary of the Cameloran Peace Treaty. Neil made a mental note to find out what that was. The story that followed was the story of an evil king, born to the throne but with no desire to live in the ways of the kings before him.

"The Camelorans are not accustomed to questioning their kings," the record stated. "The king's word, whether for good or ill, is law. The people's hearts and minds change with the kings, mirroring their rulers' without individual thought.

"King Dremlog delights in this custom. The people serve him. They labor for him. They go to war for him. They die for him. Dremlog readily sends men, women, and children to the battlefield, pressing the borders of the kingdom farther and farther into neighboring lands, subjecting new people to his will to replace those he loses. He will expand Camelora to all the seas and no one will stand in his way.

"Though he is young, Nalot of Elahnir sees the threat of Dremlog on the horizon. Nalot is subject to his own king, but Nalot will never allow any king to overthrow his own devotion to the law of good. Nalot's kingdom is weak and small. Unlike Nalot, the king would rather surrender to Dremlog than to stand against him.

"Nalot will not surrender.

"With the sound of war drums beating nearer and nearer to Elahnir, Nalot goes to the mountains. There he builds a forge and extracts ores to create a sword—a sword to defeat Dremlog and push back the forces of Camelora. In the fires of the forge, Nalot infuses the steel of the blade and the gold of the hilt with the power of the Ancients—the power passed through good people from generation to generation. Though the power is imitated by evil, its full strength never can be.

"But Nalot knows the power in the blade and hilt will not be enough to defeat Dremlog. Three elements are needed to make the power complete.

"Nalot descends into the depths of the mountain, where darkness lays as thick as a winter blanket. Inside the mountain, in the light of Nalot's torch, the walls glisten with infinite jewels and gems. Just a handful of these stones could make Nalot a rich man.

"He cares not for riches. He cares not for hands full of stones, for the sword needs only one. The strength in Nalot's soul will lead him to the stone infused with the power needed to complete the sword and defeat Dremlog.

"As he walks, the stones pull at Nalot, hoping to tempt him away from his quest, telling him to love wealth more than freedom, to buy Dremlog's mercy instead of fighting against him.

"One stone does not pull on Nalot in this way. It quiets the voices of all the other stones. It fills Nalot with hope.

"Nalot takes his mallet and chisel. He frees the stone from the mountain wall. The weight of its power is both heavy and light in Nalot's hand.

"He returns to the forge and sets the stone into the hilt. The sword pulsates with the completeness of its power.

"In his humility, Nalot fashions a shield of steel and gold. He knows that he is in the hands of the Eternal One. The shield will prove his reluctance to harm.

"The war drums grow in strength. Dremlog's army no longer rests as it moves into the heart of the kingdom. The king prepares to surrender. Nalot prepares for battle.

"As is his custom when facing a king, Dremlog himself arrives at the battlefield. The Cameloran forces attack quickly, cutting down all who oppose them, ignoring the king of Elahnir's quick signal of surrender. Swords do not stop and spears continue to spill blood.

"Until Nalot arrives. He holds his sword high, the sweep of its power halting the fighters where they stand. Nalot descends to the battlefield and challenges Dremlog to single combat. Dremlog laughs. He believes Nalot will be easy to defeat. He agrees to the battle.

"Before the battle begins, Nalot offers Dremlog the choice to retreat. Dremlog laughs and strikes. Nalot uses his shield to deflect the blows, the power of the sword filling Nalot's limbs with strength.

At last, he uses the sword. The blow is swift and hard. The sword's power turns Dremlog to dust. A gust of wind blows the dust of Dremlog, spreading his remains over the battlefield until nothing is left.

"The fighting ceases. Dremlog's men stand in fear. Their fearful expressions then turn to expressions of relief. The evil king's spell over them is broken.

"Nalot's king approaches the scene of battle and removes his crown.

He places it upon Nalot's head, pronouncing the brave young man king of the land.

"In the days of King Nalot, the lands united into one kingdom. Peace and prosperity covered the land for hundreds of years. Though such times may be forgotten with the pride of men, they may again be remembered. Let us never again forget the danger of a king's pride, nor the power of a humble man's wisdom."

Neil slowly closed the book, his mind full of intertwining thoughts. He stared at the back cover, pondering. Could Mered have sent Spenser to find Nalot's sword?

Outside the window, Camelora had grown dark. Engrossed in the story, Neil hadn't even noticed. It was a wonder he had been able to see the words of the record to read them. Garrick, he knew, would have left the palace for his home to spend the evening with his family, but Neil didn't think this new revelation should wait until morning. With the small book tucked under his arm, he slipped out of the palace.

Zahra answered when he knocked. "Neil!" she exclaimed. "It's been so long since we saw you. My husband's fault, I'm sure. What brings you here?"

"I need to talk to Garrick," he said. "It could be important."

She opened the door wider and waved him in, directing him to the table by the fireplace where the family had recently finished their evening meal. "He's tucking the young ones into their beds," she explained. "I'll go and fetch him for you."

She disappeared up the steep wooden staircase at the side of the room, leading to the floor above. Neil sat down at the table and placed the old book on it, drumming his fingers as he listened to the sound of footsteps over his head. Zahra crossed the floor and stopped. Neil heard the hum of muted voices. Heavier footsteps then crossed back to the staircase and Garrick soon appeared.

"Neil," he said in excited surprise when he was still only halfway down. "What brings you here?"

"I found something," the young man replied, holding up the book.

Garrick rushed to the table. "This looks old," he said, taking the book out of Neil's hand as he sat across from him.

"A thousand years," Neil stated. "I found it in Zaric's study, wedged between a couple of books on the top shelf. Read it, it won't take long."

Garrick did as instructed, opening the book to the first page. Neil could hardly sit still as he watched the governor read. Jumping from his chair, he paced from one end of the room to the other. The more he thought about the information the book contained, the more elated he became. With all that was happening in Camelora, something finally seemed to be going right. He feared that if he stopped moving, so would the excitement he felt.

"A fairy tale," was Garrick's simple statement when he finished.

The eagerness in Neil's body deflated. "But is it?" he questioned, clinging to a thread of hope. "I thought Helen's stories were fairy tales, and they turned out to be true."

"You're right. But I've never heard this one before."

"I don't think *anyone* has heard this story before. If this *is* the only copy, and it *is* a thousand years old, that wouldn't surprise me at all. The only ones old enough to have heard it are Zaric and Mered—and maybe Alan. I wouldn't be surprised if this is what Spenser is looking for. Do you think it *is* possible Mered knows this story, too?"

"Very possible. It would have been a legend even when Zaric and Mered were born, though. I'm not sure Zaric was born at the time of the seventy-fifth commemoration of peace. So, you imagine Mered believes this sword still exists."

"*I* believe it still exists," Neil argued. "It's not much of a stretch to think that Mered does, too. How many impossible things have we all learned to accept?"

"And they think we're keeping a magical sword with the rest of the weapons in the armory?" Garrick pointed out.

"That idea isn't their smartest, I'll admit. They must believe in the idea that Zaric would be hiding it in plain sight—the last place anyone would think to look."

Garrick flipped through the book again as he thought. "I want you to hold onto this," he said, handing the book back to Neil. "Keep it safe. Judging by Spenser's actions, he doesn't know exactly what he's looking for and I want to keep it that way. Mered is probably working from memory and not a written record. When Zaric returns, we'll bring it up with him."

"Can we keep this discovery between the two of us until then?" Neil asked, his mind drifting to Siri. He had forgotten, in his excitement, to ask if she was in the house. Even if she was on their side, Neil didn't trust her to not give away this information if she believed she could get something greater in return.

"If you'd like," Garrick agreed. "It could be nothing, after all."

When he returned to the palace , Neil went straight to his room. He looked around, wishing for the first time that the furnishings weren't so sparse. The room lacked a good place to hide the book. No one besides Neil ever came to his room, but he didn't want to take a chance with something so important.

In the end, he decided to hide it in the plain wooden trunk he kept in the corner. Lifting out a few of the items he kept in it, he set the book at the bottom, then covered it again with his spare clothes. It would have to do. Neil hoped Zaric would return soon, or that they would be able to stop Spenser and his traitors, and he would finally be able to relax.

Chapter 33

The Present

T he knock on the study door startled Neil. Well past midnight, most of the city was asleep. He would be, too, but there were only three books left to look at and he was determined to finish skimming them before going to bed. Despite finding the story of Nalot and his sword, Garrick asked Neil to continue searching the records, wanting to be sure they didn't miss something even more definite.

Siri stood on the other side of the door, fidgeting. "Spenser is planning the assassination for the morning," she blurted before the door was fully open, agitation peppering her tone.

"*This* morning?" Neil asked, stunned.

"Yes, *this* morning," she reiterated. "A group of refugees is not far away and he plans to take advantage of the situation. There's more, too. He plans to have his rebels attack the refugee camp."

"Have you told Garrick?"

"I can't find him." Her voice faltered with worry as she said this, surprising Neil with her sincerity. "I'm afraid he might already be in trouble."

"Don't worry," Neil said, for once choosing not to ignore the urge to comfort Siri. "I think I know where he is. Anyway, you said they aren't planning an attempt on his life until the morning."

Siri nodded in understanding, blinking back the water in her eyes.

"But why," Neil continued as they walked down the hallway, "would Spenser attack the camp *and* Garrick? His band isn't that large."

"He doesn't intend to destroy the camp," Siri explained, her voice still showing a hint of emotion. "The objective is the same as before: frighten the refugees until they no longer trust Zaric or the Camelorans. They won't be prepared and the rebels will be able to kill quite a few of them before anyone can stop it."

"The rebels could be killed as well. Do they realize that?"

"I doubt it. They're young and idealistic. Spenser has been giving them extra training. They think they're invincible."

Neil opened the door to the council room. His anxiety released when he saw Garrick where he thought he would . A number of maps lay strewn across the table in front of the governor, whose chin rested on his folded arms. It took a moment for Neil to realize the man was asleep. Neil opened his mouth to say Garrick's name, but Siri tapped his arm with her fingers. She crossed to Garrick, placed a hand on his shoulder, and gently shook him.

Garrick's head snapped up. He looked around, relaxing when his eyes fell on Neil and Siri. "I must have nodded off," he stated, applying the heels of his hands to his eyes, then rubbing the back of his neck. "What time is it?"

"Early," Neil answered.

"What matters is how much time we have to prepare," Siri said, wasting no time as she took a seat next to Garrick. With a hand on Garrick's forearm, she went on. "Spenser is planning the attack for this morning."

Garrick let a pause fill the space, then asked, "Are you sure?"

"Yes."

"There's more, though," Neil put in.

"More than an attack on my life?"

"Spenser plans to attack the refugee camp at the same time," Siri informed him.

"And cause them to question their safety," Garrick muttered to himself. "Many lives."

"We need to bring in the council," Neil stated, stepping forward. He didn't add that they should have been brought in days—if not weeks—ago, as much as he wanted to .

"You're right," Garrick agreed. "We need as many hands as we can get."

"Did I make a mistake?" Siri asked, the self-doubt rising in her voice for the first time. "I should never have suspected any of them would be involved with Spenser."

"No, Siri," Garrick assured her. "You couldn't be sure. None of us could. We can't go back and change it now. Do you know where the rebels will be?"

"Most of them," Siri replied, taking up a pen and dipping it in a pot of ink. "Or maybe half of them? It's another one of those things Spenser is only revealing in parts, to prevent betrayal. We never know when he'll change his mind, either."

Siri slid one of the maps closer to herself, oriented it, and made a few marks.

"We'll be stretched thin," Neil commented, noticing how spread out the marks were.

"We need to place the majority of our guards around the camp," Garrick stated. "Their safety is the most important. That is how Zaric would want it."

"But we can't lose our governor," Neil argued. "The people might lose all confidence in us if we do."

"I have an idea," Siri said, saying the words as her thoughts formulated. "Do you trust me?"

"Don't ask that," Neil complained.

"*I* do," Garrick assured her, casting a glare at Neil.

Siri straightened her back and pulled a few more maps close, her confidence building as her plan took shape.

Chapter 34

The Present

When night came, Helen didn't expect to sleep. She knew now that rest would only come in fragments.

Every day, Bernt had her brought to him. Every day, his frustration increased that there was still no sign of Zaric. It was only a matter of time before Bernt's actions became more drastic. Helen didn't like to imagine what he would do, but the thoughts invaded her mind, anyway. From the windows of the Government House, as the soldiers led her down the corridors, Helen could see a scaffold being built in the courtyard—a sign that Bernt was preparing for executions. In her cell, where the courtyard was not visible, the sound of hammers and saws haunted the air.

Fear ran through every corner of Helen's mind. She hoped that Zaric would once again visit her dreams, but he didn't come. Now, without sleep, it was impossible. She knew that she should believe that Zaric would find a way to save them, but the fear was too natural to suppress. Helen envied Aurelie, who slept quietly against her.

It was hard to tell what time it was. The world outside was dark and the only light in the room came from the guards' oil lamp, which stood on a table with a guard nearby. They sat on either side of the entrance to the room, speaking to each other only when they needed to. The lamp gave Helen something to focus on other than her fear and she stared at it, studying its shape and wick and the length of the flame.

"Zaric will come. Zaric will come," she told herself over and over. "I don't need to be afraid. Zaric will come."

The light of the flame calmed her, the feeling starting in her chest, spreading throughout her body, and settling in her mind. Helen wished the flame were a fire, giving its warmth to every corner of the room.

The flame leapt, startling Helen. Her sudden movement caused Aurelie to stir and Helen did what she could to steady herself. Had she only imagined it, or did her focus alter the flame?

Wanting to test her theory, Helen stared at the flame again, using the attention Zaric had taught her. The flame grew, climbing higher and higher. Narrowing her eyes, she wondered if her tired mind had only imagined it. But it was real. The flame rose inch by inch, like a golden sapling reaching for the sky. The increased light caught the attention of the guard sitting closest to it and he jumped from his chair in a panic. Helen cast her eyes to the floor, breaking the connection. The flame fell to its normal size.

"Did you see that?" the guard asked his companion.

"See what?" the other guard questioned in return. The first guard gave no reply as he continued to stare at the flame, rubbing one eye, then both. Helen watched him out of the corner of her eye, then decided to close her eyes, afraid that he would notice her and suspect her of playing a trick. When she opened her eyes again, he was settling back into his chair.

"Nothing," he finally answered.

"You're tired," the other guard stated. "Don't fall asleep. I won't cover for you if you do."

They fell back into silence. Helen didn't dare look at the flame again.

Instead, she pondered. If she could make the flame grow simply by willing it, relaxed while focused, what else could she do in this space? She remembered standing in a field with Neil, enclosed in a box of Ian's making. She had created a distraction then and broken the box, simply by willing it. The memory of the campfire returned, then the memory of the seaside. The success of each attempt came when her focus was unforced. Is this what Zaric had tried to tell her? Could she use what little he had been able to teach her to free herself and Aurelie, along with the rest of the prisoners?

Somewhere in the village arose the clanging of a bell. It didn't stop. Its incessant peel filled the dungeon, signaling something more serious than the passage of time. The guards exchanged a concerned and baffled glance as they jumped to their feet, running to the nearest window. Helen shifted Aurelie and rose, her body stiff as she took slow steps toward the cell's barred window. The guards were too distracted to notice.

The window overlooked the village, down to the harbor below. Out on the water, a few boats drifted, their hulls filled with flames. For a panicked moment, Helen wondered if she had caused this, but she realized that she would know it if she had. She didn't believe she was capable of doing anything without intention.

Running feet pounded on the floor above. "Stay where you are," came an order down the stairwell, directed at the guards. Helen fell to the floor before they looked toward the cell.

The two men took turns pacing the floor uncertainly, returning to the window again and again. When she was certain they were paying more attention to the doorway and the window than to the occupants of the cell, Helen woke the rest of the prisoners one by one, touching each man or woman on the shoulder and making a signal to stay quiet. As much as possible, she kept her eyes on the guards, not wanting them to grow suspicious and stop her progress. As she moved , a plan formed in her mind.

Once everyone was awake, Helen wordlessly directed them to sit against the wall farthest from the door. All the while, a nagging thought tickled her mind, asking if she was actually capable of what she envisioned. She didn't know what she would do if it didn't work, but she also didn't know what she would do if it did.

Helen knelt in the middle of the cell in front of the others, her hands resting in her lap. She looked at the barred window, thinking about the air on the other side. She focused on that air until she believed that it was tangible, capable of being grasped and pulled, like grasping and pulling strands of rope. Her mind pulled on the threads of air, bringing them into the dungeon through the bars.

"Do you feel a draft?" one guard asked. Helen's heart skipped and the connection broke.

"There's no glass in the windows," the second guard retorted. "There's always a draft."

"This feels different."

"You just want to see what's going on outside."

They fell silent again, continuing to pace the floor and look out the window. Helen waited a couple of minutes, then started again. She pulled the air through the bars, taking more and more. The intensity of the draft increased, becoming first a breeze, then a wind. The pacing of the guards stopped. Helen's work did not. She wound the wind around and around. It grew too large for the soldiers to believe it was only a common draft.

With alarmed faces, the guards turned toward the cell and pulled out their swords, the air whipping their hair and clothes. The flame from the lamp shook, then flickered, and finally blew out. Now, the only light in the dungeon was the faint light that reached down the stairwell and the dim light coming in from outside.

Helen's mind pulled harder and harder at the air and swirled it around the dungeon. At last, she knew she was ready. With a great push, she thrust out her hands, expelling her energy forward, toward the guards. The cell door and bars rattled, then shook, before finally breaking away from the stones that held them and crashing to the floor. The guards were thrown against the wall, their heads knocking against the hard stone. They crumpled, unconscious, into heaps on the floor.

"Let's go," Helen exclaimed, grabbing Aurelie's hand and picking her way through the bars on the floor. The rest of the prisoners followed.

Chapter 35

The Present

The guards above the Pharan city gate sounded a cry. Torchlight dotted the clearing east of the village walls.

But the cry was not one of fear. With enough of them banded together, the guards were certain they could eliminate this threat.

The men and women only filled a quarter of the meadow. They tried not to let their nervousness show, despite the pre-dawn darkness. If not enough of Bernt's battalion had been drawn away to the harbor, they stood no chance. It was a possibility they had prepared for, but the preparation didn't erase their fear. Some of the assembled fighters were armed with swords, but some had only knives or clubs to protect themselves. Teenage boys stood outside the group, holding sticks and stones. At a signal from a man at the front, one boy beat a rhythm, then another joined in, until soon they were all banging a pulsing beat on their crude instruments.

The ground beneath the Pharan band rumbled. The people braced themselves, spreading their feet wide as they crouched lower to the ground. Although it was not unexpected, it felt different than they had imagined.

The city gate swung open, the solid wood creating a heaviness within the group that stood before it. But they stood tall again, ready to face the enemy who emerged.

* * *

Bernt's men ran up and down the streets near the harbor, unable to determine what was happening. The burning boats were sinking, their flames extinguished by the seawater. Nothing about these boats seemed to be important—they were simple, wooden fishing boats. No other boats were out on the water. The fishers they expected to see at this time of the morning were not there. The houses and structures along the waterfront were eerily silent. Where the men expected commotion, there was only quiet.

Then, little pricks of light appeared at the end of the street. The men turned their heads to see the same dots of light at the other end. Further inland, a band of torchfire moved toward the harbor. The men stood still, too baffled to make any sound.

A warning cry from the eastern city gates rose on the air. The soldiers filling the harborside streets knew they were expected to respond, but they were locked in place. They couldn't determine the size of the group now closing in on them. There was a shout, followed by the rushing of feet, then Zaric's followers fell upon them.

* * *

Connor and Lena headed north, toward the Government House. The night was quiet, like any other night in Phara. A casual stranger would never imagine what they would find inside its walls. But for their part, the couple was glad that the Government House was at the edge of the village, its fortress-like walls serving as protection for the people. Being separated from the others made it less likely they would be captured while Zaric's plan played out.

A secret tunnel led into the house from the northern side of the forest. Many Pharans knew about it. A past governor had built it—a means of escape in case of invasion. As a boy, Connor and his friends used it to take food from the governor's kitchen. He never imagined it would be his means of saving the life of his only child. He and Lena hoped the occupying battalion hadn't discovered the tunnel themselves.

Deep in the trees, they came upon an inconspicuous mound of dirt. They cleared away some brush, revealing an old wooden door. Rust covered the hinges and the metal ring which served as a handle, causing the devices to screech and whistle as Connor pulled. The door moved only an inch. Lena wrapped her hands around the ring, next to her husband's. They both pulled with all their might. The door opened with reluctance, like a sleeper annoyed at being disturbed in slumber.

It was hard to tell if the darkness inside the tunnel spread out into the forest, or if the darkness of the forest penetrated the tunnel. Connor took flint from his pocket as Lena held out the torch she had brought. Once it was lit, they entered, Connor leading the way.

"How far does it go?" Lena asked, her whisper amplified by the curved stone walls. Her mother's grief and concern still punctuated every word she spoke.

"About a quarter of a mile," her husband answered, using his free hand to take hers.

"Do you think Aurelie is all right?" she asked, voicing the primary thought that occupied her mind.

"I believe she is. Helen won't let anything happen to her. She hasn't so far." He stopped to look into his wife's eyes. "What does your heart tell you?"

"That everything will be fine," Lena sighed. She gave his hand a squeeze. "My head just isn't sure if I believe it."

"Lena, you are the strongest woman I know. Don't be afraid to believe it."

After a few minutes, the sound of commotion drifted down the tunnel. The trespassers pressed themselves against the wall and listened. A dim light shone ahead of them. As they moved closer, the light became more defined, revealing the outline of a rectangle. They approached it with caution and found a stone door, held in place by hinges. The sounds of the house came through the cracks, but the commotion they heard before had died down. Connor extinguished the torch and adjusted his grip, holding it like a club, ready to attack if necessary. Acting in unison, they worked their fingers into the gap between the door and the wall, then pulled. Nothing happened. Soon, though, the protesting hinges yielded to their effort and the door swung inward a few inches. They stopped and listened. There was no reaction on the other side of the door. Beneath them, the ground rumbled and shook. Lena and Connor looked at the tunnel around them, wondering if it would hold. Then, their eyes locked.

"We need to hurry," Lena stated. "Zaric must be at work."

With another synchronized pull, the door opened just enough for them to slide through.

The opening dropped them into an alcove where the house's food was stored. Beyond that lay the kitchen. It was empty. Anyone who had been there before must have left in the commotion. Connor continued to grip the torch while Lena snatched up a rolling pin from the large workspace in the center of the room. They hoped the information they were given was correct, since neither of them had ever been in the main part of the house before.

Dread and apprehension tightened their chests as they made their way from the kitchen to the dungeon. They hoped there were enough shadows to utilize along the way to avoid the guards. With the panic created in the harbor, it was impossible to predict where the guards would be. Each new rush of patrols down the house's hallways increased their uneasiness. They were sure they would be caught. They wished they had better weapons to protect themselves. All the while, the floor shook and rumbled at irregular intervals.

Connor and Lena came to a long corridor. The sound of the guards grew distant and they hoped they had time to reach the end before anyone saw them. Without hesitation, they made a dash to the end, where an open doorway revealed a downward staircase.

Just as they approached the doorway, whispering voices and urgent footsteps rose from the stairs. Connor pulled to a stop and threw out an arm to halt Lena. They held up the torch and rolling pin, ready to attack.

Helen appeared before them, nearly knocking them down as she rushed around the corner. She stopped herself just in time. Once realization registered in their minds, Lena's and Connor's arms fell.

"Mother! Father!" Aurelie shouted, running to them with arms outstretched, throwing them around Lena, then Connor.

"How—" Connor began, but his question was interrupted by the sound of shouts below. "Nevermind. Let's go."

He ushered Helen and the rest of the prisoners down the hallway as Lena led them, holding onto Aurelie with the grip of a mother determined not to let her child leave her sight again.

Chapter 36

The Present

In the burial chamber, a small group of Pharans waited. Some children slept while some played. Men and women paced or shifted nervously from one place to another. Guards stood watch at the entrance.

On the floor at the foot of the stone casket, Zaric sat with his eyes closed. His mind blocked out the sounds around him, concentrating on the images he held in his memory. Beneath him, the ground vibrated so slightly, a person would have to stand completely still to feel it.

In his mind, Zaric saw the village of Phara. He walked its streets like a ghost, an unseen apparition observing the chaos caused by the fires in the harbor and the gathering forces on the plain. Bernt's men assembled in what order they could, some moving east while the others went west. He saw none of the villagers. He wanted to be sure of that before getting to work, determined not to hurt any innocent person.

Zaric found a stone building and studied it. Its state of disrepair revealed that it was empty inside. Directing his thoughts on a corner of the structure, his mind pulled at it and he willed himself not to let go, even as the stone resisted. Cracks formed in the rock and mortar, the pressure of his efforts breaking it in long seams. With a violent burst, the stones crashed down to the street below. The men nearby went silent, looking first to the stone in the middle of the street, then up to the building. With another effort, Zaric worked again, breaking away more pieces of the walls. Confused and frightened, the men scattered, breaking their formations as they fled.

Zaric's consciousness walked down the street, pulling at more buildings until their stones tumbled to the ground—sometimes striking Bernt's men as they fell and sometimes merely causing more panic. At times, entire walls crashed down. The soldiers forgot their objective, worried only about how to get away from the crumbling buildings. There was no time to wonder how it was happening. The more he worked, the less effort it took for Zaric to bring down the stones. The ground rumbled as he labored. All the while, Zaric watched for any stray villagers who might leave their homes and wander into the scene.

Rubble soon filled the streets, blocking off alleyways and cutting off Bernt's men as they tried to escape. Men lay on the ground, dead or injured. Zaric followed as the men ran, stepping over broken stones, finding more empty structures to use as weapons. Occasionally, he chipped away at the stones, breaking off small fragments, their sharp edges and corners causing just as much or even more damage than the large pieces of rock.

"Help is coming!" Zaric heard someone cry. He looked around, trying to find the source of the statement. He saw no new forces and none of the men around him reacted to the voice. "Help is coming!" the shout rang out again.

Zaric opened his eyes. His head spun as he regained awareness of his body and surveyed the chamber. Many of the people clambered to the entrance. Fear mingled with excitement as one of the guards from the surrounding woods burst through. Zaric stood, one hand on Thea's sarcophagus and the other trying to steady his head. The guard pushed through the gathered crowd and made his way to Zaric, beaming with excitement.

"A large group of refugees is approaching," the guard stated. "They're only half-a-mile away. They told me to tell you: Meira and Stephen are coming."

* * *

Bernt's men filed out of the eastern gate with Bernt, atop his horse, at their head. The Pharans in the clearing noticed that a good number of men were not with them, but they were still outnumbered. Gulping back their fear, they stood firm, despite the nervousness rippling through their band. They lacked the strength and years of preparation this battalion had. Even with fewer soldiers, Bernt's men could still hurt or kill them.

The Pharans continued to beat their rhythm. The flow of soldiers through the city gate slowed to a trickle, then stopped.

The drumming stopped, too.

Both sides stood immovable, the silence between them broken only by the rumbling and crashing of stones within the village walls. Unbroken minutes passed, neither side willing to make the first move. Feet shifted imperceptibly as bodies grew restless and weapons grew heavier.

A captain in Bernt's battalion raised his arm. The restlessness of the two bands ceased. Both sides waited. The Pharans wondered and dreaded what action the signal would prompt.

A whistling sound altered their attention as objects shot through the sky overhead. A handful of men in Bernt's battalion fell to the ground, a couple of them screaming in pain while the others lay lifeless, arrows protruding from their chests. The captain still stood with his arm in the air, but a look of confusion creased his forehead. Haltingly, his arm came back down.

Only a few seconds passed before men emerged from the forest, the size of the new group growing as though the forest itself were coming to life. More men and women followed, descending the slight slope to join the Pharans at their rear. More arrows sailed through the air and more soldiers fell.

As the surprise wore off, the captain raised his arm again, deciding not to give the new forces time to settle in. He brought his arm back down with a signaling flourish and the first two rows of men rushed forward. A volley of arrows shot out from the ramparts of the village wall. The Pharans in the front rows held their shields out while those further back raised theirs above their heads. Still more people poured out of the trees. A hastily-formed line of archers released their own arrows, targeting the archers on the wall.

Swords, spears, and lances rang out as they struck against shields. The last of the additional forces took their places. Inconspicuously, Meira and Stephen fell in among them. Zaric's people returned the blows from Bernt's battalion, cutting down the soldiers at a rate not even they expected.

Along the horizon, morning light glowed.

The cracking and rumbling of stone from inside the village grew louder, like a wave moving closer to the plain. Cracks formed and spread in the outer walls until large chunks of stone fell, bringing with them the men who leaned against them. Caught off-guard, the men below had little time to move out of the way. Many were crushed or pinned as the massive stones hit the ground.

Bernt's men in the meadow tried to ignore the scene behind them, moving forward through the Pharan ranks and pushing deeper and deeper among them. The Pharans banded together as much as they could, coming to each other's aid and striking at their enemy with great force. Doubt crept through the Pharan ranks. Sensing this, their enemy snatched more and more ground, pushing the Pharans backward. The people knew they needed more help, but had no idea where they would find it.

* * *

Lena and Connor attempted to lead the freed prisoners to the kitchen, but their way was blocked at every turn. The good fortune of the clear path they had found when they arrived had disappeared. The sound of soldiers closed in around them and the worry of being seen was tangible.

Rounding a corner, they entered straight into the sight of a pair of guards, who raised the alarm and rushed toward them. Following the only unobstructed route, they found themselves at the front door. It only took a short moment to decide to take their chances and face what was on the other side—both the known and the unknown.

Connor pulled the door open and looked out at the chaos in the street. No one watched the Government House. Even with the distractions the battalion faced, though, he didn't doubt they would recapture the prisoners once they saw them, as well as Lena and himself.

He waited for the street to offer a brief clearing, then rushed forward, calling to those who followed, "Now!"

They rushed out of the mansion and down the steps, hoping to reach the shadows of a side street before anyone noticed them or the guards within made their way out. All of the danger, all of the concealment was familiar to Connor, Lena, Aurelie, and Helen—only this time there were more soldiers to avoid. Their hearts beat faster and their senses were more alert.

From shadow to shadow they moved. Above them, morning light

and colors filled the sky. With such an abrupt change to their plan, Connor wasn't sure where he would lead the group, just that they needed to get away from Bernt's men. If they could, they would find a place to hide until the fighting ended. Lena touched his shoulder, then pointed to an alley, near where they knew an opening in the wall would be. After looking up and down the open street, Connor dashed from the shadows and the rest followed.

When they reached the alley, he stopped, throwing out his arms to keep the rest from moving forward. Silhouettes moved at the opposite end. The figures halted when they noticed the prisoners. Afraid they were facing a part of Bernt's battalion, Connor tried to turn and flee before the people had a chance to react. But the sound of his name stopped him.

In the dim light, he recognized the man at the head of the group—a group of villagers. Connor stepped forward with caution and his own group followed. The fear that these villagers were working with Bernt filled his mind.

The Pharan group was larger than it initially appeared, spreading out where the buildings ended, filling the alleyways.

"We should have listened to you," the man said as Connor and his group came closer, his voice faltering, as though he wasn't sure what else to say. "We thought things were bad, but we were willing to tolerate them. Over the past few days, they've gotten worse. That's why we're here. We were hoping to find some way to join Zaric and the rest of you, to help in whatever way we can. Will you let us help you?"

Connor smiled and put out his hand with only a slight hesitation. The man returned the gesture, grasping Connor's forearm. "Of course," Connor stated. "We're trying to find a way out of the village, to bring these prisoners to safety."

Helen stepped forward, not able to hold back any longer. The turmoil of her thoughts nagged her, telling her there was more for her to accomplish. Though she was afraid, she knew she needed to push those fears aside.

"I think I know what to do," she said. "And, with larger numbers, we won't need to hide anymore."

Chapter 37

The Present

Snow drifted, dusting the ground as an icy wind drove back the summer heat. The morning sun tried to penetrate the cloud covering Camelora, but failed. For two hours, the citizens of the city wore their fur-lined winter cloaks, brought out again at the beginning of the weather changes.

By mid-morning, the heat of the sun burned away the cloud, melting the snow into puddles before evaporating them. Cloaks were removed again. The sweltering heat was followed by thunderclouds, rolling in the wake of the report of an approaching caravan. Camelorans and refugees alike sheltered away from the lightning and rain of the summer storm. As suddenly as it darkened, the sky cleared. Garrick, Neil, Siri, and their guards trudged through the mud left behind by the erratic climate.

The calm was strange after the frenzy of the earlier morning. Neil was disappointed and concerned. He had hoped for a strong wind—a daily occurrence lately—to offset the arrows he was sure some of the rebels would choose to use. Without the hint of a breeze, the rebels were more likely to hit their marks.

The government delegation was in place when the arriving refugees emerged from the woods. It was a now-familiar sight, but the

295

emotions Neil felt were anything but familiar. He wished he could shout out, warn the people, protect their lives. Instead, he couldn't help thinking that they were using the innocent refugees as bait. Hoping the guards and council would do their part, he kept his eyes forward, trying to tamp down every thought and feeling.

Although Garrick had often invited others from the council to join him in greeting new supporters before, today he had them disguised and stationed throughout the city, ready to stop and detain anyone acting suspiciously, in an attempt to save the lives of any refugees or citizens who might be targeted by Spenser's group.

To Neil's surprise, Garrick displayed a calmness unusual even for him. He walked toward the approaching group with a grin and confident gait. He joked with his bodyguards and Neil. He invited Siri to take his arm. For her part, Siri managed to look both like she belonged with the delegation and also like she didn't. Neil wondered if it was real or just an act. In spite of all she had done to help them, Neil now realized how unwelcome Siri must still feel. Even now she was trying to prove herself and her loyalty to Camelora. Neil examined his heart for the old doubts and suspicions that had once come so readily, but they weren't there. There was no room for them. In this moment, he knew he needed to trust Siri. So far, everything she had told them had been true.

It was only when Neil looked at Garrick's hands that he noticed them trembling. Following Neil's gaze, the governor shoved his hands into his pockets.

The Cameloran guards positioned themselves around the refugees as the caravan stopped. It numbered less than one hundred men, women, and children. Sadness jabbed Neil's chest at the sight of so few people. But just this once, that sadness was mingled with relief. Knowing the danger the people were likely in, Neil was glad there weren't more to worry about protecting.

Garrick held out his arms to the group in greeting. "Welcome to Camelora!" he exclaimed. "May you find peace and safety within our walls. May you strengthen the forces of Zaric in his defense of the kingdom. May the light of the Eternal One shine down upon you."

The leader of the refugee group stepped forward, shaking Garrick's offered hand.

A whizzing sound preceded the pained cry of a guard. The man fell to the ground, an arrow protruding near his neck where his thick protective coat ended.

* * *

The guards wondered how much they should tell the refugees. Being told there would be an attempt to attack and kill the people at random, the guards had been instructed to protect them at all costs. Yet they had also been told to wear plain clothes and avoid drawing attention to themselves. Telling the people they were in imminent danger could cause a panic, tip off their attackers, and interfere with the governor's plans. Not telling them seemed like the opposite of protecting them, making them vulnerable.

Every guard who could be enlisted in a short amount of time had been. They were stationed on the edges of the camp and along the main thoroughfares. No one knew for sure where their enemies would spring. This was the best they could do. Knowing the training of most of the rebels, they were confident they would be able to at least match them. They had been instructed to spare the lives of the rebels as much as possible, enabling the governor and the council to interrogate them later.

They tried not to wonder what was happening on the plain. Garrick had given them no details, but they knew the attack they were meant to thwart wasn't the only attack planned for that morning. Although it was difficult, they would need to stay focused on the camp and let the governor take care of anything else that might happen.

If they couldn't tell the people what they suspected, though, they could at least ask them to be alert. The refugees knew each other and they knew the soldiers were not part of their numbers. Their presence told the people something was expected, but their clothing told them it needed to be kept quiet.

A shout rose up on the edge of the tents. "Drop your weapon!" a soldier commanded.

The screams of refugees came from another direction. They were matched by the appearance of flaming arrows hurtling through the air. Flames spread quickly where the arrows fell, spreading through one tent and threatening others.

The soldiers dropped all pretenses and rushed toward the sound of the commotion, directed by the few refugees who managed to keep a presence of mind. Water buckets were brought from a nearby well to douse the fires before they could spread farther.

The commotion and the screams rose up all over the camp. There weren't many areas under attack, but they were spread out, making it more difficult for the soldiers to find the source. Coupled with the fear and flight of the refugees, those under direct attack and those not, the task of finding and arresting the rebels was not as easy as it originally seemed.

Screams of fear mingled with screams of pain. Here and there, refugees fell, the victims of arrows and knives from the camouflaged rebels. Most were only injured, but some were not so fortunate.

At last, the soldiers spotted them. About a dozen hooded men and women stood out, holding weapons they couldn't easily conceal. The soldiers swooped down upon them, surrounding the traitors with drawn swords.

"Weapons on the ground," they shouted. "Now."

Only three resisted. One rush toward a soldier with his knife held high, ready to attack. But the soldier's sword was ready and the man fell.

All of them were young. The guards couldn't help noticing that fact. Some walked with defiant faces, while others couldn't hide the fear they felt. Their hands trembled as the soldiers bound their wrists behind their backs. They surrendered easily and asked what would happen to them. The soldiers didn't answer. Garrick had instructed them not to speak. Anyway, they didn't know what to say.

* * *

The attack began even faster than Neil expected.

Men, women, and children screamed as the guards rushed into formation. Archers positioned themselves, facing the city walls, standing between the unseen enemy and the people gathered in the field. Another row of guards stood in front of the archers, shields raised to deflect any more arrows. More shielded guards took a protective stance around the refugees.

Many of the refugees themselves dropped to the grass, allowing the guards to protect them, their expressions stunned and uncomprehending. Others tried to run, fear blinding them to the safety the guards offered. A few of the Camelorans attempted to wrestle the runners to the ground in their desire to keep them safe. The refugees fought against them. Those who managed to reach the woods disappeared into the trees.

Arrows flew from various parts of the wall, spread thin by the limited number of rebel archers. What they lacked in numbers, they made up for in accuracy. It pained Neil to see the Cameloran defense training used to betray their own leaders. He was reluctant himself to pull his own sword, not wanting to use it against the people he had promised to protect. Yet he knew this reluctance would end up helping no one. He needed to protect those who accepted his protection from those who chose to turn their backs on it.

Neil also worried that his wrist was still too fragile to wield it, making him less useful than he wanted to be. Although he had spent time training to regain his strength, it was not what he wanted it to be.

If Siri's hunch was right, Spenser himself planned to attack Garrick, his arrogance preventing him from allowing anyone else near the governor. Measuring his breaths and trying to see past the commotion around him—and inside him—Neil scanned the chaos for a face that didn't belong.

The arrows from the wall stopped. The Cameloran archers still stood at the ready, afraid that letting their guard down would only make the arrow-fire resume. They had returned fire, but the air was too full of screams and cries for them to know if their own arrows had found their marks.

A guard on the opposite side of the circle pivoted, pushing through the other guards to make his way to the center. The lower half of his face was shrouded in a scarf. Worried that the guard saw something he couldn't, Neil glanced over his shoulder, taking in the scene behind him. The governor was in no danger from Neil's side. Neil looked back at the guard just as he pulled his sword from its sheath, running toward Garrick. He was too far away. Still, Neil ran.

Siri appeared, holding a sword of her own. Neil pushed away the question of how she managed to obtain it. She threw herself between Spenser and Garrick, striking a blow before Spenser could throw one of his own. The haste and angle knocked them both off-balance. Siri wasn't in a good position to recover. Spenser kicked at her stomach. She grunted as the blow knocked her away.

But Siri had given the guards enough time to realize what was happening and create a defensive wall surrounding Garrick. In frustration, Spenser went for the guards, his sword raised. Back on her feet with new breath in her lungs, Siri rushed at him again. She struck out, but the strike merely bounced off. Spenser swung, but she blocked the blow.

As Spenser turned his attention and frustration to Siri, Neil reached Garrick and his guards. In a tight circle, they surrounded the governor, making him indistinguishable. A new torrent of arrows flew from the city wall, but from fewer points this time. Neil looked from Garrick to Siri—the governor in the center of a protective human cocoon while the unarmored, unshielded woman did all she could to deflect the motions of Spenser's sword. Neil ran toward them, but the unpredictable pandemonium of the field made that more difficult than he expected.

Spenser landed a thrust, his sword piercing through Siri's skirts and into her thigh. With a yell, she knelt on the ground, holding herself up with her sword. Spenser took advantage of his position and raised his sword above Siri.

"No!" Neil shouted, holding out his hand, though he knew it would do nothing.

Yet it did something. A wave of air went out from his hand, knocking Spenser off his feet and causing him to tumble to the ground.

As Neil rushed for the fallen man, Spenser stumbled to his feet and ran, swinging his sword with one hand while drawing a knife with the other, cutting his way through the guards who tried to stop him. Some of them cried out, holding their arms and legs where the blades sliced through. Once he was free of the Camelorans, Spenser sprinted across the field, heading north.

The guards followed. Neil pushed his way to the front of the group, wanting to lead the way. In his head, he prayed that they would catch up to Spenser before he reached the hills north of the city, where the rugged terrain afforded him plenty of places to hide. Neil rarely went to the northern part of Camelora and was unfamiliar with the rocky landscape. Now, he regretted that fact.

They reached the area north of the city, where an unfrequented grassy path led to the grassy, hilly plain strewn with large rocks and boulders. Ahead, Neil caught a glimpse of Spenser's figure disappearing behind a cluster of rocks. Neil expected to see him emerge from the other side, but saw nothing. He slowed his steps.

"Spread out," he instructed, breaking away from the guards and moving left.

The men did as they were instructed, fanning out as well as they could. Just before they reached the stones, Neil noticed Siri farther down the group, moving in synchrony with the guards. She had found a stick to use as a crutch as she walked, grimacing with each step, but her determination was clear. Neil knew how she would react if he told her to turn back. He decided against it.

At first, the terrain was fairly even and easy to navigate. But as the large boulders drew closer, more and more rocks littered the ground in larger and larger sizes, sometimes hidden by grass, ready to trip anyone who wasn't paying enough attention. Neil slowed his pace and picked his way through, weaving between the boulders, shifting his gaze between the ground at his feet and the space ahead of him. The occasional groan of a falling soldier reached his ears. He worried it might not be because of the stones.

The sound of loosened pebbles and stones reached him, but Neil couldn't tell where it came from. Looking ahead, he caught a glimpse of a moving form between two standing stones. He stepped forward, drawing his sword. Whenever a clear path opened up, he sprinted ahead, leaping over small stones and skirting large ones. He was forced to slow down again when each path became cluttered again.

More and more, flashes of Spenser moved across his field of vision.

The distance between them was shrinking. The looming boulders and standing stones thinned. Neil made another push, coming between two stones just as Spenser came around them. Leaping, Neil wrapped his arms around Spenser's torso, restraining the man's arms at his sides and knocking the blades from both of their hands. They fell to the ground with a hard thud, Spenser gasping for air as he broke Neil's fall. Still, he managed to roll out from under his captor, pulling a dagger from his waistband. Neil scrambled to his feet and fumbled for a dagger of his own as Spenser lunged forward.

"Stop," came a calm and authoritative command as a sword appeared at the side of Spenser's chest, blocking his path and abruptly halting his movement.

"Drop your knife," Siri instructed. With a smirk and a shake of his head, Spenser threw his dagger to the ground.

"Where did you get a sword?" Neil asked Siri, trying to catch his breath.

She nodded over her shoulder, where Garrick ran up to stand behind her, his scabbard empty. "He didn't even notice," she said with a twinkle in her eye.

As the guards reached the spot where Neil and Siri held Spenser, they surrounded the enemy, swords and knives drawn. Neil held his breath, half-hoping and half-dreading that the man would try to fight. But his sword lay on the grass where Neil felled him, out of his reach. If he tried to reach for another hidden weapon, the guards were too near for him to get it. His face contorted in anger and disgust, Spenser lifted his arms in surrender.

Garrick pulled a coil of rope from his belt and approached Spenser, roughly pulling the man's arms behind his back. Neil walked up to them, making sure Garrick was able to pull the knots tight.

"Are we arming prisoners now?" Neil asked with a grin. Garrick looked at him in confusion and Neil nodded towards Siri.

"I—" Garrick started, raising his eyebrows in surprise.

"It's all right," Neil chuckled. "It looks like it's a good thing."

For the first time, he cast a smile at Siri. And, as a first for her, the smile she returned was genuine.

Chapter 38

The Present

Above the battlefield, as if out of nowhere, a grey cloud began to form. It went unnoticed to begin with, but it soon blotted out a large portion of the morning sky and descended down toward the field, confusing the men and women below by being so out of place.

Wounded Pharans fell to the ground and were pulled to safety by their fellow fighters. The small band of young men encircled and protected their fallen friends. The storm cloud above them grew.

More arrows sailed across the sky, moving in both directions. The cries and screams of men and women filled the air. Thunder rolled as the cloud spread rapidly over the plain and village. A blinding flash halted the battle for a second as lightning struck down near the village wall. Those men who stood in reserve, not yet fighting, danced around, unsure of what had happened, breaking their formations. The captains shouted at their men and the battle resumed. Another strike of lightning hit in the midst of Bernt's battalion. Rain began to fall.

* * *

The scene in Phara was one of panic. Any order to the movement of Bernt's battalion had broken down. The ground continued to shake as buildings continued to crumble, scattering the enemy like dust and rubble throughout the city.

Helen walked in the middle of the group of Pharans, her hands held out, palms pointed up to the sky. Those who had managed to find weapons walked at the edge of the group, fighting off any soldiers who approached, though not many soldiers were left to defend the streets. Those who weren't hiding in fear were now assembled on the plain. In the sky above them, Helen's storm cloud raged.

The villagers flinched and jumped as pieces of buildings fell, ready to dodge any stones that came their way. But the stones never came near them. The buildings were silent as they passed, as though they could tell the difference between friend and foe. Many of their foes lay in the rumble that had already fallen. The Pharans snatched up the shields and weapons of these soldiers as they passed.

It had taken Helen a few minutes to push away the self-doubt and concerns that stood in her way, stepping away from the rest of the group as they did their best to organize themselves. Despite controlling the wind in the dungeon, Helen wasn't sure she could accomplish something of the magnitude she hoped outside. Not even her efforts against Ian had reached something on this scale. Her success before had depended on her ability to close off her thoughts and let the power she imagined work through her.

Now, with the help and protection of the Pharans, her plan was working. The storm she imagined was growing.

Approaching the main city gate, they found soldiers who had fallen, both dead and seriously wounded. More swords and shields were gathered. Most of the group would be armed when they joined the battle. They expected the wounded soldiers to try to stop them, but those conscious enough no longer cared. The Pharans looked to the soldiers on the wall and in the hollow space beneath the arch of the gate, surprised the soldiers hadn't attacked yet and nervously anticipating that to change. But none of those soldiers turned to see what happened in the village, as though the masses behind them were invisible. As the Pharans moved closer to the gate, rain began to fall.

In the grey cloud above them, lightning danced. Connor raised his sword above his head and gave a shout. The Pharans responded, their own weapons raised, and the group rushed forward. In surprise, the soldiers on the wall turned. Most of their arrows were already spent and there was little they could do to stop this added threat.

Holding a sword and shield, Lena shepherded Helen and Aurelie to a nearby doorway, doing her best not to break Helen's concentration. Lena stood guard as Helen continued to control the storm. Standing in the shelter of this stone structure, she realized it had been a few minutes since she last saw a stone fall.

A few Pharans rushed up the stone steps to the top of the wall, their swords and clubs swinging, hitting the soldiers stationed there. With a cry, the rest of the villagers rushed through the gate. From the doorway, Lena saw just how big the group had grown as wave after wave of Pharans passed her, their stolen weapons at the ready. Bernt's forces were far outnumbered now.

Outside the village, tramping feet and heavy rain created slick mud, causing many fighters on both sides to lose their footing. As the minutes passed, more and more of Bernt's men fell by the sword.

In a great push, Helen hit the ground in the middle of the plain with a bolt of lightning. Blinding light washed over the fighters in the field. They flew backward as mud and dirt sprayed into the air. All sound ceased. She hit the field with another bolt, and then another. Her own body vibrated from her skin to her bones, filling every appendage with pain and breaking her concentration.

The fighting stopped. Rain poured down as the dazed soldiers and fighters struggled to their feet. In the center of the field, a large crater filled steadily with rainwater.

Once they reoriented themselves, the Pharans regathered and reordered, preparing to continue the fight. Bernt's men stood with slumped shoulders, taking in the scene around them. Many of their comrades had fallen. They found themselves unexpectedly, unfathomably outnumbered. One by one, they dropped their weapons into the mud.

"Fight, you fools!" Bernt shouted from the midst of the battalion, his horse long since gone. A Pharan appeared behind him, hitting Bernt across the shoulder blades with the broad side of his sword. Bernt fell forward, mud splattering his face as he dropped his sword and caught himself on his hands. The Pharan seized him by the arms and pulled him back to his feet. Another man came forward with a bit of rope and tied Bernt's arms behind his back. A group of Pharans corralled and surrounded Bernt's men. The captive leader seethed.

Commotion rippled through the Pharan forces. The people stepped aside, letting someone through.

Zaric.

As he reached the middle of the field, Bernt was brought forward and shoved to the ground. He fell to his knees, but the men caught him before he could fall forward into the mud again. Defiant, he looked up at Zaric, whose face was set firm.

"The people of Phara have spoken," Zaric said. "They do not support Mered and they do not want his army here."

"This isn't the will of the Pharans," Bernt spat out. "This is *your* will."

"They chose for themselves to fight against you. Whether or not you believe that is no concern of mine."

"He's right," Connor spoke up, coming up behind Bernt. He moved around the man and stood next to Zaric. "We didn't fight when you came. Many of us didn't believe that we could win, so why even try?

But that has changed. This is our land and we aren't going to give it to Mered. Hand over your weapons and we will let you go."

"Or what?" Bernt sneered.

"Or today an execution will be carried out," Zaric stated. "We have no time for a rebellion."

The color drained from Bernt's face and his defiance melted away.

"We will let you go back to Mered," Zaric went on, "so you can deliver a message. Tell him the rightful king of Camelora has no intention of allowing him to take over this kingdom. King Zaric has returned."

Chapter 39

The Past

Mered's army arrived just as Althea predicted, led by Mered himself. Like a flood, they poured through the pass, over the hills, and into the valley. Forward they marched in straight lines— swordsmen and cavalry. Zaric was amazed at the number of men Mered had recruited, how many of his people had chosen to abandon the government he tried to form. He pushed against the rising doubt in his mind. He trusted Althea and believed in her plan.

Zaric's own army stood as still as they could, waiting to defend themselves, their families, and their kingdom. They watched stoically as the opposing army grew and grew, wondering if there was an end to Mered's forces. Zaric stared at the distant hill at the end of the valley, unnerved by the glint of sunlight reflecting off metal. He looked back at the castle and thought of the people inside—of Althea, of Edric. He had wanted his wife to leave before the battle began, but she refused, wanting to stay in case she was needed. Edric was old enough to fight, to do his duty for his kingdom, but not old enough to be outside the castle walls. He was part of the second line of defense, held back in reserve in case they were needed. That didn't make his father worry less.

The opposing army stopped, mirroring the orderly lines of Zaric's soldiers. Time froze for a minute as everyone stood still and silent. Mered sat atop his horse with his arm raised, ready to give the signal to his men. No words were exchanged between him and the king. The time for words had passed.

The tension built as Mered waited. Then, he let his arm fall.

The front lines of Mered's army ran forward with a shout while Zaric's army stood their ground. The battle had begun.

The distance between the armies disappeared. The sound of metal against metal rang through the air. The shouts and screams continued to fill the battlefield as soldiers on both sides fell. Soon, the division between the armies disappeared completely.

Zaric rode among his men, swinging his sword in an effort to protect them, cutting down their opponents. At times he found himself facing a mounted soldier from Mered's side. He fought them with even greater strength, knocking each one from his horse.

Zaric found Mered not more than three yards away. A smug confidence radiated across his face, knowing that his army overwhelmed Zaric's. The king gave another signal—so slight that many of the soldiers on the ground didn't even notice.

Mered's expression of arrogance changed to one of disbelief as the rest of Zaric's army emerged from the trees surrounding the valley and swept down the three hills. For a moment, a large part of the commotion stopped as the invaders tried to decide which way to turn. They weren't prepared for a battle on all sides. Many of the soldiers in the rear were struck down before they had a chance to react.

Snarling, Mered picked his way through the battle as quickly as he dared, cutting down soldiers without thought as he made his way to Zaric. When he reached the king, he swung his sword with all his might.

Zaric's cool courage contrasted with Mered's heated rage, allowing the king to prepare for the attack. Zaric defended himself with shield and sword, but the blows came with more fury than anyone could block. The king's horse reared and threw his rider to the ground. Zaric managed to roll and get to his feet before Mered finished dismounting and rushed toward him.

Once on firm ground, it was easier for Zaric to deflect Mered's blows. Mered fought with anger, but Zaric fought with skill. Soon, he had the upper hand, pushing Mered back. As Zaric's strokes grew stronger and more intense, Mered began to bend. His legs gave out and he fell to the ground, Zaric standing over him with his sword at his enemy's throat.

"Surrender," Zaric said. "Surrender, Mered, and spare the lives of these men."

"And what will I gain from that?" Mered retorted.

"It's not about you. These people don't deserve to die to satisfy your ambitions. Why can't you see that?"

"This coming from the man who wants to be king forever. Don't the people deserve to have a say in *that?*"

The words cut into Zaric's heart and he pulled his sword away a few inches. Mered smirked in triumph. In a black haze, he dissolved from the spot where he had lain .

Zaric spun around in undisguised surprise, trying to find his cousin's face among the soldiers surrounding him, prepared to deflect a blow. He knew that Mered hadn't gotten up or rolled, but he was nowhere to be seen. Zaric's fear increased as the image of Althea came to his mind.

Fear would not help him. He thought of a device—the only one Alan had tried to teach him so far—and hoped it would work. Focusing on the image of where she should be at this moment, he closed his eyes and concentrated.

When he opened his eyes again, he was in the room at the top of the keep. No one was there. Ignoring the rattling, spinning sensation in his head, he ran to the open door and descended the stairs, not caring that his steps echoed through the stone cylinder. Stopping on a landing two stories down, he heard the sounds of a struggle, then Althea shouted. Zaric flew down the next two flights.

He found Mered and Althea in the second-floor banquet room. Althea lay sprawled on the floor as though she had been thrown there, scratches and marks marring her skin. Tears rolled down her face as Mered towered over her. Seeing Zaric in the doorway, Mered's eyes widened and he grabbed the queen, wrapping one arm around her neck while the opposite hand held a dagger to her throat. "I knew you would find me," Mered sneered. "Hoping, actually."

"Mered—cousin," Zaric pleaded, "this isn't going to give you what you want. Let Althea go."

More footsteps were heard in the echoing tower and Edric burst into the room. From the post where he had been stationed, Zaric realized, he could easily hear his mother's screams. The young man tried to rush forward, but his father grabbed his shoulder. Edric tried to twist from Zaric's grip, but it was too firm.

"This is good," Mered chuckled. "I didn't realize I would have the chance to show your son the man you really are."

"He already knows who I really am," Zaric responded, confused. Undefined fear seeped through him as he wondered what Mered was trying to do.

"Does he? Does he already know the choice you're going to make, before I present it to you? You see, Zaric, I'm willing to make a trade. You give me the kingdom and I will spare your wife's life. Nothing more, nothing less."

Zaric's heart shattered and his spirit tore into two. As a husband, Zaric was willing to do anything to protect his wife. As a king, he was duty-bound to protect his people and his kingdom. The man

Mered had become—so far removed from the cousin and friend Zaric had loved—would follow through with his threats with obstinacy and relish. Zaric couldn't turn his people over to the hands of a tyrant, yet he couldn't lose Althea. Their lives were one.

Althea's and Zaric's eyes locked. She shook her head so slightly, he wasn't sure if it was real or imagined.

"Is this the man *you* are?" Zaric asked. "Willing to kill an innocent woman to get what you want?"

Mered stood unmoved, neither his grip on Althea nor the blade slackening.

"Mered," Zaric begged, his emotion rising to his eyes, "please."

"Do you see, Edric?" Mered said with a chuckle. "Your father has made his choice."

He let go of Althea and time slowed. Zaric rushed forward, hoping he could reach her before Mered's next action—an action his mind could see, though it hadn't begun yet—but knowing he wouldn't. Before Althea could take more than a step forward, Mered pulled back his arm and shot it forward, plunging his knife into the queen's back. She opened her mouth to scream, but the sound came out as a weak cry. She hung suspended in the air, her back arched, until Mered withdrew the blade and she crumpled to the floor. Zaric's feet stopped, rooted where he stood.

"Mother!" Edric shouted, running to her, passing his frozen father in the middle of the room. Seeing his son fall to his mother's side, cradling her head in his young hands, brought Zaric out of his shock and propelled him forward, too. He fell next to his wife, taking her hand in his.

His disbelief was cut short when a movement out of the corner of his eye caught his attention. With a shout, Mered pulled his sword and rushed toward Zaric, who barely had time to raise the sword he still carried and block the blow.

A great surge of power swelled in Zaric's chest and filled his arms. He pushed against Mered's sword, causing Mered to stumble backward.

"I have allowed you to make your own choices," Zaric said, his voice booming with the power inside of him. He held up his free hand and a forceful wave of air hit Mered in the chest.

He stumbled, but regained his footing.

"I hoped that you would realize your selfishness," the king continued.

Another blast struck Mered just as his form grew hazy, pulling him out of his transport. He fell back, but scrambled to his feet again.

"But you wanted to take what the people chose not to give you—trying to erase *their* choice."

The force of the next blast knocked Mered to the floor and pushed him across its surface until he hit the wall. For a few seconds he lay still before trying to lift his head.

"For too long," Zaric went on, approaching his enemy in three swift steps, "we have let you act without consequences. But that ends now."

Zaric raised his sword with both hands and brought it down again into Mered's chest. Mered looked up at the king in surprise, gasping for breath. Tears pooled in Zaric's eyes—for Althea, for Mered. "I'm sorry," he whispered.

The eyes that looked back at Zaric were filled with hatred. Mered shivered, put his hands against the blade of the sword, and grunted as he pushed it out of his body. Mustering a shout of rage, he dissolved into a black mist that rose up and disbursed into the air.

Zaric dropped his sword and ran back to Althea, falling to his knees beside her, but Edric held her tightly and wouldn't relax his grip. "She's gone," he managed between sobs. "She's gone and it's all your fault."

"Edric," Zaric said, tears rolling down his own cheeks. "Let me hold her."

"No!" his son shouted, his face twisted in pain and rage. "She's dead because of you!"

Zaric reached for his wife's pale and lifeless face, noticing the blood drenching her dress and staining Edric's clothes. His heart broke even more for Edric while devastation filled his own soul. This wasn't supposed to happen. Althea wasn't supposed to die. They had planned so much together. Edric needed his mother. If only Zaric knew where Alan was...

"Please, let me take her," he pleaded, but Edric only tightened his grasp.

"You could have saved her. You could have given Mered what he asked for."

"It isn't as simple as that."

"How was it not simple?"

"I'm a king. I couldn't hand the people over to Mered."

"Then I never want to be a king. I would never let my family die. Your people aren't worth more than my mother."

Edric pulled Althea's body closer while Zaric looked on, helpless.

Chapter 40

The Present

As they led Spenser through the city, he carried an air of arrogant defiance. He said nothing, spat no insults. He didn't protest his innocence or complain that this was a gross injustice. His haughtiness irritated Neil, who pulled the man's arm with a roughness he might otherwise not have used.

Nearing the palace steps, another group of guards emerged, leading more bound rebels. Rufus was among them. Fear radiated from the young man's eyes as he pleaded, "Spenser, help us!"

"Don't look to me," Spenser replied with a sneer. "You made your choice. No one forced you."

Garrick had Spenser taken to an empty room and assigned a guard to stand at the door. It was pointless, he explained to Neil, to question this man first. He would likely ignore every query. Instead, they would question the Camelorans who worked with him—those who chose Mered instead of Zaric.

The rebels were all taken to separate rooms where the council members could interrogate them individually. Although it was obvious Rufus was the weakest and most likely to give them everything they wanted, the governor was more curious about Riva. He and Neil went to the room where she was held, not arguing when Siri followed

317

them. It was a small meeting room and Riva sat in a plain wooden chair in the center of it. Garrick pulled up a chair of his own and sat across from her.

Neil and Siri sat apart, at the edge of the room. Riva turned to look at them. Her look of surprise at seeing Siri turned to one of anger and hatred. "You said you were one of us," she hissed. "You're a traitor."

"Yes, I am," Siri agreed, unaffected by the accusation.

"We can say the same about you," Garrick pointed out.

His eyes scanned the young woman, taking in her appearance. She wore the clothing common to Camelora—good quality, clean fabrics that were comfortable without being too fine. Her hair was modest, her frame healthy. Nothing about her stood out at first glance. The only uncommon thing was an exquisite bracelet of fine jewels, peeking out from under the cuff of her sleeve. It was unlike any jewelry available in Camelora.

"You like jewelry," he stated, waving towards the bracelet.

Riva's opposite hand flew to her wrist, covering the bangle. "There's nothing wrong with that," she replied, red spots appearing on her cheeks.

"You're right," Garrick agreed. "There's nothing wrong with that at all. I suspect, though, that you don't just like it because it's pretty, but because it makes you different from the other women in Camelora. *Better* than them. It makes you stand out."

"Maybe I am better than other women," Riva retorted, raising her chin. "Why should we live without the fine things they have in the Southern Lands?"

The governor's eyebrows rose. "The Southern Lands wanted nothing to do with our ancestors. If it weren't for that, we would trade freely with them. What do you think you know about the Southern Lands, Riva?"

"They can have everything they want," Riva answered. "Even the most common women wear the finest jewels."

Neil stifled a laugh. "Is that what Spenser told you?" he inquired.

"He also told me that you would deny it," Riva said, glaring over her shoulder, "because it doesn't suit your story." She turned back to Garrick. "I didn't know what I was missing out on until Spenser came. All my life I thought I had to be like everyone else, when I could have been enjoying jewels and beautiful clothes and power and freedom. Just like Neil and Helen enjoyed, before they decided they needed more. Spenser told us all about their plan—how they came to Camelora to take advantage of the old legends, all so they could steal the kingdom that rightfully belongs to Mered. He wants to protect the people, but *they* only want to control and destroy us."

"Spenser seems to know my mind better than *I* do," Neil inserted, "and I've never met the man."

"You thought no one had figured out your plan?" the girl smirked.

"I didn't know someone had gotten it so wrong."

"You put your trust in the wrong person," Siri said, getting up from her chair and crossing to the corner of the room behind Garrick, folding her arms. If Riva's words hurt or amused or touched her in any way, she didn't show it. "Mered doesn't protect anyone but himself."

"Of course *you* would say that," Riva spat, disgusted. It didn't escape Neil, though, that she also showed a hint of envy. "You betrayed him simply because he had the courage to say no to you. Your thirst for power is the reason you joined Neil."

Siri's demeanor didn't change. "I'm glad we stopped you before you could run off to Mered," she said, a new kindness entering into her voice that Neil had never heard before. "You should know how evil he is—how he treats and uses girls like you—but I don't want you to experience it to find out."

For the first time since the beginning of the interview, a flash of doubt appeared in Riva's eyes, but she shook it away, adopting again the defiance she had shown before.

"Riva," Garrick inserted, his voice as gentle as always, "I am Cameloran, like you. My whole life, I have lived the way you live, been taught what you are taught. In your heart, you know what Spenser told you isn't true."

"You are a fool, Garrick, willing to believe every lie Zaric ever told you. I choose to believe the truth that Spenser tells me."

"Let me guess," Garrick said, leaning forward. "Spenser has promised you all of the jewelry, power, and influence you could ever want. You have been told that you will have a place of prominence in Mered's court. I could ask Siri to tell you how she was promised the same things—how her *mother* was promised the same things—but I'm afraid you wouldn't believe her."

"The land south isn't a land of freedom," Neil stated, "it's a land of oppression. When Mered promised our governors all the lands and power they could ever want, what do you think happened to the rest of the people? My village was very poor, very simple. We were happy enough, but we dreamed of enjoying the same things as you. We dreamed them because we didn't have them."

The three interrogators fell silent, allowing their words to sink in. If Riva felt anything from hearing their words, though, she didn't reveal it. The hardness of her eyes burned with sharp coldness.

"Siri, Neil, let's move on. Perhaps, with time, Riva will come to appreciate being confined in a Cameloran prison, instead of being stifled in Mered's court."

They filed out of the room, where a Cameloran soldier stood ready to guard it. From the other side of the closed door, they heard Riva's voice, but couldn't make out what she shouted.

Entering the next room, they saw Rufus by the window, midway through a nervous pace, his fingers wound through his hair. He turned his head as they walked in and the color drained from his face.

"Please, have a seat," Garrick said as he closed the door.

"Am I in trouble?" Rufus asked, visibly shaking.

"Have a seat."

"He told me to do it."

"Have a seat."

Rufus stood frozen for a few seconds, his mouth hanging open as though he were about to say something else, then he closed it and rushed to a chair, plopping himself down. He rested his elbows on his knees, his hands covering his face. Garrick pulled up a chair while Neil and Siri stood behind.

"People died today," Garrick stated, his voice stern. The usual kindness he spoke with was nearly undetectable.

"He told me to do it," Rufus repeated through his hands.

"You chose to obey the order. You didn't have to."

Rufus's eyes opened wide and he threw his arms out, prepared to argue. He inhaled, preparing to speak, but sighed instead. "Ask whatever you want," he said as his arms dropped. "I'll tell you everything you want to know."

"We want to know... everything."

"It started with my friend Olin. He was helping in the refugee camp with his father when he met Spenser. Olin didn't really want to be there—he never does—and Spenser could tell. Before Olin and his father left, Spenser asked Olin to meet him at the edge of the camp. He promised Olin all of the things he's always wanted but never thought he could have. That's what Olin told me, anyway.

"Olin came up to me the next day and took me to Spenser. He promised some great things—the sorts of things no one talks about in Camelora. Here, everyone is the same. We don't want to be the same."

"You think we're all the same?" Garrick asked.

"Well, we all have the same things," Rufus relented. "I grew up with three older brothers and I don't want to become like them. I want to be *better* than them, show them I'm not just the runt. Mered promises power and land and wealth. Zaric has never promised us that. Well, at least not the power. And the wealth we have to share. I'm tired of sharing."

"Most of us *choose* to share," Garrick stated. "We aren't forced to. *No one* is forced to."

"What else could I choose to do?" Rufus argued. Then, he calmed down again. "We were recruited to create panic. If we could succeed in making the people think you don't know what you're doing, they would turn against you and it would really mess up everything Zaric has planned. Then, we would receive the things Mered promised. I swear, I didn't want to hurt anyone. I just want to get out of this stuffy place."

"What about the thefts?" Neil asked.

"The thefts?" Rufus was visibly confused.

"The weapons," Garrick explained.

"Oh, those. Spenser told us to steal some weapons. We didn't ask too many questions about that, even when he was very specific about what he wanted. I assumed it was to arm ourselves to rise up against Zaric. We used some of them today, but there were others we took that we haven't seen again. Spenser also asked me to search old records for any stories that mentioned weapons."

"Did he say why?" Garrick asked.

Rufus shook his head and leaned back in his chair, resting his hands on his knees. Garrick stared at the young man without saying a word until his gaze intimidated Rufus into a wilting posture.

"Are you sure people are dead?" he asked. "They could just be hurt. I don't mind helping to repair the damage I've done. I would rather stay here and help you than run to Mered now."

"I wouldn't lie about people dying, Rufus," Garrick stated sternly. "I don't need to lie to learn what I need . And you and I both know very well that you were never going to get the things Mered promised. You made choices, Rufus, and those choices have consequences."

"I'm sorry. I promise I'll never do it again."

"You aren't a child, Rufus. Pretend all you want, but I think you understand how serious your actions are." Garrick rose, towering over the young man. "If you accept the consequences, your punishment will be less severe." Rufus opened his mouth, but Garrick held up his hand. "Don't say anything right now. You will only say what you think I want to hear, and that won't help either of us. Take some time to think."

Without another word, Garrick rose and left the room, with Neil and Siri not far behind.

"Wait!" they heard Rufus call through the door once they were in the hallway. They ignored his shouts.

Garrick led the way now to interview Spenser.

Neil was sure Garrick was piecing together the same picture he was. With the information they gained from Riva, Rufus, and Siri's infiltration of Spenser's group, their own theories were confirmed. Joining himself to a group of refugees, Spenser was able to hide undetected until his rebels were recruited. He found and exploited the weaknesses of some vulnerable young women and men in Camelora and the refugee settlement. He played on those weaknesses and made promises he knew he wasn't likely to fulfill.

Desperate for something different, they believed him.

Spenser's position now was no different from those who had chosen to join him: sitting in the center of a meeting room on a plain wooden chair. Leaning back and resting the ankle of one leg on the opposite knee, his air was nonchalant. His manner was disinterested as he watched Garrick and Neil enter. When Siri walked in, though, his face darkened and a toothy sneer spread across his mouth. "Sirena," he said, "the prodigal daughter. Which side are you pretending to be on today?"

Siri smiled sweetly, but said nothing.

"Spenser, is it?" Garrick stated. "Although, we're pretty sure that isn't your real name."

Spenser shifted his eyes to Garrick, then back to Siri, expectant.

"Oh, don't look at me," she said. "I still haven't been able to remember your actual name. You're lucky I even recognized your face."

Anger flared in Spenser's eyes. He tightened his lips.

"You don't have to speak to us," Garrick went on. "I'm not sure there's much you could tell us that we couldn't find out another way. Rufus is more than willing to talk. He already has, actually."

"Rufus," the man scoffed. "It didn't take long to realize he was a bad choice. I made sure he never knew too much."

"And Riva, too. The others are being questioned as we speak, so I'm sure we'll have a very clear picture of your actions, intentions, and plans by the end of the day. No one person has to say too much for us to learn everything, you see."

No reaction—sound or movement—came from Spenser.

"I also know that you haven't been able to contact Mered for weeks," Garrick continued. "If you're as far removed from Mered's inner circle as Siri suggests, I doubt he'll send anyone to rescue you. He didn't come searching for Ian, after all. You won't be able to take anything back to him. You've failed."

Still no reaction came from the man.

"If I know Zaric as well as I think I do, he'll treat you well. Before your execution, anyway. You might as well tell us your name."

The man stared at the corner of the room, his arms folded across his chest and a slight pout lowering the corners of his mouth. The governor watched him for a moment, betraying no emotion, then went to the door without another word. Siri and Neil followed.

"Oh, I think I remember," Siri said, turning back to the room and smiling at the prisoner. "Zaraham, was it?"

The man's face wound in rage. "My name is Alazar!" he shouted.

Siri, unflinching at this outburst, chuckled as she followed Neil and Garrick out of the room.

Chapter 41

The Present

"She's dead because of you."

Hundreds of years had passed, but these words rang in Zaric's ears as though they had been uttered only minutes before. Standing with his hand resting on Althea's stone face, his touch was as gentle as it would be if she lay before him in the flesh. He was a stronger man now—a stronger king—than he had been then, but he still missed his wife with an ache that never lessened. He still missed his son.

"Zaric."

The king turned his head to the mound's opening, where a woman's silhouetted figure stood. Helen. Zaric beckoned her in and she stepped down into the chamber.

"The caravan is ready," she said, coming up to the foot of the tomb. "It's time to go home."

"Home," Zaric mused. He silently took in the face beneath his hand. "I was just saying goodbye."

"I understand."

Zaric placed his hand on the stone cheek one last time. It took a great effort to pull his eyes from Althea's face, so he closed them as he turned, then opened them again upon Helen. "I haven't had a chance to tell you how well you did," Zaric said. "Receiving only half of a message, but not letting that stop you from finding a way to escape the dungeon. The work you did in the battle, finding the strength to use your powers —many people owe you their lives."

Helen flinched. "I only did what you taught me. Seeing you in my dream, I knew there would be a way. And I didn't want anyone to lose their life, just because they can't see Mered for who he really is."

"Your dedication gave Aurelie back to her parents. I know that they, at least, are in your debt."

Warmth filled Helen's cheeks. As she tried to shake off her embarrassment, a thought came into her head. She reached into her pocket and pulled out a roll of papers. "Speaking of Aurelie," she said as she carefully opened it, "I found this when I was going through records. I don't believe anyone has looked at it in decades. It's a genealogy."

Zaric took the papers from her hand and his eyes moved across the top sheet, then visibly froze. Helen knew what caught his attention. "'The Family of Edric,'" he finally read out loud.

When the shock wore off, he shuffled the pages until he reached the last. Halfway down the partially filled sheet was a name he had come to know well, the name of a child who was now a man: Connor.

"I think Aurelie is the person we were searching for," Helen stated. "You must have realized already that she has abilities—abilities she inherited from her foremother. Zaric, Connor and Aurelie are your family."

"My family," Zaric said, disbelieving . Then, a light glowed in his face. "Have you told them yet?"

Helen shook her head.

Zaric dragged his hand across the stone coffin in a final goodbye as he headed to the entrance of the chamber, braced now to leave behind the dead to find the living.

The caravan waited for its king, men and women and children making final preparations as they did so. Zaric scanned their faces, looking for those he had come to know the best. His family stood on this plain, alive. The full import of these words hit Zaric when his eyes fell on Connor.

He walked up to the man, studying his features and face, looking for a hint of his son, his wife, his father. He found his father in the squareness of the younger man's shoulders, but he found young Edric and Althea in Connor's mouth when he smiled—a smile he had hoped for hundreds of years to see again.

"Zaric," Connor said, "we're ready to go to Camelora."

His smile turned to an expression of confusion when Zaric threw his arms around him and embraced him, then drew back with his hands on Connor's shoulders.

"What's going on?" Connor asked.

"Will you walk with me?" Zaric asked. "I have a story to tell you."

Chapter 42

he's dead because of you.

S This single statement occupied Zaric's mind in every quiet moment after the battle ended. The sounds of the battle died—the screams, the cries, the clashing of swords. But Edric's words remained. Althea's body rested in a Pharan tomb, along with the remainder of the fallen. Many other families lost people they loved. Everyone mourned. Zaric didn't need Edric's words to feel responsible, but they intensified his guilt.

When Zaric walked, it was without purpose or destination. When he sat or stood still, he thought of the people who had been lost, contemplated what he had done wrong. He wondered where Mered had gone when he disappeared—if he was alive or if he was dead. He was apprehensive for the day his enemy came back.

Most of all, he thought of Althea.

With the disappearance of Mered came the ripple of surrender from Mered's forces throughout the kingdom. But it wasn't the end of doubts, of fears, of dissatisfaction, on the part of the people. Rumors flowed from one city to another. Neighbors gossiped and whispered that King Zaric was not strong enough to protect them. Traitorous noblemen and women, intent on taking advantage of the weaknesses

Mered exposed, insinuated that Zaric was no longer fit to be their king.

The rift between Zaric and Edric put Evander in a difficult position. He met with Zaric upon his arrival in Phara, but their reunion was brief and stiff. Zaric understood: the father had lost his only daughter. Both men were alone in their own way. It didn't surprise Zaric when he learned that Evander went to Edric after their visit and was now spending his time with his grandson. As Edric refused to see his own father, Zaric was glad the boy had Althea's.

After a week, the King's Council trickled into Phara from their various battlegrounds across the kingdom, ready to convene a meeting with their monarch. They sat around a large wooden table in high-backed chairs, every eye fixed on their king as his turmoiled mind struggled to find the words to begin the assembly. In his imagination, their looks were accusing and condemning. Zaric wondered now if he should have tried harder to be the kind of king his own father had been. Would this conflict ever have taken place?

"We have lost much," he finally began, keeping his voice as flat as possible. "I as much as anyone. Our kingdom has been deep in war for far too long. All have lost people they love. I still wonder where I went wrong, what I could have done differently to prevent all of this."

"If Mered had been given a place on the council..." one man posited, the trailing off of his voice saying more than his words did.

"Don't say that," another man shot in return. "The people didn't want him. Zaric wanted to *stop* the government from forcing the people to accept what they didn't want."

"He wasn't the right man for the job," Zaric said, grateful for the voice on his side. "Surely that is evident now. You do not give a child everything he wants simply because he throws a tantrum."

"I'm sure we could list many things we could have done differently," the second man went on. "They're all easy to see now. But, at the time, we did what we felt was best. The people chose the council—we can't fault Zaric for not overriding the people."

"Well, the people are beginning to feel differently than they did before," a woman to Zaric's left interjected. "Many of them no longer want Zaric to be king. I concede that most of them *are* speaking from grief, but if they choose to hold a vote at this time, aren't we obligated to comply with the result?"

"Do the people have the *option* of calling for a vote?" another woman questioned.

Voices began to buzz, but Zaric stopped them with a raise of his hand.

"What do they want?" Zaric asked, a pit opening in his chest.

"To split the kingdom into pieces, essentially. They want regions overseen by independent governors, with their own laws and regulations. Much like the current duchies, but without the unifying kingdom. *We* may know that Mered is responsible for what happened to Camelora, but many of the people blame *you,* your majesty. They have lost faith in you."

These words tore at Zaric like metal claws. For a second, Edric's face—grieving, accusing—flashed in his mind. Despite losing the war, it seemed that Mered had still managed to accomplish his objective. He had managed to take Camelora away from Zaric.

* * *

Zaric sat in the empty council room, staring at the table, replaying the meeting in his mind. He knew he had no choice but to let the people vote—not if he wanted them to trust him again—but he was afraid of what they would choose. A fractured kingdom was a vulnerable kingdom and he still didn't know where Mered had gone.

Edric was never far from his mind. His son still wouldn't see or speak with him. Instead, he set himself up in a cottage near Phara—near his mother's resting place—and vowed to give up his right to the throne. He supported the election of governors, though he himself didn't want to be one.

Evander made a similar choice. Finding a distant relation, he turned over his estate in Veren and remained with his grandson in the coastal region. Zaric could have borne the loss of the people's trust if it hadn't come with the loss of his family.

"Your majesty," a voice said, breaking into Zaric's reverie. He turned to find Alan standing behind him.

"Have a seat," Zaric said, waving his hand at the empty chairs surrounding the table. He forced a smile. Alan said nothing as he sat, simply watching Zaric as the king stared at his hands.

"I've thought of blaming you," Zaric eventually stated, "but there's far too much of that happening right now—far too much passing the blame. I know what I chose and I don't believe I made the wrong choices."

"But it still hurts."

"Yes."

"Good."

Confused, Zaric cast uncomprehending eyes at the mysterious man. He thought his mind was playing tricks or he had misheard.

"That means I chose the right man," Alan continued. "If you could no longer feel—or could feel only anger, like Mered—we would have a problem."

"I didn't think it would turn out this way."

"It was always going to turn out this way, your majesty. You were given a gift to save the kingdom in a future time, not now."

"Not now?" Zaric repeated, his surprise boiling with irritation. "What better time could there be than now?"

Alan didn't even flinch. His mouth remained closed and his eyes still revealed understanding.

"I'm sorry," Zaric exhaled, rubbing his eyes with his fingertips. "It's not your fault, either. If only I had done more…"

"Mered is gone. As bad as things seem, you prevented them from becoming worse."

"I've lost the confidence of the people. And my son."

"Some of the people still support you. Think of that. Edric… I wish I could say what will happen with him, but *that* I just don't know. This I *can* say: one day, one of your descendants will join you in defending the kingdom. He or she will bear a gift—a gift like Althea's—that will help you defeat Mered once and for all."

"So Mered is not dead."

"But he's gone for now. It's time to look forward and prepare for the future of Camelora. The time *will* come when the people trust you again. And then, they will need you."

* * *

Zaric stayed in Phara until the votes were taken throughout the land. By the time all the results were counted, he wasn't surprised by the decision of the people. He knew before the first vote was cast. The people chose to split Camelora into regions and appoint their own governors. Zaric would be given uninhabited land at the northern edge of the kingdom, far away from the rest of the people. He was not to interfere with the new Cameloran way of life. The word wasn't used, but the meaning was clear: exile.

And, still, Edric refused to see his father.

The sun had yet to crest over the horizon, but Zaric stood with his cart at the top of a hill east of Phara. At dawn, he would set off for the land north with anyone who wished to join him.

He stood alone.

He had never seen the kingdom as *his.* All he had ever felt was a deep responsibility for it. That feeling was still part of him, as well as an obligation toward the people of the kingdom. He would respect their wishes to not be governed by him, but he wouldn't stop watching over them. As best he could, he assured the kingdom that if they invited him to return, he would come. When they one day chose to accept his help again, he would be ready.

The light on the horizon intensified as yellow pushed the darkness farther from the sky. The tip of the sun appeared and Zaric sighed. He took a heavy, labored step forward and his cart rolled with it.

"Your majesty!" came a shout from behind. Baffled, he stopped and turned. As well as stripping him of his responsibilities, the people had stripped him of his title.

A small group, trailing two carts of their own, crowned the top of the hill. He counted six men, four women, and seven children; some he recognized and some he did not. At their head was the man from the council meeting a few weeks before—a young man he had come to know well in the time since. Of all the former council members, this man had proven to be the most hopeful.

"Adan," Zaric said with unmasked surprise.

"We couldn't let our king go on his own," Adan replied.

"I am no longer a king."

"We don't agree with the decisions of the kingdom," Adan asserted. "We have no place in this new society. When the people come to their senses, we want to be there with you, to help rebuild Camelora."

Seventeen people. It was far from the number of supporters Zaric hoped for, but seventeen more than he thought he would see just a few minutes ago. A broad and bright smile—the first of its kind in weeks—covered Zaric's face as he looked over those who came out to join him. "My friends," he addressed them, then stopped. He found he didn't know what to say.

Seeing the brightness in the people's face, he realized that words didn't matter. They already understood.

Chapter 43

The Present

The journey from Phara took longer than Helen expected. Although the original journey to Phara had taken them through Nubiim, the direct return to Camelora felt just as long. Of course, the addition of the Pharans and those people recruited by Meira and Stephen made their progress slow. And despite their victory over Mered's forces in their own village, the Pharans needed to be cautious as they moved through unknown territory. They sent spies out to watch for unexpected opposition or bands of Mered's soldiers out gathering support of their own. Days became weeks. Helen realized now the luxury it had been to travel with such a small party before.

But the weeks passed. She cheered herself each day with the thought that she would soon see her father and Neil again. The journey couldn't last forever. Zaric pointed out the signs that indicated they were close to reaching their destination. As they moved farther inland, some of these signs became familiar to Helen, too.

Every time Zaric turned his gaze to the Pharan people, journeying to an unfamiliar place without complaint or dread, he marveled. The contrast to the small band that left Phara with him almost a millennium ago was striking. Seventeen replaced by hundreds. Many more supporters stayed in Phara to preserve it as a stronghold and save it for their neighbors to return when all of this was over. If the supporters gathered in Camelora were at all like this, Zaric was confident they stood a chance against Mered.

The caravan neared a hill, topped by a new guard tower in a clearing at its crest. Sunlight glinted off what Helen assumed was a telescope. She imagined all the groups which had passed this way in the recent months, but she knew that the sight of Zaric at the head of this caravan made it much more significant. As they passed up the hill, Helen saw a figure run from the base of the tower in the direction of the city.

Approaching Camelora was different from leaving it. The anticipation was overwhelming. They heard the city before they saw it: the sounds of voices and work and life in the valley just beyond the ridge of a hill.

Down the hill the caravan swept, working to hold back the carts that threatened to shove them forward. The travelers saw segments of structures and all kinds of colors peeking between the trees. They poured beyond the forest and Helen and Zaric found themselves facing a Camelora much different from the one they had left a few short months earlier.

A new wall was being constructed, taller than the existing wall. The green fields surrounding the city were mostly filled with tents and cooking fires, with only a small area relegated for crops. People of all ages moved through the spaces within the large camp, working and playing and visiting. A wide path led through the camp to the southern gate of the city.

The sight of the city was accompanied by strong emotions, an excitement and happiness that swelled and burned deep within Helen's chest. The brief thought crossed her mind that this was the second time she had approached Camelora, but she would never remember the first. This feeling of elation was what she had hoped to experience

337

that first time, fueled further by the prospect of seeing those she cared about the most—and the prospect of being able to rest.

No one paid much attention as the caravan moved down the wide path. It struck Helen that none of these people knew that the king they had come to support was returning. To them, he was only the leader of another group of refugees, arriving to meet with the governor.

Ahead of them, a tiny cloud formed above the city, dropped rain, then disappeared. "Helen?" Zaric asked in confusion, stopping long enough to glance at her. "Are you playing a trick?"

She shook her head and shrugged in response, just as baffled as he was.

A crowd appeared at the open city gate. They walked out in a kind of formation, approaching the caravan. The man at the front walked with quick steps, forcing the others to match his speed.

When he was close enough, Helen recognized him as Garrick. A broad smile covered his face. "Your majesty!" he exclaimed. Helen expected him to knock the king over in his rush, but he stopped himself short and the men clasped right forearms.

"I am so glad to see you, Zaric," Garrick continued, taking a step back.

"And I you," Zaric said. "We have much to speak about. But first, I would like to get these people settled. I have already vetted them and can vouch for their commitment."

"I trust your judgment better than mine," Garrick said, "but that's a story for a private discussion."

The two men continued to speak and give instructions to the guards, who trailed behind Garrick, but Helen stopped paying attention. She searched the faces behind the governor for the ones that mattered the most to her. A calm, warm feeling flooded her when her scanning eyes fell upon Neil's face. He flashed a familiar smile. Helen smiled in return and took a step forward, then stopped.

Her eyes had picked up a glimpse of another familiar face—one that had just as quickly disappeared behind the guards. She wondered if it was real or imagined. Surely it couldn't have been Siri.

Helen turned to Lena with a quizzical look, but the woman's elated face only responded with confusion. It took a moment for Helen to remember that Siri had been a young girl the last time her aunt saw her.

Thoughts of Siri were set aside when Neil closed the space between him and Helen by stepping forward. She flung her arms around his neck and he returned the embrace.

"It feels longer than just a few months since I saw you," Neil said.

"Not as long as seven years, at least," Helen retorted. "But definitely too long. I've missed talking to you."

"I've missed you lecturing me, too."

"That's not what I said."

Neil ignored the statement and tugged on Helen's hair. "I'm glad you're safe. Your father's here."

Helen exhaled in relief. "Is he doing better?"

The pause that followed this question was too long. In that pause, Helen received the answer that Neil didn't give. She both wanted to and dreaded seeing her father, fear constricting her chest like a heavy stone. The way Neil looked at her, Helen knew he could tell what she was feeling. She remembered just how well he understood the grief and fear she felt.

"You must be tired," he said.

"Yes, I must be," Helen agreed. "I thought I saw someone who couldn't possibly be here."

Neil turned, scanning the Cameloran crowd behind him as though he were looking for someone .

"I wasn't imagining it, was I?" Helen stated.

"Siri's here," Neil told her.

Helen's heart pounded against the wall of her chest. "Lena!" she called over her shoulder, then pressed her way forward without turning to see if the woman followed.

Making her way past the guards, Helen pushed through the crowd which had formed to see their king return. She searched the faces surrounding her, staying on the outskirts of the crowd, where the people stood farther apart.

Movement was easier once she passed through the gate of the city. She was able to make her way toward the palace unhindered. A few dozen people moved about, unaware of their king's arrival and the commotion outside the city gates.

Helen saw a figure advancing faster than the rest before it disappeared behind a building. She hurried and turned the corner. A dark-haired woman walked away from her, farther down the street. "Siri!" she called.

The woman stopped, but for a few seconds only stood still with her back to Helen. Then, she slowly turned. Siri flinched when her eyes met the young woman's and she looked away. Helen advanced down the street in quick strides, not entirely sure what she was going to do. Her eyes took in Siri's face, her expression, and the clues her posture gave. She stopped a few feet short of her rival.

In a way she couldn't quite explain, Helen felt that she understood Siri. The stories Lena had told her rose in her mind. She thought of the little girl, taken to live in Mered's court because her parents had been deceived by his promises. Helen wondered what her own life would have been like if her own parents had made the same choice.

For a few seconds, Helen stood before the other woman, both of them fixed in place. Then, Helen threw her arms around Siri.

Siri stood rigid beneath the weight of Helen's arms, but she quickly relaxed and returned the gesture. A wave passed between them—a wave of remorse from Siri to Helen and a wave of forgiveness from

Helen to Siri. Helen didn't know what had brought Siri to Camelora, but she sensed in the woman's attitude a shame for everything that had passed between them. Helen had an overpowering desire to ease that emotion. The fact that Siri stood in the street, free to move as she wished, showed that she had gained the trust of not only Garrick, but Neil, and everyone else who held a position of trust in Camelora—the women as well as the men.

When the women parted, Siri looked over Helen's shoulder, her gaze locked on someone else. Helen turned to see that Lena had understood her call and followed her into the city. A glimmer of recognition lit Siri's eyes.

"Siri!" Lena exclaimed, part whisper and part cry, both a question and a statement. For a moment, all she could do was stand in place, staring. Helen stepped away as the women rushed toward each other.

As they embraced, the embarrassment melted from Siri's face, replaced with a smile of joy. "Hello, Aunt," she said quietly.

Any reservations Helen had left dissolved at the sight of aunt and niece together. She found her perception of Siri changing, looking at the woman now through Lena's eyes.

"Who is this?" Zaric's voice asked over Helen's shoulder. She turned to find the king standing with Garrick, Neil, Connor, and Aurelie.

"This is Siri," Neil told him.

"Siri," Zaric repeated, his eyes lightening with the knowledge he had of her. His countenance didn't change, revealing still the calm joy he experienced at being home. Helen realized that the king had already made the connection when she herself realized it: Siri was Zaric's descendant as well.

"You've come to join us," he said, stepping forward to place a gentle hand on Siri's shoulder.

At this statement, Siri burst into tears. All of the strength she had shown to this point evaporated at the sight of the king. Without hesitation, he pulled her into his arms and held her against him, allowing her to cry, releasing the shame and guilt she felt from her past actions, choices, and mistakes.

"I won't make excuses for everything I've done," Siri said when she finally pulled away, wiping her eyes with her fingers, "but, please, can I stay here? With you? Can I help you?"

Zaric cast a glance at Helen, who inclined her head. "We are glad to have you," he said.

"Siri has been a great help to us in your absence," Garrick pointed out, taking a step forward. "It's a long story that I can tell you when we reach the palace, but I will say now that Siri was instrumental in helping to save the city. She has Zahra's approval, too."

"Is that right," Zaric stated, amazement and admiration mingling in his expression. "I understand you're Lena and Connor's niece."

Siri nodded.

"Will you take them, and your cousin, to the palace?" he went on. "I'll give you some time to catch up, then I would like to meet with you, to discuss some important things. Garrick, if you will go with them and make sure a room is prepared for the family, I would appreciate that."

Zaric, Helen, and Neil watched as the others went down the road. "I imagine you want to see your father," Zaric said to Helen.

"Very much ," she responded.

"Neil, please take Helen to Cyrus. After I have a chance to speak with Siri, I want to meet with the two of you, as well as Garrick. I believe we have a lot to discuss."

* * *

A typical afternoon rain shower pattered against the window of Zaric's study. Camelora's weather gradually stabilized throughout the day

342

with the king's return. The oil lamps on the walls, desk, and table had been lit to counteract the darkness of the sky outside, casting the room in a warm glow.

Helen sat in an armchair, her legs curled up beneath her, resting her head against the soft wing of its back as she watched the rain. This was her last meeting of the day, then she would be able to retire to her room for an early night. After the long journey, she was looking forward to a long sleep.

Neil sat in an armchair matching Helen's, his elbows resting on his knees as he gazed at his friend. They had spoken briefly about Camelora and Phara between seeing Cyrus and meeting with Zaric, but it wasn't enough time to really understand what each other had been through. There was new light in Helen's face—new worries and new strengths. He wondered how she felt about the information Zaric had just given them.

"Siri is your descendant," Garrick said in surprise. He stood near the bookshelves with his hands clasped behind his back.

"If the records are correct," Zaric replied. "Connor descends from my son, Edric, and Connor's sister is Siri's mother."

The king leaned against the windowsill, his arms folded as he surveyed the room, unable to ignore the stacks of books on the desk that had once sat neatly on the shelves. "When I said to make yourself at home..." he began, his words directed at Neil.

"I know where they all go," Neil assured him. "I'll put them back when I'm done with them."

"Siri really has been helpful, then?" Helen asked.

"Yes," Neil responded, continuing to watch Helen's face. Her eyes were still bright and untroubled. "I didn't think she would be —"

"That's an understatement," Garrick inserted.

"—but I'll admit she has changed my mind," Neil finished. "Your father suggested that I give her a chance."

"I *always* believed she would be helpful," Garrick said, "as soon as she asked to see Zaric and offered her assistance."

"How do you feel about this, Helen?" Zaric asked. "Can you forgive her enough to work with her?"

Helen took the time to think of her response, wondering if the emotions she felt in the street were genuine. "I can and I do," she finally answered. "That's what I would hope for in her position. I've learned things about Siri that help me understand her now."

"I believe Siri will be very useful to us," Garrick reiterated. "She has already given us some information about Mered's court and plans. Perhaps when you meet with her again, she will tell you even more."

Zaric nodded pensively.

"Connor's daughter," Garrick went on; "do you believe she's the person you were looking for? The one with the gift?"

"I don't intend to use her," Zaric stated forcefully. "I'm not sure I even want to tell her. The gift takes a toll—physically, emotionally, mentally... And not just on the person with the gift, but everyone who cares about them."

Memory flickered in his eyes, visible to everyone else in the room.

"Have you told her parents?" Helen asked, hoping her words would pull Zaric out of the past. "Auri already knows there's something different about herself. Her parents should know, too."

"That's true," Zaric admitted. "They can decide how much to tell Aurelie."

He pushed himself away from the windowsill and took a plain wooden chair from the side of his desk, setting it near Helen and Neil.

"Neil," he said, settling his attention on the young man, "have you made any progress on the task I gave you?"

"Yes!" Neil exclaimed, brightening with excitement and leaping from his chair. He strode to Zaric's desk, moving papers and books aside until he uncovered the thin book he had found on the shelf. "This is why I haven't put everything away."

Holding the book out to Zaric, he asked, "Do you recognize this?"

Puzzled, Zaric took the thin tome and examined its cover . Brightness dawned as he turned it over in his hands, then opened it with an eagerness Helen had never seen in him. "I haven't seen this in years," he said after reading the title page. "Centuries, even. It was before my time long before it *was* my time. Where did you find it?"

"On a top shelf, over there, tucked between two larger volumes. I assume you've read it."

Zaric nodded, still staring at the book. "It's about an ancient hero, although I can't remember his name. As a boy, I imagined he was still alive, watching over Camelora. I wondered if I would ever meet him. As I grew older, I wondered instead if he had ever even existed in the first place. It's not unusual to tell cautionary tales with made-up characters."

"And now?" Helen questioned. "Do you believe he's real or imagined?"

"When you get to be as old as I am, you're much more willing to believe what you once thought was impossible." He closed the book again and directed his words to Neil. "I would have to read this again to remind myself of the details. You think this holds the answer to defeating Mered?"

"It's the most promising record I've found," Neil replied. "It mentions a weapon that once destroyed an evil king. If I can just find a secondary record to back it up, I think we should search for it."

"We're not the only ones looking, though," said Garrick. "Those rebels I told you about, Mered instructed them to look for a weapon, too."

"He could be working from this same book," Zaric mused. "No doubt his father had a copy as well."

345

"Whatever he knows," Neil said, "he needs to learn more, and he believes the answer is here in Camelora."

"Some weapons have been stolen from the armory," Garrick said, "and one of the young men spent a lot of time in the library, going through books about weapons. At least now that the rebels are captured, we know Mered won't be receiving information any time soon."

Zaric flipped through the book again. "What is the weapon?" he asked.

"A sword," Neil answered.

"Not surprising," Helen remarked.

"I can question Rufus again," Garrick suggested. "He's eager enough to talk now. Maybe he came across something he didn't realize was important."

"As long as you don't reveal too much about what *we* know," Zaric responded, "I think that's a good idea."

Everyone sat still, watching Zaric as he tapped the book against his leg. When he looked up, a broad, bright smile covered his face. "I have a good feeling about this," he said. "Neil, I believe you have found a way to save the kingdom."

About the Author

Like P.G. Wodehouse, Vibeke Hiatt has been writing since the age of five. By the eighth grade, she knew she would one day major in English. She graduated with an AA and BS in English from Utah Valley University. After graduation, she worked as a phone book editor, then a data analyst, before leaving the corporate world behind to become a full-time mom. *The Fragmented Kingdom,* the sequel to *The Forgotten King,* is her second novel. She lives in Utah's Salt Lake Valley with her husband and four children.

You can connect with me on:
- http://moonriseonjupiter.com
- https://twitter.com/VibekeHiatt
- https://www.facebook.com/vibekehiatt

Also by Vibeke Hiatt

The Forgotten King
Every city falls in the end... except Camelora.

The land is under attack. The governors of the regions are betraying their people. Mered is plotting to take power.

And no one can see it.

No one except Helen.

Enlisting the reluctant help of her childhood friend, Neil, she embarks on a journey to find the forgotten king—the only man who can stop Mered. But the journey is fraught with unexpected dangers and not the journey they imagined. It is a race against the truth Helen doesn't want to face: if they fail, all hope for the land will fall.

www.ingramcontent.com/pod-product-compliance
Lightning Source LLC
Chambersburg PA
CBHW032148190726
48290CB00005BB/1457